Kay

God loves you
so much!

Patricia

From Ages
Three *to* Thirty

The Life of Jesus

Patricia Griffin Dunlop

LifeRich Publishing is a registered trademark of The Reader's Digest Association, Inc.

LifeRich Publishing books may be ordered through booksellers or by contacting:

LifeRich Publishing
1663 Liberty Drive
Bloomington, IN 47403
www.liferichpublishing.com
1 (888) 238-8637

ISBN: 978-1-4897-2359-8 (sc)
ISBN: 978-1-4897-2357-4 (hc)
ISBN: 978-1-4897-2358-1 (e)

Library of Congress Control Number: 2019910711

Print information available on the last page.

LifeRich Publishing rev. date: 08/13/2019

ONE

3

"Just a few more miles, and we'll be home, Mary! It's been almost four years. There must have been a lot of changes," Joseph said as they neared Nazareth.

"For us too, Joseph. When we left, it was just the two of us, and now we've added the two boys. Oh, Joseph, I'm so excited! Look! Isn't that Abraham, son of Hiram? My, he's grown!

"Abraham! Come closer," Mary called. "Tell us what's been happening. Are your parents well? How are your sisters?"

"Hi! A lot's happened, and a lot's the same. But I can't tell you, because Mother heard that you were coming and threatened to eat anyone who talks to you before she does!" joked Abraham.

"All right then. We'll see you soon, I hope," Mary said and chuckled.

Joseph, Mary, and the boys continued another quarter hour before seeing the outskirts of town. Many of the elders, women, and children were outside and waved as they passed by.

"It's good to see so many people. Oh, Joseph! Look! There's Miriam in front of our house," said Mary.

"Mary! Oh, Mary, I have missed you so much," said Miriam as she ran toward Mary and hugged her.

"Who are these adorable little boys? This must be Jesus! He had just been born when we left Jerusalem after the registration. And this is …?"

"This is James, our second son. He's a little over a year now," Mary replied. "Oh look, Joseph. Our house! It looks like nothing changed while we were gone."

"Mary, this is just the beginning. Come see what your neighbors have done," Miriam said as she led the family into their home.

Mary was astounded. The house was clean. Fresh bread, figs, and fresh flowers were waiting for them, and the garden had been weeded and was growing in nice straight rows. Mary knew that Miriam had planted the garden and had been instrumental in having everything ready for them.

"Now no more talk until after dinner. You two unpack. I'm taking the boys with me. You're coming to our house for dinner. No arguing now," said Miriam as she and the boys left for home.

"Well," said Joseph, "that was some welcome home! Let's unpack."

It didn't take them long. They washed up and were on their way to Hiram and Miriam's place. What a welcome. It was as though the two families had never been apart.

Hiram said, "We'll eat first because once you women start talking our dinners will be forgotten. Come on, everyone! Dinner on the roof tonight, where it's cool."

After a dinner of cold lamb, fresh bread, and fruit, Hiram and Miriam filled Mary and Joseph in on all that had happened while they were gone—births, deaths, injuries, crops, politics, and so on. Then it was Joseph and Mary's turn to tell of their travels to and from Egypt.

"Tell us everything, Mary," said Miriam as she settled deep in her chair.

Mary began, "It's really beautiful in its own way. It's hot and very sandy. That sand gets into everything—even the food!"

"Their homes are a little different though," said Joseph. "Their courtyards are completely fenced in, and the homes can only be entered from there. They have a wooden ramp instead of stairs built outside the house to reach the roof. The children love to run up and down those ramps. It makes quite a racket!

"They eat a lot of bread and fruits, and they drink a kind of beer," he continued. "Their beer is really different. It's thick, and everybody adds different herbs and spices to make it taste different. It was good, but I prefer our thinner beer."

"They really like sweets. Sometimes their breads taste more like cakes because they fill them with things like honey and dates," said Mary.

Hiram asked, "I hear they have a lot of gods. What's that like?"

"They do," replied Joseph. "An unusual thing about it is that they pray to the 'correct' god, and if their prayers are answered they're delighted. But if their prayers aren't answered, it doesn't seem to bother them. It's almost like 'Better luck next time.'"

"Did you learn the language when you were there?" asked Hiram.

"A few words, but there were hundreds of Jews in the area, so we could always find people and businesses who spoke Aramaic," Joseph replied.

"An uncle of mine once told me that the Nile floods every spring," said Hiram.

"Almost every spring. It's really a blessing though," replied Joseph. "It floods over a wide area, but when it recedes, it leaves behind really rich soil, which is good for growing crops. In a good year, the harvests are huge. But people are careful with them. They try to save enough each year in case it doesn't flood the next year. No one really goes hungry though. All crops are stored in the middle of town, and you just take what you need when you need it."

"One thing is that you can't drink the water from the Nile without boiling it. Sometimes that's kind of inconvenient, but you get used to it," said Mary.

"Fader! Moder!" called Jesus as he came running from a corner of the roof. "I foun' a birdy! Yook! Yook!"

"You certainly did!" said Joseph. "But, Jesus, this bird is not living. He must have been very sick. We must bury him."

"No, Fader. He is my birdy, an' I yove him!" said Jesus.

"Jesus," said Mary, "birds fly in the air. We can't hold them in our hands. They need to be free. When they're done flying, they need to be buried, sweetheart. How about if we cover him now and tomorrow we'll all go out behind the courtyard and bury him?"

"No, Moder. Birdy fly. My birdy fly! I yove him, Moder!" Jesus bent down and kissed the bird on the head.

The bird shivered, stretched, spread his wings, and flew off. "See. My birdy fly! Bye, birdy. Yove you."

Mary and Joseph looked at each other and smiled. Hiram and Miriam stared in amazement. "Did you see that?" said Miriam.

Hiram said, "That bird must have just been cold."

"Well," Joseph said, stretching. "It's time to get the boys home and into bed. It's been a long day for all of us."

"It sure has," said Mary. "Thank you so much for all you've done for us. We really owe you for this. Dinner was amazing! It's been a few years since we've had our regular food."

Hugs, good nights, and promises of seeing one another soon ended the night. Mary and Joseph and the boys headed for home and their beds.

As Joseph and Mary climbed onto their mats, Joseph said, "I need to see Benjamin at the carpentry shop first thing tomorrow to see if he has a job for me. Good night, my Mary. I love you. Oh, I am so glad to be home."

The next morning, Joseph went to see Benjamin. The man who had been working with him had been hit by a runaway cart and had died of his injuries a few days later. Benjamin had heard that Joseph and his family were coming home, so he had waited to see if Joseph might be interested in working with him again. He was.

Two

5

"It's a girl! It's a girl! It's a girl! We have a sister!" Jesus and James yelled as they ran and skipped through the neighborhood.

Everyone they met got the same news. "Her name is Elizabeth, and she's really little and she cried, but now she's sleeping. We got to hold her, and she wiggled and made funny faces, and she's so cute! I just love her! And we can't call her Lizzie."

Back at home Mary was changing Elizabeth when fourteen-month-old Judas woke from his nap. Joseph had gone to work after making Mary promise to take it easy. Neighbors were already bringing food. It seemed there would be enough food for several days. Mary picked up Judas and cleaned and changed him.

"Oh, little Judas. You weren't the baby in the family very long, were you? Don't you worry. You are going to get just as much attention and loving as the others. You must remember that you are very special. I am going to hug you and cuddle you and give you *prrrrts* on your tummy and make you giggle and giggle. You are my happy boy! Mommy loves you so much, little one."

The family was together for supper that evening—a supper of bread, cheese, figs, and fresh vegetables. Both Elizabeth and Judas began to fuss.

"Sorry, Mary, but I need to get back to work for an hour or so. Will you be okay with both of them fussing like this?"

"Go," she replied. "I'll be fine. I've had fussy children before."

"Mother, I'll hold baby Elizabeth," said Jesus. "I don't care if she cries. I'll just sing and rock her."

"Thank you, Jesus," Mary said as she put Elizabeth in his arms. "Be careful that she doesn't fall. And be sure to hold her head, or she can really get hurt."

"I know, Mother. I remember from when Judas was little." Jesus began to rock his little sister. He rocked her back and forth and sang his favorite psalm to her.

After just a few minutes, she was sound asleep. Mary finally got Judas settled and went over to Jesus; she thanked him for being such a good helper.

"Thank you for letting me be a big boy today, Mother."

"You are welcome. You are my big boy!"

"I want to ask Father something."

"I expect he'll be home for Family Time tonight. You can ask him then. How about if we review today's lesson?" asked Mary as she began to feed Elizabeth.

Later when Joseph returned home and they'd all had dinner, he said, "Well, boys! Let's gather round. Let's start with prayer. "Father God, bless our talks this evening. Open our hearts and minds to receive Your message. Thank You, Father God, for all You do for us. Amen," Joseph prayed.

Jesus raised his hand to speak. "Yes, Jesus. What is it?" said Joseph.

"Father, what's a lie? I mean, I know if I do something and say someone else did it that that's a lie, but what about other lies?

"What kind of other lies, Jesus?"

"Well, one of the kids at school was getting in trouble for something he did—just a little thing. I know his father is mean, and when he hears about it, he'll really whip him. I wanted to say I did it so he wouldn't get in trouble. Would that have been a lie?" asked Jesus.

"Well, boys, what do you think?" asked Joseph, knowing this was a very deep subject for such small children and wondering just how he was going to answer this question.

James rushed to answer. "Mother and you say not to lie, so I don't!"

"Thank you, James. That is a very good answer. What do you think, Jesus?"

"Father, I know that what isn't the truth is a lie. But," he said, pausing for a moment, "even Abraham lied when he said Sarah was his sister. I don't want kids hurt by anyone, and if I had said I did it, I would have been scolded and made to do extra homework. But he's going to get such a beating. Would it really have been wrong? I want to know, Father."

"Oh, Jesus. The answer is, yes, it would have been a lie. But would it be wrong? The answer to that question has been searched and debated by the priests and scribes and Pharisees for ages. 'When is a lie not a lie?' Personally, I think you did the right thing, especially for your age. I also think that it's very good that you ask questions like this. Don't ever stop wondering about things, Jesus. By questioning, you are thinking, and that's where answers finally come from. Let's look at the story of Abraham and Sarah," said Joseph.

A wise boy, he thought.

THREE

7

"Are you sure you're up to this, Mary? It's about a four-day journey to Jerusalem," Joseph said as they were packing. "This will be our fifth child, and the younger two are still quite small. Actually, all of them will need watching."

"Don't worry, Joseph. Hiram and Miriam will be there, and their children are almost grown. Oh! I didn't tell you; Enoch and Mary have taken in their grandchildren, so Martha and Mary and young Lazarus will be coming too. I admire them for taking in the three children. It won't be easy, as Enoch and Mary are older. But they adore those children."

"That's really nice of them. I did hear it at the shop today. I think they'll do well. Okay. I'm done packing this stuff. What's next?" asked Joseph.

"I think that's it. We'll probably both remember something as we're falling asleep tonight," Mary said as she stretched.

Joseph reached over and gave Mary a hug. "I love you more every day, Mary. You're a wonderful mother and a friend to so many."

"Thank you, Joseph. You're not so bad yourself! I too love you more every day. I thank Father God every night for bringing you to me."

"Thank you, my Mary. Well, I guess we'd better get some sleep. We leave early in the morning," said Joseph as he gave Mary a good night squeeze.

They rose early the next morning. It seemed everybody in town was doing the same. Joseph hitched the donkey to the cart and began loading—leaving room for his small children and, possibly, Mary.

After a breakfast of bread and dried fruit, they started off. Most of the town met at the synagogue so they would travel together.

"Hold on a minute, everyone!" called Matthew. "I've been talking with some of the older boys, and we have games planned for the boys four years old and older. So if you wish, each day during the mornings and the afternoons, those children may come to my cart, and the older boys and I will keep them safe and busy. How does that sound?"

The crowd cheered. "Just the boys or the girls too?" shouted someone from the group.

"Girls too! If any older girls want to come and help with the younger ones, that would be great. But I know that many of you girls have younger siblings to watch," answered Matthew. "Let's start this afternoon then."

Miriam's daughter, Hannah, and one of her friends volunteered to work with the girls.

They started off. It seemed to Joseph that Mary had packed enough food for an army, but he knew better than to mention it.

After lunch, Jesus and James joined the other children for the first afternoon of games. As promised, Matthew kept them busy—so busy in fact that they were more than willing to crawl into bed after dinner. Matthew had set up races and challenges of every kind, inventing games that would keep the children ahead of the townspeople.

With most of the children off and safe, the women could relax a bit. Younger children could be carried or could ride in the carts.

What a happy time this was for the women! Although they were tending the youngest children, they were able to meet and talk and talk and catch up on the latest news. One of the women had learned a new stitch that seemed to give a little when stretched. Another found a new way to prepare vegetables. They had so many new things to exchange.

Because the Romans were now in charge of the entire area, the men's main topic of conversation seemed to focus on one question: What would this mean as time went on?

The men took careful charge of the carts and possessions. Occasionally, a wheel or an axle or something would break, and they would all stop and repair it before moving on. But Matthew's father, the wagon maker, had stocked his cart with every part he felt might be needed.

Things went well that first day and a half. About midafternoon, Matthew's father fell while leading the mule pulling his cart. The caravan stopped, and everyone rushed to his side.

"Miriam! Can you run to find Matthew and send him back here? Then can you stay and manage the children or else bring them back here?" called Joseph.

Miriam had always been a good runner, and she ran to Matthew. Matthew left immediately. Miriam tried to keep both the boys and girls playing, but after a while, she gave up. They wanted to know what was happening.

Miriam's daughter, Hannah, laid down rules for them. "There is a crisis. You may not be noisy, and you may not bother the adults while they're helping others. That means all of you! Do you understand?"

She looked at each child individually and got each one's solemn promise to leave the adults alone until the adults called them. The children picked up, cleaned the area, and then ran back to the caravan—Miriam right behind them.

Matthew's father had died. A burial service was held for him late that afternoon. Rabbi Carpus led the service; he spoke of the goodness and love of Father God; he spoke of how the Torah tells us of our reuniting with our loved ones when we pass. The entire group was very still. They buried their beloved

11

friend in a shady spot and set stones over him as a marker. Matthew's father was sixty-two years old. Matthew was now all alone in the world. His parents had each been the only child who had survived childhood illnesses in their families. His mother had died from a severe cough when Matthew was five.

The next day was a somber day. Everyone seemed to be thinking. Without having to be asked, the older children took charge of the little ones in order to let the adults be.

Everyone was up and getting ready to leave before daybreak that morning. Mary said, "Jesus and James, please take this breakfast to Matthew. Ask him to have dinner with us tonight after we stop traveling for the day. Oh, and don't take no for an answer."

Jesus and James found Matthew praying. His eyes were swollen and red. They gave him the breakfast, but he said he wasn't hungry.

Jesus said, "Then we'll just stay here until you eat." After a few minutes, Jesus said, "I think Father God must think you're special. Not many people are all alone. I would like to be your friend. Then you'll always have someone."

"Me too!" said James. "I'll be your friend."

Matthew smiled and began to eat a little of the bread and then a few of the figs and dates. He then drank some water, and soon the food was gone. "Wow!" said Matthew. "I guess I was hungry. I didn't eat much yesterday. Thank you for being my friends. I need friends. We'll be almost like a family. Now I need to finish my prayers and get ready to start out. Please tell your mother that I thank her very much! It was very nice of her to think of me. And tell her I will be pleased to have supper with all of you this evening."

As they walked back to their cart, James asked Jesus, "What does it mean to be a friend and almost family?"

Jesus said, "I think it's kind of like having another brother or maybe an uncle who's kind of more like your brother. You know, we can call him Matthew, instead of sir or mister. And maybe he'll teach us stuff—stuff like how to build a strong cart or a barn for animals for when the weather is bad."

Things started off well on the third day of their trip to Jerusalem. The sun had set red last night, so the weather should be fine today. Miriam and Hannah decided to work together and take the children for their much-needed playtime. It was a brilliant day with the sun shining, a few clouds skimming by, and a slight breeze.

The boys decided they had had enough of those running-ahead games and wanted to play ball. Miriam wondered how they were going to do that and still keep up with the caravan. "Hmmm," she said. "What kind of game can we make with the ball?"

"We have three balls. We could throw them far away and then go get them," offered one of the boys.

"Could we play Sting Me?" suggested Jesus.

"And maybe we could play Frog Line Over," offered James.

"Great ideas!" said Miriam. "Let's do all three. We have all day to play. First, though, we have two younger boys who have never played these games. Let's teach them how. Jesus, you explain Sting Me, please."

"Sure. One person is the stinger, and everyone tries to stay away from him. When he catches up to someone and touches him, then that person's the stinger and has to try to touch someone else."

"Good job!" said Miriam. "James, would you explain Frog Line Over?"

"Everybody but one person lines up, and they bend down on their hands and knees. Then the person standing at the back puts his hands on the last one's back and hops forward and then on the next person's back until he gets to the first person, and then he bends down and the one in back stands up and does the same thing," explained James.

"Good job, James! The one doing the hopping needs to pull the back hem of his garment to the front between his legs, or he'll fall flat on his face!" added Miriam.

There were no more complaints about not wanting to run. The day passed quickly.

The girls seemed a bit whiny, so Miriam left the directing of the boys to Hannah and her friend and went to see what was going on with the girls.

"Miriam, we don't want to play hop the rocks anymore," said one of the girls.

"What do you want to do? Do you have any ideas?"

"No. I guess we're just bored. We're usually kept busy at home all day with chores."

"I have an idea. We need to keep walking so we don't lag behind the carts. Actually I have two ideas. We could walk and sing the psalms or make up our own songs. Or we could see how many times we can go through the alphabet naming an object that starts with each letter—taking turns of course. Does either one of those ideas sound interesting to you?"

"Yes!" they all shouted at once.

"Can we do both?" asked one of the older girls; she seemed so excited. "Maybe first one and then the other and then the first one again?"

"Of course," said Miriam. "You can't repeat anything though—not any of the psalms and not any of the words for each letter. What do you think we can do for the two smallest girls?"

The girls made several suggestions. "Can't they just learn?" one said.

"We can have our hands do different things as we talk or sing, and they can do that," someone else said.

"We can carry them or let them ride on our backs when they get tired, and maybe they'll fall asleep even," suggested a third.

The day was a success! Some bumps and bruises, and some very worn-out children, a very tired bunch indeed, returned to the caravan.

The men had again pulled the caravan into an almost circle. Everyone gathered as a group around several small fires. The fires were blazing, and the women were cooking. It smelled wonderful. The adults had decided to have a combined meal—everyone sharing whatever they had planned for the meal. The children rushed to tell their parents—and anyone else who would listen—about their day. The men were checking their equipment and getting ready for tomorrow, when they would arrive in Jerusalem, at last.

It was a very special night. Everyone stayed up late singing and talking and teasing around the fires. Slowly, people started off to bed. It was so quiet sleeping under the moon and stars that night. They were all looking forward to their arrival in Jerusalem tomorrow.

In spite of being up late that night, everyone seemed to be up and getting ready early the next morning. Morning prayers were said as usual. While the women fixed breakfast, the children did some quick studying, and the men made a final inspection to make sure everything was in good working order. They would walk to the area close to the temple, where they had stayed in previous years.

"We should be there about the fourth hour," Joseph told the family at breakfast. "The plan is for all of us men to go to the temple, buy the lambs, and have them sacrificed—hopefully at the second of the three groups. That will give us some leisure time before dinner tonight."

"Father," said James. "What is sac-saca ..."

Joseph replied, "Good question! Would you ask mother after I leave? I'm sorry, but I need to rush to meet the men and go to the temple. I love you."

"I can tell him," said Jesus. "I remember Mother telling us. Have fun today, Father."

"Thank you, Jesus. Okay, everyone help Mother. I'll be back in a few hours, and soon after that our celebration will begin. I love every one of you!"

"Joseph," said Mary, "please ask Matthew to have dinner with us tonight. Don't let him say no."

Joseph smiled, waved to his family, and went off to join the men for the walk to the temple.

Mary smiled as she cleaned up after the meal and planned the day. Jesus was answering James's questions.

"We're celebrating really three festivals while we're here. We start by coming to Jerusalem and spending our time in tents instead of houses. Next the trumpets blow to tell everyone we're starting. In ten days, we will be very quiet, and we'll think about all the things we've done wrong.

"We always want to be good, but sometimes we're not. Then we have to tell Father or Mother what we did and say we're sorry, and maybe we'll get punished. But we like to say we are really, really sorry to Father God. So the priest puts his hand on a goat, and he puts everyone's bad things on the goat and that means that we are really sorry and that we love Father God. That goat is called a sacrifice. The goat walks away with all our wrong things. It means our wrong things are taken away. The goat is the sacrifice for what we do wrong."

Apparently bored, James said, "Jesus, I'm thirsty."

"I'll help you get a drink, and then we need to help Mother. I think Elizabeth is waking up from her nap, so maybe you could play with her while I help Mother."

The men returned sooner than they had expected, each one bringing his sacrificial lamb to be served at dinner. The group was in a high celebration mode, until they heard a crash and some of the children began screaming. One of the little girls had tripped and fallen into one of the fires. Her hair and cloak caught fire; she had several burns. The fire in her hair and clothing was put out quickly, but she was screaming from the pain.

Jesus grabbed James's hand, and they rushed to see what was happening. As they got there, the adults were hurrying to their carts to see what they might have to help. The girl's father and mother and a few others were trying to calm her. Jesus and James ran to her. Jesus took her hand and said, "Don't cry. Father God, please make her well."

By the time the others returned with ointments and strips of cloth for binding, she was sitting in her father's lap and no longer crying. The women crowded around to put ointment on her burns, but they couldn't find any. They were amazed! The only sign of her having been burned was that a good part of the back of her tunic, and some of her hair were burned away. People were amazed.

Finally, it seemed to the children, it was time for dinner. Jesus always loved the ceremony involved with the festival meals. He felt that they filled his heart. This meal was no exception. The meaning of these days of festivals had such deep meaning, not just for him but also for many others. "Thank You, Father God. Thank You," he prayed.

The next morning, one of the groups from a nearby town was off to the side stoning a man for thievery. One of the rocks bounced and hit a little girl in her temple. There was a lot of screaming, and James ran to Jesus and said, "Come on! Someone's hurt bad!"

They ran to where the commotion was, and there lay the small girl. She was completely still, and no one seemed to know what to do. Some were trying to find her parents. Others just ran off, ashamed of what they were doing on a festival day.

"Quick! Let's pray," said Jesus.

The two boys ran past the adults, knelt down, and took the little girl's hands. And Jesus said, "Father God, please heal this little girl. She didn't know she was going to get hurt."

The little girl stirred. Soon she was sitting up. When she saw the boys near her—boys she didn't know—she tried to pull away. Her mother had been preparing the meal near her cart and came running. She picked her up and held her close.

"What happened?" she asked James and Jesus.

"She was watching the men, and a stone hit her on the head. She wasn't moving, so we asked Father God to heal her," answered Jesus.

The mother looked at the boys quizzically and said, "Thank you, boys. Maybe you should return to your family? I'll take her to our cart, and she'll be okay." She carried the little girl to their cart. Others around the site were very quiet—not sure what had just happened.

After the days and celebrations of the Festival of Tents, the trip home was uneventful—except of course for the usual scrapes and bruises, broken parts on the carts, cranky kids, hot sun, and the number of clothes that needed mending. One thing did seem to stand out. Matthew and Hannah seemed to find it very nice to be with each other!

FOUR

10

It was raining again. It looked like this would be an all-day rain. During the past few days, they'd had some sprinkles and even a few heavier rains, but this was different. Joseph said, "I guess it's going to rain most of the day. So, boys, you and I are going to give the carpenter's shop a new layout. How about it? I think if we arrange equipment in a different way, we can do our work more efficiently. We'll be back for dinner. Elizabeth, help your mother."

And off they went for a day of working together.

As soon as the men left, Elizabeth whined, "Mother, I don't want to stay home. I want to go with the boys!"

"I know you do, Elizabeth. But, sweetheart, that's not going to happen. You're needed here to do what needs to be done. I need to weave more clothing for all of us. You children are growing so fast it's hard for me to keep up. I want you to dust all the furniture and wipe any spills or sticky spots you find. Get started now please," said Mary.

"Yes, Mother. But why can't I work with the boys?"

"You know, Elizabeth, I would love to say, 'Because I said so.' But let me say this; when Father God created this world He saw all the work that needed to be done. He thought, *What if everyone only wants to plant and harvest crops? Or what if everyone only wants to cook?* And He thought a while and said, 'I guess I'll tell them what to do.' So He made some chores for the men to do and some chores for the women to do. That way everything will get done, and people will know what they're supposed to do. Do you understand?"

"I guess so," said Elizabeth. "But I don't like it all the time."

"So what are you going to do now?"

"I guess I'll go dust. Can I go out in the courtyard first and see if the new baby lamb is okay?"

"Yes. But don't be long. Soon baby Simon will be awake, and I'll need your help so I can get this cloth made."

Elizabeth seemed appeased. She grabbed a piece of oiled cloth to cover her head and ran out to see the lamb. True to her word, she didn't stay long. When she returned she seemed happier, more ready to accept the chore of dusting.

Joseph and the boys were working hard. First they emptied the shelves. Joseph had to remind them over and over to lay things down neatly and in the order that they removed them, telling them it would make putting things back much easier. They settled down and were doing a remarkable job, especially considering how young they were.

When everything was removed from the shelves and the shelves were wiped down, Joseph said, "Boys let's have some fun. The hard work is done. Putting things back will be much easier."

Joseph proposed that they use the shadows from the candles to make figures on a wall and then take turns making up stories to go with those shadows.

Seven-year-old Judas held his hand up with the thumb spread away from the fingers and said, "Hey, look! It's a turkey! If I put up both hands, they can talk to each other!" That started a time of using their imaginations—and their silliness.

The boys loved it! They shared lots of laughs and a lot of very strange stories. What imaginations young boys have. They seemed to be invigorated by the time spent playing and almost enjoyed putting things in their new, hopefully more readily available, order.

FIVE

11

"Father," said Jesus, "next Sabbath is 'Kids' Game Day,' and I was thinking about something new. You know how we try to get a strong stick to hit the ball? Well, I was thinking about trying something more like the paddles that are used with a boat—you know, something that has a small stick thing to hold on to and a wider paddle on the top to hit the ball."

"Hmmm," Joseph said. "Sounds like something to try. Would you like to make it in the carpentry shop?"

"Yes, Father, but the paddle part is what confuses me. I don't know if it should be flat or if it should rounded in a little bit or if it should round out. What do you think?"

Joseph smiled and said, "Why don't you make one of each. You can try them all at game day and then decide which works best."

"Thank you, Father! May I use some of the scrap wood? May I start now? I need to decide how big to make them. I can't wait to try them." Jesus ran off to find just the right pieces of scrap wood.

Between school and home chores, Jesus worked on the paddles every minute he could manage. Finally, Kids' Game Day arrived. There must have been about twenty children from ages five to maybe fifteen who came to play the various games.

So many games went on at the same time. A few ropes had been tied to branches on a few trees so the youngest could swing. Some of the girls were throwing rocks and hopping on one foot to pick them up—trying not to fall. The older boys were having their usual races. They ran around the outside of the field, from one tree to another, or they would hop arm in arm with their legs that touched each other tied together. What a game that was, with all the participants trying to be so macho and yet falling, one pair of boys after the other. It was hilarious!

Jesus had brought his paddles. The older boys examined each one and gave their opinion, but finally they decided to try each one and see which worked best. It was decided they would play a game using each of the paddles and then decide.

The game was to hit the ball and run around the far tree and back before the ball was caught and you were touched with it. Jesus was given the first at bat. He chose the paddle that rounded in. The next game they used the paddle that rounded out, and finally they tried the paddle that was flat. It was decided that the paddle that rounded out was the best.

What a day it was! All were sweaty and exhausted and covered with dirt. Being boys, that's when they were most happy. The girls weren't much cleaner.

Each child brought his or her own lunch, and when seven-year-old Judas blew the sheep's horn as a signal to eat, they sat together and ate—boys under one tree and girls under another. What a rowdy bunch they were. The older ones teased the younger ones, and the younger ones gave back as they could.

They spent the rest of the afternoon playing more of the same games.

It was almost sundown when they stopped to go home to wash up before dinner and Family Time. But first, every scrap of mess was cleaned up, broken branches laid by the firepit, and the dirt smoothed. And thus ended a wonderful Kids' Game Day—until next time!

SIX

11

The birth of baby Anna was very hard on Mary. Mary had fallen asleep right after the birth, and the family found it hard to wake her, so they let her rest, hoping her body knew best how to heal her—through rest.

"Boys," Joseph said to the three older boys. "Mother is ill today, and she may be for a few more days. The birth of Anna was very hard on her. Miriam is with her daughter Rebecca, who delivered her third child yesterday, so she's not able to help us. One of you boys will need to miss school today and stay with the younger ones. I'll talk with Rabbi Carpus."

"I'll stay with them, Father," said Jesus. "I'm ahead on my class work, so it won't be a problem for me."

"Thank you, Jesus. As I said, I'll speak with the rabbi."

"Father, when James and Judas leave for school, would you have a few minutes? I have a serious question I want to ask you."

"Of course. Okay, boys! Time to get ready for school now. Remember to behave yourselves!"

As Joseph helped the older boys get ready for school, Jesus cleared the breakfast table. When Joseph came to the table, they sat across from each other.

"What is it, Jesus?"

"Father, I'm not like others, am I?"

"What do you mean?"

"Well, memorizing and understanding the Torah and even understanding the Prophets is not difficult for me. They seem so clear," said Jesus.

"That's a very good thing, isn't it?" said Joseph.

"Yes, Father. But it's more than that. I feel that Father God is with me all the time. I think he kind of shows me things. I don't know how to explain it, but it makes me feel good inside."

"Jesus," replied Joseph, "you are a very special person. Father God has a definite plan for your life. I want you to continue to be open to His word. As you grow, you will feel this more and more. It's a very good thing, Jesus. Always keep Him close to your heart."

"Thank you, Father. I really love Father God as I love you and Mother and even my brothers and sisters. My heart seems to get bigger when I think of Him."

"Jesus, I am honored to call you my son, to watch you grow, to watch how you treat others, and to watch your curiosity. And I grow in my love for you each day. You are a great blessing to your mother and to me. Continue to be the loving person you are. Don't let things that happen change who you are. You are as Father God wants you to be. Do you understand?" Joseph continued.

"Yes, Father. I think I understand." As he stood Jesus said, "I need to start Elizabeth and Joses and Simon on their Torah studies now. Mother is such a great teacher. I'll do my best. Thank you, Father. I love you too, Father."

The day started off well for Jesus. Even two-year-old Simon seemed willing to learn. At the fourth hour, Jesus put out figs and dates for midmorning snacks for the children to eat while he took water and a cool damp cloth in to his mother.

"Mother! What's wrong?" Mary was so pale, and there was a lot of blood on her mat.

Jesus turned and called, "Joses! Go to the carpentry shop and get Father. Tell him to come home *now*! And then run and get the physician. Hurry! Elizabeth, watch Simon and keep him safe and happy."

Jesus rushed back to Mary, taking her hand in his. Feeling her forehead, he cried out, "Father God! Please! Heal my mother."

At that, Mary stirred and Joseph walked into the room. "What's going on? Oh no, Mary! My love," he cried. "Be well! Mary. Be well."

Elizabeth, carrying two-year-old Simon, brought the physician into the room. "Okay," the physician said. "Everybody out! I'll take it from here."

Back in the living room, Jesus and Joseph said together, "We need to pray. Now!"

Simon crawled into Joseph's lap and said, "God will always love us." This was his regular prayer. The five of them held each other and prayed and prayed.

About the seventh hour, the doctor came out of Mary's room. "She's sleeping now. I gave her some medication, and she'll probably sleep for another hour or so. She's much better now than when I first got here. Jesus, you did a great job of reacting quickly. You did just the right things. I am proud of you, young man."

"Thank you, sir. I did the only things I could think of; I sent for help, and I prayed."

"I know, Jesus. Your mother told me how you prayed. Your mother was very seriously ill. Most women do not live through this. I believe it was your prayer that saved your mother. Never be afraid to pray, Jesus.

"Joseph, may I have a word with you?" the physician added as he prepared to leave.

He and Joseph walked outside. "Joseph, this was very serious. I must tell you that Mary will not be able to have more children. I don't know of another woman who has lived through this. She must do nothing for perhaps weeks. You will need help. I'm sure women will bring food for all of you.

I'll send a wet nurse to nurse the baby, but maybe we can find someone to come in to help with the younger children while the boys are in school."

"I'll see to it," said Joseph. "Thank you for coming so quickly. And ..." Joseph hesitated, "thank you for reaffirming to Jesus the strength of prayer. The younger ones heard you, and I know they'll remember it also. Thank you, my friend."

"Joseph, it will be maybe even three months before Mary will be back to herself. I'll be back tomorrow and again next week to check on her, but she is very fragile."

"I understand. Thank you. See you tomorrow then," said Joseph as he went back into the house to check once more on Mary and the youngsters before returning to work.

The next morning, Mary was up before everyone and was starting the cooking fire when Joseph got up. "Mary! What are you doing out of bed?" said Joseph.

"Good morning, Joseph! I feel fine! I'm hungry though, so I thought I'd make a big breakfast for all of us. Ah, I think I hear the children. Oh! And baby Anna and the wet nurse! I guess the day has started."

The usual morning clatter seemed a little subdued that morning. The children were amazingly quiet and almost formal. It was as if the house itself knew a miracle had happened here, but still some things about Mother were incomprehensible. Jesus did stay home one more day. Joseph emphatically told Mary to get lots of rest—giving Jesus the look that said, *I expect you to see to it, young man!*

When the physician came to see Mary, he couldn't believe his eyes. She was well, and he told her so. She was even able to feed baby Anna. He made a big deal of telling her to continue to rest every day.

Later, as he made his rounds of patients around town, he had to tell everyone of the miracle at Joseph's house. Mary was well!

SEVEN

12

"Great dinner, Mary!" said Joseph as he gave her a hug and a kiss on the cheek. "All right, everyone. Time for Family Time."

Mary finished the dishes and picked up her mending. *The tradition of tearing your garments in sadness is sometimes a big pain,* she thought.

"Open our hearts and minds, Father God, that we might do Your will," Joseph began. "Yes, Joses?" Joses had raised his hand to speak.

"Father, I don't understand about our learning," said Joses.

"What do you mean? Can you tell me what you're thinking?"

"Well, Father, I know Daniel, son of Joshua, became a bar mitzvah last Sabbath ... but I don't know how all this education works for that to happen."

"Joses, that's a very good question. Why don't we take this time to talk about it? First, Mother does the teaching until all children reach the age of five. She makes sure you understand how to listen, how to remember what she is teaching you, and the beginnings of how to understand the simpler ideas of the Torah. Understand?"

"Yes, Father, but sometimes Simon doesn't sit still and listen to Mother."

"Guess what? You were the same way! In fact, most people are like that at three years of age. That's one reason mothers need to be so patient.

"From ages five to ten, boys begin going to school and are taught from the Torah. Did you know that the Torah was first written down not too many years ago? Before that every boy needed to memorize the entire Torah! The Torah is what Jesus and James and Judas are studying now. Can you imagine having to memorize the whole Torah?"

"Wow!" said Jesus, Judas, and James together.

"I'm glad I didn't live in the old days!" added Judas.

"Now Jesus is finishing his studies to become a man, a bar mitzvah—not only a man at home, but also a man in the synagogue as well. Wait, Joses. I can see you're going to ask what that means, but I'm going to turn to you, Jesus, and ask you to explain what you understand your role will be when you are a bar mitzvah." Joseph turned to Jesus with a smile, a wink, and a small nod.

Jesus blew out a breath and said, "Joses, you know that we must have ten men at synagogue in order to have a service. Well, if there are only nine, and I am there, then we can have the service. I will be permitted to take part in services—usually doing readings. I will be a 'son of the commandments,' and the thing that's nice for Father is that he won't be responsible for anything I do that's wrong. I will have to take responsibility for myself. I will be considered a man."

"Just in the synagogue and stuff? Or will you be a man to us too?" Of course it was Joses asking this question.

Joseph replied, "He will be a man everywhere, with a man's responsibilities."

Joses looked puzzled and said, "Jesus, you'll be done with school then. So what will you do all the time?"

Mary, Joseph, and Jesus smiled at this. Jesus said, "There is continuing school, where I can study legal issues, but I don't know if I'll do that. I might just take one class at a time. But I'll still teach the younger students at school as a rabbi, and I'd like to spend more time working with Father and Benjamin. The business seems to be growing fast."

"Joses, have we answered your questions?" asked Joseph.

"Yes, I think so. I just think that I'm glad that my brothers are older than I am so I can see what happens to them."

"Good. Time for bed now. So,"—Joseph smiled at his inquisitive son—"Joses, why don't you say a closing prayer tonight?"

"Father God, thank You for helping me understand. There's so much to learn; I'll try to learn all of it. Help me and help everyone. Amen."

***

The day arrived when Jesus would become a bar mitzvah—a son of the commandments. He had just turned thirteen. Jesus spent extra time with his morning prayers. He went to the synagogue ahead of the family to prepare and to see what part of the service would be his responsibility. When the rabbi told him he would be reading *maftir,* he was amazed.

"Father!" he called when he was able to join the family. "I am to be maftir!"

Three-year-old Simon wanted to know what that meant.

Joseph said, "It means he will be the very last person in the service. It's really an honor. He will reread a little of the Torah reading for the day, the maftir, and then he will chant the *haftorah,* a reading from the Prophets." Turning to Jesus, he said, "I am very proud of you, Son! You are a wonderful man. I love you so much!"

"Thank you, Father," replied Jesus.

"Father," said Simon, "how come Jesus gets to talk and you don't?"

"But I do. The rabbi will call me up at some point in the service, and I will say a blessing. I will thank God for guiding Jesus and ask Him to watch over Jesus as he goes on in life. You see, now he is responsible for his own decisions, and that is a very big responsibility."

The service went very well. Even little Simon, now three appeared to understand some of what was said.

Later that night as they prepared for bed, Joseph and Mary turned to each other and smiled. Joseph shook his head and said, "A man already! He's a good man, Mary, a fine man. I am so proud of him." He said as he held her.

Jesus felt even closer to his Father God. He was now a man; he was now a son of the commandments—a bar mitzvah!

"Thank You, Father God. Please always hold me close to You and help me to do Your will. Thank You for all You've done for me and for my family. Please continue to watch over and keep us safe," prayed Jesus.

EIGHT

13

"Mother!" complained Joses. "Elizabeth's climbing trees!"

"Oh?" said Mary

"She can't do that!"

"Why not?" asked Mary

"Because she's a girl!"

"Yes, Joses. Elizabeth is a girl."

"But Mother, girls aren't s'posed to climb trees!"

"Why?"

"I don't know! They just aren't. No one else does."

"Maybe they will now that Elizabeth is climbing."

"No! That's just for boys," insisted Joses.

"Joses, is she climbing the trees you boys want to climb so that she's in your way?"

"No. She's going up that old tree that we climbed when we were little."

"So she's not in your way?" asked Mary.

"No. But the guys laugh, and then they tease me about having a monkey for a sister."

"Ah, so that's the problem. Which is worse—that they tease you or that they call your sister a monkey?"

"They aren't going to call her a monkey again, cuz I told them that I am the team captain in school, and if they do that I'll be sure they can't play ball."

"Joses! That was wonderful! I am *very* proud of you for sticking up for your sister. I am going to tell Father about this

31

because he needs to know what a wonderful young man you are becoming."

"Thank you, but does that mean that she's still gonna climb trees?" asked Joses, not really mollified.

"Yes it does! And if the other girls want to climb trees, I want you boys to leave them alone. Or, better yet, if you see that they could use some advice from you boys, who have been doing it for a long time, I hope you will give them advice," said Mary.

"Okay I will; but I don't feel very good about it," groused Joses.

"This will give you a chance to develop leadership skills. Just do your best," said Mary as she went back to her loom. Joses went off to meet the boys. Mary noticed that he started walking slowly and kicking dirt but soon walked faster and, finally, broke into a run. *I hope that will help him grow,* she thought.

At Family Time that evening, Simon, now five and ready to start school, said, "Father, I think I want to be a rabbi."

Joses broke out laughing.

"Joses!" said Joseph. "That was not acceptable behavior. You will apologize to your brother right now! And you will tell him what you did wrong. Now! Then you will sit quietly the rest of the evening and not say another word."

"I'm sorry I laughed at you being a rabbi. But they're old like Jesus, and you're just a kid."

"Thank you, Joses," said Simon. "Is it okay if I want to be a rabbi, Father?"

"That would be awesome! Can you tell us what you're thinking?"

"Well, you know, sometimes when Anna gets kinda stubborn and whiny, Mother looks at me kinda like for help. I like it. Sometimes Anna's really stubborn, but I just think about it and try different things, and almost always she stops whining and learns what she's supposed to do. And I love being with Benjamin in the carpentry shop now. He waits for me to learn the things he's showing me, and if I have an idea about something he lets me try it, and sometimes it works!"

"Mother and Benjamin have both told me about those times, and I have been very proud of you. How do you feel when Anna learns?" asked Joseph.

"I feel like—I don't know—like I won something or like I did a good job. I feel good!"

"You might really be rabbi material. I wonder if the word you were looking for was that you feel blessed by our Father God?" asked Joseph.

Simon thought for a little bit and then smiled and said, "Yes, Father! That's how I feel. Blessed by Father God!

"Simon, I'll be here for you," said Jesus. "If you want to talk about something or if you want to know what something means or if you want to know what I do, just ask me."

"Thank you, Jesus. When I see you working with the kids, I know I want to help kids learn. I think that, if kids learn stuff early, they can learn more," said Simon.

"You're so right. That's why what mothers teach children their first five years is so important. They are learning how to learn," said Joseph.

"Jesus, is it hard to be rabbi?" asked Simon.

"Every job, everything you do, has hard parts and easy parts. I work hard on the hard parts and enjoy the easy parts," answered Jesus.

"Jesus?" asked Elizabeth. "Things are hard for you? I thought you just did everything and James and Judas too. All you do is 'do,' and it gets done."

"I wish!" said Judas, who was only a year or so older than Elizabeth.

Judas felt proud that his sister thought he was grown up.

"Elizabeth, I'm glad we seem that way to you. All adults have something that's hard for them—everyone! That's a good thing because somebody else can do it. It's like Jonathan the leather maker; Jonathan can't make a brick that will last a long time. But the brick maker can. The brick maker is not at all good at working with leather, so he depends on the leather maker. Does that help you understand?" said Jesus.

"Yes, but I thought when I got big, I could do everything—well everything that all the women do. Not so, huh?" asked Elizabeth.

"We all wish we could. We all thought that when we were younger. But you know what, Elizabeth? When you're older, it all makes sense. You don't even think about questions like, What do I not know that someone else knows? You see the whole picture," said Joseph.

"But I'm not grown up, and I don't always know what to do sometimes. Jesus, you're a rabbi. What do you do when something is hard?" asked Elizabeth.

"I have two secrets. You already know those secrets. I read from our Hebrew Bible, not just from the Torah but also the Prophets. But I think the most important thing is that I pray and ask Father God to help me.

"That reminds me," explained Joseph, "when you ask Father God to help you, that doesn't mean that you can go off and play and He'll do the work. Nope. It means that you keep looking for the answer, and God will help you find it. Something interesting happens; you'll be reading or thinking about the problem, and all of a sudden, you'll find the answer!"

"Wow! You're going to do that, Simon?" asked Elizabeth.

"I think everybody should do that all the time—not just rabbis but little kids and big grown-ups," said Simon.

"One last thing, Simon," added Joseph. "Don't ever be afraid to change your mind. Because that is where you are led now does not mean you can't change your mind later. Do you understand?"

"I do, Father, but I'm sure!" Simon is so sure!

Mary and Joseph looked at each other, smiled, and both were thinking, *Possibly another rabbi? Thank you Father God!*

NINE

14

"Rabbi Jesus!" A young boy came rushing into school.

"Yes. What is it?"

"Your brother's fighting with Lazarus!"

"Really!" said Jesus. "Let's go see."

Sure enough, Joses was on top of Lazarus and throwing punches.

Jesus picked up Joses and said, "What on earth is going on here?"

"He's just such a wimp."

"Joses, what do you mean by a wimp?"

"Well, he can't do anything. He can't hit a ball. He can't run. He can't even pass the little kids in a race!" said Joses.

"Really! Why do you think that is?" asked Jesus.

"He's just a wimp."

"Hmmm. Let's look at this. Joses, what was your score in mathematics last week?"

"Seventy-two," replied Joses.

"Lazarus, what was your score?"

"A hundred, Rabbi."

"I see," said Jesus. "Joses, what was your score in Torah class last week?"

"Seventy-eight, Rabbi." Joses was starting to see a pattern here and decided to address Jesus as he should his teacher.

"Lazarus, what was your score?"

"A hundred, Rabbi."

Jesus asked Joses, "What was your score in memory work last week?"

Meekly Joses answered, "Seventy, Rabbi."

"So," said Jesus, "you are good at sports like running and hitting a ball and games. However, Lazarus is very good at mathematics, Torah class, and memorization. If Lazarus is a wimp at sports, does that mean that you're a wimp at schoolwork? I think you both have a lot to think about. I want you two boys to sit over there and talk things over. I mean *talk* things over, not just sit."

The boys sat but just looked at the ground for a few minutes. Finally Lazarus said, "I'm sorry I'm so bad at sports. I want to do better, but I don't know how. No one ever taught me how. You have big brothers to show you. I don't."

Joses looked at him. Then he said, "I could teach you. Maybe my brothers will even help. Do you really want to run and hit and stuff?"

"I really want to. I always wanted to. I watch you, and you can do everything. It makes me feel really dumb," admitted Lazarus.

"Well, I feel dumb at school when I see what you can do. I would really like to be smart, but I'm not."

"I can help you with schoolwork. Maybe we could trade. You teach me games, and I'll teach you class stuff," said Lazarus.

"Yeah. We could do that. I don't know how though. Maybe we could work here after school or maybe at one of our houses or maybe ... I don't know." Joses was thinking out loud.

"Maybe, maybe Rabbi Jesus could help us set a time or maybe our parents," offered Lazarus.

"Let's talk to our parents tonight. I would kind of like to do it here at school because there's the big area where we can bat and run, and sometimes Rabbi or one of the older kids is here if we have a question about our classwork." Joses was really getting into this helping each other thing.

The next morning before class, Joses asked Lazarus, "Did you talk to your parents last night?"

"I did. Can we meet at that same place after school today and talk about it?"

Both boys needed to concentrate on schoolwork all day. Their minds tended to be looking forward to their meeting. Finally, the class day ended, and they could meet.

"Grandfather Enoch said he would feed the baby animals so we could have two hours after school," said Lazarus.

"My family said they were very proud of the two of us for finding a way to help each other. They said they couldn't believe how grown up we were acting. I guess we made them proud. I didn't hurt you yesterday, did I?" asked Joses.

"Not too much. Just some bruises. Grandfather said I would probably get a lot worse than that in my lifetime. Okay. How should we do this?" asked Lazarus.

"We could do one first one day, and then the next day we could do the other one first," said Joses.

"Or we could do the running and batting first every day because we've just been sitting in school, and it would kind of wake us up," suggested Lazarus.

"Okay. Let's try that and see how it works. We can always change it. So let's start with you running a little bit. Okay?"

Lazarus started running. It made Joses laugh.

Lazarus was not happy. "How can you teach me anything if you just laugh at me?" asked Lazarus.

"Sorry. I'll try not to do that again. How about let's start with your flopping hands and arms. Bend your arms at the elbow and make your hands into fists. Try that," said Joses.

Lazarus tried.

"Okay. That was better. Now let your arms move. When you step on your left foot, let your right arm swing out, and when you step on your right foot, let your left arm swing out. Like this." Joses ran a big circle around Lazarus demonstrating how to use your arms when running.

"I'll try. You make it look so easy." He tried. Joses had him do it a few times, and Lazarus seemed to be getting better each time.

"That was a lot better!" said Joses. "Now let's look at your legs. Can you lift up your knees when you run? Like this. Oh, and stand up straight with your head up." Again Joses ran large circles to demonstrate.

"Like this?" Lazarus asked.

"That was better. Keep trying. You'll get better and better." He did get better.

"Let's do classwork now. You've really been working hard. I guess that means I have to work hard on my studies, right?" said Joses.

They started with mathematics. "It really isn't that hard. Just remember that things are always the same in math. Two plus two will always be four. Nine times nine will always be eighty-one. Like that. So kind of like, if you can remember it once, then you always know it. I think we should start with last year's numbers 'cause that's where we really got into math. Okay?"

"Really? It doesn't change? I guess I never thought of that. Oh, man! I promise I'll try hard. What's first?"

The two boys worked really hard every day, Sunday through Friday after school. After two weeks, they had formed a strong bond. They found a rhythm to their teachings, and both improved—a lot. Lazarus was able to hit a ball once in a while, and Joses got a score of one hundred on one of his tests—on only one test though. They both learned it was okay to laugh at and with each other.

Because others were helping with their work at home, the boys eventually studied and played only twice a week. But it became fun for them.

Sabbath days—the days of rest—was a game day when the young boys of the town would gather for races and ball games.

It didn't take long for Lazarus to begin to enjoy it. Although he would never be the best man on the team, his cheering and encouragement of the others added a great deal to the games— and he tried!

TEN

15

The day was one of those golden perfect days. Mary prepared a supper that could be eaten on the roof. After dinner, Joseph decided that the roof was the perfect place to have their Family Time.

Joseph opened with prayer and then surprised the family by saying, "This is a special night. It could mean a big change for all of us. Benjamin and I have been working together for many years, but he wants and needs to stay home. His arthritis is so bad, and he wants to just stay at home and take care of himself and his home. He's almost sixty-two and not many of us live to be that old."

He continued. "I offered to provide money to him on a regular basis so he could have what he needs, but he said he's been putting money away, and he'll be fine."

"Wow!" Jesus said. "I wonder how he could do that. He's usually the first person to give when someone needs something."

"He is, Jesus. But he assured me that he'll be okay—not that we can't visit him often and just make sure. Well," said Joseph, "This means I will need more help in the carpentry shop. Jesus, you're a rabbi during school time, you're taking a class, and you help out in the shop every day. James, you're taking a class and working for our leather maker every day. Judas, you're in school and working for the brick maker every day. Joses, I could use your help after school, and Simon I would even have a job for you."

"Would I get paid?" asked Simon, now almost six.

"Sure," said Joseph.

Simon was excited.

"Now, here's what I need to know. I can find someone to hire to do the work if that's what we decide. Yes, I said *we* decide. However, if any or all of you would like to work at the carpentry shop, there will be a place for you. We would have a family business. I want all of you to think about this, and we'll talk more tomorrow night at Family Time. Remember, you do not have to work in the carpentry shop. I just need to know if anyone wants to."

"I've noticed that the work seems to have really picked up," said Jesus. "So there'd be plenty of work for all of us. But a family business. I kind of like that."

"I do too, Jesus. Any more questions?" Joseph asked the boys. "Good. Think about this a lot, and we'll talk tomorrow. Elizabeth, would you please close with prayer tonight."

"Dear Father God, thank You that all the boys might be working together. I don't know why I can't too, but I know that You know best. Please bless all of us and help the boys think. Good night. Amen."

The next evening, Mary and Joseph were surprised at the energy the boys brought to the dinner table. It seemed they were just bursting to tell everyone something. After things were finished for the day, the family sat down for Family Time.

"Mary, would you mind sitting closer to us? Can you leave your mending for tonight?" asked Joseph.

Mary smiled, put down her never-ending mending, and moved closer to the family group, eager to talk.

Joseph opened with prayer and reviewed what he had said last night. He asked the boys to tell him their thoughts. "We don't have to make a final decision tonight," he said. "I just want to hear from all of you what you're thinking.

"Jesus, I am assuming that you will be staying on. Is that correct? I'd like to say you do not have to if you have a wish to do something else. I would just like to know."

"I would very much like to stay! This is a big change for all of us, no matter what we decide," answered Jesus.

"James, what are you thinking?" asked Joseph.

"I spoke to Jonathan at the leather shop today, and he was surprised. He said his wife's nephew is looking for work and had asked him for a job. His wife said he had to hire him, and he didn't know how to tell me. He said I could have a day or so to decide, and if I decided to leave I could leave when I wanted to. Also, I really would like to work here. I have some new ideas for leather, and I'd like to discuss them with you—oh, and the brothers," answered James.

"How do you feel about leaving Jonathan?" asked Joseph.

"I'll miss seeing him every day, and I'll miss the smell of leather, but I've had time to think about it and I think it would be a great opportunity. Um, I would really like to see us expand the business though, but we can talk about that later."

"Thank you, James. I appreciate your honesty. Yes, of course we will all discuss changes to be made. A business always needs to grow," said Joseph. "Judas, what are your thoughts?"

"Father, at first I didn't want to do it. I didn't want to change from working with brick to working in carpentry. But then I thought about how it's so hard for the brick maker to work some days. His back is sore, he has arthritis in his hands and knees, and I think maybe brick making is a young person's job. I don't think I want to be doing it when I'm older," said Judas. "So I started thinking about what it would be like to work in carpentry and work with my family. Father, right now I am so excited about it, I can hardly wait to get started!"

"Thank you, Judas," said Joseph. "You're showing your maturity by the way you think. I'm proud of you. I imagine you'll have to continue working there until the Brick Maker can find help though."

"Yes, Father. I talked to him about it today, you know, like 'if,'" and he said that there's a new family building a home quite close to him; maybe one of those boys would like a job. He's going to check with them."

"Good. Mary, what do you think of all this?" asked Joseph.

"Oh, Joseph, I am so proud! As I listen to these boys, I see they're thinking and talking as men. My thoughts are like this: We would be able to schedule things according to our activities, we won't need to work around other families' work schedules, and everyone will be close. I like that. My only concern or thought is that Benjamin was the bookkeeper, and someone will have to do that now."

"Thank you, Mary," said Joseph. "I've been thinking of the process of getting all the work done on time and in order and of which boy would do which part of each job. I didn't even think of the bookkeeping. We'll need to give that some real thought as we make plans for a family business. Thank you."

"I was also thinking that, when we have more stable times, maybe we three girls could make things to sell. Elizabeth is already very good at the loom. She's even learned to make patterns with the same color thread. Anna is young, but we can work with that. She's at the age where she needs to learn more," said Mary.

"That's quite a task ahead of you. But knowing you, you'll do a fine job of implementing it. I really like that idea, Mary." Turning to Joses, he said, "Joses, I'd like to hear your ideas."

"I think there are things I can do. I was thinking that I'm strong enough now to fetch the wood for you. I can be the one who runs errands, like if you run out of a … you know, the stuff you need to make things smooth or anything, and I can learn to do all the work," said Joses, quite excitedly. Mary and Joseph looked at each other and smiled.

"Thank you, Joses. It shows that you have also been thinking. I appreciate that. Well, Simon, what are your thoughts?"

"Well, I know that my main job will be picking things up off the floor and putting them in the right place, and I know that I will need to sweep. I was thinking that I could really scratch some of the stuff if I'm not careful with the broom, so I know I need to be really careful. Remember a while ago when I put one of the dishes in the wrong place? I could see that Mother wasn't happy, so I don't want to put something in the wrong place again," said Simon.

"Simon, I am very proud of the way you're thinking at such a young age. Thank you! You're right about your jobs. They will be keeping the shop picked up and cleaned up. I know you will do your best," Joseph said with a smile.

"Joseph," said Mary, "maybe you could make a broom with a handle that is the right height. I think that's the biggest problem when sweeping. The handle is so long it knocks things over."

"Good idea. Does that sound good to you, Simon?"

"Oh yes, Father. But I will try to always do my best. I know I am the littlest boy, and I have to be more careful," said Simon.

"Good. Now we all need to think. It sounds like everyone is thinking this is a good idea. And it sounds like we're all eager to get started," began Joseph.

"Could I say something?" said Elizabeth. "And maybe Anna too?"

"Of course," said Joseph. "I'm sorry I didn't ask the two of you for your opinions. Please tell us what you're thinking."

"Well, I want to work with Mother. But when we sell things, will I get paid or does the money go to the whole family? I want to start to have some money of my own," said Elizabeth.

"Of course you'll be paid," said Mary. "It sounds like this entire family will be involved in a business of one kind or another."

"I don't want to work," said Anna. "I just want to play after lessons."

"Anna," said Joseph, "we are a family, and everyone has things he or she must do, whether we want to or not. You will have chores assigned to you."

"Yes, Father," said Anna. Then quietly she added, "But I don't want to."

Mary told her, "Anna. Don't worry about it now. Elizabeth and I will help you."

"Then it's agreed! We will have a family carpentry shop. Let's call it the Shop! Yes, James, we will think about adding new things to what we do. For tonight though, I think we've done enough talking. Let's plan to keep talking and to start working together. How about if we start our new Shop two weeks from today?"

They all agreed—even Anna. "Jesus, will you please close with prayer?"

"Father God, we thank You for always being here for us. We pray that this new direction for all of us is Your will. Hold us tightly in Your hands. Guide us and help us to work for Your glory. Thank You. Amen!"

ELEVEN

15

Mary and the children were in bed. Joseph and Jesus were on the roof talking of some preliminary plans for putting this new business in place. It was a clear summer night; even the animals seemed content.

Suddenly, they heard Hiram call to them. "Joseph! I need help."

"Coming, Hiram." called Joseph. He and Jesus went to the door to meet Hiram.

"What is it, Hiram?" asked Joseph.

"I'm sorry to be so late. Miriam's sister came to us this afternoon. She's really sick. She coughs almost all the time, and she's running a fever. Miriam has been feeding her broth, but she can't even swallow that now. She says she is freezing cold, and she just can't get warm. Joseph, it's so warm outside that we let the coals burn out, and I just have a few logs to heat the warming stones. Can you help me?"

"Of course!" said Joseph. "Let's go to the courtyard. We had a fire for our dinner, and I'm sure there are still hot coals."

As they retrieved the coals and more logs, Jesus said, "I'd like to go with Hiram, Father. I can help him carry things so he'll have enough logs for tonight and tomorrow as well."

Joseph hesitated a minute. After all, what the sister had could be contagious. "That'll be fine, Jesus. I'll check the animals and the house one last time before heading to bed." To Hiram, he said, "If you need anything else just let me know."

Mary came out with a pot of honey. "I heard you, and I thought maybe some honey would be nice to soothe her throat. I'll say prayers for her tonight."

"Thank you, Mary. I don't know whether or not we have any honey left. Thank you," said Hiram.

"Father God's peace and healing be to your home tonight, Hiram," Joseph called as Hiram and Jesus started off for Hiram's home.

As they neared the house, they could hear the awful coughing. It seemed to be constant—almost like she couldn't catch a breath.

"Miriam, Mary sent honey for her throat. I didn't know if we had a lot of it, so I accepted it. Here, Jesus, just lay the logs here. I'll get a fire started in no time."

Jesus walked over to the sister and said, "Hello. I'm Jesus, son of Joseph and Mary."

She just nodded. Her coughing wouldn't stop.

Jesus said, "I've had some experience with people who are ill. May I feel your forehead to see if you have a fever?"

She nodded yes. Her red-rimmed eyes seemed to plead with him to do something.

He touched her, looked her in the eyes, and said, "Be healed by Father God."

Hiram had the fire going and put stones along the sides to warm. Miriam brought a spoon for the honey and another cool cloth for her head. Jesus said, "If there's nothing else I can do, I'll leave now. Good night, everyone. May Father God be with all of you," he said as he left for home.

Before breakfast the next morning, Hiram, Miriam, and her sister were at Joseph and Mary's door.

"Come in, come in!" said Mary. "Can you sit for breakfast?"

"Mary, is Jesus still home? Sister would like to talk to him if it's okay with Joseph and you."

"Of course it's okay with us. You are family here. Here he is! Jesus, Sister wants to talk with you."

"Hello, Sister. Are you feeling better today?" asked Jesus.

Sister rushed to Jesus and threw her arms around him. Crying, she said, "Jesus! I have not coughed since you touched me. This is a true miracle. Thank you so very much. I wish I had something to give you! Oh, Jesus! Thank you for making me well."

"Our Father God is the healer, not me. He is an awesome God. He heals all who ask. I am so glad you're well. You were very sick last night, and I wondered if you would live and if Hiram and Miriam might also get that cough." Smiling, he said, "Did you get warm?"

Sister joined his laughter. "I did, Jesus. But now the whole house is very warm. Hiram built that great big fire, and it's going to take a long time for the house to cool down."

By now, the entire family was up and ready to eat breakfast. Elizabeth set out three extra places for the guests. What a fun meal that was—all of them good friends and all of them telling and retelling what happened the night before.

"Okay, boys!" called Mary. "Every one of you is going to be late for school if you don't leave right now. Elizabeth and I will clean up today. But!"—she paused for emphasis—"only today. Don't think it will become a habit around here. Scoot!"

Kisses and hugs were shared all around.

After the boys were gone, the men were off to work, and breakfast was cleaned up, Mary asked Elizabeth to go over lessons with the younger two. Mary, Miriam, and Sister took cups of tea to the roof.

"Thank you for breakfast, Mary. It was such fun! The kids are getting so grown up! I like the way they take care of each other," said Miriam.

"Thank you. That was something Joseph and I talked about even before Jesus was born. We wanted children who were kind—not perfect for goodness' sake! But kind," said Mary.

Sister asked, "Mary, what Jesus did last night was a miracle. I don't understand it. How did he do it? Does he do it all the time?"

"Not 'all the time,' but there have been several times when Jesus and his brothers have prayed for healings. If you ask him, he will tell you that it is not he who heals but our Father God. He tells us that we can each heal in our own way. I'm not sure I understand it myself. We're just honored to be his parents. We accept it and feel blessed."

The three of them sat thinking for a while, Mary with a smile of remembrance on her face.

After a bit, Miriam said, "We need to get home and get our work done, Mary. Thank you for all you do and for being a great friend."

"Yes. Thank you, Mary. I am just so overwhelmed," said Sister as she and Miriam hugged Mary and then left for home.

TWELVE

16

Things were falling into place for the Shop to become a family business. Benjamin was retiring, and James and Judas were training others to take their former jobs as leather worker and brick maker. Another Family Time would be devoted to the Shop.

Joseph began with prayer and then opened the topic for discussion.

Jesus said, "Father, I know Benjamin said he didn't want anything—that he had been saving money, and he was well off. I know his arthritis is bad especially in his hands and knees and feet. I was wondering if we could make a special chair for him as a gift from all of us."

"Jesus, that sounds like a great idea! Do you have something in mind?"

"Yes, Father. I was thinking about making something like a curved wood under the legs on each side of the chair so that it moves backward and forward kind of like it would rock. He could lean back and relax more, and I think it would be easier for him to get out of the chair. The only thing is I wonder if the seat could be made softer than hard wood, or maybe instead of a flat seat, we could round it a little like an almost flat bowl."

"It sounds like you've been doing some thinking! Boys, what do you think?" said Joseph.

"Father, let me think about the seat being softer. I think we may find a way with leather. I don't think it can be used instead of wood but it is softer," said James.

They talked about it for a few minutes, but the hard seat still seemed to be a problem.

"Joseph," said Mary, "What if the seat and the back are gently curved but you make a pad of leather and I stuff it with lamb's wool. It would probably need to be about four inches thick, but if it got flat he could just shake it, and it would regain its softness."

"Mary, that's a really good idea! Boys, what do you think?" asked Joseph.

"I think Mother is the smartest person in the whole world! Oh, and you too, Father," said Joses.

"Me too!" said Simon.

Elizabeth offered, "I can help Mother with the stuffing."

"I would like to help Jesus design the chair. The things to make it rock sound a little tricky, but I like that," said Judas.

"I think we want this made just to Benjamin's size. It would be nice if we could figure out his size before we start—you know, like how far from where he sits to the top of his head and how far from the back of his back to the back side of his knees," said Jesus. "If it isn't tall enough, it will hurt his neck, and if the seat is too long or too short, he won't be comfortable. Judas, how about you and I work on that right away?"

"Father, the other night, we talked about who would keep the records. I would be willing to try. But I'll need a lot of help. Do you think I could ask Benjamin to work with me until I really know what I'm doing?" asked James.

"James, I was hoping you'd be our bookkeeper. Thank you for offering. Yes, by all means, ask Benjamin to teach you, and I'll do my best to make record keeping as easy as I can for you. Benjamin has taught me to keep all records of time and material up to date, and I'll expect that of all of you." Joseph grinned.

"Enough for tonight, I think," added Joseph. "Jesus and Judas, you'll begin working on the size of the chair and the rockers. James, you'll work on preparing the leather for the seat and contact Benjamin about teaching you bookkeeping. Mary and Elizabeth you'll take care of the stuffing and the final details for that seat. I'll find the very best wood I can for this very special chair. Let's pray."

"But, Father!" said Joses. "What can I do? I'm bigger!"

"Yes you are, and that's very grown up that you want to help. The very best help for all of us is if you would play with Simon and Anna and keep them busy so we can get this work done. Do you think you could do that?"

"I don't want to play with them!" Joses said petulantly.

"Well then, I guess there's nothing left for you to do," said Joseph. "Maybe when you get bigger, you'll be able to help. That's enough for tonight. Let's pray."

"Dear Father God, thank You for being with us every moment of every day. Thank You for giving Mary and me the very best children. Please guide our every move as we begin this new part of our lives. Lord, thank You for being our God. Amen," prayed Joseph as he ended Family Time for the day.

THIRTEEN

16

"Father," Elizabeth asked during Family Time, "I have two questions."

"Wonderful! What are they, sweetheart?"

"Well, Mother and I were talking about things in the Torah today while we were sewing, and we were talking about the seven days of creation. I don't think it was possible for God to make all this in just seven days."

"Elizabeth that is a good question. And I'm glad to hear about your working with your Mother and that you're thinking about what you're learning. It's good that you don't just memorize things, especially what is written in the Torah," said Joseph. "Jesus, how would you answer your sister?"

"Thank you, Father. From what I can see, when the earth was first created, there were no names for time except for 'day' or 'night' or later 'time' and 'half time.' Do I think it was a day as we have days today? I don't know. I think each event had its own time period, and it was described as a night and a day.

"However," Jesus continued, "our Father God can do anything, and if He means it was a day like we have now, well then that's what it was."

"You know what, Jesus?" asked Elizabeth. "I think you're right about the name of the time, cuz there are an awful lot of animals and fish and birds and plants and trees and everything."

"Hey! You know what?" asked Joses.

"What, Joses?" said Joseph.

"I think Father God had a contest and He asked all the Angels to draw different kinds of animals and different kinds of plants. Then He saw that all the ideas were good, and so He made all of them!"

Joseph, Mary, and the older boys tried hard not to laugh—just to look at each other and smile. Joseph said, "Wow, Joses! That would be a lot of fun. I can picture Him setting the rules like 'fish must breathe water,' 'all animals need to have hearts,' 'everything must be able to reproduce,' and so forth."

"Father! They had to make worms and bugs too! I bet the mean angels made things that bite like snakes and mosquitoes." Joses was really getting into this.

Joseph just rolled his eyes. "Elizabeth, you said you had two questions. What is the other one?"

"I know we're not to sin, you know, do what's wrong. Well, what about King David with Bathsheba and Joseph and his Mother getting the inheritance for Joseph? Those were really big sins, but God still let them become great men, and He still loved them," said Elizabeth.

"What a very hard question you've asked! Yes they did a big wrong. Yes God forgave them, and He guided them to do great things for Him. Everybody does what is wrong—no matter how we try, we do things we shouldn't. What these stories tell us is that, when you do wrong, you need to tell Father God what you did, and then you need to tell Him you are sorry and that you won't do it again."

"Okay, Father," said Elizabeth. "I think I understand."

"Elizabeth," added Jesus, "the most important thing is that Father God will forgive you if you are really sorry. Remember Father God has a very special plan for everyone, and He only wants the best for all of us."

"But if everyone is really sorry, why doesn't everybody do great things like King David and Jacob?" asked Elizabeth.

"Because there aren't a lot of really big jobs like theirs. Each of us will do something special at some time if we do what Father God wants us to do," replied Jesus.

"Great discussion tonight!" said Joseph. "James, will you lead us in closing prayer?"

"Most holy Father God, thank You for questions and thank You for answers. Please keep our minds open to You and to what You want us to do. Thank You for being our God. Amen."

Fourteen

16

"Father," Simon, now seven, asked, "how come I don't have a grandfather or a grandmother living with us? All the other kids do."

"Very good question, Simon. I know we all miss a lot by not having them here. Grandparents provide so much love to a family. They know a lot because they've lived a long time, and they even make really good babysitters!

"Grandparents are the mothers and fathers of your mother and father. Did you know that?" continued Joseph.

"No, maybe, yes; I guess I don't know if I knew it or not."

"That's okay. I was the youngest in my family, and my parents were pretty old when I was born. I don't remember very much about them. They all died in a fire when I was not yet two years old. My mother lay on top of me during the fire, so I was saved." said Joseph. "I was raised by the priest and his housekeeper. He was so much fun. He liked to take extra desserts, so when the housekeeper went to get dessert for the next meal, she would put her hands on her hips and sternly say, 'Father!' He would answer from his study that he was busy just then, but would she please call him when the meal was ready. She would shake her head and grin. It was almost like they played a game."

"My family used to live very near here—in this very town!" said Mary. "My parents and a younger brother died of a sickness, a plague, that came here about five years before

Father and I were betrothed. I went to live with my father's two brothers. They knew nothing about raising a child, but they were very loving. They had lived together all their lives, so they told me that I needed to remember my manners and the way to behave as a lady that my mother had told me. I was to be sure to act that way all the time, no matter how they did things. That was fun!

"I also had a younger sister," Mary added. 'She wasn't as sick as the rest of us, and my mother's sister and her husband took her to live with them down south; I think it was near Beersheba. I haven't heard about her since then, so I don't know how she is. I was very sick for a long time, but I recovered. And your father and I were betrothed and then married."

"So we don't have a grandfather or a grandmother? I think that stinks!" said Simon.

"I'm sorry, but it happens that way sometimes. There are a lot of elderly people in our town who would be happy to talk with you and tell you things. All you have to do is ask them," said Joseph.

"Like Benjamin?" asked Simon.

"Yes, like Benjamin," said Joseph

"Okay! I'm going to go see him and tell him to tell me all the grandfather things!"

"You do that," said Joseph, smiling. "Just remember a couple things—older people get tired when they have to listen for a long time. They are not used to a lot of noise, so try not to be too rambunctious. Another thing, remember what your mother has taught you about respect—respect for Benjamin and respect for all of his belongings. You may not touch any of his things without his permission. How about just a short visit at first?"

"Okay, Father. Maybe I can help him a little?" said Simon.

"Of course. I'm sure he would appreciate it. However, be sure to do what he wants you to do, not something you think you could do. Do you understand?"

"Yup! Maybe he'll let me sit in his chair."

"Father," said Jesus. "That reminds me. I have an idea for something to go with the rocker chair. I know that sometimes when my legs are tired, I sit sideways on a bench with my legs out in front of me and then they feel better. I was thinking of making a small stool maybe about a foot high that he can use to put his feet on. What do you think?"

"Great idea, Jesus!"

Elizabeth added, "Maybe Mother and I could make a cushion for the stool, and maybe it could match the one we made for the chair! Okay, Mother?"

"Okay, Elizabeth. That would be a great thing to do. You were certainly a big help with the chair padding, so I'm sure the stool will be an easier project. Is that okay with everyone?" asked Mary.

Thus started another great project for this awesome family.

"Simon," asked Joseph, "would you like to close with prayer tonight?"

"Sure. Father God, please take care of my grandfathers and my grandmothers. Please help us make the stool for Benjamin. Thank you Father God. Amen."

***

When the stool was finished, Jesus and Simon took it to Benjamin. He was in so much pain. It hurt Jesus just to see Benjamin like that.

"Benjamin, Simon, let's pray." The three joined hands, and Jesus prayed, "Father God, our Benjamin is in so much pain. I know that people have to have diseases, and Benjamin has accepted his. But Father God, please take away the awful pain that he has. Thank You so much. Amen."

Tears came to Benjamin's eyes. "Thank you boys for praying with me. It means so much to me that you love our Father God.

I need to tell you something; I am already feeling less pain! Our Father God is so good!"

Although the arthritis continued, the pain Benjamin had been having was gone. He now felt only the stiffness and the difficulty when moving.

"Boys, you two and your amazing family are all the family I need. For so many years, my wife and I wanted children of our own—our own family—but Father God has shown me that sometimes your family is not only the family born to you. Sometimes it's the people who love and care for you. Do you understand?" asked Benjamin.

Jesus smiled and nodded.

Simon said, "I know what you mean! Father told me that we don't have grandparents, but he said you could be my grandfather. That's what you mean, isn't it?"

"That's exactly what I mean," replied Benjamin, hugging both boys.

FIFTEEN

16

"I'm not going to school anymore, Father!" stated Joses. "I hate it, and I'm staying home."

"Hmmm. What is it you hate about school?" asked Joseph.

"All of it! I just want to stay home."

"But you and Lazarus seem to be doing so well in school."

"We do, but I just don't want to go anymore," whined Joses.

"Well, let's look at this. What would you do at home all day?"

"I don't know. Just nothing."

"Let's go through a day and see what happens. You wake up, get dressed, roll up your bed, and then what?"

"Eat breakfast," said Joses.

"We all have chores around the house, and that means we earn our meals. If you are not going to school, which is your main chore, have you earned breakfast?"

"What? I have to earn breakfast? What about lunch and dinner?"

"Yup. That too. That's what a family is. Everybody does work, and then we all get to eat, have clothes to wear, and have a house to live in. That's a family."

"Really? But I don't want to go to school and feed the animals and clean my room and empty my morning pot and all that stuff. I just want to sit or maybe play games with the other kids," replied Joses.

"Where do you think the other kids will be?" asked Joseph.

"Oh no! They'll be in school. I just have to wait until school is done!"

"So let's look at this, shall we? Mother has to work to cook for you, and Mother and Elizabeth have to work to make clothes for you and your brothers, and your brothers and I need to do your share of the work. Is that right?"

Joses sulked. "Yes. No. I don't know. I just don't want to go to school and do anything. Just sit."

"Let's see what kind of work you will be able to do when you get older if you don't have any schooling. What do you think you could do? Or do you still plan on doing nothing?"

"Father, I don't know. I like it when all the men get together and talk about their work and I like it when they come to our shop and talk. I really want to do that."

"Good planning. I see that you're thinking about your future. Now what kind of job do you want to do?"

"Maybe I'll be a doctor, and I could help people. Or remember when James worked for the leather maker? I'd like that. Or Judas worked with bricks. No, I don't think," he started to say, before adding, "But maybe that would be good. I'm strong, you know."

"Joses," said Father, "every one of those jobs requires mathematics. Every one of those jobs requires you to be able to read and write, so you'll need language studies for that. You will need to have very good grammar when you speak with businessmen, and you learn that in school. Joses, I could go on and on about why you need to go to school. But it all comes down to this—no matter what job you want as you get older, you need to go to school."

"Noooooooo!"

"Yes. And I'll tell you a little secret. When you have to do something, you have the choice to make it easy or hard."

"Really, Father? How?"

"You can choose to be grumpy, and that will make everything much harder. Or you can choose to make yourself happy about it. And believe me—that will make everything a lot easier not only for you but also for everyone around you."

"How can what I do make everyone feel bad?"

"Let's see. When Anna is cross and cranky and really, really fussy, how does that make you feel?"

"I get kinda mad, and I just want to go away from her. Sometimes I think she's just a whiner."

"Don't you think that, if you were crabby about going to school, you'd be crabby about everything, because all you'd think about was that you had to go to school? Now do you understand how it would make all of us feel?"

"Yes, Father. I don't know what to do now." Joses looked so sad.

"I have an idea. Why don't you go into your room and sit there and do nothing but think about this. Don't think about anything else—just this. Will you try it?"

"Okay. How long do I have to think?"

"How about one hour or until you've made a decision. I shouldn't be too busy at the Shop today so come and tell me what you decide. Okay?"

"Okay."

About an hour later, Joses came to the Shop.

"Father, I'm going to go to school, and I'm going to do my chores. Sometimes I won't like it, but I'm going to remember that I'm doing this so I can have a job when I get old. I want to talk with the men, and I decided I even want to be a bar mitzvah someday. So is that okay?"

"Joses, I'm proud of you! Did you think of all that by yourself?"

"Well, I asked Mother why I had to decide—why couldn't I just be told what to do? And she said that was something I had to think about too."

"Very good, Joses! When will you start?"

"I have to catch up on my morning chores, so I guess I'd better start now."

Sixteen

16

It was Family Time, and Elizabeth had a very big question.

"Father, why are some big brothers and sisters mean?"

"What do you mean, Elizabeth?"

"Well, some of my friends' big brothers are mean to them. They chase them away. They call them names like 'idiot' and 'stupid.' Sometimes, they pinch them, and that leaves big bruises. Sometimes they pull their hair, and sometimes they take their sandals and throw them around—all kinds of mean stuff."

"Have the girls told their parents?" asked Joseph.

"I don't know. I don't think so, because wouldn't their parents stop it?"

"Boys, I think it would be best if you helped your sister with this problem. What do you say?"

The boys were quiet, so Joseph said, "It's okay. Think for a minute."

Joses, ever ready with an answer, said, "Tell their fathers! That's what I'd do."

"Me too!" added Simon. He seemed to always want to follow his Joses.

Judas said, "That's just going to cause trouble. The boys will find out who told, and then those boys will come after you and you'll probably get beat up. Give us a minute to think."

After a moment, Jesus asked, "Where does this teasing happen? At their homes or on the playgrounds?"

"I think it's mostly around outside, but it's not nice. And you guys don't do that!"

"No," said James. "That's because Father and Mother have taught us to always be nice. Come to think of it, I wouldn't want to face Father if he found out I was mean to someone!"

"Father," said Jesus, "we could tell the girls to stay farther away, but that won't stop the boys from following them. I see this as a real problem. Maybe we could deal with this at school. I think Rabbi Carpus and I should talk about this and study the Torah for ideas. And maybe we'll have to do some serious teaching on how to treat one another. Elizabeth, do you think this might help?"

"Well, what if they hear that the idea came because I told?" asked Elizabeth.

"That won't happen. This will be a class based on the Torah and the Prophets and what they have to teach us. Actually, Elizabeth, I think this is a great set of lessons for everyone. Thank you for bringing it up. Rabbi Carpus and I will begin work on it tomorrow. If you feel comfortable, why don't you ask the girls to pray for their brothers? You don't have to say anything about tonight. Just wait until someone mentions it, and then tell her to pray about it. Could you do that?" asked Jesus.

"I think so. I can see if I can do it when something comes up. Would that be okay?"

"That is amazing. Thank you all for making such a great discussion and for coming to a wonderful conclusion. I'm very excited about this new lesson strategy, Jesus. Thank you for thinking of it," added Joseph. "Elizabeth, will you please close with prayer tonight."

"Father God, I want to help my friends. Thank You that Jesus has a wonderful idea. Help me tell the girls to pray for their brothers. I'm a little scared to do it. Thank You for all Your help. Amen."

SEVENTEEN

17

"Hey, Joseph! I broke this table, and I need it for most of the work I do. Can you fix it for me? I'll need it as soon as you can do it," asked Jonathan the leather maker as he struggled to drag the table he'd wrapped in a blanket.

"Jonathan!" said Jesus and James as they came rushing over. "What happened to your arm? You're bleeding."

Jesus said, "Here. Sit down. Let us look at your arm. Jonathan, I think it's broken—and badly. I see the bone, and there's some stuff in there."

"Boys, first I need to know if you can fix my table soon. I really need it," said Jonathan.

"Of course" said Joseph. "We'll have it ready for you tomorrow. Now let the boys look at that arm of yours."

James said to him, "It was that big heavy arm that fell, wasn't it? Please let us clean your arm and see what we can do. Judas, would you mind going for the physician?"

"I'm gone!" answered Judas as he took off at a run.

Elizabeth saw Judas running and ran to the Shop. "What can I do?" she said.

Jesus answered, "Does Mother have any boiled water at home? It doesn't need to be hot, just to have been boiled. We need as much as you can carry. Hurry please."

"Father, I know you need to stay on that rush job. We can do this," Jesus said to Joseph.

They removed Jonathan's left arm from his garment and began removing the larger pieces of whatever the stuff was in his wound.

"There!" said Jesus. "I think we've removed all that we can. Oh great! Thank you, Elizabeth! You're just in time."

Jesus held Jonathan's arm as James carefully poured water to wash out the remaining "stuff."

"James, let's pray," said Jesus. "Father, Jonathan, Elizabeth, please place your hand on Jonathan and pray with us."

"Father God," James prayed. "Jonathan is a good man. He was kind and a great teacher to me during my working with him. Please, Father God, heal Jonathan's arm. We thank You. Amen."

Jonathan cried out in pain. Yet as Jesus was holding Jonathan's arm, it healed.

In tears, Jonathan prayed, "Thank you, Father God. I have done nothing to deserve Your healing. Forgive me, Lord. I thank You. I have no other words, but I thank You!"

Judas returned. "I was unable to find the physician. Someone told me he went to Bethany about a possible infection. He probably won't be home until tomorrow. Wow! I see you're healed, Jonathan! My family prayed for you, didn't they?"

Jonathan couldn't stop the tears. He merely nodded to Judas.

James said, "Father, I'd like to walk him home. Okay? I won't be gone long."

"Thank you," said Joseph. There were hugs all around and James walked Jonathan back to his leather-making shop.

"Father, may Judas and I look at the table?" asked Jesus.

"Go ahead. This job I'm on is finally going well, and I should be done sooner than I thought."

Jesus and Judas were assessing what would need to be done to the table and checking the supplies for matching wood when James returned.

"I went into the shop with Jonathan, and it was that arm that fell. I don't know what could be done to make it stronger, but I never did trust that thing."

Joseph said, "Give me a few more minutes, boys, and we'll look at it together. Do you have things to do?"

"Of course we do, Father! There's always plenty to do!" said James, almost ruefully.

Later, Joseph finished and joined the boys. "Let's take a look at this entire problem—both the table and that arm. James, explain what that arm is and what it's used for."

"Let me draw it out. When he's making something big, Jonathan uses the arm to hold the leather above the table, above his head, and out of his way—but within reach. It stands next to the table and is tall enough for him to walk under. It sits in a block about eighteen inches high and about eighteen inches across. It should be stable, but sometimes when you pull on the leather, the other side of the arm leans down toward the table. That's what happened, and the arm snapped and fell on his arm. I think this is a good picture of it."

After a while, they figured that the arm needed to have a matching support on the other side of the table. That presented another problem—how to get the leather on and off the arm, as sometimes the leather needs to be wrapped around the arm more than once.

It took time, but they came up with what they thought was the only solution. The top of the poles where the arm fit needed to be open at the top so the arm could be lifted up. That presented another problem—how did you keep the arm from popping out of those top slots? Tie strong leather straps around the pole ends? Make the post top slots deep? A deep slot seemed to be the answer.

They decided to surprise Jonathan. When they took the repaired table to him, they would bring along the new support. It worked!

"Joseph and sons, if there is ever anything you need, just let me know!" Jonathon told them. I owe you big-time. I don't even have enough words to say thank you! Thank you!"

Heartfelt handshakes and slaps on the back all around.

EIGHTEEN

17

The news reached the family early in the morning. Enoch had passed away during the night. His funeral would be this evening.

Mary and Elizabeth went to be with Enoch's Mary and the children. The wailing women were already there. Enoch's Mary had just finished bathing Enoch, and she and the girls were wrapping him in his burial cloths. Enoch's wife asked Lazarus if he would like to place the special cloth on Enoch's face. What a little man—with tears in his eyes, he carefully placed the cloth over Enoch.

Elizabeth held on to her Mother. "Mother, this is so sad, but it feels kind of nice too."

"Yes. We saw a very special moment. Mary showed her grandson that he was an important part of their lives. It was a sign of the love they have for Enoch."

People from the village began coming to visit, many bringing gifts of food for the family and for the meal after the funeral. Soon, the men came to carry Enoch to his family's burial cave outside of the village. The wailing women followed, but it was the women of the village who led the walk. A solemn service, followed by a meal at Enoch's Mary's home that seemed to slowly bring things back toward normal for everyone.

Back home, Anna was cranky. Even Simon trying his best couldn't get her to stop fussing. Finally, she let James pick her up, set her on his back, and run around the living room like a donkey. Things quieted, and Joseph thought it might be good to have Family Time, even though it was late.

"Father," said Joses, "will Lazarus have to move now?"

"Why do you ask?

"Well, Grandma Mary is old and … I don't know."

"Let's think about this. I think you're right about Grandma Mary. Maybe the children will need to move back to their hometown. I don't think anyone is thinking about that right now."

"I am!" said Joses. "Lazarus is my best friend. What can I do, Father?"

"First," replied Joseph, "you're probably right. Martha, Mary, and Lazarus may move back to their hometown. But there's a lot of planning that needs to take place first. The thirty days of mourning must be observed, and we need to see if there's family in their hometown to care for them. A lot of this is for the adults to take care of. I know you're going to think about this a lot, but there isn't a lot you can do. I promise I will do my best to tell you about the plans as soon as I know them."

"I guess that's okay. But I have to do something."

Jesus said, "Maybe Lazarus will also be worried about moving and leaving you. What if the two of you talk about it? Maybe that will help both of you."

"I can try. I just feel so bad," said Joses.

"That's a good thing," said Joseph. "It shows that you care. The world needs people who care. I know this is awful now. But, Joses, it can make you stronger. You do have a choice. You can get angry and waste your life with anger, or you can accept it and use this as a path for your life. Do you understand any of this?"

"I think so, but I don't want to."

"Joses, I'll be here for you," said Simon.

"Me too!" said Elizabeth. "I'll help you with your studies if you want me to."

"Thanks," said Joses. He was so sad.

Joseph said, "Joses. Will you please close with prayer tonight?"

"Yes Father. Father God, I am so sad about Lazarus. I will miss him so much. Will You promise me You'll take care of him? Oh, and help Enoch's Mary and Martha and Mary too. Amen."

NINETEEN

17

It was late. Joseph, Jesus, James, and Judas had been at the city gate visiting with friends. The boys had played a few games of ball and everyone was tired. They saw a young man sitting by himself. Joseph walked over to him and said, "Young man. Are you a visitor here?"

The boy answered, "Yup. I arrived a couple of hours ago, but I haven't been able to find a place to stay tonight."

"We always have room for others. Come stay the night with us. My boys are just a bit younger than you are, so you'll find company," said Joseph. "I'm Joseph, and these are my sons Jesus, James, and Judas. We have more children at home, but they shouldn't be too much trouble, as they're probably in bed. What is your name?"

"I am Barabbas. I've been on my own for years since my family was killed by marauders. I would appreciate a good night's sleep in a safe place."

Joseph and the boys were hungry. Mary had left a loaf of bread for them. James poured beer for the five of them. Barabbas was very hungry.

"How long has it been since you've eaten?" asked Joseph.

"I was able to find a honeycomb and some grains still in a field, but that's it for the last couple days."

"Where are you from?" asked Judas.

"All over. My parents traveled all the time, and so that's what I do. It's okay, though. I get to see a lot of stuff I wouldn't have seen. I've seen a lot of travelers and sellers who travel the highways. Some of the stuff they carry is really different. If I want something, I can usually work for it. Almost everyone has work that needs to be done. Even if they can't give me money, they usually give me a meal and some bread to take with me. I get along fine."

"You're welcome to stay the night here," said Joseph. "Tomorrow you'll join us for breakfast, and if you are continuing your journey, we will also give you bread to take with you. Boys, I'm off to bed. Good night."

The boys cleaned up the area and rolled out mats for sleeping. There were always extra mats for visitors.

Barabbas lay down near Jesus and James.

"Hey! Boys!" Barabbas whispered after a while. "Let's go outside."

"Why?" asked Jesus. "We have a busy day tomorrow and are already up late."

"Come on! It'll be fun! I do it all the time."

"What?" asked James. "What can we do at night?"

"We can see things—things like who's doing something sneaky or who's fighting, or maybe we can find something."

"Find something? Like what?" asked James.

"I don't know. People leave stuff outside, and maybe we could use it or sell it."

"Barabbas," said Jesus. "Please stop talking. This is absolutely something we are not going to do. Also if I can, I will be sure you do not do that in this village. Now roll over and go to sleep. I'll pray for you!"

Barabbas was not at all happy. But he remembered the good bread he'd eaten that night and the promise of more tomorrow, so he did as Jesus asked; he rolled over and went to sleep.

The next morning, both Jesus and James stayed close to Barabbas. They made sure to limit his contact with Mary and the younger children. When they left for school, they took Barabbas with them.

As they parted at the schoolyard, Jesus said to Barabbas, "Please be on your way. Be safe. I'd like to ask you something. When you think of taking something that belongs to others, consider how you would feel if someone took something of yours."

"Jesus, I don't have anything. I've never had anything. So I guess it really doesn't matter to me."

"I'm sorry, Barabbas," Jesus said. "I will ask our Father God to guide you."

"Don't bother. I can take care of myself. Thanks for the meals and sleep. You've got a nice family. Maybe I'll see you around?" And Barabbas went on his way.

After school, when Jesus was at work at the Shop, he asked Joseph if he and James could talk with him for a bit.

"Of course, Jesus. Give me just a bit, and I can stop what I'm doing."

"What's going on?" asked Joseph.

"We want to talk about Barabbas, who was here last night." They told Joseph what had happened last night and this morning. "Father, we both feel really uncomfortable about this, and we don't know what to do about it."

"I'm sorry, boys," said Joseph. "I had an odd feeling about him, but the Torah tells us to take in strangers. I think we did the right thing by taking him in."

"I think so too," said James. "But I just don't feel good about it. In fact I'm almost afraid of what could happen.

"And, Father," James continued, "the other thing is that I prayed for him last night, and I expected he would be different this morning. He wasn't. I'll continue to pray for him. But that doesn't make me feel—I don't know—I'm worried."

"Sometimes God sees how a person will be no matter how we try to change him or her. Sometimes people can't be changed because they really don't want to. This could be one of those times. If it is, we need to trust our Father God."

"Thank you, Father. I'll pray for him again but I'll pray harder for Father God's protection for all of us," James replied.

TWENTY

17

"Good morning, young men!" called Rabbi Carpus. "Today we'll do final tests for this past year. No booing. And then! Tomorrow we have two weeks of *no school and no homework!*"

The boys roared. From the youngest to the oldest, it was an amazing surprise.

"However, that doesn't mean you have no assignments. You have two. You must do something nice for someone else, *and* you must do something nice for your family."

"Now," continued Rabbi Carpus, "are you ready for your final tests? Another surprise—some of you will have written tests, and some of you will have oral tests. There will be different tests for each class. Understand?"

"What if I get all written tests? That'll take a lot longer, and the other kids will get to go home while I'm still writing!" complained Joses.

"Joses, Joses, Joses, learn to trust your rabbis. Everyone will be dismissed at the same time. If some are finished before others, we have things for them to do."

"Rabbi, is it okay if I ask what kind of things?" Joses asked sheepishly.

"Mmmm. I don't think I'll tell you exactly what they'll be doing. I think I'll ask everyone to trust Rabbi Jesus and me. How about that?"

"But, but, but—" stammered Joses.

"No buts. Just trust. Now, off to your classrooms. And have a wonderful two weeks!" Rabbi Carpus sent them off.

"That's my brother!" said Jesus.

"Yes, but I think he has great promise. He's a little self-centered, but I have a feeling he'll put that to good use some day."

"With constant prayers!" Jesus said shaking his head.

"Hey, Jesus," said Joses later in the day. "That was kinda fun! The stuff I didn't really know was when I had to write, so I got to think. The easy stuff I could just talk. I liked it."

"I'm glad, Joses. Learning is so important. I love it when Rabbi Carpus and I can make it fun. You're a great kid! Just keep doing your best. Okay?"

"Thanks Jesus! Hey, there are my friends! See you later." And off he went.

As Jesus walked to the Shop, he was thinking, *I wonder what kind of responses Rabbi Carpus and I will be hearing in two weeks. We have great hopes that it will be a great learning experience for each of them.* He prayed, "Guide them all please, Father God."

***

The community had organized a Town Day to take place during the two-week break from school. Everyone came together, and from the newborn to the oldest, there was something to amuse or challenge everyone.

"Grandma" Margaret, at seventy-three appeared younger than some of those in their fifties. The older boys made carrying chairs with their arms to make sure everyone was included. (Place your right hand on your left arm above the wrist and then connect with someone doing the same thing. It makes a really safe chair.) Those who had difficulty walking were carried. Benches were brought for the adults. (Joses wanted to know why he couldn't sit there—why he had to sit on the ground. Oh, Joses!)

Matthew had been planning a special event ever since he heard about Town Day. He made three boxes—a larger one for the smaller children, a medium one for the other children, and a smaller box for the adults. Each box had a hole in the center. The smaller boxes had smaller holes, so it was more difficult for the adults. He gathered rocks and balls and sticks.

The day of the game, he set up the three boxes parallel to each other but about ten feet apart. Matthew lined up the participants and placed rocks and balls and sticks near all three lines.

"Now," he said, "this is for boys and for girls. The idea is to get rocks and balls and sticks in the opening of the box in front of your line. You each have two chances with each thing. When you've had your turn, just get in line again for another try. I'll try to pick up the stuff and return them to the box for the next person. Take turns and let's see what happens!"

Miriam had a trick up her sleeve too. "Everyone not playing, gather over here by Grandma Margaret. We are going to do some rhythm movements." As the women and small children gathered, she said, "We're going to begin to clap our hands in a rhythm. Then as we go along, we'll start clapping at different rhythms, like this!"

The women really got into it. Sometimes they slowed the beat, and sometimes they clapped on every other beat. Eventually they began swaying and then the girls began moving as they clapped.

What an awesome day! Everyone took part. By the time it was time to eat, everyone was exhausted. But everyone was happy. As the women were cleaning up, the men and boys decided to try to kick the ball. They pretty much stayed in their same lines, but the object now was to see who could kick the ball the farthest. You could kick two balls at each turn. But while the next person was kicking, you needed to get the balls you kicked and bring them back without getting hit by the balls being kicked.

The day ended with everyone tired and happy. Everyone helped clean up the area and then home to wash up and get to bed.

The next morning, Joses asked his mother, "Mother, we have to do some stuff for school, and one is for our family. I want to do something for you. What do you want me to do?"

"That's very nice of you, Joses," answered Mary. "I do have something that would be a great help to me. I have a big order for linens, and if you could take little Anna for a walk or do something to keep her busy for a while, I would really appreciate it. Is that something you'd like to do?"

"I think I could do that, maybe. I think she still takes a nap, so when would be a good time?"

"That's right. She naps right after lunch. Maybe you could go now? Then you could be back by lunchtime, and she could take her nap. Sound good?"

"Okay, I'll go get her," said Joses as he rather reluctantly but determinedly went to find his sister.

"Anna, would you like to play with me today?" asked Joses.

"No!" said Anna belligerently.

"Why? It will be fun. We'll do what you want to do. Okay?" tried Joses.

"I want my babies!" demanded Anna.

"That's okay. You can bring all you want to."

"My sissy and my brother and my lamb and my baby goat and—"

"Sure," said Joses. "How 'bout if I take a blanket, and we can carry all of them at once?"

"I wanna hold sissy. You can hold the rest," stated Anna.

"Okay. How about this blanket? It's nice and soft, and it's big enough to hold all your friends."

"They're not my friends! They're my babies!"

"Okay. Let's go." Joses took her hand and swung the blanket stuffed with the babies over his shoulder.

At lunchtime, they returned. "Mother!" shouted Anna as she ran to Mary. "I had fun! Joses showed my babies how to throw things. And then I wanted to, and he showed me too. He said I have to look around me so I don't hit anything or people. I almost hit a big rock sometimes. Mother, it was so much fun! Can I do it again?"

"You'll have to ask Joses. You know he is very busy with his friends," said Mary.

"Okay! I will!" Anna ran off to find Joses and asked him, "Joses can you take me out for a walk again?"

"When do you want to go?"

"Tomorrow when Mother starts work? Like today? I promise I'll listen to you just like I did today. Please?"

Joses hugged her and said, "Okay. But I can't do it every day."

"I know. Mother says you have to be with your friends."

"I'm hungry," said Joses. "Let's help Mother get lunch ready. The big boys and Father will be home pretty soon."

The next day went just as well. Joses taught her to hop and to jump. He wanted to teach her to skip, but she would have nothing to do with that.

When they reached home, Anna said, "Thank you, Joses!" She reached up and gave him a hug. "I love you!"

Mary smiled and said, "I love you too, Joses. You were really a big help to me. I was able to finish the entire order in these two days. Thank you!"

Later, Joses remembered that he needed to do something for someone or someplace that was not his family or his family's home or Shop. He had an idea but he didn't know why. He thought, *Why am I thinking of helping Benjamin straighten up his animals' area when I don't like to work? But it's all I can think to do. I better ask Father if he has an idea for what I could do.*

He walked to the Shop and asked his father.

"Have you had any ideas of what you'd like to do?" asked Joseph.

"Not really. I thought you might help me," said Joses.

"As I understand it, you're to come up with the idea and then implement it. Maybe this will help. What kind of thing do you think you might want to do?" asked Joseph.

"Father, I just don't know," whined Joses. "I've been thinking, but I need help."

"I'm afraid I can't help you. All the advice I can give you is that, if you get an idea and it feels like a strong idea, it's probably the idea you should work on."

"Father, I have an idea, but I don't think I want to do it," explained Joses.

"Why don't you think you'll like doing it?" asked Joseph.

Joses thought for a minute and then said, "I guess I was being lazy. I wanted to do something easy. Okay. I'll do it. I'm sure Benjamin would like my help."

"Benjamin. You're doing something for Benjamin? I like that. He's been very good to our family all our lives. I'm proud of you for doing whatever it is."

Joses walked slowly to Benjamin's. When Benjamin came to the door, Joses said, "At school, we're supposed to do something for someone so I will work on the spot where you keep your animals."

"Joses, that's very thoughtful of you. I've been having difficulties these past few days, and I've not been able to get out there as I should. I really do need your help. Thank you."

"You're welcome," said Joses, without much feeling.

"May I just tell you where to find the things you might need? I'm just not able to walk that far," explained Benjamin.

"Sure," said Joses as he followed Benjamin to his rocker. Benjamin told him where to find the tools and told him about the small lamb with only three legs.

Joses found the tools and then found the lamb. As Joses cleaned the area and put out fresh water and hay, the lamb followed him. "Hey!" said Joses. "Are you trying to help me? I sure could use it. Tell me, can you do anything? What about go around and around? Hey! You did it! I was going to ask you to stand on your back legs but you only have one. What can you do? Here's an old cloth. Can you catch it?" Joses began moving the cloth in a circle—the lamb chased it. He then started walking and then running, and the lamb followed him! After a while he said, "I'd better get back to work. Oops! I should say *we* had better get back to work."

When finished, he went in to talk with Benjamin. "I got the whole area cleaned up. That little lamb helped me all the time. We even played! It was fun. Oh, I saw that a couple of the boards on the pen were loose, so I fixed them."

"Thank you, Joses. I am so grateful!"

"Can I tell you something? I wasn't too sure I wanted to do this, but I couldn't think of anything else to do. We have to do something while we're off school, so I decided I'd just better do it. I'm glad I did. It feels good to do a good job, especially when I had fun too. The lamb helped me!" Joses giggled. "I mean he followed me all over, and then he chased me for a while. We had fun!"

"I'm glad to hear it," said Benjamin. "Did you learn anything?"

Joses smiled. "You sound just like my father. I learned that I can do a job and not have to be told what to do."

"I think you learned something else," said Benjamin.

"I did? I can't think what else."

"Well, I can think of two other things."

"What? I know I felt better after I did it," said Joses.

"That's also important. Maybe you could remember that you really didn't want to do the job, but you started in, and it wasn't so bad," explained Benjamin.

"That's right! I guess I didn't think of that. But you said two things. What's the other?"

"You took a few minutes to play. It's important to take a few minutes at an appropriate time. It makes the work go better. That's a good thing as long as you remember to limit the time you spend away from work," explained Benjamin.

"Benjamin, you're nice. I gotta go home now. I'm glad I came here. Bye."

"I'm glad you came here too. Thank you very much, Joses. You come by anytime!" called Benjamin as Joses began walking home.

TWENTY-ONE

17

School resumed. The rabbis kept the children together as they shared their stories of what they had done for others and for their families.

An older boy told the group, "One of the walls on my grandparents' house was leaking, so I helped them repair it. It was easier than I thought it would be."

A younger boy reported, "I set the table and cleared the table every day except two."

"My grandmother hurt her leg and couldn't walk, so I got a big stick and cut it. But that wasn't enough, so I got two sticks. And then she could walk," said someone else.

"A neighbor's chickens got out," one boy said. "So I helped him catch the chickens, and then I helped him fix the fence."

"At synagogue, I saw that one of the benches looked scratched, so I worked with Rabbi Jesus to fix it so it looks nice," said another.

"The wheels on my neighbor's cart were wobbly, so he and I took them off and fixed the wheels and the axle." someone else volunteered. "It was kind of fun doing it!"

Then it was Joses's turn. "Benjamin's arthritis was really bad, and he couldn't clean his courtyard, especially the part where the animals stay. So I helped him clean it. He has a lamb with three legs, and he was a lot of fun," he said.

"Philip," said Rabbi Jesus, "I know you did something unusual. Would you tell us about it?"

"My grandpa is really sick, and Father said he is going to die because he is so old. So my father and I made his casket for him. I feel sad."

"That's a good thing you did. It's never easy to lose a grandparent or anyone else close to us," said Rabbi Carpus. "In years to come, you will remember this, and it will make you feel better."

"Rabbi, I kept my area clean, and I rolled up my bed every day, and I tried to remember to say please and thank you," said one young boy.

"Great job! Great job, everybody! Anyone else? Joses you look like you are mulling over something. Will you share this also with us?" said Rabbi Carpus.

"Well, my mother had a big order, so I took little Anna for a walk. It's kinda hard to talk about it because—well—she's kinda whiny, and she only wants to do what she wants to do. So I thought it would be a really bad day. But it was fun. I taught her to hop and to jump and to throw a ball and a stick. We went for a walk for two days, and it was kinda fun. I didn't think it would be."

"Thank you, Joses. Thank you everyone. Anyone else? No? So now, for another part of this experiment, we're going to go to our classes and talk about two things. What did you learn? And how did it make you feel?" said Rabbi Carpus.

***

In their classes, the boys were really quiet. It was as though they weren't sure what was going to happen. The younger boys were wiggling. They weren't sure that they learned anything. And how were they going to say how they felt?

"Boys, it's good to see you back in class. It sounds like you had a really good time away from school," began Rabbi Carpus. "All of you did something really nice. Would you please tell me how it made you feel?"

The room was very quiet. The boys looked around as if they had no idea what to say.

"Philip, you said you feel sad about your grandfather, but how did you feel when you finished his casket?"

"Kinda good because I made something for him. And it's something that he'll use. My grandmother cried when she saw it. She said it was so beautiful. That made me feel good."

"Thank you, Philip. Thank you for telling us, and thank you for being the first one."

"When I set and cleared the table, I felt like a grown-up."

And that started it. They all wanted to talk at once! After a couple minutes of letting them talk, Rabbi Carpus said, "Now please tell me what you learned."

"I learned that my little sister can be fun," said Joses, laughing.

"I learned that my grandmother was smiling when she could walk again."

The boys shared and shared.

"Great!" said Rabbi Carpus. "Let's think about this. You helped others—your families and your neighbor. It made them feel better, and it made you feel better. What do you think we can all say we learned from this?"

Philip said quietly, "I think we should always do things for others, and if we do, everybody will be happier."

The boys started talking again, and it was agreed that Philip was right. Doing things for other people was the best thing to do.

Later in the day, Rabbi Carpus and Rabbi Jesus met and discussed this entire experiment. It seems the older boys had come to the same conclusion as the younger boys. Helping others was a good thing.

"Well, Jesus. What is your final thought about this?"

"Rabbi Carpus, I think this is something we should incorporate into the curriculum every year. I was really impressed with the things the boys found to do to help others.

I thought that some, if not most of them, might just pick something easy and play the rest of the time."

"I did too. I agree. We'll make this a routine event every year. Rabbi Jesus, I'd like to tell you something. I'm very proud of your teaching and of the way you treat the children—especially the ones who are troubled."

"Thank you. I love teaching!" said Jesus.

TWENTY-TWO

17

"Judas! Run to the school and tell Jesus to come if at all possible!" said Joseph. He and the boys had gotten to the Shop and found damage inside. It looked like someone had been inside causing real trouble.

"Jesus," said Judas, "can you get someone to take your classes for a while? You're needed at the Shop."

Jesus was teaching the older boys, so he called one of them, told him what to teach, and asked him to take over.

"What's wrong, Judas? Has something happened to Father or Mother?" asked Jesus.

"No. The Shop was broken into, and there's been damage done. Father wanted you here so we can all figure out where to go from here."

Joseph, James, and Hiram met them at the door of the Shop. "It's not too bad, but it's a real mess. I sent James to bring Hiram here, but we decided to wait to do anything until the two of you got here," said Joseph.

A newly made table and two of the four chairs had been broken. One of the shelving units had been knocked over, spreading everything stored there all over. The largest of the oil lamps was smashed, and the lumber sorted in the back had been thrown around that entire area.

Benjamin arrived, walking with the help of two sticks. "Joseph, I saw Judas bring Jesus home from school, so I figured something bad had happened. Wow, what a mess!"

"Thanks for coming, Benjamin. I just can't figure out who would do this to us. The boys and I try to treat everyone as we want to be treated. I just don't know what we did that would cause this type of reaction!" said Joseph.

"Joseph, may I speak to you alone?" said Benjamin. They moved outside. "Do you remember that young man who stayed at your house a while back?" Joseph nodded. "I saw him near the gate yesterday. He was really scruffy looking. I didn't want to say anything in front of the others because I don't know that he had anything to do with this, but I wanted you to know."

"Thank you Benjamin. I appreciate your telling me. I think we should keep this between the two of us until we look into this some more. Okay?" asked Joseph.

"I agree. If I can do anything, please let me know. I'm sorry this happened," Benjamin said as he walked, with difficulty, back to his home.

"Father," Jesus said, "we were working on the lumber in the back area, and we found something."

"What is it?"

"We think it's the foot of a hare," said Jesus.

"A hare? How would that get here?" mused Joseph.

"Father, Barabbas had one like this when he spent the night at our home," said Jesus. "He showed us this white streak right here. He said it was unique like he is. I think this is his."

James said, "I remember it as well. I'm sure it belonged to Barabbas."

"You may very well be right, boys. Let's think about this while we clean up the mess. I need to tell Jonathan that we'll need another few days to rebuild his table and chairs."

It was quiet as they cleaned up. Each one thinking of how to handle this situation. Was it Barabbas? Probably. Why? Because? Where do we go from here? Contact the Roman authorities? Try to find him? What?

Mary brought Anna to the Shop.

"I saw Jesus and Judas, James, and Hiram and then Benjamin come over here and figured something was up. What a mess! What's going on?" asked Mary.

"Let's go outside so the boys can keep working," said Joseph as he walked outside with Mary.

"Somebody broke in and did some damage. The boys and I are putting things back in order. We'll be ready to work tomorrow, so it's not too bad. We'll tell our customers that things might be a day later than we had said at first, but most people will understand. We should be okay. Don't worry, Mary."

"I'm just glad none of you was hurt. Is there something I can do? Maybe bring lunch here so you can keep working?" said Mary.

"That's a good idea. Thank you. Maybe something extra to drink? It's pretty dusty in here with all this moving around."

"Will do. I'll send Elizabeth with lunch. I know she'll want a reason to see what's going on. Be careful! I love you!"

"Mary, I love you too. Thank you for thinking about lunch."

Elizabeth brought lunch, but the men decided not to stop and eat but to eat while they worked. It didn't surprise anyone that Elizabeth made herself useful without even asking what she could do.

Hiram was able to stay for two hours but then needed to get back to his work. Joseph and the four young people worked until sundown and then went home to clean up and have dinner.

"Joseph," asked Mary when they were alone, "do you have any idea who would do something like this?"

"I don't want you to repeat this just yet, but it may have been Barabbas, the young man who stayed with us one night. The boys found a hare's foot that looked like the one he showed them when he was here," explained Joseph.

"I'm sorry. I had a bad feeling about him. I was glad when he left. But now to do this? He must be a very troubled person."

"We'll talk about it at Family Time. Do you think Joses, Simon, and Anna will be okay with the discussion or should we fill them in ahead of time?" asked Joseph.

"I've already talked with them. I didn't want them to be afraid, so I made it more that we are solving a problem," said Mary.

That night, Joseph opened Family Time with prayer and then opened the night's topic. "Tonight we are going to try to solve a problem. We know there was damage at the Shop, and most of it is cleaned up. But there are things broken that need to be fixed, and there is lumber needed for other orders that needs to be replaced. Any ideas?"

Simon, now eight, said, "I think you should fix stuff."

"Thank you, Simon. That's a very good idea," said Joseph, smiling.

Joses said, "I was really mad that you left me in school. I can do stuff too, you know."

"Yes you can, Joses. But you had a pretest and then a test in mathematics, and that is what I feel is more important," said Joseph. "We will not discuss that further."

Elizabeth said, "Thank you for letting me work with you. I really liked that. You know I like to make things look nice."

Ever the one to find the bottom line or get to the bottom of the problem, Judas said, "I think we should forget about finding him. We can tell those who ask us that we don't know who did it, and we go about our business as if nothing happened. I think our first priority is getting new wood and then fixing what's broken. Then we can catch up on orders."

Jesus said, "Well said, Judas! I think that's it, Father."

"I do too!" said Joseph. "James, will you take responsibility for determining what wood needs to be restocked and then purchase it? Judas, first thing you and I will do is repair the table and chairs. Then by the time Jesus, Joses, and Simon are done at school, we should be in good shape, and we'll be able to work on the rest of the orders. Okay, everyone? Jesus, please lead us in prayer tonight."

"Father God, we thank You for being with us today and every day. Please take charge of the person who did this to the Shop and keep all Your people safe. Thank You that we have the strength and the knowledge to solve this. Please continue to bless us as we go about Your will. Amen."

The problem was solved—together—with the strength of Father God.

TWENTY-THREE

17

The day came when Martha, Mary, and Lazarus would return to their hometown of Bethany. It was a sad day for everyone, especially, it seemed, for Joses and Lazarus.

In school, Rabbi Jesus said, "Today will be a day of saying goodbye to our friend Lazarus. We will all miss him, and I know he will miss us. Let's be extra nice to him and to each other today."

"Rabbi Jesus?" asked one of the boys. "I want to tell Lazarus that I'm really proud of the way he caught the final out in our game last week. That gave us the win!"

A few of the boys had similar things to say.

James Bar Jonah said, "I can't believe how he went from a kid who couldn't even run to a kid who was okay at games. He just kept trying, and I learned from that. I hope we get to see him when we're grown-ups. I want to see what he does when he's older."

After a few minutes, Rabbi Jesus asked, "Joses, is there something you'd like to say?"

"I feel really sad, but I won't forget him ever! I wasn't doing very well here at school, and he taught me how to learn. I can never forget that. I know he has to go, but I don't want him to. Jesus, I have to see him again!"

"I will pray that you do. Maybe you could pray about it and ask our Father God to give you both the blessing of seeing each other again."

After school, Joses walked Lazarus back to his home.

Lazarus said, "Joses, I have a good feeling that we'll see each other again. I promise I'll keep praying for you and that we do meet again."

"I'll keep praying for you too. Do you know the people you'll be staying with?"

"Kinda. They're my mother's cousins. I saw her a few times before we moved here, but I was kinda little. She had a couple children, but they died when they were real young. The oldest one lived to be about seven, but she got the fever and died."

"Is she nice?" asked Joses.

"I remember she always smiled. The man is pretty big, and when he laughed, it made me laugh. I'll be okay, Joses. I'm gonna miss you though. Thank you for teaching me how to run and hit and all that stuff."

"Thank you for teaching me how to learn. Let's make a contract—you know, like the men do in business!"

"Okay. Like what?"

"Like, I promise to always do my best at learning, and when I get stuck on something, I'll remember you and keep trying. Okay?" asked Joses.

"Okay! And I'll keep trying at sports. I know I'll never be really good, but I promise I'll keep at it. Okay, we have a contract!"

They reached Enoch's Mary's house. Mary and the girls had everything packed. The man Lazarus would be living with was there to take him and Martha and Mary to Bethany. The man was well dressed, and his cart looked very sturdy. Joses thought that maybe the man would be okay for Lazarus.

Elizabeth and some of the girls from town were already there to see them off. Mary had sent breads for the children to eat along the way.

Everyone hugged everyone, and the cart started off. Elizabeth and Joses and some of the other children walked to the city gate alongside the cart and then waved as long as they could see them.

The children headed home to finish chores before dinner. Elizabeth, now twelve, returned to Enoch's Mary's house and found Enoch's Mary crying so hard.

"Elizabeth, I have lost so much—first Enoch and now the children. I feel so empty," cried Mary.

Elizabeth put her arm around Enoch's Mary's shoulder and said, "Let me help you put a few things back in order, and then I'm taking you home for dinner tonight. No arguing."

"Thank you. That will be nice." There wasn't too much to do, but it was better to do it now than to have to do it after dinner.

After dinner, Enoch's Mary helped Mary clean up the dishes. "I've been thinking," said Enoch's Mary. "I don't think I can just sit and take care of myself. I'm too old to take in children again, and I have a lot of time that I could do something. I love to draw. I think I would like to make drawings of people and places around town. What do you think, Mary?"

"That's a great idea! No one in town does that. It would give you some income too! I think you might find some business in this house. I'll talk with Joseph and see what he thinks."

"I was thinking that some people wouldn't be able to pay, but they could pay with produce. Almost everyone has a garden, and almost everyone has goats or chickens or sheep. I would accept those things, and then with my little garden, I would only need to buy a few other things."

Mary hugged her. "If you need help getting started, just come to me. Actually, Elizabeth is a good planner too, so we'll both help you! Would you like to stay for our Family Time or do you need to go home?"

"I'd like to go home. But first, I want to tell your whole family thank you for the way they helped me today."

As the family gathered for Family Time Enoch's Mary said, "This was a very difficult day for me today. I want to thank all of you for taking such good care of me. I really do feel better. Thank you for making me feel so welcome."

"I can walk you home," said Simon, a big boy at eight.

James, ever the gentleman, said, "Great, little Simon. I'll walk with you. C'mon."

It turned out that Joses and Elizabeth also wanted to walk. When they returned home, Joseph opened Family Time.

"Father," said Joses, "when Jesus was rabbi today, he really helped me with missing Lazarus. I'm glad he's my brother!"

"Thank you, Joses! That was very nice. Know what? I'm glad that you're my brother. It's been fun to watch you grow from that angry little kid to a determined one," Jesus said as he jostled Joses.

Twenty-four

17

"Father, before we start work today, could we have a Shop meeting?" asked James.

"Certainly," said Joseph.

"I think Judas and I are pretty much up to date on the different kinds of work here in the Shop. So I was thinking, I'd like to incorporate some leatherwork. For instance, we made those cushions for Benjamin; I think we could offer that to our customers.

"Also," continued James, "I was thinking how some of the work, like metal work and forging, can have sparks that burn arms and burn the front of men's clothes. We could offer leather aprons and cuffs that reach from wrist to elbow. That could stop a lot of burns and scars. What do you think?" said James. "Cushions and cuffs and aprons?"

"I think we could do it," said Judas with a grin. "I'll have to learn leather working. I was trained in brickwork, and I think they're probably very different."

They all laughed.

"Father," said James. "What do you think?"

"I think we're ready to expand," agreed Joseph. "I think we should talk about the pros and cons of whether we start all of the projects or just one at a time. For instance, should we offer just cushions? That will mean a lot more work, I think. We'll need to carefully measure everything we need the cushions to cover. Probably no two items will be the same.

"If we start with cuffs and aprons we would probably need"—Joseph thought for a moment—"maybe three sizes for the aprons and maybe two sizes of cuffs? James, how do you plan to attach the cuffs to a man's arm?"

"I was thinking that, near the wrist and near the elbow on both long sides, we would attach a leather thong so that they could cross and then tie together, but I don't know how the men could tie them with one hand."

"Hmmm. I see. Let's think about this as we work today. We'll need to consider things like how to attach the cuffs; when we would work on patterns; when we think we can offer these items; and, of course, what to do first. When Jesus gets here after school, you can bring him up to date, James. Then we'll take time before we leave for the day and talk about it. Let's get to work now."

When Jesus returned from teaching, James filled him in.

Later at the meeting, it was decided that they would begin offering aprons and cuffs in two weeks. That would give them time to train Joseph, Judas, and Jesus on working with leather and to have a small supply on hand. The cuffs would be permanently closed at the elbow leaving only the cuff end to be secured.

At the end of a few months the leather aprons and cuffs became regularly requested items—so much so it was decided to let Jonathan the leather maker make the cushions. That would free Joseph and the boys from having to deal with things like measuring for the exact size and then where to get and store the stuffing.

It didn't take long for women to want both the aprons and the cuffs! They needed them for weeding gardens, cleaning the courtyards, cooking—which could involve splashing and sometimes sparking—and carrying wood for burning. It was exciting to see a well-received new product coming from the Shop.

TWENTY-FIVE

17

Mary and Elizabeth, now twelve, had a small but steady business with their cloths. Women loved the sashes they made—especially the sashes with texture.

On their last trip to Jerusalem, they had learned a new technique called "sprang" that gave a more open look to the cloths. Sprang was made on the loom, but strings were knotted or twisted in various patterns to make each cloth unique. Their women customers liked this sprang for head coverings and sashes and even sacks for carrying several items.

One day, a distant cousin of Miriam's came to visit Hiram and Miriam. Japeth had been a traveler and a salesman of fine goods for many years. Miriam was wearing one of the sprang head coverings, and he became very excited about it. "Miriam!" he exclaimed. "I can sell these! I can sell a lot of these. Who made it? You?"

"No. My friend next door makes these. She and her daughter have a small business making things like sashes and head coverings and carrying bags for the women in town," said Miriam. "Would you like to meet them?"

"Please!" said Japeth.

Miriam walked next door to ask Mary if this was a convenient time to bring a visitor.

"Sure!" said Mary.

"I'll bring him and Hiram over soon. Thank you!" replied Miriam.

"Elizabeth, run and see if Father would be able to come home for a little while," said Mary.

Joseph was tied up so James was sent to see what was going on.

Hiram, Miriam, Japeth, and James all arrived at Mary's about the same time. Miriam introduced everyone, and Japeth started right in talking.

"I am a traveler dealing in fine goods. I have never seen anything like Miriam's head covering! I may want to carry them. She says you make other things as well. Would you mind showing me your work?"

"Of course," said Mary. "Elizabeth you're the primary maker of sprang cloths, so would you show him some of your work?"

Elizabeth said, "I've made three different patterns, and I use all of them in sashes and head coverings. This pattern appears to be sturdier, so I use that one for carrying bags. These scarves show the three patterns."

Japeth listened. He carefully examined each item like a man of his occupation would do. "I love the textured items, and I love the sprang items. I would love to carry your things with me to sell them. I have no doubt that they will be great sellers!"

James and Hiram were asked to join in the discussion. Should they do this? And if so, under what terms? At the end of the discussion, James wrote the contract.

1. Japeth would buy all of the texture and sprang items Mary and Elizabeth had on hand and any they could make in the next three days before he left. These items included textured sashes and head coverings, sprang sashes and head coverings in all three patterns, and the carrying bags.
2. Mary and Elizabeth were not to sell any of these items to any other salespeople, but they may continue to sell to people in and around Nazareth.

3. For this current supply of merchandise and the others they could make before Japeth left, he would pay them 5 percent above what they were currently asking from their customers.
4. Japeth would return in about four months and will buy no fewer than fifty of each item (equaling at least four hundred pieces) at another 5 percent increase.
5. James would draw up the papers, and contrary to current policies, Mary and Elizabeth's names would be on the contract, as well as those of Japeth, Joseph, and James.

That evening, James and Joseph drew up the final contract, and the family talked it over during Family Time. The entire family was excited! Two things came from this discussion. James suggested that one-half the price for the next approximately four hundred items would be required before Japeth left. This would give Mary and Elizabeth the money to buy materials.

The second thing was the family praising the work of James. Joseph said, "I am so proud of you, Son! I knew you were good with our bookkeeping, but you showed that you have a real head for business. Thank you!"

"Thank you, Father. And thank you for trusting me," said James.

"James, would you lead us in closing prayer tonight?" asked Joseph.

"Dear Father God, thank You for helping me today. Thank You for helping Mary and Elizabeth. Please help all of us to do our very best every day. Amen."

***

Anna was of the age where she needed to find work for training—to work with one of the women in town or possibly to join Mary and Elizabeth in creating cloth. Convincing Anna to do any kind of work was not an easy task. Anna continued to insist that she wanted to just play with her dolls.

What kind of work might Anna do? This was the topic of discussion at Family Time.

Joses said, "She's just lazy. You can't get her to do anything."

"Was that helpful?" Joseph asked him.

"I guess not; but— Nothing," Joses said as he saw the look on his father's face.

"I've seen her playing with her dolls, and she pretends she has things for the dolls—things like a bed and clothes and chairs and friends. Maybe we could show her how to make those things, and then she wouldn't have to pretend," Simon said.

Jesus nodded and said, "If she likes to do that, maybe she'll find some part of it that she really likes to do, and that could help her decide what kind of work she would do when she is older."

"Good idea," said Joseph. "Let's talk about how to make that work. First, what do you think of that idea, Anna?"

"I'm not sure what it means. Will I have to work?"

"I don't think it would be real work," said Jesus. "It's more like, when you play with your dolls, you'll make real clothes for them and a bed and all kinds of things. The only thing is, you will really make those things all by yourself. You know none of us knows as much about dolls and what they need as you do. We have to let you make the decisions."

"I get to make decisions? Really? Then I think I will like to make things for my babies."

Simon said, "I'll help you learn to make wooden things."

Elizabeth added, "And I'll help you learn to make the clothes. Okay?"

"Really? You big kids will really help me?"

"Sure!" said James. "We have pieces of wood at the Shop that you can have. We'll look tomorrow and bring some home for you."

"And Elizabeth and I have material you can have to work with," added Mary.

"Oh, I have to think," said Anna. "I will be so busy. I don't know if I'll have time for my chores." Ah, Anna! Ever trying to do nothing but play.

"It doesn't work that way, Anna. We all have chores, and we all have things we need to do outside of the routine work around the house," said Joseph.

Anna looked like she was going to argue.

"Anna, please close with prayer tonight," Joseph asked.

"Father God, I have a whole bunch of work added to my work now. Father says we all do. I don't know how I'm going to do all this. I need Your help. Help me, Father God. Thank You. Amen."

TWENTY-SIX

18

The boys may be eighteen, sixteen, and fourteen, but they were still boys. For some reason, they felt this was a good day for wrestling in the living room. What a ruckus! As they rolled around, they'd hit a piece of furniture and say, "Oops!" Then they'd set it back in place and get right back at it.

Mary had been on the roof setting up her loom when she thought she heard a crash downstairs. Simon was on the roof helping her move her loom. "Come on," she said, and the two of them went downstairs to see what was happening.

"Jesus, James, and Judas! What on earth are you doing?" Mary asked.

Jesus came over to her, leaned down, put Mary over his shoulders, picked her up, and spun her around three times.

James and Judas decided this was a good time to be sure that everything was put back in order—quickly!

"Jesus! You scalawag! All three of you! You know better than this. Now! Off to work and school."

"Ah, woman! I guess we were a little noisy. Boys, let's move before we get in some real trouble." Jesus kissed Mary on the cheek, and the three boys left for work and school.

"Woman," said Simon, "I'm going to school now too."

"Wait just a minute, young man. What did you just call me?"

"Woman—just like Jesus did."

"Please do not do that again. Let me see if I can explain this. Jesus is a grown man. Sometimes when we're teasing each other he calls me 'woman.' That is his love name for me, and it is not to be used by anyone else," Mary explained. "If anyone else used that name, it would be like they were showing disrespect to me. Can you understand?"

"I guess. You mean it's like a special name—kinda like when anybody says your name they say Mary. But most of the time when Father says your name, it's kinda soft. So is that a love name too?"

Mary nodded. "Yes. Now off to school!"

"Mother," asked Simon, "do you have a love name for me?"

"Yes I do! Every time I say your name 'Simon,' I think 'my Simon.'"

"Oh, Mother! I love you!" A hug, and he was off to school.

Mary prayed as she returned to the roof, "They are such great kids—no, men. Thank you, Father God, for my amazing family. You have blessed me in so many ways. You've blessed all of us in so many ways. I am so thankful! Please always guide them and please always guide me. Thank you, Father God. I love You."

James and Judas were laughing as they entered the Shop.

"You're both in really good moods today. What happened?" asked Joseph.

"I guess we're not as grown up as we should be," said James as he went to his workstation.

"We were wrestling in the living area. I guess we were making a racket—you know, crashing into things and laughing. Mother came down from the roof and tried to give us the riot act, but Jesus picked her up and twirled her around. We cleaned up the area, and as soon as Mother shooed us, we left. We did make it well away from the house before we broke out laughing."

Joseph shook his head and prayed, *Father God, bless my Mary. She is quite the woman! Thank You, Father God for the gift of Mary and for my awesome family.*

Twenty-Seven

18

About midmorning just as the rabbis were getting the students ready for recess, Rabbi Carpus said, "I'm not feeling well, Rabbi Jesus. Do you think you can take all the children out for recess? I'd like to lie down."

"Of course. Let me feel your head and see if you're running a fever." Jesus put his hand on Carpus's forehead and said, "Be well. Lie down until the boys and I come back for classes. You'll feel better by then."

"Thank you, Jesus. Be sure the younger children find their equipment by the big tree. I set it out there earlier."

"Of course," replied Jesus. Jesus led the way outdoors. "Okay, men. Let's let out some steam so we can get back to learning."

Outside, the older boys were playing bat and ball when the ball hit an outfielder and knocked him down. He landed hard on his left arm. His arm looked like it was lying at a funny angle. Jesus ran over to him and said, "That was a really good try to catch that ball. Let's have a look at that arm." Jesus ran his hand over the boy's arm and then used both hands to gently straighten the arm as he prayed, "Father God, please heal this young man."

"Better?" Jesus asked him.

The boy wiped his eyes and said, "I think so. I tried to catch the ball, but I missed."

Jesus told him, "It's not important whether you actually caught the ball, but it is important that you tried your best."

"I did. I think I got kinda dirty though."

"Nothing that won't wash off with the cloth and water in the washing bowl. Can you get up now?"

Just as the boy stood, the younger children started screaming. As Jesus looked up he saw Joses take off running. What they saw startled all of them. A young goat was running toward the younger children, head down, at top speed. The goat appeared to have been caught in the thorn bushes and was bleeding from a good many puncture wounds.

Joses reached the goat just before it reached the children. He still held the ball paddle in his hand so he raised it and hit the goat on the nose with the edge of the paddle. The goat went down. Joses sat on it until Jesus and the older boys got to him.

"Joses! That was wonderful! You saved the children from being hurt. Some of them could have been badly hurt. I am so proud of you!" said Jesus.

"Thank you," said Joses. "I didn't really know what I was doing. I just did it!"

"That's the Spirit of God at work in you. Are you okay?" asked Jesus.

"Yes. Just kind of shaky."

"Can you stay on the goat while I check to see how badly he's hurt from these thorns. He's starting to wake up." He turned to the older boys. "Boys can you help hold the goat down while I remove these thorns? Be gentle, but if enough of you try, you should be able to hold him down without hurting him any more than he is already."

Jesus began removing the thorns. There were so many. The poor goat was really punctured and scratched. The wounds weren't deep, but there were so many of them. When Jesus finished removing the thorns, he said to the boys, "While you're still holding him, let's ask Father God to make him not too afraid now and ask Him to heal all his sores."

"Can we pray for animals, Rabbi?" asked one of the younger boys.

"All are Father God's creatures. Do you think we can pray for animals?"

"I want to think so. Soooo, yes! I believe he can heal animals!"

"Shall we pray for him?" Jesus asked the boys.

"Yes, Rabbi," was the unanimous reply.

"Father God, this goat is afraid, and he has many wounds. Please calm him and heal him. Thank You. Amen."

The goat stood up slowly, shook himself, turned around, and headed back in the direction of his farm—healed and sure-footed.

"Okay! Let's put things away and get back to lessons," Jesus said.

Instead of returning to school, Simon was looking through the thorns and seemed to be picking out certain ones.

"Simon," asked Jesus, "what are you doing?"

"Mother and Elizabeth use these to hold scarves and stuff. Some of these are kinda big and some are twisted. I thought I'd get some for them."

"That was very thoughtful. Let me help you, and we'll get done more quickly. Okay?" asked Jesus.

"Sure! Look at these!"

They picked out about twenty or so to take home.

"We'll clean these on the way home today. Let's get to class," said Jesus.

After school, Simon insisted on starting to clean the thorns while Jesus finished with his classroom prep work. When he got home, Simon went running into the house yelling, "Mother! Elizabeth! Look what I found for you! We washed them so you can use them."

"They're perfect!" said Elizabeth.

"Beautiful!" exclaimed Mary. "Where did you find so many?"

"Well, a big goat came to school and was running at the little kids. He was hurt, and Joses hit him on the nose, and he fell down. Jesus took out the thorns, and then we prayed to Father God, and then he was okay. He ran home, and then you want thorns, so Jesus and I picked them, and I washed them. And here they are!" exclaimed Simon, all out of breath.

"What a great story, Simon! Thank you for thinking of us. Yes, we are running out of thorns, and these will be just right for our work! Thank you, Simon."

Mary and Elizabeth wrapped him in hugs. They smiled at each other, knowing that the full story would be told soon—but this was enough for now.

TWENTY-EIGHT

18

"Joseph, there's been an accident! Can you spare one of the boys?" asked Hiram.

"Of course," answered Joseph. He turned to Jesus and said, "Jesus, you've just come from school. Can you go?"

Jesus nodded.

"Father, I'd like to go too," said Joses, now eleven. "I know I can help."

"Thank you. Please remember you are to do only as you are told. Even if it's dirty and messy, you are to help. Understand?"

"Yes, Father."

As the three of them ran, Hiram said, "Men were coming into town with two carts, their supplies, animals, women, and children. The donkey leading the back cart was spooked and bolted forward right into the front cart, and the donkey in front reared. The result is that some people are hurt, their animals have run off, their belongings are all over the road, the carts are damaged, and a lot of things are broken. Here we are!"

What a scene! Children were crying; mothers were trying to comfort the children. There were about a dozen people, plus their cattle and goods. No one seemed to be badly hurt, but there were a lot of cuts and bruises.

Several others had come from the town and were busy salvaging items thrown from the carts, repairing the carts, and trying to find the animals that had run off.

One woman seemed to be in labor. Jesus asked if anyone knew where the physician was. It seems he had been called to a town about three miles away. Jesus turned to Joses and asked him to run, find the physician, and bring him back quickly. He ran off.

The woman's husband was at her side, holding her hand, and wiping her forehead. "It's too early! We just can't lose another one!" he told Jesus.

Jesus knelt down and said, "Tell me, when is the baby due?"

"Not until later next month. We've tried so hard to have a child! We just can't lose this baby!" cried the man.

"Are you Father God's people? Do you believe in Him?" asked Jesus.

"Yes!" said the man. "He has brought us safely this far."

"Join me in prayer!"

Jesus and the man placed their hands on the woman, and Jesus prayed, "Father God, thank You for bringing these people this far. This baby, not yet born, is Your child. We ask You please, Father God, to take charge of this family. Please let the child be well. Thank You, Father God." Jesus turned to the woman and said, "Be well."

The baby boy was born about two hours later. He was a small boy, but by the sound of his cry, he would be a strong young man. Jesus held him for a moment and smiled his gentle smile. "You are Father God's child. Stay close to Him always," he said as he cradled the baby in his arms.

"Jesus, come here!" called Hiram.

A man had walked a short distance from the carts and was sitting on the ground holding the front of his neck. Hiram was trying to help him. "Sir. Sir! Can you hear me?"

The man nodded, but his eyes were wide open in fear! Hiram leaned him forward and tried to pound him on the back, but nothing happened. When Jesus got there, he and Hiram stood the man up and bent him over their arms. Jesus gave him a slap on the back, and a large piece of fig flew out of the man's mouth. He coughed. His eyes were watering. He said, "I was eating a dried fig when I tripped."

There was a thump! Another man had sat down hard. He was bent over, holding his chest and having a hard time breathing. They ran to help. There were two rather large branches at his side. It looked as if he'd picked them up—perhaps to support the carts. He was having trouble breathing and unable to talk.

The man seemed to be older than the others. Suddenly he became unresponsive. Jesus turned to Hiram. "Pray with me. Father God, in Your great goodness we ask that You heal this man to Your glory. Thank You, Father God."

There was no change. Jesus prayed, "Father God, please show me what to do!"

They laid the man down and waited a few seconds and when nothing happened Jesus took his knuckles and, with pressure, rubbed them up and down the man's chest several times. The man began to move. "Thank you, Father God, for showing me what to do," Jesus prayed.

After watching the man for a while, Jesus said, "Hiram, please stay with him until the physician gets here. He needs to rest. Keep him down. I'll check to make sure everyone else is doing well, and then I'll return. Come get me if anything changes."

After Jesus left, Hiram talked to the man about what had happened and assured him that all of the others were being cared for.

The townspeople were amazing. Those who weren't tending to the injured were picking up the spilled items, gathering the animals which had run off, or trying to repair the carts.

Jesus went to see how the animals were doing. Most of them had been found and returned to the area. He checked to see if those mending the carts needed help. They were doing fine, so Jesus returned to the man who had had the heart attack.

Just then, Joses came running. "I found him! He's coming!" he called, panting hard as he neared Jesus. "He was just starting on his way back. He needed to check someone's bandages, and then he's going to come right here."

Some of the town's folk heard and cheered! Joses was given water to drink and told to sit in the shade for a while and to splash the water on his face and body to help him cool down. (What boy wouldn't like to be told to do that?!) The physician, in his cart, came shortly after.

Jesus updated the physician on what had happened and what had been done. The physician was impressed. He spent time with the man with the heart attack and with the new baby boy. He assured them that they were doing fine.

He did have special instructions for the new parents. One suggestion had them giggling. "It's okay to let the baby sleep on his own mat; you don't need to hold him every minute."

He stopped at the man who had had the heart attack. The man's son was now sitting with him. The physician questioned both men regarding his symptoms and questioned Jesus about the treatment.

"It was a heart attack; that's certain. But I can't see anything else to do for him right now," said the physician. Turning to the man, he said, "I want you to stay quiet tonight. And then I want you to stay 'even' for three months. By even, I mean don't get sad, excited, angry, or upset in anyway. And I want you to lie down for at least an hour every afternoon. No arguments. After that, you should be strong enough to *gradually* go back to your usual work." Looking at the man's son, he said, "If he won't stay quiet around here tonight, I need him to spend the night with me. It's important."

"He has never been a man to sit quietly, especially when there's work to be done," replied his son.

"Then he's coming home with me. Can you manage things without your father?"

"We sure can. However, if you ask him, he'll tell you that no one, other than himself, can do anything right," said the son with a grin on his face and an elbow bump to his father's arm. You could see that there was a lot of love between father and son.

"Good! Then he'll come home with me. I'll put him to work. I've been gone a few days, so he can help me with my bookwork," the physician teased.

"That's worse than the heart attack," said the man, grinning.

Jesus noticed that the men had been able to restore both carts and that the women from town were coming toward the carts with various pieces of pottery and items of food. They were able to replace almost every piece that had broken and had brought enough food to feed the people until they reached their destination.

The travelers decided to stay where they were for the night and start out in the morning.

Twenty-nine

18

"Father, I'm now eleven, and I need to find work to do. I think I would like to work in our shop with you and my brothers," said Joses.

"Really?" asked Joseph. "Let's see. What do you see yourself doing when you work?"

"I don't know. I'll just do what I'm told I guess. I know I have to do something. And no matter what I do, it'll probably be boring. So I might as well work with the family. At least I'll be able to know what everyone's talking about."

"That's really not what work is about though," said Joseph. "You'll be working for many years. You need to find work that makes you feel good. I want to tell you some things about work. First of all, no matter what work you do, it has a lot of boring stuff to do. A lot of our work is not just cutting the wood. Then we have to sand it to make it smooth, oil it, rub in the oil, wipe off the extra oil, and put all the pieces together. We spend a lot of time sanding to make things smooth."

"But you would tell me what to do, wouldn't you?"

"Sometimes that makes people angry—having someone always telling them what to do. When that happens, a person gets angry, and that puts everybody in a bad mood."

"I remember we talked about that before," said Joses.

"Right. I'm glad you remember. Let's start all over again. What kinds of things do you like to do?" asked Joseph.

"I like to play games. I like to run. I like to be with my friends. I think I like to do things with my hands," said Joses.

"Good. Now tell me what you do not like to do."

"I don't like to study! I don't like to do chores. I don't like it when Anna sulks."

Joseph said, "It sounds to me like you like to be very active and not just do the same thing all the time, and you like friendly people. Does that sound about right?"

"Yup. But I don't care if it's the same thing—just so it's kinda fun."

"I think you have just done a very good job of deciding what kind of a job you'd like," said Joseph.

"I have? What did I decide?"

Joseph smiled. "You want a job that challenges you—that changes all the time, a job that is around friendly people and one that you don't need to be told what to do all the time. Right?"

"I guess—I think. Well, maybe I just don't want to work," groused Joses.

"Joses, a little patience please. You're doing a very grown-up job of thinking about this. This is very important. You learn something different with every job you hold. You do not have to stay at the same job forever. You can change jobs if you want to. There is nothing wrong with trying more than one type of work."

"Thank you, Father. I guess I have to think some more about what I want to do."

"That's fine. You can come to work with your brothers and me for a few days and see how things go. It'll be easier to see if carpentry is the right job for you if you give it a try. But if not, maybe you'll be able to think of what kind of work you want. Shall we try it?"

"I guess so. But what if I'm not very good at it?"

"No one is very good when they start a job. That's one thing you do not have to worry about. What you need to worry about is doing the best you can at whatever job you do. If you try your best all the time, you will do well in any job you do," explained Joseph.

"Thank you, Father. I don't think I'm always good at doing my best. When would I start?"

"How about today?"

It was decided. Joseph and Joses went to join the brothers for this new adventure.

"Boys, Joses would like to try working with us for a few days. He thinks he might like this kind of work, so let's get him started. Either one of you have a project that needs help?" asked Joseph.

"I do!" said Judas. "I'm making a cabinet for Mother and Elizabeth to store the items they're making for the next time Japeth is in town."

It's a good thing Judas was a patient person. Teaching Joses was a challenge! No matter how hard he tried, Joses seemed to be all thumbs.

"Joses I'm going to have you practice on a piece of wood that's not for this project but will be for another project." Judas showed him a smaller piece of wood. He carefully explained about the grain of the wood, about the importance of sanding and oiling with the grain of the wood, and about taking pride in a piece well done.

Joses tried. At least Joses tried as hard as Joses was capable. After a few tries, Judas saw that Joses was absolutely not able to sand evenly along the grain of the board. Joses wanted to press hard in the center of the board and let up on the edges.

Judas could tell that Joses was getting tired of trying to sand the board, so he brought him to the special cabinet.

"This is what I'm working on. It's going to look kind of like a big box. I'm using wood that's pretty thick. See here? That's so I can sand down around the edges on the outside of the top, and then the cover of the box will fit tightly. Mother and Elizabeth need to keep the items safe from mold and critters like spiders and moths for a few months, so the cover must be tight"

"How do you sand it smaller?"

"First, I take this chisel and gently tap it with a hammer so it takes out very small pieces of wood. When I have all that chipped out, then I can sand and sand and sand it," explained Judas.

"Can I try to chip stuff?" asked Joses.

"Sure. Let's get some wood for you to practice on, and then I'll show you how."

Joses took to that. Actually he was quite good, even from the first. When Jesus came after school, Joses ran to him saying, "Look Jesus! I'm learning how to make tight covers!"

"Good job, little man!" said Jesus as he tousled Joses's hair.

That night at Family Time, Joseph asked Joses, "Joses, what did you learn at the Shop today?"

"I learned that I'm not good at sanding and kinda a little bit good at oiling, but I really like chipping out pieces of wood! It's kinda hard because, if you hit the chisel too hard with the hammer, you can really make a mess. So I have to concentrate."

Joseph and Mary smiled at each other.

The next morning, Jesus said, "Father, I have an idea for Joses. I think he'll like it. Could we, all of us, have a short meeting when Joses and I are done with school today?"

"Sure. Have a good day, everyone! Off to school and work!" said Joseph as he kissed Mary on her cheek.

Joses could hardly sit still all day in school—all day just wondering what Jesus had in mind. Finally, it was time to "go to work."

Jesus and Joses walked together to the Shop.

"Jesus, can you tell me what you're going to say?" asked Joses.

"Sure. It's about you, and I think you just may like it!" Jesus teased.

As soon as they entered the Shop, Joses said, "Time for the meeting!"

A customer was inside talking with James. "Well, young man, you sure are excited about something! I'm almost finished talking, so he'll be with you in a minute."

Finally, they were all together!

Jesus said, "Joses, I think you really like using the chisel and hammer. If so, what if we explore having you make decorations for people. I was thinking we could make a drawing of something—something like a bird or a hare or a lamb or even a person—on a piece of wood. Then you could try using the chisel to chip around the animal so it would kind of stand out. Do you understand me?"

"I think so. But how big would it be?" asked Joses.

"Whatever size you would like it to be. Maybe different sizes. The largest ones could be hung on people's walls. Would you like to try?"

Joseph, James, and Judas all began talking at once. It seemed that everyone thought it would be a great idea.

"James, you're good at drawing. Could you help him with that? Father, you know about wood. Could you choose wood for him to work with? Judas, you know about tools. He may need something special or a special size, could you help him with that?"

Joses was so excited. He went with Joseph to pick out the wood. "Father, why does the kind of wood I use make a difference?" But that was only his first question. It seemed that Joses had found something that really interested him.

When the wood was chosen and the drawings were made, Joses was able to try two animals with quite nice results on the second one. That night at Family Time, Joses said, "Mother, this is my new job, and I would like you to have the first one. Well, it's really the second one, but the first one was just practice."

"Oh, Joses! This is a beautiful little lamb! Elizabeth! Simon! Anna! Look at this."

To Joses's delight, the entire family was impressed.

It was a wonderful start to a new career.

THIRTY

19

Almost the entire town was going on this trip to Jerusalem to celebrate the New Year and its festivals. Benjamin arranged for four Greek men to watch over the town and the few people who were unable to travel. Barabbas was always on the minds of the townspeople.

Along the way the townspeople of Nazareth were met by other groups from towns also going to Jerusalem. One young man, Philip, from a small town called Nain not too far from Nazareth found Elizabeth intriguing, and she didn't seem to mind. The two of them somehow managed to keep the people of the two towns in close proximity to each other.

One evening as the families were sitting near a fire, Hiram and Miriam were at their happiest—each holding a grandchild. "Our eight-year-old granddaughter thinks she's the ruler of the world. These two, her younger brothers, are two and four and totally involved in their little world. I hope they always continue to be each other's best friend," said Hiram.

"They will." Miriam changed the subject. "Joseph, I've told Mary and Hiram about something and asked them to keep it a secret—yes, even from you. We thought I had a woman's problem that might significantly change my life, possibly take my life. The three of us prayed about it, and we all agreed that, if it continued, we would ask your entire family to pray with us. Father God was merciful and granted His healing. The physician has agreed that I am healed. I give our Father God so many thanks!

"Whew!" Miriam continued. "I didn't know if I could share this, but now that I have, I feel so much better! I feel like a load is off my shoulders."

Joseph said, "I'm glad that you're healed, and I understand that it's hard to share personal things—especially woman things—but I'm so glad you're okay. Thank you for including my Mary. She and you are so close, and I think that's great for both of you."

Later that evening, Rebecca was sitting next to Miriam watching her Mother and her own boys. She said, "These three little ones are such a blessing to me. When our second child was stillborn I thought my heart would never stop aching. Then I had these two boys, and soon we'll be adding another one!"

Congratulations from everyone. Her sister Hannah hugged her and said, "I didn't know that!" She looked at Matthew, and he nodded. "Matthew and I were going to tell everyone sometime on this trip that we're with child. Maybe they'll be born close together! Wouldn't that be great."

More congratulations were shared all around.

***

On the third evening, Philip, who was spending a lot of time with Joseph and his family, was asked to share who he was and where he saw himself in the future. "I'm hoping to be a tent maker. I finished my apprenticeship about four years ago, so I'm working with my father. I've been able to save some money. My thinking is that tents don't last forever, and sooner or later, everyone will need another one. Therefore, I hope to provide a good living when I have a family."

"What kind of man do you see yourself as?" asked Joseph.

"Wow! That's a heavy question. I've never really thought about it. Let's see. I am a Jew, and I love Father God with all my heart. My thoughts are always that, whatever I do, I want Him to be pleased with me. I'm honest. That sounds like I'm perfect, but the truth is I'm far from it. For one thing, I'm kind of messy. I try to remember to clean up after myself, but that isn't very often. My work, my family, and my friends are also very important to me—right next to Father God," said Philip.

He continued, "I'm fussy about how I make tents; they have to be good enough that I would live in them. It makes my father proud, and it makes me feel good. I eat everything put in front of me. I love children; regardless of their ages, you can teach them something. And that makes me feel good. I like playing ball and racing. I'm not really good at either one, but I'm probably in the middle somewhere. Is that enough for now?" Philip looked at Joseph.

Joseph and Mary looked at each other, smiled, and nodded.

It had been quite a night. Joseph offered the closing prayer, and everyone stood to go to his or her tent. In just a couple of days, they'd be in Jerusalem.

The journey to and the celebrations in Jerusalem were basically uneventful but wonderful! There were a few broken wheels, a broken arm, and some bruises and headaches, but nothing out of the ordinary. Soon the celebrations were over, and they were on their way home.

***

It felt good to be home. It always did. What was it about home that made people feel so comfortable? The men went back to work and the women and children unpacked. That evening, they held a town dinner and invited the four Greek men who had guarded the city while they were away to eat with them.

One of the Greek men sat with Joseph and his family. About halfway through the meal ten-year-old Simon asked the man, "Do you know our Father God?"

"I don't know. What's His name?"

"His name is in our hearts. It's so holy that we cannot speak it."

"Tell me more about this God," said the Greek, smiling at this young boy.

"Well, He is the one true God. He's the God of love. He gave us laws that we must obey, and He's always with us," answered Simon.

The Greek man looked to Joseph as if asking permission. Joseph nodded as if to say, "Go ahead."

"We have many gods, and each one has a special thing he or she does for us. One god leads us in war; another rules the moon and the stars. Another god rules the weather; and another god gives good health or bad health," explained the Greek man.

"But our one Father God does all of that and more. He loves us and He forgives us when we do something wrong and we're sorry. I don't think I would want to live with a lot of gods. What if they don't agree? What if one says the sun will be out today and the other says it will rain? Won't they fight and that will cause a mess for everyone?" asked Simon.

"I guess I never thought about that. We're just taught that this is the way it is and this is what we should believe," said the Greek man.

"I think you should love our Father God. You would have a better life if you followed Him," stated Simon.

"Hmmmm. How would I know which is right? Is the way I live right or is your One God right? How would I know?" asked the Greek man.

"Just ask Him. Tell Him you heard about Him and ask Him if He is the true God. He'll let you know."

"How? Will He just talk to me and say, 'I'm real'?" asked the Greek man.

"Kind of. It's like … you just know. One day you'll be doing your work, and you'll just know. Like that!" explained Simon.

"Just like that!? Well, young Simon, I just may do that some day!"

"Thank you. I will pray for you that you find the truth. May I call you my friend?" asked Simon.

"I would be honored, my young friend. Now we have a contract. We are friends! Let's shake hands on it," said the Greek man.

"May we also share a man hug?" asked Simon as he rose to hug the Greek man.

This hug would be remembered in the years to come.

THIRTY-ONE

19

Mary and Elizabeth were doing well sewing the items for Japeth to sell. On this trip through Nazareth, Japeth brought his eleven-year-old son. The boy wanted to begin working but also wanted to travel and see more than just his local area. Although the boy was small for his age and appeared to be shy, he was able to help his father with the organization of the cart and with the bookkeeping. Japeth's eyesight was failing a bit, and doing the bookwork was difficult. It appeared to be the start of a good business partnership.

"Hi, everyone! I'm back! How is everybody?" called Japeth.

Judas had been working at home that day to replace some bricks that had come loose in their home and in Hiram's.

Anna ran to the door, followed closely by Elizabeth and Mary.

"Welcome!" said Mary. "Come in!"

The boy was introduced, and Elizabeth, Mary, and Anna took the two of them to the storeroom to show them what they had prepared. They had a surprise for Japeth.

"What is this?!" said Japeth. "It looks like a soft flower!"

"It is. We've made a few of them for the women in our town, and they love them," said Mary.

"They attach them to their head coverings and sprang items with a large thorn," explained Elizabeth.

Mary said, "They wear them for special occasions like weddings and visiting around here but also when they visit family and friends in other towns."

"May I sell them?" asked Japeth.

"We were hoping you would say that," said Elizabeth. "We made a hundred of them just in case you might like them."

"I do! We need to talk finances, but I would like to buy all that you have. I noticed that each one seems to have its own color. How do you do that?"

"Elizabeth felt that each lamb seemed to have a slightly different color in its wool. Not only that—it also appeared that different parts of their bodies had a slightly different color. We keep the different colors separate. It's a bit of work during shearing time, as we need to be right there by the men. But it seems to work better when we sort the wool there at the beginning, rather than try to match pieces of the wool after the sheep have been shorn and the wool thrown in a pile," explained Mary.

"We're thinking of making smaller ones for girls to wear." said Elizabeth.

"Son, what do you think of these flowers?' asked Japeth.

"Father, I think the women would like them, but I think that the girls would like them even better. You know how my little sisters are always trying to be pretty."

"You're right, Son." To Mary, he said, "Let's talk finances."

A price was agreed upon. Japeth said, "I'm going to take a chance. I would like to have double this number next time I'm through here—maybe half this size and the other half in various smaller sizes. Deal?"

***

Miriam and Hiram and all their children and grandchildren invited Japeth and his son and Joseph and his family to eat the noon meal with them that Sabbath. Mary and Elizabeth insisted on helping with the food and the preparations. The women enjoyed being together. It wasn't often that all of Mary's children and all of Miriam's children were able to be together.

After the noon meal, Japeth regaled everyone with tales from adventures on his travels. His favorite story was the one about the male goat that, for some reason, decided to ram one of the wheels on Japeth's cart.

He and his son had stopped at a roadside inn and were enjoying a soup that was strange to them, when they heard this awful *bang!* A few seconds later, there sounded another *bang*. After the third *bang*, they heard a lot of laughter and cheering outside, so they went to see what was going on.

It seemed that a huge male goat had decided to ram one of the wheels on Japeth's cart. As they came out of the inn, the goat charged a fourth time. The goat was stunned, and the wheel of the cart broke. Everything shifted inside the cart. Some of the bystanders ran to keep the merchandise from falling out. The owner of the goat came running. He was angry at the goat and embarrassed.

It turns out that the owner of the goat was a craftsman dealing mainly in building and repairing carts. He apologized and told Japeth he'd have a new wheel on the cart first thing the next morning. What had caused the goat to ram the wheel? It seems a hare had been caught and jammed between the wheel and axel, and that goat wanted that hare!

While the adults were talking, Japeth's son kept the older children occupied with hand and finger images he made on the living room wall behind a lamp.

All of a sudden, there were terrible screams from Japeth's son and the children. It seems that the boy had moved his hand suddenly and the part of his tunic near his hand had caught fire. They were able to put out the fire, but the boy's left hand was burned. Some of the oil from the lamp had landed on his hand and caused a huge blister.

Japeth, tears streaming down his cheeks, grabbed the boy and held him tightly to his chest. James and Jesus rushed over. James rubbed the boy's head and softly talked to him, while Jesus tried to look at the hand. The boy would have nothing to do with that and kept jerking the hand away from Jesus.

Jesus said, "James, please hold his arm still for me."

As James held the arm, Jesus said, "Father God, please heal this boy."

The boy stopped crying, looked at his arm, and then looked at Jesus.

Jesus said to him, "Be well, young man. Our Father God loves children." He turned to the rest of the children and said, "If you'd like to, you may continue to play, or you can come with the rest of us. I think the mothers have a surprise for us."

It seems everybody had come to the room to see what had happened. After explanations were made and things calmed down, they decided that everyone would return to the roof. The women did have a surprise for them—a tray of cheeses and fruit.

The boy came over to Japeth and said, "Father, the sleeve on my tunic is burned. I don't have another one. Mother will be angry."

"Son, when Mother hears what happened, she will not be angry," Japeth told him. "She'll be so glad that you're well. Don't worry about your tunic, Son. We'll get by."

Overhearing them, Jesus went up to the boy. "Please let me look at your tunic," he said. "Hmmm. It isn't too bad. You put out the fire very quickly. If you hadn't gotten oil on your skin, you wouldn't have burned your hand. Here, let me smooth your tunic out a little and see if that will help."

The boy watched in awe as Jesus rubbed his sleeve. "Thank you, Rabbi Jesus! It was just wrinkled a lot. Oh, thank you!" And he threw his arms around Jesus and gave him a hug.

Japeth looked at Jesus with a smile of appreciation and nodded his thanks.

Things settled down, and the children went outdoors to play.

After a short time, they heard an awful scream. Simon was the first to reach a small boy. He and three other neighbor boys had been playing nearby. Blood was literally gushing from a wound in the boy's upper leg. Simon put his hand on the site and yelled, "Father! Brothers! Hurry!" He turned to Joses and said, "Joses go find them, fast!"

Little Anna got there before the men, and Simon told her, "Hold his hand or rub his forehead or his hair or something so he can feel you. He's scared, and he needs you to be quiet and gentle. Please, Anna! He needs you," he said, as Anna seemed ready to move away.

Anna began to touch the boy's hair. "Look at me. I'm not scared. My father and brothers are coming. You'll be okay," she said over and over.

Joseph, the boys, and everyone else seemed to arrive all at once.

Jesus said, "Good job, Simon. I'm going to put my hand next to yours. Count to three, and then I want you to quickly move away from my hand. I'll take over. Understand?"

Simon nodded. Jesus counted, "One, two, three!" Jesus took over.

Joseph asked Mary to get cold water. He asked Miriam and Elizabeth to get clean cloths and strips for bandaging. James and Judas each held a hand to keep the boy calm. Anna continued to stroke the boy's hair and tell him he would be fine.

Jesus looked quickly at all those around him and said, "Let's pray."

Both families prayed. "Father God, we know this is a bad injury. In Your gracious goodness, we ask that You heal this young man right now. We thank You, Father God. Amen."

Jesus held the site a little longer. He asked the boy if he was feeling better, and when the boy nodded that he was, Jesus slowly removed his hand from the wound. The blood had stopped, and the wound was healing.

"What on earth were you boys doing?" asked Hiram.

"Here let me show you," said one of the boys. "See this tree here? Well, we would all start here and run as fast as we could, and when we got to that line over there, we would throw our stick and see whose stick would go the farthest. Well, he got kinda far on his first turn, but he wanted to try again. So when everyone was done, he grabbed his stick and started to run. But he tripped, and the stick got stuck in his leg by his tummy. When he got up, the stick fell out, and he started squirting blood. We just screamed!"

The injured boy asked, "I'm kinda tired. Was I bad?"

"No," said Jesus. "It was an accident. You'll be fine. Maybe you could watch a little better where you're running. Okay?"

The boy's father arrived. When he heard what had happened to his son, he knelt in front of the boy and pulled him to his chest in a great big hug. "Oh, Son! I couldn't live without you." His father had tears running down his cheeks. "Oh, my son!"

Joseph filled him in on the details of what had happened. The boy's father turned to the group and said, "I have no words to thank all of you. If any of you ever need anything, please come to me. I'll do my very best to help you! Thank you! Thank you."

Miriam asked the man and his boy to join them for fruit and cheese.

It turns out that the man was a metalsmith. He had heard that the metalsmith in town was getting older and was looking for someone to help him. "My wife died a few weeks ago. She has always been sickly. So now it's just my boy and me. I was ready to leave the area where I worked, so we came here about a week ago.

"I work with gold, silver, and copper, but I especially like working with copper. It seems to come alive in my hands. Right now, my boy is beginning to work with me to learn the art of metalsmithing. He's doing well, but it's up to him to choose his work. Oh! What would I have done if I had lost him?" Again tears slid down his cheeks.

After cheese and fruit, it was time to return to their homes. Hiram asked Jesus to close with prayer.

"Father God, what would we do without You? You provide for us every day. You send new friends to us. You heal us as we pray. Thank You, Father God. Thank You for being our God and for being so patient with us. Amen."

***

The next morning, Japeth and his son accompanied Joseph and his sons to the Shop. Japeth has traveled quite a bit of the world and was awed at the quality of furniture made by this family. Joses pulled him aside to show him the designs he was making.

Japeth was surprised. "These carvings are wonderful! I think I could sell these as well. I love that they're different sizes—small ones and then these large carvings for wall decorations!"

"James," said Japeth, "what's that you're working on with leather?"

James showed him the aprons and the sleeve protectors, explaining what they were used for and how they were attached. Japeth was amazed and examined them carefully.

"James and Joses, I'm going to be here for perhaps another two or three days. Could we meet and talk about these items? I need to think about it, but I think I just might want to sell all of them," said Japeth.

The next day at their meeting, it was decided that Japeth would take with him the supply of cuffs and aprons and the carvings that were on hand, and then he ordered a supply for his next visit. A contract was drawn up, much like the contract with Mary and Elizabeth.

That evening, Joses approached his older brothers. "Guys, Japeth had the idea of making rounds into some kind of toy for children. I was thinking about it, and I think I want to make them kind of like a wheel, like something that kids can get rolling and run alongside. Does that sound like it would be possible?"

The four brothers tossed around the idea for a few minutes, and Jesus said, "Well, little brother, it seems we all think this is a really good idea. Go ahead and work on it. If you want—and I mean want—help, just ask any one of us. Okay?"

James added, "I am impressed, Joses. You have a great idea. Go for it!"

"Little brother, I knew you had a brain. Proudin' at you, kid!" said Judas.

Another possible item for the family's Shop?

THIRTY-TWO

20

Family Time arrived, and James was both excited and incredibly nervous.

"Everyone, I would like to discuss something tonight. You all know Lois. Her father is the pottery maker in Nain. I would really like to approach her family and ask that we be betrothed."

The family went wild! Mary and Joseph looked at each other as if they were saying, *Are we this old? I knew this day would come, but we're still so young!*

Joseph said, "Congratulations, Son! That is a great deal of responsibility, but you have a good head. You're certainly of the age, and I think Lois is a wonderful young woman!"

"Thank you, Father. I'm so excited. She is beautiful inside as well as outside. I've always known that the woman I marry had to love our Father God as I do. I asked her about it, and, Father, she loves and trusts our Father God! I feel we can make a loving family just as you and Mother have."

"James, will you be living here in Nazareth?" Mary asked, almost as if she was afraid one of her family might go far away.

"Lois and I haven't discussed it, but it would seem we would live here. I haven't said anything to anyone, but Benjamin told me that he's now sixty-seven, and his arthritis is getting really bad. It's harder and harder for him to get around and to do things around his house and yard. He asked me if I would like to live with him beginning soon, and he would leave his home to me. That would be a perfect place to make our home. I haven't said yes or no. What do you think, Father?"

"I think that's a lot of responsibility. Caring for a person as he ages may get harder and harder as time goes on. At the same time, I feel that Benjamin is a strong man and won't let you do more for him than is absolutely necessary. What he probably needs most is someone to keep up his home, his yard, and his few remaining animals. The more I think of it, the more I think it could be a good thing for both—I mean all—of you. My opinion is that it is definitely something to keep in mind. I have always loved that man! That's really a remarkable offer!"

"It'll give us another place to hang out once you have your own place. Oh, that sounded awful! I didn't mean it to sound like that. I meant when you have your own place and your own family, we'll have another place to visit. Oh, did I say anything right?" said Judas.

Even nine-year-old Anna was laughing at him.

James said, "I know what you mean. In a way, this is kind of scary. I'll be moving but … nuts! Nothing's going to happen immediately, so we all have time to think."

"I want you to have a little girl so I can make dolls and clothes and furniture just for her—something I won't make for anyone else," Anna said dreamily.

Jesus said, "Well, little brother! You sure are growing up. I can't wait! My little brother betrothed and then married and then with children. Hey! I will be Uncle Jesus. I'm going to like this! If it means anything, I think this is all great! Mother, if I bring home those special lamb chops that the butcher seasons, would you make those as a special dinner tomorrow? We need to celebrate!"

"Yes of course! Elizabeth has been thinking about a special dish to make sometime. So maybe tomorrow, Elizabeth?" asked Mary.

"Mother, that would be great. But what if it isn't as good as I think it will be?" asked Elizabeth.

"Then I'll eat all of it!" said Joses. "You've never made anything bad, so it can't be too bad."

"Thanks, Joses. Maybe I'll let you have an early taste."

Joseph asked, "Well, James, where do you go from here?"

"I would like Jesus and Judas to come with me on Sabbath next, and we would go to Nain to ask Lois's father. I'm unsure. Should I send a messenger to him that we're coming? Or do we just go?" asked James.

"If you talked with Lois and told her you might come on Sabbath, then I think you all should just go. Just for general information, your mother and I bless you and Lois and your life to come, and we'll pray for both of you."

"Thank you, Father. Simon, you've been quiet. What are you thinking?" asked James.

"My heart's stuck! I feel that all my words are stuck in one place in my throat, and they don't know how to say what I want. May I say the prayer tonight, Father?" asked Simon.

"Of course. Sometimes the best way to say something is to let Father God say it through you. Please pray, Simon," Joseph said with a smile of pride in his youngest son.

"Father God, thank You for all You are and for all You do. James is making a big decision, and we ask that You bless him all the way. Father God, we all need You so much. Hold on to us and help us to always do what You want. Thank You for being our God. Amen."

THIRTY-THREE

20

Joses was thinking about making that toy for children. The idea of the wheel—a wheel a little like a carriage wheel but made smaller and lighter—kept running through his mind. He figured they would need to be at least two different sizes, one for smaller kids and one for older kids.

He worked and worked on his project. Finally, he determined that the spokes had to be evenly spaced inside the wheel. But how does one make the spokes go from one side to the other without using an axle, as that makes it too heavy. Joses tried to make the spokes in rows parallel to each other, but the wheel wouldn't roll properly; it only went sideways. He tried making the outside edges of the wheel rounded, but that really didn't work.

After a week of trying, Joses asked Joseph, "Father, I don't know what else to try. I think we can really make a play wheel. I think it will be interesting for kids, but I don't know enough to accomplish what I want. Could I talk with Matthew? He's the carriage maker, and maybe there's something else I don't know. Jesus and James see him often, so maybe I could go over when they do?"

"That's a good idea, Joses. I like the way you've been trying and working on different designs on your own. It shows you're growing. You'll be a good man when you grow up. I think Matthew is just the one to help you. And you'll get to play with the baby for a while. Good job, Son!" said Joseph.

"Thank you, Father. When I grow up, I want to be just like you. You're so nice to everyone, and you don't yell when someone does something wrong."

"Thank you, Son."

Next Sabbath after dinner, Joses walked with Jesus and James the two miles to see Matthew—and Hannah and the baby, of course.

"Good Sabbath!" said Matthew as he welcomed the boys inside the house.

"Good Sabbath, Matthew. Would you have some time to help me with something I'm working on?" asked Joses.

"Of course. Come see Hannah and the baby first," replied Matthew.

"Boys! Welcome! It's so good to see you," said Hannah.

"I wanted to talk to Matthew about a problem I'm having on my project, so I came with my brothers. Our whole family sends greetings, as do your mother and father, Hannah. I've been told by everyone to give you and the baby hugs from everyone," Joses said as he hugged Hannah. "Maybe one big hug will do for everybody?"

Hannah laughed. "I agree. We might get worn out hugging for everyone. See how big the baby is now? Hardly a baby anymore."

"I've been making these small rounds for some of the small children. May I give one to the baby?" asked Joses.

"Joses! It's beautiful! You really make these?" asked Hannah.

"I do. I try to make each one a little different. I make them different sizes as well as with different designs. Some of the girls and women wear them on their head scarves, so those need to be kinda small. Sometimes people like them for a wall for their homes, so those are larger but with different designs," replied Joses.

"Look! The baby loves it. Oops! Now she's chewing on it," Matthew said as he picked up the baby and tickled her to make her laugh.

"It's okay for her to chew on it. A lot of the littlest ones do. They always leave scratches from their teeth. One of the mothers said it helped stop the hurt when their teeth came in," explained Joses.

"Well, young Joses," said Matthew, "let's you and I go to my workshop and see if I can help you with your problem. Jesus and Judas can continue playing with the baby."

Joses explained to Matthew, "I'm making a lot of those small rounds, but I want to make something like a wheel that the children can push and run alongside. Do you know what I mean?"

"I think so. Have you thought about how they would keep the wheel moving?" asked Matthew.

"By pushing it with their hand every few feet or maybe using a stick and pushing it between the spokes? I won't be able to decide until I get a working wheel."

"Joses, I think that just might work. In fact, I'm sure it will! May I work on this with you? We'd sort of be in business together, but I won't charge you anything. I just may want some of the rounds for my children and maybe a few for gifts. We can work that out once we get the project up and running. Does that sound like a good business deal?" asked Matthew.

Joses nodded. "Father said I can trust you and that you'll be fair and not treat me like a little kid. He was right, wasn't he?"

"Let's shake on it." They did—just like two men!

Matthew took Joses to his workshop outside but near the house. "These are wheels to carriages, Joses. Let's take two of them out back and see what happens when using wheels that we know are stable."

"No working today, Matthew! It's Sabbath," warned Joses.

"Right, Joses, but I think it'll be okay if we play for a little while."

The two of them tried and failed and laughed, but both felt they had a better understanding of what was needed. These wheels were just too heavy and too unwieldy.

"Joses, let's both work on it this next week and meet here next Sabbath. But if one of us finds a real solution, I think we should meet some evening. In that case, I'll come to your home. I don't want you walking alone at night. Sounds okay?"

"Thank you, Matthew. I feel like giving you a hug, but I know men shake hands." And he offered his hand to Matthew.

Matthew took his hand, shook it, and then drew him in for a big hug. "I'm a man who loves hugs!" he said as he let go.

On his way home, Joses felt as if he were flying. All he could think of was his rounds for kids. "Hey!" he said to Jesus and James. "That's what I'll call them—Rounds for Kids!"

Next Sabbath at services, Matthew and Joses talked. "Matthew," said Joses, "I think if we meet tomorrow that will be work, and I don't think that's right."

"I've been thinking the same thing. What If I come to your house after sundown? Then we can compare notes and decide where to go from there. Will that be okay with you? Or is your family planning something?" asked Matthew.

"I asked Father before synagogue today, and he said that sundown at our house would be great. I'll see you then?"

The sun had just gone down when Matthew arrived. Joses seemed kind of quiet. Matthew asked him, "How did things go? Did you solve the problems of the world?"

Joses giggled. "No. But I'm sorta disappointed. I really tried, Matthew. But I have more questions. What did you find out?"

Matthew said, "First of all, it is never 'nothing' when you try. Everything you try is a lesson, just like in school. You learn more by trying then actually doing. So from my point of view, I think you did a great job. Now, let's compare what we've each done this week and then see where we are."

Comparing what each had tried during the past week, they did make some progress. They talked for a while and came up with a slightly different idea. They would try something much smaller—what they would call Twirlers. The Twirlers were small "wheels" that kids—and adults—could put on a finger and spin.

Joses would start on these immediately while they both worked on developing the Rounds for Kids.

The Twirlers took off! Contests developed. People came up with ideas like moving the Twirler from one hand or one finger to the other, spinning while walking or running, and trying acrobatics while twirling. There were days when Joseph, James, and Judas had to help so there would be enough Twirlers to fill the orders. The Shop decided they would try to make a supply to have available for Japeth the next time he returned.

THIRTY-FOUR

21

The year of James and Lois's betrothal went by quickly. It was a busy year for the entire family. Japeth loved the Twirlers and began to carry them. On one of his trips, he said, "Soon I'm going to have to just carry your things. As a family, you are certainly creative. Please let me handle the sales for whatever you invent!"

James had worked hard helping Benjamin. The house was now in good repair, the garden was growing well, the animals were strong, and several had had babies. Benjamin was failing though. It took all his energy just to take care of himself. It hurt James to see how much trouble it caused Benjamin just to move. But somehow, Benjamin always found time to be with Simon—as his grandfather.

One day, Benjamin asked James to sit with him for a while. "James, you have been so good to me this past year. I never expected you to do so much. I have asked the scribe to come over here tomorrow, and I am going to sign my property over to you right away.

"I spoke with the doctor again this morning," he continued, "and he agrees with me that, soon, this stiffness will make it so that I will no longer be able to take care of myself. He tells me that Enoch's Mary is now a qualified physician's helper. She's looking to tend to two people who cannot care for themselves. Her home has been set up so she can work efficiently. She and the doctor have worked out a plan. A man from Nain will also be living there. I want you to have my home."

"Benjamin, I don't know what to say. I've loved every minute I've spent here with you. You have never been a problem or a hindrance. If you do this, I will miss you a great deal. Are you sure you want to do this so soon?" asked James.

"Yes, James. It's time. This is what I want to do. Enoch's Mary and the doctor and I have planned for me to move this Friday after breakfast, so I can be settled before worship on Sabbath."

James said, "I really want to hug you, but I'm afraid I'll hurt you. I can only promise I will pray for you every day, and I will visit often."

"Thank you. I want to tell Simon tomorrow. It's been a great blessing sharing what I know with that little man. He's a great kid," said Benjamin. "I'm exhausted, James. I really need to get some sleep now. I think I'll just sleep here in my chair. Your family gave me a great gift when they gave me this chair. Be sure to thank them again."

Benjamin moved that Friday morning and settled in nicely. Not having to take care of himself allowed him to rest. He felt better. *It was a good move!* he thought.

***

The day of James and Lois's wedding finally arrived. Lois had only her father as a close relative, so it was decided to hold the wedding in Nazareth.

A wedding was a joyous celebration, not just for the families, but also for the entire town. The women of the town were busy making new clothes; the men closest to Joseph and his family made small gifts according to their work. Matthew made a beautiful storage chest and lined it with cedar. Jonathan made leather cloaks to cover them when they needed to go outdoors in rainy weather—perhaps to tend the animals. The metal maker made what he called wind music—a metal disc with small metal rods that hung from the disc so that, when the wind blew, it made a very pleasant sound.

Mary, Elizabeth, and Anna were busy making and drying fruits and vegetables to be served during the week. And cleaning! They did a special cleaning of not only their home but also the town square, where the days of celebration would be held. Miriam insisted on working right along with them. Two weeks before the wedding, Miriam came to see Mary and brought a large package.

"Mary, you are not to say anything when I give you this. The only thing you are allowed to say is, "Thank you," said Miriam.

"Really? What on earth do you have there?" asked Mary.

Mary opened the package and saw that Miriam had made beautiful new tunics for Mary and the girls. "Oh, Miriam!" exclaimed Mary. "I don't know what to say. I've been trying to figure out when I would have time to make these. Miriam, I accept your gift with very humble thanks. Thank you, my friend!" With tears in her eyes, she threw her arms around Miriam.

"I wanted to help. I want to be a real part of this celebration. Thank you, Mary. Do all the boys have new tunics?" asked Miriam.

"I have just finished ones for Simon and Joses; they're both growing so fast. Joseph and the older boys decided they were going to splurge and have the tailor make theirs. So I don't have to do anything there. Oh, Miriam! Thank you so much. You are the best friend a woman could ever have!"

On the day of the wedding, the family went to the synagogue, together with Lois and her father. As weddings were, it was a small and brief ceremony. Rabbi Jesus officiated, the documents were signed, and the group left for the celebration.

Hiram and Miriam and their families had overseen the bringing of the food and wine to the square. It looked lovely.

It also looked like there was enough food and wine to last for a month—much less a week! Rebecca and Hannah sent their children to the children's fathers and were busy helping Mary and her girls with preparations.

Soon the entire town seemed to be there. Oh, how James and Lois were being teased! It was great fun!

Then it was time to eat. Jesus, as rabbi, opened with prayer. "Father God, we thank You for this time together. We ask You to keep James and Lois close to You and guide them in a loving marriage. Bless all of us who are here today, and keep each one of us as Your child. Thank You, Father God. Amen."

The days (more like evenings) of celebration moved quickly. Joseph and the boys watched the supply of wine and water and carried anything heavy that had to be moved. Rebecca and Hannah took over the filling of the food as the food on each platter emptied. That left Joseph and his family a lot of time to visit with everyone.

Early on the first evening, Mary noticed that Jesus, James, and Judas were missing. *Hmmm*, she thought, *I wonder what they're planning.*

All at once, the crowd started cheering! Mary ran to look, and there were her three sons! They had gone to Enoch's Mary's house. Two of them were carrying Benjamin, and the third was carrying his chair. Mary and Joseph looked at each other with pride and love.

"Set him here," said Joseph. "This will be out of the commotion and will still be where everyone can reach him. Benjamin, welcome! The celebration is now complete. Thank you for joining us!"

"I didn't have a choice. These boys of yours just came over and said I was going. I couldn't be more proud or more happy." He turned to the boys. "Thank you, young men. You have made me the happiest man on earth. And before you say anything, no, you did not hurt me in the slightest when carrying me. How did you learn to make that chair with your hands and arms?"

"We each take our right hand and hold it a ways above our left wrist and then clasp our left hands below the other person's elbow. It makes a nice, soft, sturdy chair. The person we carry sits on our hands and then holds onto our shoulders and we walk a little sideways. It seems to work well." replied Jesus.

"It was very comfortable. Thank you boys." said Benjamin.

James came over to him and bent down to talk with him face-to-face. "Lois and I didn't want you to miss our celebration. You're so important to us. I asked my brothers to help me think of a safe way to get you here, and this is what we came up with. I'm so glad we didn't hurt you. We'd like you to be here every day if possible."

With tears in his eyes, Benjamin said, "Thank you, my boy. Thank all of you! Now, where's Simon and where's Joses and where are the girls?"

"Right here!" Simon said. "James tells me we can't hug you or shake your hand cuz we'd hurt you. Can I touch your face? Would that be okay?"

"Yes! And you may gently ruffle my hair too. My head is the one thing that isn't stiff," said Benjamin, laughing.

"Lois," continued Benjamin, "in my tunic pocket on this side is something I want you to have. You won't hurt me. Look."

Lois reached in, and there in a soft cloth was a necklace of silver. The chain was very fine. There was a fairly large emerald surrounded by silver hanging from the chain. "This belonged to my wife. We had always wanted to pass it to our daughter, but that wasn't to be. I want you to have it. Will you accept it please?"

With tears in her eyes, she stooped down and said, "Benjamin. I accept it most humbly. It's the most beautiful necklace I have ever seen. Thank you so much." She turned to James. "Please help me put it on." After a moment, she asked James, "May I tell him?"

James stooped down and put his arm around her and nodded.

"Benjamin, James and I have decided that our first son will be named Benjamin. We owe you so much. You are an awesome man and an awesome friend. Thank you, Benjamin. Thank you for being wonderful you!" She reached over and lovingly kissed his cheeks. Both of them were crying. Those around them had tears in their eyes.

Lois's father came forward. "I don't know how to thank you for loving my daughter as you have. Joseph and his boys are always talking about you and about all the good things you've done all your life. It's a great honor to meet you. Thank you! May I call you friend?" He rumpled Benjamin's hair.

"Yes, please. Father God is my example. I have been blessed so much throughout my life. I want to make others feel a little better if I can. I would be honored to be your friend! You've raised a wonderful daughter. You are welcome to come visit me any time you're in town. I'll look forward to it. I've always wanted to learn about making pottery. It's something I've always wondered about. Will you visit me?"

"Most assuredly! You have my word. In fact, I'll be staying with James and Lois a few days after the celebrations, so I'll visit with you before I leave."

"Thank you!" said Benjamin.

"Mother! I'd like you to meet someone," said James as he and Lois and another young woman walked over to Mary. "Mother, this is Priscilla. Priscilla, this is my mother, Mary. Mother, Priscilla is Lois's best friend. They've been neighbors since they were babies."

"Welcome, Priscilla! It's nice to meet you. You are welcome at our home any time you're in town," said Mary, taking the girl's hand in both of hers.

"Thank you. It's very nice to meet you too. Lois has told me so much about you and your family. She says that she wants to model her family after yours," replied Priscilla.

"Lois, that's very nice of you. I know we'll have a lot of wonderful times together," said Mary as she gave Lois a hug.

"Mary!" interrupted Miriam. "Would you please come over here?"

As they walked away, James turned to Lois and Priscilla. "That looks like a minor interruption in food plans. Mother and Miriam are neighbors and close friends. I've never seen any situation that the two of them couldn't handle. Sometimes it seems like they're thinking the same thing at the same time."

The rest of the week went well. The rabbis and the children attended school during the day, the men tended to their work, and the women tended to household chores. But in the evening, it was a time of celebration.

To add a special note to the celebration, Benjamin was able to spend two more evenings with the celebrants!

Lois's father was as good as his word. He visited Benjamin twice before returning to Nain. The two men hit it off as if they'd been friends for years. Benjamin told him that he'd always wondered how one knew the right amount of sand and clay to make pots. And how did you know how fast to move the wheel? On his second visit, Lois's Father brought a small wheel and a variety of sand and clay to show Benjamin.

Lois's father wanted to know how designs and lines and curves could be made in wood—especially in the doors of furniture. Benjamin explained it to him. Both men seemed to have the same sense of humor—the making of good friends.

***

Judas found that he enjoyed being with Priscilla. For the week or so after the wedding, he spent evenings at James's house spending time with James, Lois, Lois's father, and, Priscilla. Priscilla enjoyed being with Judas as well. The four young people got along well together.

Judas joined James and Lois as they accompanied Lois's father and Priscilla to Nain on the Sabbath. Judas would be making this trip many more times.

Priscilla's parents invited all of them to lunch. After the others left, Priscilla's parents asked her about Judas. From what they had seen and heard, they liked the young man.

As Judas, James, and Lois were leaving town, they met Philip. "Hi, Philip!" called James. "Good to see you!"

They stopped to talk for a minute, and Philip asked, "How is Elizabeth? I'd really like to see her again, but Father hasn't been well this past year, and I can't leave."

"I wondered why you hadn't been around. I'm sorry about your father. But I have an idea," said James. "I have a feeling we'll be coming here often with Judas so he can see Priscilla. We'll try to bring Elizabeth with us—if she wants to. Sound good?"

"Yes! If you would! I would really like to spend some time with her. Father's latest treatment from the doctor seems to be helping his stomach a little bit, so let's pray that I can soon do the traveling too," replied Philip.

The boys told Elizabeth about their meeting with Philip. Elizabeth tried not to show her excitement—but failed. "Of course I'll go. If Mother says it's okay. Mother?"

"Yes. It's okay with me. I just might need to go to Nain for some supplies and you could come with me."

"Oh, Mother!" said Elizabeth as she nearly squeezed her Mother to death. "Can we go soon?" She stepped back. "I'm being pushy aren't I?"

Mary grinned.

The middle of the next week, Mary ran low on the strings to replace the worn-out strings on the largest of her looms. Instead of waiting for the traveling seller of cloth goods to come to town, Mary said, "Elizabeth, tomorrow let's you and I and maybe Miriam go to Nain for the day. I need some supplies, and I'd rather not wait for the salesman."

Miriam did accompany them. Enoch's Mary needed some special soft cloths for the men's needs, and they promised to get them for her as well.

Joseph insisted that Judas accompany them. The four of them started off early in the morning. About halfway there, Judas said, "I had no idea women could talk and laugh so much. You're like a group of young girls!"

That only set off more laughing and talking.

When they reached town, it seemed the entire town was there to greet them. A small boy had seen them coming and had run to tell Priscilla and Philip and then announced it to the neighborhood.

Judas walked up to Priscilla. "I'm so glad to see you." He turned to her mother and said, "May she take the time to go with us to the store that sells cloth?"

Her mother said teasingly, "I don't know if she would want to go with you."

"Mother!" said Priscilla. She turned to Judas and said, "I would love to."

Before they reached the store, Philip found them. "I guess you can't just come into town. Two kids came running to tell me you were here."

"Mother and I need supplies from the cloth shop. If you could go with us, you could talk with Judas while we shop," said Elizabeth.

"I'd love to," Philip replied, almost afraid to breathe.

While the women shopped, Judas and Philip planned a lunch. "Mother and Miriam brought food, but I think it would be nice if we found a shady spot to eat. We could get cold water from the well and have things ready when they finish."

"Good idea," said Philip. "There's a large tree not too far from our tent-making shop, and we can stop at the well on the way. Why don't I get a pitcher for the water? Want to come with me? You can meet my father. I'm sure it'll take the women a while to shop, and we can come right back."

Philip introduced his father and Judas to each other. Judas looked in the man's eyes and could see he was really hurting. "What seems to be your trouble?" he asked.

"It's my stomach. No matter what I eat, it seems to hurt me. We're trying raw goat's milk and raw honey now, and it seems to help a little. Oh, I don't take them together; I just try to eat mainly those two things."

As they were leaving, Judas reached over to Philip's father, hugged him, and said, "Father God, please heal this man."

Philip's father looked surprised and then smiled. "Off you go, you two. Say hi to young Elizabeth for me."

They still waited a while for the women, but the men didn't mind at all. When the women were done shopping, Judas would have time to talk with Priscilla, and Philip would have time to talk with Elizabeth as they ate lunch.

The place Philip chose for the picnic was perfect. The two couples each found a spot a short distance away where they could talk. Mary and Miriam didn't mind sitting alone. They always found things to talk about. It was a pleasant day, but soon they needed to leave to get back to Nazareth before sundown.

"Philip and Priscilla, thank you for making this such a special day," said Mary. "I look forward to the next time we need supplies. Greet your parents for us, and we hope to see you soon."

That evening, Elizabeth asked Mary, "Mother, what do you think of today?"

"I think you mean what do I think of Philip," said Mary. "Right?"

"Yes, Mother," said Elizabeth blushing.

"I told your father before dinner that I thought he was a very thoughtful young man, who seemed to put other people and their needs ahead of himself. He's well mannered, and I think he will make a great husband and father some day."

"Thank you, Mother! I kind of hope I might be his wife but—I know—we'll see."

Two Sabbaths went by before James and Lois and Judas and Elizabeth could make another trip to Nain. When they arrived, Philip met them before they even entered the town.

"I'm so glad to see you. Please come first to our tent-making shop to see my father," said Philip.

Elizabeth had not met him, so Philip introduced them. Philip turned to Judas. "Do you notice anything different from the last time you were here?"

"Your father! His eyes are bright, and he's standing tall. He's well, isn't he?"

"I am, young man. When you prayed for me, I felt something inside. And by sunset, I felt well. I slowly began to add regular foods to my meals, and I can now eat anything! Thank you! Thank you."

"Please don't thank me," said Judas. "Thank our Father God. He is the healer."

"Oh, I have! I find myself telling Him thank you all day long. I feel so well!" He gave Judas the biggest bear hug he'd ever had.

This trip was just one of many they would make to and from Nain.

THIRTY-FIVE

21

A few months passed, and Judas made his announcement during Family Time. "I would like to ask Priscilla to marry me—to be betrothed to her," he told the family.

"Great!" said Joseph. "Your mother and I wish you the very best, Son."

Lots of hugs and a whole lot of commotion ensued. Everyone was talking at once.

Simon, almost twelve, said, "I wish it was a couple more years from now so I could be a rabbi at your wedding."

"Well, we'll work on something over this next year. Okay?" said Judas.

"Have you spoken to her parents?" asked Mary.

"Not yet. I wanted to tell my family first. When James and Lois and Elizabeth and I go to Nain this Sabbath, I plan on talking to them. I sure hope they bless this betrothal," said Judas.

"Elizabeth, you'll be next, won't you?" asked Anna.

"What? Where did that come from?" asked Elizabeth, blushing.

"Well, you're the next oldest, so I just thought you'd be next."

"I suppose that could happen. Can we please not talk about it?" asked Elizabeth.

"Okay, but I just want to know when it'll be my turn," explained Anna.

The whole family was shaking their heads and smiling.

Joseph said, "That's enough talk about betrothals for tonight. I heard something today that I wanted all of us to discuss."

"Is it bad, Father?" asked Anna.

"I don't know how to answer that," said Joseph. "I'm sure you'll all remember the boy Barabbas who spent a night with us a few years ago. He's a full-grown man now and seems to be creating havoc wherever he goes. He's picked up several other men, all of whom appear to be as wrongdoing as he is. They've been marauding and pillaging throughout Judea. The Romans have arrest warrants out for them and are actively seeking them."

"May Father God protect our people!" said Simon. "Why are they doing this? What can we do about it?"

Joseph answered, "There isn't much we can do about it. We need to be aware of who he is and what he's doing. Other than that, I'm afraid there's nothing we can do but ask Father God to protect His people."

Joses said, "Father, if we pray hard enough, won't Father God stop him?"

Joseph looked to Jesus. Jesus said "Simon, there will always be crime; there will always be bad things happening. If there wasn't evil, we would be in heaven with Father God. There are some people who cannot be changed through prayer because they don't want to be changed. They don't want Father God's help. To answer your question, yes Father God could help him, but he won't accept it. We can pray for protection for our people."

"That makes me sad," said Anna. "I don't want anyone around me but good people!"

"That's what everyone wants. We won't have that peace until we reach everlasting life with Father God," said Judas.

"One more thing," continued Joseph. "It seems that they are trying to join with others and form a rebellion against Rome and its authority over us. Let me say again, this is not something to worry about; it is something to be aware of, and we should be on the lookout for possible signs of trouble. So far, Barabbas and his men seem to want to stay in Judea."

"Father, may I pray tonight?" said Simon.

"Certainly."

"Father God, why are there bad people? And why do they hurt good people? Why do they think they can take things that belong to others or hurt people? Is it because some people are just plain bad? Help us to understand. Help us to know what to do. Thank You, Father God, for all You are and for all You do. Keep all of us in Your love and keep us safe. Amen."

THIRTY-SIX

22

The next Sabbath when James and Lois and Judas and Elizabeth walked to Nain, Philip met them and asked Elizabeth if he could talk with her a minute.

"Of course," said Elizabeth. They walked a short distance from the others.

Philip began, "Elizabeth, I love you with my whole heart. I want to marry you and raise a family with you. I'd like your permission to speak to your parents next Sabbath. What do you think?"

"Oh, Philip! I love you so much! Yes, I want to marry you and raise a family with you, but I won't be able to keep this a secret from my family for a week! May I tell them?" answered Elizabeth.

"Of course. Elizabeth, I promise I will do my best to be the best husband a woman could want—and the best father when that happens!"

It seemed to Elizabeth that she was walking on air on her way home. That night at Family Time, she said, "Father! Mother! Philip is coming up here next Sabbath, and he's going to ask you if we may be betrothed!" She almost jumped off her chair as she said this.

"Hmmmm!" said Joseph. "We'll have to think about that."

"Father! Are you serious? Philip is a good man, and he promised he would be the best husband and the best father ever!" exclaimed Elizabeth.

"I'm teasing you, Elizabeth. I think I'll have a little fun with him. But if you still want him next Sabbath, he will have the blessings of your Mother and me."

***

The year of the two betrothals was an eventful year. The man staying with Benjamin at Enoch's Mary's house died. A woman with atrophy began to live there. She needed a lot of very special care.

Simon, thrteen, was now a bar mitzvah and teaching some of the younger children at the school.

Anna, now eleven, continued her work with dolls. Some days, she was bored with the whole thing, and some days she just wanted to sit and play with the dolls. It seemed that, on those days, she would be inspired with another item to add to her collection of "Things for Dolls."

Joses's carvings evolved. Some of his designs had openings in them—for instance, the carving of a cutout tree standing alone in its frame. Other items, like a fish jumping, had no frame. His items were sought after—not just by the people of Nazareth, but also by Japeth and his son's customers as well.

One day, Rabbi Carpus told Jesus he'd decided he just wanted to teach one or two classes per day; the administration of the school, the setting of the curriculum, the entire running of the school would fall to Jesus. And so Jesus became the school's administrator.

The most important event that year was the daughter born to James and Lois. The little girl was healthy and, of course, "the most beautiful baby in the world." She was given the name Leah. James and Lois doted on her. If she cried—even if it was the middle of the night—they would have a "discussion" to see who got to get up with her.

Joseph and Mary were a little skeptical about becoming grandparents. But when baby Leah was born they, as all grandparents, seemed to have regressed to become slaves of the little one.

Anna loved being the "big girl," as she called herself. It seemed her main focus was to make every kind of doll and doll accoutrement for baby Leah. James tried to explain to her that she needed to wait to give the baby some of the things she was making. Finally he asked Joseph to tell her.

Joseph told her, "Only soft things that can be washed until Leah is two years old!" That worked pretty well.

***

The weddings would be just two months apart. Judas and Priscilla's wedding and celebration would be held in Nain, Philip and Elizabeth's in Nazareth.

"Mary mother of Judas, may I speak to you for a minute?" asked Priscilla.

"Of course, dear. Let's go up to the roof."

"I would like your opinion on something; I've asked my mother, and she said I should discuss this with you. I've gotten very close to you and your family this past year. I know that Jesus and Simon are rabbis. I was wondering if there was a way I could have them take part in the wedding ceremony."

Mary hesitated. "How do your parents feel about this? I think that's the first thing we should consider."

"Mother said that this is my wedding and my celebration, and I should be able to have parts of the ceremony the way I want them. She said she didn't think our rabbi would mind but that I should see how you feel. Father agreed with her."

"You have a very wise mother. I am honored that you're talking this over with me. Jesus and Simon would be honored, and I'm sure they'll let your rabbi take the lead and let him decide what parts they would have. Does that sound reasonable to you?" asked Mary.

"I haven't asked my rabbi yet, but he's pretty old and has arthritis in both feet. So I can't see that he would object to having Jesus and Simon there," said Priscilla. "I'll see him when I get home. Do you think it will be all right if Judas talks to Jesus and Simon today?" asked Priscilla.

"I think that would be wonderful! Priscilla, I want to tell you that I'm very pleased you will soon be a part of our family. You are a wonderful young woman, and you seem to think of other people and their concerns, as well as your own. That's very important in leading a life as Father God has instructed," said Mary.

"Thank you. I feel blessed to be a part of your family. We'll have the wedding and celebrations in Nain. Would you tell me how you feel about that?" asked Priscilla.

"It's the right thing to do. I'm just so glad that Nain is close. We'll be able to visit each other often. Let's go see what the others are doing," said Mary as they moved to the stairs.

Priscilla ran over to Judas, took his hand, and whispered, "She said great!"

"Jesus! Simon! May I see you outdoors please?" asked Judas.

"Guys, you know that my wedding is soon. Priscilla and I were talking, and we'd like my two rabbi brothers to take parts in our wedding ceremony. Would you do it? Would you be a part of our wedding?" asked Judas.

"Yes!" they answered together.

The three of them discussed the ceremony and which parts they might take. They went inside to take the discussion to the rest of the family. Joseph and Mary smiled at each other—a smile of love and contentment.

The wedding and the celebrations were wonderful in the small town of Nain. Priscilla's parents had made room for Joseph and Mary to stay with them. The rest of the family stayed in a large tent made especially for the celebrations by Philip and his father.

Joseph was very impressed with the tent. Because the rainy season was just ending, they were unsure of the weather, so Philip and his father made a floor that they attached to the tent. It was the same material as the tent, but they doubled it and sealed all the seams with wax. It worked out very well.

During the week of celebration, Philip and Elizabeth carefully watched Judas and Priscilla and all the activities around a wedding. They also took it upon themselves to watch over the older people. They took time to talk with them, to listen to their stories, and to get food and wine for them as they needed it.

Philip's grandmother was there and said she just had to tell Elizabeth about Philip as a child. "He walked when he was less than a year! From then on, we had to really watch him. He loved opening doors and crawling up the steps to the roof. You know, he could have fallen and really hurt himself, so we had to watch him close. I told his father that he should put a rope around him so he could only go so far, but his father got mad at me for suggesting it.

"One day, we were all going on our trip to Jerusalem when we met a goat herder who was riding on his mule. Well, Philip here decides that he can ride on animals too. He was only about three years old, and he decided he was going to ride one of the goats. He walked over to one that was lying down and laid his arms across its back and grabbed the goat's hair so he could hang on. That goat just sat there for a minute and then decided that was enough of that, and he stood and kicked up his legs. He sent Philip flying! You should have heard him howl. He wasn't really hurt—just a few bruises—but he was so mad at that goat!"

"Okay, Grandma," said Philip. "Elizabeth will be in our family for a long time, and you'll have plenty of time to tell her all your stories. I'm going to take her away and see if we can be of help to someone." They moved on—Elizabeth smiling and Philip shaking his head.

***

Judas and Priscilla were able to find a small house in Nazareth and settled in. Judas's training at the Shop came in handy, as that house needed a lot of fixing. Priscilla told Judas, "I never really cared for house cleaning at home, but I find it's sort of fun in our own home. It feels good when it's clean. You've done a lot of fixing up around here, and it looks nice."

"Thank you. I love the way you've sewed so many little things that make it look comfortable. I think we make a great team. I love you, sweetheart!"

***

Two months later, Philip and Elizabeth were married in Nazareth. The week of celebration was held, as usual, in the town square. The weather was perfect that entire week. Philip told everyone that Elizabeth "is the most beautiful woman on Earth!"

Philip and Elizabeth made their home in Nain. At first, they were going to live with Philip's father, but that just didn't work out. The house was very small, with only a small place for a garden and a very small area for keeping animals. They were so excited when they found just the right house close to work and close to Philip's father. They seemed completely happy!

***

One night after the two weddings, Mary turned to Joseph and said, "Our family is getting so small here at home. Jesus is at the school morning and evening and at the Shop during the afternoons, and James, Judas, and Elizabeth are now married. That really leaves just the three younger ones at home with us."

"I know. But it's okay. I think the three older ones have made good marriages, and Jesus is an awesome rabbi and administrator. We are so blessed."

"We are blessed!" said Mary. "Father God has been so good to us. You're such a wonderful man, Joseph. I feel that you are my biggest blessing. I have loved you for so long."

THIRTY-SEVEN

22

"Benjamin died during the night last night," Enoch's Mary told Mary and the girls as they were at their work at home. "He slept in his rocker chair as usual, but when I went to get him ready for breakfast I saw that he'd been gone for some time."

"Thank you for telling us, Mary; I'll tell my family right away. Is there anything I can do to help you?"

"Yes, if you would. I have a neighbor watching my lady, but I need to get back and tend to her. Could you please ask your two rabbis to make all the arrangements for the burial later today? I'll wash him at home, but I need to stay with my lady."

"I'll be happy to. I'm certain the boys will make the plans. As soon as I've talked to my family, I'll come over and help you. Anna, will you please go with Enoch's Mary? Her lady will need a lot of her attention," said Mary.

"Yes, Mother. I can go right now," said Anna.

"Thank you. I'll see you a little later then, Mary. I'll go to the Shop and the school right away, and then I'll come over to help you."

Mary went first to the Shop to tell Joseph and the boys. Joseph said he would send James to tell his wife and send Joses to tell Philip and Elizabeth in Nain. Joseph said he would take the responsibility of making sure bread and wine would be available for the mourners. Mary then went to the school to tell Jesus and Simon.

"She would like the two of you to take charge of all arrangements for the burial. I told her you would. I hope that's okay," said Mary.

Simon said, "He was such a good friend to me. I'll miss him a great deal. I know, I know! He's well and happy now. But I'll still miss him. We met and talked at least once a week. He was truly the grandfather I never had."

Jesus smiled at Simon. "We'll all miss him. You and James have been very special friends to him. He loved you a great deal. You'll always have that love with you wherever you are."

"I know; thank you. Thank you, Mother, for coming to tell us. We need to get back to our classes. I love you, Mother."

"I know, Son. And I love both of you," Mary said as she left the school.

Shortly after Mary arrived at Enoch's Mary's house, James arrived. "Mother, Mary, I don't know if Benjamin told you, but he has a burial site already prepared. His family is buried in a cave just east of town."

"I didn't know that," said Enoch's Mary. "He did leave some money with me when he first started staying here. He said it was to cover his last expenses."

"Then would you mind if I go over to the school? They should be almost done for the day. I'd like to talk with my brothers about further plans," asked James.

James had to wait a few minutes while his brothers finished their class work. The three hugged and began making plans. James said, "He was so kind to me. I need to be a part of this part of his life."

"I was thinking that one of us needs to hire the mourners and the musicians. Would you like to do that? Simon and I will take care of the rest."

"Thank you. Benjamin told me he wanted them to play and sing psalms—something mournful rather than keening. What do the two of you think?" asked James.

Jesus said, "That would be a great idea. Okay, Simon, he was your friend, and I want your input."

"I think he'd like that. He said he could never see the reason for what he called 'all that hollering.' My heart feels so heavy, but my head says he's so much better off," said Simon.

"People are already at the house. What do you think—have the service in two or three hours?" asked James.

"Let's see if we can make two hours—if the mourners and musicians can be ready. Then Enoch's Mary will be back in time to care for her lady before sundown," said Jesus.

The mourners and musicians were able to be there in two hours, as were Philip and Elizabeth.

As was tradition, friends and neighbors took turns carrying the body to the cave. Benjamin's body was laid to rest with his family.

Joseph, his family, and Enoch's Mary stayed a few minutes after the stone was rolled in place. They would return to Enoch's Mary's home, where wine and bread would be served to the mourners before they returned to their homes.

"I would like to pray right here if that's okay with you, Enoch's Mary," said Simon.

"Of course, dear. Maybe we could all say a prayer."

Simon began, "Father God, our hearts are so heavy. Hold Benjamin tightly in Your arms to comfort him for all he's been through. When we feel sad, help us to remember how much better he feels. Love him for us please, Father God. Amen."

The others joined in, each with his or her own prayer.

Enoch's Mary went to be with the townspeople. She was so thankful that the neighbor staying with her lady was able to stay for a while. Miriam and her family were already there serving the bread and wine. After the townspeople went to their homes for dinner, Joseph and his family stayed to help Enoch's Mary straighten up the house. Joseph and his family then went back to their home for a small supper and for a Family Time with their entire family.

Thirty-eight

23

Mary looked to see if anyone was outside. She only saw Hiram. "Hiram!" she called. "Please run to the school and get Jesus and Simon and tell them to run home."

"Will do!" replied Hiram as he moved quickly to get Jesus and Simon.

"I'll watch the classes. Run home! Your mother asked me to run and get you!" said Hiram as he literally ran into the classrooms.

"Mother. What's wrong?" called Jesus as they entered the house.

"Quick, boys! We're in the sleeping room. It's Anna. We were working, and she just doubled over and said her stomach hurt. She's running a fever, and she's really sweating. The doctor's in Nain tending a sick baby. I'm afraid of what it could be," said Mary.

Jesus took Anna's hand, smiled, and said, "Anna, show us where the pain is."

"Right here," Anna pointed to her lower right abdomen. "It really hurts, Jesus. Pray for me please! Right now! *Please!*"

The rest of the men of the family came rushing into the house. "Mary," called Joseph. "What's wrong?"

"Come. Let's pray. I'll explain later."

They all placed their hands on Anna and prayed.

"Father God," began Jesus as he held his hand over the spot that hurt, "my little sister Anna is in a lot of pain. I ask that You please heal her now, Father God. Please! Thank You!"

Immediately Anna quieted. "I don't hurt anymore; I feel better. Thank you, everyone. I knew if we all prayed, I'd be okay. Thank you!"

"Lie still a little while longer. Mother's getting some water for you. After that, you may get up—if you're still feeling better," said Joseph.

Joseph went to the kitchen to talk with Mary. "What happened, Mary?"

"We were each working on our projects when she just doubled over and said her stomach really hurt. Joseph, I've heard others talking about something like this. I think she had appendicitis. I was really worried. How did you know to come?"

"Hiram sent one of the older boys to the Shop and told us to run home *now!*" said Joseph. "So we ran home *now*. Appendicitis is serious, isn't it?" asked Joseph.

"People usually don't survive. Oh, Joseph, hold me for a minute please. I feel so shaky; I was so scared!"

After a minute, Joseph asked, "Feeling better now? Anna told me she wanted to get up, but I told her she needed to lie down until she'd had some water. We'd better get back to her."

Anna was sitting up in bed. "I'm fine—really. I told the boys to go back to work and back to school, but they said I had to wait until you got back here. Can I get up now?"

"*May* I get up now, Anna. As your father said, as soon as you drink some water. One other thing. You will stay by my side all day. No argument about it," said Mary.

"Yes, Mother. But make them get back to work and school."

Mary turned to Joseph and the boys. "I guess she's feeling better—trying to be the boss. I think she's right. Go back to work and school. Be sure and thank Hiram for me, will you?"

Mary decided that she and Anna would do some baking together. Mary really didn't think she could concentrate on her work. She wanted to watch that Anna didn't overtire herself. But she needn't have worried. Anna was humming as they baked.

"Mother, let's make something and take it to Hiram and Miriam. I really made a mess of their day, and I want to thank them," said Anna.

"I think some of the green olives are old enough to pick. We could make that olive and leek bread. I think everyone likes that," suggested Mary.

"That would be great! I know Hiram likes it especially. Let's make enough for us for dinner too."

A little later, Anna asked, "Do you think we could ask Hiram and Miriam to dinner tonight? I just feel so good—like I'm light!—like it's a special day."

"It is a special day, and I hope you will always remember it. The breads are just about done baking, so why don't we run over and ask them when we take the breads from the oven?" asked Mary.

Hiram and Miriam were happy to come for dinner. Miriam said, "I just finished making a lamb stew. May I bring it over? There should be a little for all of us."

What a wonderful dinner!

Joses teased Hiram. "Are you thinking of becoming a rabbi? I hear you sent Jesus and Simon home so you could teach the classes!"

That set off everyone laughing and trying to one-up the other.

Jesus, Joses, and Simon walked Hiram and Miriam to their home. On the way back home, Joses said, "Remember when I was a little kid I said that maybe Father God had a contest for the angels and told them to design plants and animals for the sky, on the earth, under the earth, and in the water?"

"No," said Simon. "Maybe I was too little. What did you think happened with that contest?"

"I thought that Father God saw that they were all awesomely good, so that's why we have so many different kinds of plants and animals and things," answered Joses.

"Oh. Why are you talking about it now?" asked Simon.

"I don't know. As old as I am, I still think that could have happened. It could've, Jesus, couldn't it?' asked Joses, feeling a bit like a kid again.

"I really don't know, Joses. With our Father God, everything is possible. I guess you'll just have to wait and see," said Jesus.

"You mean, wait until I'm with Father God, and then I'll know," said Joses.

"Exactly! There are millions of questions we have. Some we'll discover the answers to, and some we just have to wait and see. When you have kids, I hope they're just like you—full of unanswerable questions!" Jesus teased.

THIRTY-NINE

23

Japeth and his son arrived early one morning a few days later than usual and explained to Joseph, "We had to change our route because we're carrying so many of your things! Going this way, we can have an almost empty cart when we get here, and all of our customers get a chance at your goods. Boy, people love your things!"

"That makes us feel good," said Joseph. "Right now we have a huge rush order. I don't think we have time to help you pack our things. Could you come back in an hour or so?"

"Not a problem. I need to stop and see Mary and Anna and see what they have for me. It's really not appropriate for us to enter your home without one of you or Miriam with us, so I'll just ask them to drag the chests to the door, and then they can help me pack our cart. I know that Anna loves to pack the cart. Why, I cannot imagine!"

"Of course. Thank you, my friend. See you in a bit." And Joseph went back to work.

Japeth apologized to Mary for being late and told her the wonderful reason.

Mary said, "That is certainly good to hear! Come inside and see what we have for you. Miriam saw your cart coming into town, so she's here as well. Elizabeth brought a lot of items last Sabbath. She's been experimenting with more colors and some intriguing patterns."

"May we see them?" asked Japeth.

Mary took them inside and showed them the items in the chest.

"I'm impressed! Be sure and thank her for me."

"Joses has been making a lot more items as well. Wait until you see them!" said Mary. She showed them the rest of their items.

"We're going to need a bigger cart! These are all great items—very unique," said Japeth as he and his son, and Anna, were packing the cart.

"I have some news for you, Mary. There appears to be a sickness that's starting to go around. Some people in Cana and some as far south as Jerusalem have had a high fever and a really deep cough. It lasts about two or three weeks. Some young children and some older people have died from it. The physician in Cana is asking everyone to begin drinking the Roman drink called *posca*."

"What's posca?" asked Miriam, who had joined them at the cart.

"Vinegar, honey, and water heated until the honey melts. Some folks add things like seeds for flavoring while it's heating and then strain them out before drinking."

"That makes sense, I think," said Mary. "Vinegar is used for sores and achy stomachs; it probably kills germs."

They settled the account and agreed on the order for Japeth's next visit.

"Well, we need to get to the Shop and pick up what the men have finished. Thanks, ladies! We'll see you on our next run!" said Japeth.

"See you then," Mary said as she waved goodbye.

Joseph and his sons were just finishing when Japeth and his son reached the Shop.

"Great timing!" said Joseph. "Come see what we have for you. See if you like anything."

"Mary told me that Joses has new items for us. I can't wait to see them," said Japeth as they all walked to the back of the shop.

"Joses! These are far better than any I have ever seen! We'll take all of them—that is, if it's okay with you," teased Japeth.

Joses grinned and said, "I guess it'll be okay. At least that'll give me room to make more."

"Father, we need to get one of these larger tree designs for our place. Remember how Mother loved trees? It will remind me of her every time I look at it," said Japeth's son.

Japeth smiled at his son and nodded his approval. He put his arm around his son's shoulders and turned to Joseph and said, "My wife died about three months ago. She was never a strong woman and suffered a lot the past few years. She told me a few days before she passed that she just wanted to be with Father God. Then one morning, I woke up, and she had passed quietly during the night. My girls are now married so now my son and I are partners for life."

"I'm sorry," said Joseph and the boys together.

"I think she's happier now; she's well. She told me that she was sickly for almost her entire life," said the son.

"I'm glad she knew Father God," said Simon. "That's really important."

They helped Japeth pack the leather and the wood items in his cart and settled the finances. Yes, the cart was almost three-quarters full!

"Now I'm happy. Come on, Son. Let's go sell this merchandise!"

Japeth and his son waved as they moved toward the next town.

***

"Miriam," asked Mary. "What do you think about this illness and the vinegar drink?"

"I don't know that it would hurt us. I think I'll try to make some. It sounds like it might be something to think about," said Miriam.

"I'll try it too. Tomorrow we can compare results," said Mary.

Miriam left for home, and Mary and Anna returned to their work.

The next morning, Miriam came over to Mary's with a cup of her final results. "This is what I finally decided tastes best. Hiram said he could drink some every day if it would keep that cough and fever away. I brought a cup for the two of you to taste."

Mary and Anna tasted Miriam's.

"It tastes just like what we came up with!" said Anna.

"Let's compare our final recipes," said Mary.

They both decided that one cup of vinegar, a half cup of honey, and four cups of water seemed to make a wonderful drink.

"Anna and I poured some for dinner last night. The men seemed to like it as well," said Mary. "I think we'll start making it once in a while."

"Hiram and I drank some warm and some at room temperature. It was good either way. Hiram thought that, when we're cold, we could drink it hot to warm up," explained Miriam.

"I think we should tell people about that illness and about this," said Mary. "Maybe tomorrow I'll go to the well with Anna and talk to the women."

"Should we check with the physician first?" asked Miriam.

"He's been called out of town on an emergency. But a physician in Cana suggested it, so it's probably okay," said Mary.

"Okay. I'll meet you at the well in the morning," said Miriam as she returned home.

The physician returned two days later. Mary and Miriam went to see him to ask about the disease and taking posca.

"There's been talk of that disease going around. A lot of people are drinking posca—some as a preventive medicine and some after the disease has started," explained the physician. "I've heard of only a couple of cases where people couldn't tolerate it—it seemed to be too strong for their stomachs. I would caution people to take just a little to start. It can't be too bad; Roman soldiers have been taking it on their marches for over a hundred years."

"Really!" said Miriam. "I guess it must be okay for most people then."

"The Romans have found that it quenches thirst better than water. I think we just need to keep an ear out and hear if people are drinking it and then watch for possible ill effects," added the physician.

Several townsfolk began drinking it. Some drank a small amount daily and some once or twice a week. After two weeks, there were only two people who had felt slight side effects, and posca became a part of the lives of many of the town's people.

FORTY

24

Joses, seventeen, was the next to fall in love, become betrothed, and marry. Earlier in the year, a new family had moved into town. The man was a potter. The town's potter had decided to move to be closer to his married children, so there was a need this family filled well.

The new potter brought his wife and four daughters, ages eight to fifteen. Joses met Claudia, the oldest daughter, in the synagogue the first week they arrived in town. From the very first, they were attracted to each other. After just a few months, Joses asked her parents if they might be betrothed. Her parents were happy for the two of them and readily gave their permission.

"Joses," said Claudia, "you know how I love to sing. I want you to sing with me."

"Me? Why? I sing with my brothers and some friends when we're being loud and rowdy, but you sing our psalms in synagogue in such a beautiful way. I can't sing like that."

"Will you try?"

"No." But then he saw the look on her face and changed his mind. "Oh, okay. I'll try but ... what should we sing first?"

"How about the psalm we sang this past Sabbath?"

They were good together.

"Will you try something with me?" Claudia asked.

"Okay. What do you want me to do?" asked Joses, apprehensively.

"I want you to sing like we've been singing, and then I'll sing harmony."

"Harmony? What does that mean?" asked Joses.

"It means that when you're singing one note, I will sing a little higher or a little lower. You just need to keep the regular melody. Okay?"

"Okay. I'll trust you. Let's see what happens," said Joses.

It was amazing! Their voices blended very well.

After a while, Joses said, "Let me try the harmony."

By the end of the first psalm, Joses was able to move over and under Claudia's notes.

Jesus was walking nearby. "I was heading to see James and his family when I heard you singing. It's beautiful! I'd like to hear everyone sing like that!"

"Join us," said Claudia. "You and Joses sing the regular notes, and I'll show you what we're doing."

"Wow! How do you know what notes to hit?" asked Jesus.

"You just try. It's kind of like you listen and then sing something that sounds like it goes with it. Try. We'll just keep singing, and you just try singing the harmony," explained Claudia.

He did.

"Jesus, you caught on fast," said Joses.

"I have an idea. Would the two of you teach our family to sing like this? Maybe this Sabbath? I think that this Sabbath everyone will be here," said Jesus.

They decided to not say anything to the families ahead of time. After dinner, when everyone was relaxing, Joses stood up and said, "Jesus and Claudia and I have something we want all of you to try. First, we'll demonstrate."

Claudia started singing. Joses and Jesus joined her. The three of them took turns singing harmony. It seemed that the further they got into the song, the freer their harmony became.

"Well done!" said Joseph as the entire family began clapping and cheering.

"Are any of you interested in singing like this?" asked Joses.

Some said, "Yes!" Some said, "I don't know." But Joseph took charge and said, "Let's all try it. I think it's a wonderful way to not only have something new for our families to do together but also to praise our Father God in a beautiful way. And by the way, no laughing at anyone who's trying."

That didn't last long. Soon everyone was trying, and everyone was laughing at themselves and at each other. Elizabeth and Judas seemed to have the easiest time with this new singing. The children tried, and Claudia said she thought maybe there should be special songs for them, and she would work on that.

"Claudia, does your family also sing?" asked Jesus.

"We all do. Father comes from a family who sang all the time—I mean all the time. Father sings while at the potter's wheel. Mother sings while cooking or cleaning. My sisters and I sing when we do our chores," explained Claudia.

"Maybe some Sabbath our families could get together and sing," said Anna. "This is so much fun and I feel … I don't know … happy after singing like this."

Joses turned to Claudia and said, "How about if you and I make the arrangements for our families to get together?" It was agreed.

A month later, they were able to get together. Hiram and Miriam were spending the Sabbath at home with their families when they heard the singing—and laughing.

"Hiram, instead of us just sitting here and trying to listen, why don't we take a couple of benches and move closer so we can really hear them? It sounds so beautiful!" said Miriam.

Hiram, Miriam, and their children and grandchildren all gathered closer to hear and enjoy the singing.

Mary saw them sitting on benches and blankets and walked over to them. "Hi!" she said. "This is so much fun! What do you think of our singing?"

Hiram answered first. "I hear the men's voices and the women's voices blending, and it makes me wish I could do something that's that awesome!

"We were just talking, and we were saying how we'd love to do that," said Miriam.

"We'll plan it. Claudia has a wonderful way of making it so easy. I'll talk with her, and we'll arrange it. I need to get back. Claudia's family is here with us."

"You go ahead," said Miriam. "We'll just sit here a while and listen. But don't forget about having Claudia work with us as well!"

FORTY-ONE

24

The year of the betrothal went by quickly.

The family had a surprise for Joses. The morning of the wedding, Jesus asked Joses to go with him for a few minutes. Surprised, Joses agreed. Jesus walked him to the home of Enoch's Mary. As they walked toward the home, the door opened, and Lazarus walked out!

"Lazarus my friend!" yelled Joses as he hugged him. "How on earth did you get here?"

"You'll have to ask Jesus. He did everything possible to see that I was here! Martha and Mary are here too. Come on inside." Huge grins spread across the faces of both men as they clasped shoulders and entered the house.

"Does our family know they're here?" Joses asked Jesus.

"Of course. While you and Claudia were visiting with James and Lois last evening, the rest of us were home having a great reunion!"

Martha and Mary swooped in for hugs. "Joses, you're so grown up!" exclaimed Martha.

"And so handsome!" added Mary.

Lazarus asked, "We've only a few minutes until time for your wedding, but I need to ask you something. Are we invited to your wedding and celebrations?"

"Oh, my friend! Now that Father God has brought us together again, I can't think of a greater honor than to have the three of you and Enoch's Mary at my wedding. Wait till you meet Claudia! She's beautiful and kind and wise—and, and—she loves me!

The wedding was lovely. Jesus and Simon served as rabbis. The vows were exchanged, Joses and Claudia became man and wife, and the week of celebrations began.

Lazarus, Mary, and Martha were greeted by everyone from the town. They were careful to be sure the attention remained focused on Joses and Claudia.

The families had decided that, at the celebration in the town square, they would all sing one of the psalms. The townsfolk were amazed. The singers received so many compliments. By the end of the day, several people asked Claudia to teach them to sing.

Claudia's mother had a surprise for the townspeople. She played the lyre! While folks were eating, she played soft music.

When the men finished eating, they started their usual rambunctious singing and dancing. At that point, Claudia's father brought a strange-looking box and set the lyre into, yet on, it. It seems that the men were not very good at keeping the beat of the song. Some sped up, and some slowed down. When they heard the beat of the lyre, they clasped arms and danced and shouted and danced and shouted—together. And Claudia's mother played that lyre. No matter what dance the men wanted to do, she was able to keep that rapid strong beat and to play it in the key they were "singing."

After quite a while, she begged off. "I need to get something to eat and drink," she said. There was a lot of, "Just one more!" But Mary took her to a table and sat her down. Miriam brought a heaping plate of food and a glass of wine. Mary told her, "Thank you so much! This is a wedding that no one will ever forget."

"That was amazing!"

"Have you ever heard the lyre played like that?"

"Did you know she could play?"

"I don't know anyone who can play like that."

"I thought the lyre was just for accompanying the psalms or holy music."

"What a blessing!"

Those comments were the gist of what everyone was saying.

Joseph turned to Mary and said, "I think our new potter and his family have become great assets to our community."

Joses came up to Claudia's mother and asked, "How did you make that sound? We have a neighbor who's been trying to play the lyre, but he says the only sounds he can make are quiet and smooth."

"You probably didn't notice, but before I started playing for the men's dancing, my husband lifted my lyre onto a special box."

"Will you show me?" asked Joses.

"I'll come with you, but my husband will have to explain it to you."

"I had to try a few times before I got this right," Claudia's father explained. "I made a frame large enough that the lyre could sit a ways into it. The frame needed to be pretty thick. I made it open at the bottom and then made several holes near the bottom to carry the sound. Then I had to have wood supports underneath in strategic places to give it stability while she's playing. On the sides and about half way down the inside of the frame I covered the wood slats with a thin piece of leather. That seemed to act as a magnifier for the sound."

"I am impressed!" said Joses. "Was it by experimenting that you learned how heavy a frame was needed and how thin to make the leather?"

"Yes. The frame needed to be high enough to amplify the sound but not too high to impede the playing of the instrument. There can't be too many support parts on the frame, or that will impede the sound. The leather needs to be sturdy enough to be stretched tightly but not too thin as to again impede the sound or to tear. You seem to be interested in this," said the potter.

Joses looked around for James. When he saw him, he signaled for him to join him. "This is my brother James, who works with leather," Joses said as James came up to them. "James, look at this frame he built to enhance the sound of the lyre."

"I wondered how that strong beat was made. May I look it over?" asked James.

After a minute James said "This is wonderful! I am so impressed! How on earth did you think of this?"

"We were living in a very small town, and we love to dance and sing! But kind of like today, some of us went faster and faster and some slower and slower. We needed something to keep us together. The only thing I could think of was to use the lyre. Did you notice that, when my wife was playing for the dancing, she didn't play all the notes of the song? She just played the strong notes—usually the first or the first and third beats."

That night at Family Time, the singing, dancing, and the lyre were the main topics of conversation.

"Joses, would you please close with prayer tonight."

"Dear Father God, thank You for blessing my life with my Claudia. Thank You for introducing all of us to new aspects of music. The family You have sent to our town is a real blessing to all of us. Father God, please help all of us to realize and then put to Your use the many talents You have given to each of us. Thank You, Father God, for all You are and for all You do. Bless us all as we grow in Your love. Amen."

FORTY-TWO

25

About a year later, during Family Time, Jesus said, "Father, may I make a suggestion?"

"Of course," said Joseph.

"I was thinking about how our family is no longer under one roof. I know we're blessed that we don't need to go farther than Nain to see our families, but I wonder if we could all go on a vacation together. I'd like to see us all go to the Sea of Galilee. We could play in the water and maybe go fishing. The kids would love to pick rocks and shells, and it would be a time away from work and a time for all of us to just be together."

"Jesus, that sounds wonderful! It'll take some real planning, but I think it can be done!" said Joseph.

"What a wonderful idea!" said Mary.

"It will take about a day to get there and a day to return home," said Jesus. "If we left right after sunup on Sabbath, we could stay until the next preparation day."

"Joseph tomorrow is the Sabbath, and the children and their families will be here. Maybe we could do some planning then," suggested Mary.

"I think the hardest part will be to see if Philip can take the time at the same time our school is closed. Neither Simon nor I could leave the school unless it was during that time," said Jesus.

"Let's talk with everyone tomorrow," said Joseph.

The next day was the usual exciting day as the entire family came together. After dinner, Mary said, "Let's put the small children down for naps. Jesus has an exciting plan we will all want to discuss."

Surprisingly, by the time the food was put away and the kitchen cleaned up, the children were sound asleep.

Jesus presented his idea, and the discussions began. It was decided that it was a go and that the two weeks school was out would be the perfect time.

"Philip," asked Jesus, "will you be able to take a week off from your tent-making business?"

"I'm sure I can. It's still a way off, and Father and I will just need to plan around it."

***

The day of the vacation finally arrived. The day before they were to leave, everyone met at Joseph and Mary's house. The girls had not only prepared the food they had planned, but each one had also brought several additional items.

"We've enough food here to last for two weeks!" said Mary, laughing.

They packed up before services on Friday and were on their way early on the Sabbath morning. The day was absolutely beautiful—a great day for traveling.

"Joseph," said Mary. "It feels like Father God is right here with us! I know; He is. But I feel like I imagine heaven will feel."

"Mary, you are such a dear person. As odd as it sounds, I feel the same way."

"Father God has given us so much! Seven healthy children— five wonderful sons and a son-in-law, two daughters and three daughters-in-law, and these wonderful grandchildren! I love you, Joseph!"

"You always make me smile. We are blessed! By the way, I love you too. You were the first blessing for my family," answered Joseph.

"Grandmother," called almost-four-year-old Leah.

"Yes, Leah. What can I do for you?" asked Mary.

"Uncle Joses says that we're going to lay down on the water. What's he talking about?"

"It's called swimming, and yes, we are going to lie down on the water *and* we're going to wiggle our feet and move our hands and look at the clouds."

"Really? Why do we have to look at the clouds?" asked Leah.

"We don't have to; we want to. Sometimes the clouds look like something else, and it's fun to look at them," answered Mary.

"They don't look like clouds?"

"Well, yes, they look like clouds, but their shape can be a whole bunch of things, like a lamb or a goat's tail—almost anything. You can look at the clouds anytime, and sometimes you see things.

"Look. See that cloud over there?" added Mary, pointing. "It looks a little like a fig. See?"

"Grandmother, you're silly," said Leah as she ran back to her parents.

At sundown, Joseph said, "We'll set up the tent here. We made good time today. The Sea of Galilee is only about a mile away. Mary, I'm starved!"

"As always, Joseph. We'll get dinner ready while you and the boys take care of the animals and check the carts."

Joseph offered the prayer after Family Time. "Father God, thank You for being with us today and every day. You have blessed us in so many ways. There is no way we can ever thank You enough for all You do for us. We are so blessed to have this week together. Thank You. Please walk with us this week and keep us safe. We love You, Father God. Amen."

The next morning was beautiful. "I don't think we've ever eaten breakfast so quickly!" said Mary as the last of the breakfast dishes were stored in the cart.

Within an hour, they were at the Sea of Galilee.

"Father!" exclaimed fourteen-year-old Anna. "The water doesn't end! Everyone said it would be like this, but it really is!"

None of them had seen the sea before. All but the youngest children just stood there, amazed. As far as they could see, there was water. And the waves! One after the other! They just stood there and looked.

"Leah," said James, "what did I tell you about the rules here by the water?"

"I have to hold your hand. I have to. I can't say no!"

"That's right. One more thing though. Do you remember?" asked James.

"I have to listen. I have to listen to all the big people. Can I go by the water now?"

"Sure. Come on."

Mary hugged Jesus and said, "Jesus, this was a very good idea. Thank you!"

"Thank you, Mother! I see other families are setting what looks like their beds on the sand and sitting on them. I think I'll go get a couple of ours," Jesus said as he walked back to the carts.

By the time he set the beds on the sand, everyone else was walking in the water. What a lot of laughing and giggling! Parents were introducing their little ones to a big lake of water, while the others were splashing and chasing each other. Mary and Joseph played in the water with them—grinning.

The second day, they met a man who was a fisherman from Capernaum. He owned a huge boat and had taken a run south to find possible new customers for his fishing business. He approached Joseph and said, "I've been watching you and your family, and I would be most honored if you would allow me the pleasure of taking all of you out on the lake in my boat tomorrow."

"Really?" asked Joseph. "I never thought I would ever be in a boat! May I speak with my family? I'm sure they'll all want to go! What do we need to do? I have no idea what to expect!"

The man laughed. "It's a little like riding in a cart or riding on a camel, but you're in a boat on the water. I have nets if you would like to try to catch some fish."

"Oh, thank you! Can you wait for a minute? I'd like to bring my family over to meet you. I haven't even introduced myself. I'm Joseph, the carpenter of Nazareth." Joseph signaled the family to come to him.

"It's nice to meet you, Joseph. I am Zebedee, a fisherman of Capernaum."

Joseph introduced his family and explained Zebedee's invitation.

The girls squealed, the men cheered, and everyone was hugging. Eventually Mary stopped and went over to Zebedee. "How can we thank you," she said. "I never even dreamed that I would someday ride in a boat! I just want to hug you and cry!"

"I'd love a hug!" Zebedee said as he looked at Joseph. "No need to cry, but I can tell you that it will make me very happy to take all of you out tomorrow. Best we go right after breakfast. Okay?"

"What can we do?" asked Mary.

"It might be a good idea if most of you could learn to lie down on the water and float. May I show you how?"

"Why do we have to learn to lie down on the water?" asked Joses.

"It's very rare, but once in a great while, a very large wave comes up, and the boat will shift, and if you aren't hanging onto something you could land in the water. If that happens, I'll bring the boat around and pick you up, but it's best if you know how to float. Here," Zebedee said. "This is all you do. Remove your robe and pull your tunic between your legs and secure it with a belt, or your tunic will get heavy and try to pull you down. Lie back, chin up, tummy up, toes up, and keep breathing. Try to relax like you're going to sleep. Then gently move your arms and legs like this. You just need to practice a little."

Joseph and the boys decided they'd try first. Zebedee stayed for a while watching. He told Joseph later that he hadn't laughed so hard in a long time.

The children woke from their naps, and the men decided it was up to them to teach the children how to play in the water. The women stayed awfully close!

Mary and her girls waited until sundown. By then, the men thought they were teachers and had to "help" the women. The women were amazed. They had to work a little harder than they'd thought they would because their clothes were heavy. But after a while, they too began to relax and float.

That afternoon before he left, Zebedee told them to put olive oil on their skin every hour or so. "The reflection of the sun on the water will give you a bad burn. If you can spend some time in the shade of the carts or under a tree, that will help. Until tomorrow then!" he called, and off he went.

Leah thought that the small rocks all over the shore were the best part of the whole experience. She was forever finding a wonderful treasure, which she just had to share with everyone. "Look, Grandmother! Look, Uncle Jesus! Look, Grandfather!" was heard all day long. It was such a joy to watch her discover the world.

Late that afternoon, another family came to the shore, stopping not too far from Joseph and his family. It seemed they were more familiar with "being at the lake," as each person seemed to know what to do to get things ready.

They appeared to be a family of parents and three older children. Joseph and Mary waved, and the new family began walking toward them. Joseph and Mary went to meet them.

"Hello!" called Joseph. "Isn't this a beautiful spot?"

"It is!" answered the man. "We try to get here twice each summer—have been since we married. Actually this is where we first met, and that's why it's such a special place for us."

"That's really nice," said Joseph as he extended his hand. "I am Joseph, the carpenter from Nazareth, and this is my wife, Mary. We're here with our entire family. This is our first time; in fact, it's really our first vacation!"

Mary said, "Can you come and meet the rest of our family? We're so excited that we were able to arrange to have all of us come at the same time."

"All of you in three carts! Wow! That must have taken a lot of planning," the man said.

The families came forward, and the boys introduced themselves and their families.

"I'm Jesus. It's nice to meet you. I'm the oldest. I am senior rabbi and administrator at our school." And so went the introductions.

The man was a pharmacist, and his wife and sons worked with him. The boys were eighteen and sixteen, and the little girl was ten.

Anna, now fourteen—almost fifteen—and the older boy, Timaeus, appeared to be drawn to each other. In fact, until Anna left for home, the two of them spent a lot of time together.

Right after breakfast, early the next morning, a huge boat came near the shore. "Is that the boat we're going on?" asked Mary. "It's almost as large as a house!"

Zebedee greeted them and helped everyone climb on board. Leah needed to be reminded to hold hands, and she literally dragged her father around the entire boat. "It kinda smells, Father, and listen when I jump! It goes boom!"

Zebedee said, "Men, come and I'll show you what makes the boat move." He walked around the boat, showing them the different areas, and then he showed them what to do in case something should happen and they would need to act quickly.

"Nothing's going to happen, but it's good to be prepared. Now, let's get started!"

After sailing for a while, Zebedee said, "If you would like to try to catch fish, I brought along a small net. The large ones are pretty hard to handle. Do you want to try?"

"Yes!" said all the men—and Elizabeth.

Zebedee showed them what to do and what to expect. The boys stood apart, held the same side of the net, and tossed the rest of it overboard. What an experience. Best of all—they caught some fish! And no one fell overboard.

Leah found new playmates—the fish! She squealed; she ran; she poked them. She wanted to hold one of the fish in her hands, but it wriggled out. Zebedee went over to her and said, "Here. Put your hand in the gills like this, and you can hold it. See?" She held first one and then another and then another and then … She was a very happy little girl.

James thought, *She's old enough; I think she'll always remember this day. Thank You, Father God.*

After returning to land, Zebedee taught them how to clean the fish and how to prepare them to be cooked over an open fire. At dinnertime, they built a great fire, and as it burned down, they all put a fish on a stick and cooked their own dinner. It was a time that everyone would remember forever.

"Zebedee, we can never thank you enough!" said Jesus, shaking his hand and patting him on the back. "Thank you. I will ask Father God to bless you in a special way. May Father God see that we meet again, my friend!"

Thursday evening, Timaeus asked if he might speak to Joseph. "Sir, I know I have only known your Anna for a couple of days, but I feel I love her and would like to spend the rest of my life with her. I am asking your permission to be betrothed to Anna."

"Sit down for a minute," Joseph said. "I need to tell you a little about Anna. Her mother nearly died giving birth to her. That gave all of us a feeling that we needed to protect our little girl. I'm afraid that she wants to do what she wants to do. She can be difficult. I've found that I often need to take a deep breath and then speak to her firmly so she understands that sometimes things have to be a certain way—even if that is not what she wants."

"I did see that. But I have also seen that she respects you and her mother and appears to often listen when others are talking."

"She's not going to change. You need to do some serious thinking about this. Is her determination something you can live with the rest of your life?"

"Right now I say yes. I'm very sure I can live with her and hopefully our family for the rest of my life," answered Timaeus.

"I want you to understand that I love my daughter very much! I want only the best for her. She is very special and very caring, but she does want to do things her way and on her time schedule. You will need to watch that things get done. She's a cuddler, not an ambitious doer.

"Anna has been making dolls and doll clothing and doll furniture for years. In fact, she has her own little business with dolls. So I have no doubt that she will be a very good mother, but you would need to keep your eye on everything— the cooking, the cleaning, the animals, and the garden. She does not take well to harsh words. You'd need to be firm but gentle," continued Joseph.

"She was telling me about her doll business and about the man who sells them for her. She said that almost everyone in your family makes something for the traveler to sell," said Timaeus.

"That's right. However, back to Anna, I can't give my permission right now. From what I have seen, you are a wonderful young man, and I really have come to like you. However, I want the two of you to spend more time together. Given that the two of you live quite a distance apart, what if you spend as much time as possible together the next three months, and then if you still feel the same way, I'll give my blessing. Will that work for you?" asked Joseph.

"Thank you, sir. I'll make it work. May I tell Anna and my family what we've talked about?" asked Timaeus.

"Our conversation in general, yes. But the things I told you about who Anna is—that's between you and me. I do not want that discussed with others. Understand?" explained Joseph.

"Yes, sir. Thank you, sir. May I shake your hand?"

"You're a good man. I hope things work out for the two of you," Joseph said as he shook hands and gave Timaeus a pat on the back.

Before everyone left for home, Timaeus approached Anna's brothers. He told them of his plan and asked their input on how the travel to and from Cana could be arranged so that he could spend the most time he could with Anna.

James and Judas and their families decided to each make a three-day trip once a month for these three months so Anna could visit Timaeus and his family. Apparently his family was quite wealthy, for they had a small house just for guests.

The trip home from the sea was a mixed event. The children were cranky because they didn't want to leave the water. Many of the adults felt the same way. Their vacation was over, and they needed to return to everyday living. Before they reached home, however, things changed. The children thought about telling their friends about their adventure. The adults realized they had had a wonderful experience that would stay with them all their lives, a very special family vacation!

***

The plan to help Timaeus and Anna spend time together was put into place. The families enjoyed their visits to Cana; staying in the little guesthouse proved to be a real treat. Jesus was only able to make one trip with Anna. He was encouraged that the entire family seemed to love Father God as his family did.

Jesus, Timaeus, his father, and his brother talked after dinner, discussing many things, including many of the stories from the Torah and the book of the Prophets.

Timaeus said, "I find so much hope in scripture. For instance, Aaron, Moses's brother, made a huge mistake when he made that golden calf. Yet Father God forgave him and still used him—and not just for minor parts of His plan; he continued to take a major role. I try to do what's right, but when I fail, I remember Aaron."

Jesus smiled. "Our amazing wonderful Father God! You're right, Timaeus. If we really study scripture, we begin to know Father God and His great forgiveness and the wonderful plan He has for each of our lives."

The men were amazed by Jesus's understanding of Father God. "I've been teaching since I was thirteen, so the law and the Prophets seem to be quite clear to me," Jesus shared. "It seems, though, that the more I study, the more the things I read are new. Every time I read a portion of scripture, it's like I'm reading it for the first time. Sometimes I just shake my head in wonder."

Timaeus's brother and uncle usually came with him to Nazareth—every other week—and stayed at the homes of either James or Judas. It really would not be proper for them to stay in the same home as Anna.

The three months passed quickly. Timaeus asked to speak to Joseph again.

"It's been three months, sir. I would like to ask you again if I may be betrothed to my Anna. If you have questions for me, please ask me anything," began Timaeus.

"No questions. Mary and I will be very proud to call you our son. You have both my permission and her mother's permission. Welcome to our family!" With that said, Joseph gave him a great hug.

"Thank you, sir! Thank you! If you ever have a concern about Anna's and my family, please feel free to talk to me about it," said Timaeus as he turned to go to the other room to reach his Anna.

"He said yes! You are mine! We need to make plans. Oh, Anna. I'm so happy! I love you my little girl," he said as he picked her up and gave her a hug.

FORTY-THREE

26

Benjamin was born! Leah was so proud of her little brother. It was the day of his baptism, and the entire family was together—a time of love and celebration.

About midafternoon, Simon said, "Okay, family! It's time we all work together to find a wife for me! James, Judas, and Elizabeth each have a son and a daughter. Joses will soon have his first child, and Anna's wedding is coming up shortly. I'm being left behind!"

"Timaeus has a younger sister," offered Anna.

"Thanks, I think," said Simon.

"I'll tell you what," said James. "Next time each of us is in Cana or Nain, it will be our duty to be on the lookout for a wife for you. How does that sound?"

"Wow. Thanks. You're really a big help. I might as well go work on tomorrow's test for the boys," Simon said as he walked off, shaking his head.

"I guess he really does feel bad," said Jesus. "Maybe we really should start looking for a possible wife for him."

"She'll have to be really special," said Elizabeth. "He's quieter than the rest of us, and he seems to have the love of our Father God as the main point of his life."

"His wife will have to be just as committed to Father God, or they'll have a very difficult life," added Jesus. "I think that we can depend on Father God to send someone to him. So far, he's done that for the rest of you. Remember?"

"You're right, Jesus," said Joseph. "We need to trust Him. Let's all remember to pray for his wish for a wife."

***

It was soon time for the wedding of Timaeus and Anna. Anna told everyone that she had several things for the celebration about which she was very firm! She wanted wine only to drink; a table of her dolls and all the things that went with them; all women and girls to have a flower of some kind on their tunics but no sprang, as she would wear one. "And I will sit, and everyone will come and talk to me."

Timaeus said, "My Anna, would you come for a walk with me, please?"

After they went out the door, Joses turned to his brothers and said, "He sure has a job on his hands!"

As they began walking, Timaeus said, "Anna, you are making some wonderful plans for our wedding!"

"Really? I'm so glad you think so. My brothers think I'm being selfish."

"Do they? I think some of your ideas are wonderful—like having some of your dolls and their furniture on a small table for everyone to see. That's a great idea! And I like having all the women and girls wear flowers. But some people may not be able to afford them, so how about if I buy a lot of them and we provide them for the women and girls? People would think that we are being very generous."

"I didn't think of that. Would you really provide flowers for all the women?"

"For you, I'll do almost anything."

"Oh, thank you, Timaeus!"

"I do have a request to make of you. I don't care for wine, and I do like beer. Could we have both? If it won't be too much trouble."

"You don't? But it's your wedding! Okay. We'll have beer too," stated Anna.

"One other thing. My grandparents will be at the wedding, and there will also be some other people who can't get around very well. Do you suppose that we could do some walking around and talking with people? I think they would really like that," suggested Timaeus.

"I should have thought of that! You're right. I'll walk around and visit. That way, everyone can see my new tunic. Mother and I are using a very special dye for both the tunic and the sprang so that I will be very beautiful. I want this to be a very special day, Timaeus! My day!"

"It will be my day too, my Anna. Don't forget that. You need to look at me once in a while; otherwise, I'll feel that it's not a special day for me. Do you understand?"

"Oh, I'm sorry. I was being selfish again, wasn't I? You have to help me not do that. Father says it makes other people not like me."

"I'll always love you, my Anna. Never forget that!"

When they returned to the rest of the family, Anna said, "I've changed my mind about some things for the wedding."

Inwardly, eyes rolled.

The wedding and celebration went well. They did serve beer and wine. Anna and Timaeus did walk and greet people. In fact, Anna rarely sat down the entire week of celebrations! She appeared to be the happiest of all those attending.

FORTY-FOUR

26

The next year brought more grandchildren for Joseph and Mary! Their family and their businesses were growing.

One morning, instead of going to the Shop, Joseph stayed behind and asked Mary if they could talk. They sat at the table facing each other.

"Mary, you know that I love you above everything. I want you to know that you are the best thing of my entire life. But I have to tell you something."

"You're scaring me, Joseph. What's wrong?" asked Mary.

He took her hands in his. "I've waited until after the wedding and celebrations to talk with you. I've not been well for some time now. I didn't think it was anything serious, but now I know it is. I've seen the physician a few times, and he has told me that what I have cannot be cured," said Joseph.

"My Joseph! I've noticed that you aren't eating like usual, but you don't look like you're losing weight. So I thought maybe the changes in the family this past year were a bit much for you. Oh, my Joseph! What can I do for you?"

"At this point, just understand. It's hard for me to eat. There are some things that I've found are easier to eat than others. So maybe we can focus on those."

"Of course! I'll do anything for you! Just tell me what's good and what's not. The two of us and Jesus and Simon will pray tonight, and we'll tell the families, and they'll join us in prayer. Father God will help you, I know He will!"

"The physician says that what I have is spreading. He thinks it started in my lower stomach but is now in other organs and that it will keep spreading."

"Joseph! Are you telling me you're dying?"

"Yes, my Mary. The physician feels I have just a few months left."

"No! We will get all the families here this Sabbath, and we will pray and pray and talk until we reach a solution together. That's it, Joseph. That's it!"

"Yes, Mary—from your mouth to Father God's ears. But it's not going to happen. Everyone has an end time, and I am comfortable that this is mine. I should get to the Shop. Are you okay for me to leave you?"

"Leave me? To go to work, yes. The other stuff? I'll fight to keep you!" Mary hugged him and let him go off to work.

Mary got down on her knees and had a long talk with Father God. When she finished praying, she felt a special calmness. She knew that Father God was in charge and that things would work out according to His plan.

That Sabbath after services, the entire family met at Joseph's for dinner. They had all spent the night in Nazareth—something everyone looked forward to.

The next day, they gathered on the roof. "Joseph and I have something we want to discuss with all of you. I've asked Miriam and her oldest two granddaughters to take all of our children to the town square for a couple of hours so that we can all talk. They'll take mats for the children to nap on. Okay, everyone?" asked Mary.

Everyone agreed, but there was a stillness—like waiting for the other shoe to drop. The mothers nursed the youngest children and put them down for naps, while the rest of the children went off to the square.

Joseph took Mary's hand and began. "Thank you all for coming. As always, it's a treat for your mother and me every time we're all together. I know it wasn't the easiest thing for some of you to come here today, but the reason we asked all of you to come is because I am not well."

Everyone was alert. Some asked the questions they were thinking. Joses stated, "Well, we'll pray! Father God will heal you."

"Joses," explained Joseph, "it isn't always like that. Each of us has to leave this earth and return to our Father God. When it's that time for each of us, we all need to listen to Him.

"I've seen the physician a few times, and it seems that what I have seems to eat different parts of my insides. They don't have a name for it, but they know that it gets worse, and we know that my time is fairly short—maybe a few months."

Anna cried out and began sobbing. Timaeus held her and asked her if she wanted to go outside or stay and listen to the others. She wanted to stay.

"Father, how are you feeling?" asked James.

"I'll be honest with you. My lower abdomen hurts all the time. After I eat, it feels worse—especially after eating things with a strong taste. The pain is now also in my back, and sometimes I have a hard time breathing. I don't want to worry you. I want you prepared. Remember something—when it's my time to leave you, I won't hurt anymore; I will be healed. I know I will miss all of you, but we have time to spend together before it's my time."

Simon said, "Father, when it was Benjamin's time and we knew he would be leaving us, we prayed that he would not have pain. Please, may we do that for you?"

Joseph hesitated because he felt he was no one special and did not deserve to be treated as a special person by Father God.

A quick discussion by the family changed his mind—quickly!

"One more thing—could my funeral be like Benjamin's? I mean not having the women keening but having everyone sing psalms?"

Mary reached over and hugged him as tears ran down her cheeks.

"Jesus, will you please lead us in prayer? I would like you to pray for all of you as well," said Joseph.

Jesus fell to his knees, and with tears running down his face, he prayed, "Father God, we need You so badly! Our father has always been a great man, especially to all of us. He has led us, directed us, taught us, and loved us all our lives. How do we say goodbye to him? Our hearts are so heavy. Father God, he is in a lot of pain. We ask that You remove this pain from him. Please, Father God, remove his pain. Father God, our families also need Your help; we ache. His leaving us will cause a big hole in our lives. Father God, take charge of all of us. Please, Father God, remove his pain and help him and us. We all love You and trust You completely. Thank You for Your healing. Amen."

FORTY-FIVE

26

It was a glorious day, warm with a slight breeze. "Mary," said Joseph, "do you think we could go outside for a while? It's such a beautiful day!"

"I'd love to. It'll take me just a few minutes to tie up the cloth on the loom, and then I'll be right with you," answered Mary.

Joseph reached for the walking sticks the boys had made for him and was reaching for another tunic when Mary finished. They walked slowly to the nearby oak tree. Mary helped Joseph sit against the tree, where the filtered sun could reach him. She made sure his extra tunic was across his shoulders. He got so cold so quickly now.

"Thank you, Mary. I'm feeling a little stronger today and wanted to feel the warmth of the sun and feel the breeze on my skin."

They sat for a while—each with his or her own thoughts. It was so peaceful.

"Joseph, what do you remember about your family? I know you were young, but do you know how the fire started?" asked Mary.

"I was only two or three when it happened. I was told that it was after sundown and some boys were playing with fire behind the house. I never knew if it was my brothers or other boys. But a wind came up suddenly, and the fire quickly surrounded the house. I was told that my brothers went inside to warn my parents, but all of them were trapped. Mother lay on top of me, and that's what saved my life. I had a small burn on my right foot, but it healed, and I've had no problem with it."

"I'm sorry. The priest and his housekeeper took you in, didn't they?"

Yes. He was my father's brother. He never married so he had no children. They made a wonderful life for me. They taught me kindness and consideration for others. He insisted that I memorize major portions of the Torah, so knowing and loving Father God has always been an important part of my life. I have so much to thank them for.

Mary asked, "Do you know anything about your parents or your brothers?"

"Not really. I think we raised sheep or that we farmed; I'm not sure. I remember there were a lot of sheep, and I remember playing with them. Father whittled. He would sit on the stump of a tree and tell stories while he whittled. I remember a small lamb that he made. I wonder … I suppose it burned with everything else. My brothers were quite a bit older than I was. They weren't around a lot. They were probably in school and then working.

"I don't remember much about Mother; it's more feelings. I remember her cooking. She seemed to be always smiling. I feel warmth when I think of her, so she must have been a loving person. I think she was quite thin." He shook his head. "That's about all I remember."

There was quiet for a while—each one thinking.

Joseph said, "I was just thinking; I'll soon see all of them. The priest and his housekeeper! I'll get to meet my parents and my brothers! I wonder what that will be like."

"Oh, Joseph! That will be amazing! I think that thinking about that will help me when I miss you so much." Mary thought for a moment and then added, "I think I'll share that with the family. We're going to need it."

"Mary, tell me about your parents and your brother and sister. Would you please?"

"I was so happy! Both Father and Mother had a sense of humor. They loved to tease each other and us kids. When Mother made a meal that was especially good, Father would say, 'This is sour. I better eat all of it.' The two of them would laugh, and my brother and sister and I would just roll our eyes.

"My brother was a rascal! Sometimes he came very close to breaking the rules, but somehow he always came out of it okay. Just before they all got sick, he had met a girl, and we all thought that they would probably be betrothed. I liked her. She wasn't funny like we were, but she was so kind. She always thought of what would make someone else feel good. I've tried to do that because of her, I think. I wonder what happened to her. Her parents moved south near Egypt while I was still ill.

"My sister was younger than I was, but she didn't get as sick as the rest of us. An uncle and aunt took her as their own and moved someplace south of here. I've never heard about her since then. I hope she's okay. I went to live with two of my uncles.

"They were very kind to me. They told me that they didn't know anything about raising a child—especially a girl—so they told me that I needed to remember what my mother had taught me and that I must always act the way that would make her proud.

"They loved Father God, so He was a very important part of everything we did. I have a lot to thank them for as well."

"I'm so glad they took good care of you. And I'm sorry about your sister. Maybe someday you'll see her again. I think I need to go inside now. Do you think you'll be able to help me?" asked Joseph as he tried to stand.

"Sure. The physician showed me how so I don't hurt you or me, and with the special sticks the boys made, we'll be fine."

As they were walking to the house, Mary said, "I wonder how the boys figured out that the stick should be used with the three smaller branches on the ground instead of as most people use them as a handle at the top. It certainly makes it easier for you to walk. You've done a great job of teaching the boys to think things through, Joseph—not just make something and then try to use it as best you can."

A few days later, they went outside again. This time, Joseph just sat on the nearby rock. He couldn't walk farther. "Things get harder and harder, Mary. It just feels good to be outdoors, but I need to go back inside. I'm sorry."

"Not sorry, Joseph. Every moment I have with you is a special blessing."

This was the last time Joseph was able to be outdoors.

A few days later, he was gone. It happened very early one morning.

"Mary," said Joseph, "I think ... my time ... is near. I want ... to ask you to ... please ... go on ... cheerfully. Don't be ... sad. Promise me?"

With tears in her eyes, Mary held Joseph close to her and said, "I'll do my best. I love you so much. I want you to know that. I want you to know that you have given me a wonderful life and a remarkable family. Thank you, my Joseph."

Joseph smiled, drifted off to sleep, and quietly moved to his eternal life.

Jesus and Simon had heard the murmur of their parents' voices and knew the time had come. When they heard Mary softly weeping, they called softly, "Mother?"

"Yes, boys. Please come in. Your father has passed. I want to stay here with him for a little while, but we need to let the families know. Will you two take charge?"

"Yes, Mother," they said. "We'll handle everything."

"Not everything Jesus. It is my responsibility and my honor to wash and dress your father. I want to do that. It's the last thing I can do for him."

"Of course, Mother."

Jesus and Simon both laid their hands on Joseph, and with tears running down their faces, they prayed and kissed their Father on his forehead. They then turned and hugged their Mother. "I love you, Mother," they told her.

"He is the best father ever! He taught us so much. He leaves a big hole in my heart," said Jesus.

They walked to the living area. Jesus said to Simon, "I think that first we need to tell James and Joses and send them to tell Elizabeth and Anna. If they take carts, they should be home by midafternoon. Will you tell Joses and ask him to go to Nain for Elizabeth? I'll tell James and have him go to Anna in Cana.

"We'll need to tell Miriam and put a sign on the Shop and contact the keening women and the musicians. When I leave James, I could tell Miriam and contact the keening women. Would you also put the sign on the Shop and contact the musicians?"

It was agreed. James and Joses used carts in order to travel faster. They wanted to hold the service for Joseph about the ninth hour.

Miriam was there quickly to help in any way she could. She tried to get Mary to eat a little, but she would only drink a few sips of water. The keening women arrived just as Mary was finishing dressing Joseph. She placed the special cloth on his face and kissed his forehead one last time. The musicians arrived a short time later. Jesus had asked them to please sing and play psalms. And remembering Benjamin's funeral, they agreed.

A simple but meaningful service was held late afternoon—after all the families were able to come home. Joseph's family had its own burial cave and Joseph was laid to rest there just before sundown.

Many people from town attended, and many brought food for the family. Miriam left with one of the neighbors for a while, and when she returned, she said, "Mary, the women have made a meal at the town square. Will you and your families join them? They want to honor Joseph and felt this was the time and place to do it."

"Of course. I don't know how sociable I'll be though," said Mary.

Miriam hugged her as they all walked together to the town square.

Mary was very glad she had gone with Miriam. So many people told her of the things that Joseph had done when their families were desperate—things he had kept to himself, things so personal to these people.

Two mornings later, Miriam ran over to Mary's. At the doorway with tears in her eyes, she grabbed Mary's hands and said, "Hiram died sometime during the night last night."

Mary grabbed her friend and held her close. "Oh, Miriam! I am so sorry!"

"He's been tired lately, but when I asked him, he said it was just because he was getting old. I never expected this! Are Jesus and Simon still home?"

"I think so. They always say goodbye when they leave, and they haven't yet."

"Jesus! Simon!" Miriam called as she and Mary entered the house. She told them of Hiram's passing and said, "Abraham is out of town. Will the two of you make the arrangements and get the musicians and the women? Ask them if they would again sing psalms please. I'll tell my girls and send someone to get Abraham."

And so, two close friends were laid to rest just two days apart.

FORTY-SIX

27

The entire year was an eventful year. Miriam's grandson, Abraham's oldest son, began his internship at the Shop and was doing well.

The physician retired to his daughter's place on the Island of Tyre. He felt the water would be beneficial to his health. The townspeople planned a dinner and wished him well.

A new physician moved into town. He and his wife had two daughters, fifteen and thirteen, and a young son about seven years old. Although the physician was born and lived most of his life in Hebron, he'd attended medical school in Rome. He had a wonderful caring way about him and immediately fit in with the townsfolk. His wife worked with him—mostly with his records and keeping his instruments clean, in order, and readily available to him.

His oldest daughter, Suzanna, brought her brother to school the first day. Jesus's class was having final tests in Torah history and he couldn't leave, so Simon enrolled the young boy. After being filled in on the boy's studies, Simon felt he needed to explain to Suzanna that sometimes when boys have older sisters, the boys get lazy and the girls get too helpful, and that was definitely not good for the boy.

Suzanna promised that she and her sister would let the boy do his own studying, helping only when needed and then keeping the amount of work they would do for him to a minimum. Suzanna also agreed to do her best to help him get up to date with his lessons, and she would ask her sister to do the same. They agreed that they would meet again in two weeks to "see how things are progressing."

After that, Suzanna would come to the school about once a month to check with Simon on the boy's progress. Simon and Suzanna sensed something happening between them.

One day, Simon asked Suzanna if they might go for a walk and get to know each other better. After a few walks, he asked her folks if they might see each other regularly. Her parents agreed, and they saw each other as often as a chaperone could be arranged.

By the end of six months, Simon approached Suzanna's father to ask if he and Suzanna might be betrothed.

"I was wondering when you were going to get around to asking me," her father said. "From what I can see, you are a fine young man. I will expect you to treat her with respect, and I expect that, when you have a family, you will do your best to make it a loving family. And one more thing—I expect you to keep your family close to our Father God. Is there anything you want to tell me?"

Smiling, Simon said, "You've pretty much said all I was going to say. I will treasure our family. I will work with Suzanna. I will do my best to instill Father God in all of our family's hearts. I love Suzanna, and I want to spend the rest of my life with her."

"Thank you, young man! Other than that, welcome to our family!" And while shaking Simon's hand, the physician reached out and gave him a quick hug.

The brothers gave Simon a bit of a hard time—reminding him that, at one time, he had been concerned about finding the right girl.

"I know. I remember!" Simon assured them. "The answer you gave me was that Father God had sent someone for each of you, and He would do it for me. Well, He sure did! I am so blessed."

Our Suzanna was such a gentle girl. After the year of betrothal, the two were married. A priest her family had known in Hebron came to officiate at the wedding. Jesus took part with the agreement of the priest. Simon asked James to read the part normally read by the groom's father.

Theirs was another wedding blessed by Father God.

On an evening after the week of celebrations, Mary took a glass of wine to the roof. "I miss you, my Joseph—especially at times like this," she said softly. "I wish you had met her. She is a lovely young woman. I think she'll be a good support for Simon. But at the same time, I think she'll find a way to make her thoughts known when it's important to her. Rest in peace, my love. I love you, and I miss you. Walk with Father God."

FORTY-SEVEN

27

"Woman!" called Jesus as he rushed into the house. "Woman, where are you? Oh, there you are!" He picked her up and spun her around.

"Jesus! What on earth?!"

"Mother, let's go up on the roof. I have the most amazing news!"

As they sat down, Jesus said, "Mother, I've been asked to go to Capernaum for about two years as rabbi of a school with a few more children then we have here."

"Oh. Jesus! That's wonderful. How did this happen?"

"Three men came to the school today to talk to me. One was a priest from Jerusalem, and the other two were a young rabbi from Capernaum and a man acting as his companion. It seems that the younger man's father was administrative rabbi at the school. He passed away a short time ago, and they want the young man to take over. However, he's only nineteen, almost twenty, and they feel he should be covered by an older rabbi for about another two years. So they came to literally tell me that I am assigned to fill in! I am so excited, and yet I wonder if Father God really feels I'm ready. I think He does, and I am so humbled! I'm rambling. What do you think, Mother?"

"I think it's the best thing for you! You have so much to share with people. The people here know you and depend on you. For you to spread your love and your knowledge to others is something that fills my heart. When would you be leaving?"

"When we leave for Passover in three weeks, they would like me to go home from there with them. I am so awed!"

"I believe you're ready, Jesus. And I believe the timing is perfect. I say go with Father God's and my blessings. I love you, my son!"

"I love you too, Mother! I'm so excited I don't know what to do next!"

"Did you ask the men to dinner with us? I hope!"

"I did. I knew you would want me to, but the priest needed to get back to Jerusalem as soon as he could and the others to Capernaum by sundown. I need to go now and have a long talk with Simon. He'll need to take over completely. See you at dinner time, Mother!" And off he went.

The three weeks were full of activity. Simon needed to be filled in on his new responsibilities, and a new rabbi had to be found to replace Simon. Abraham's son was selected. He was a great young man who dearly loved his Father God and had been assisting both Jesus and Simon at the school while also working in the Shop.

Jesus's main worry was that Mary would be alone in this great big house. He wasn't worried that living alone would be a bother but that all the work involved in keeping a home could be way too much for any one person.

There was another stop Jesus wanted to make—Enoch's Mary. He shared his news with her and then asked, "Enoch's Mary, I remember that you used to draw people. Could you draw a picture of my mother for me to take to Capernaum? Just a small one. I won't have much space in my room, so it can't take up much room."

"I would love to, Jesus! Thank you for asking me. I am honored."

They agreed on a price and the time Enoch's Mary would need. Jesus left smiling.

When the families met at Mary's house the next Sabbath, Jesus told the family of his two-year move to Capernaum. This met with varying responses.

Anna stated very primly, "I'm sure you will do a good job there, too."

Simon added, "I'm sorry to see you go, but I know it's the best for everyone. You've been a wonderful teacher and rabbi, and you are respected both as a teacher and as a man in this entire community. I promise you, I will do my best to implement all that I've learned from you. I wish you Father God's peace as you leave us."

"Your nephews and nieces will also miss you. But we'll see you in Jerusalem on the feast days, won't we? So it's not like you'll be gone forever," said James.

"I will see you on feast days in Jerusalem. I promise to do my best to see to it that I spend some quality time with you then, so I can catch up on all that's happening," replied Jesus.

Hugs (accompanied by Elizabeth's tears) were shared all around.

Forty-eight

28

The entire family was together the following Sabbath also. "Family," said Timaeus, "Anna and I would like to talk with you for a minute. My parents have been dreaming for a few years of expanding their pharmacy. They've been looking for the right town. They have asked if we would all allow them to take over the vacant pharmacy here. They would put me in charge, and it would be my business. Anna and I have talked about it, and we would love to move here. But we want to hear what all of you think."

There wasn't a lot of discussion; everyone agreed that this would be a wonderful plan. Anna told everyone that she was so ready to "come home." She added, "I love Timaeus, and his family is wonderful, but I miss my family. We talked and said that his family would always be welcome in our home, and when we have children they will be a big part of the children's lives. I would really like to come home."

Everyone offered to help in any way possible.

Mary said, "Have you considered where you would live? As Jesus said, taking complete charge of this home is a very big chore. I would be very open to discussing your living here. I'm sure we could work out any kinks and make a pleasant home for all of us."

"Oh, Mother! We were hoping you'd say that. Yes! We would love to live here with you. Timaeus said that things between us might be a little different though. He said that the three of us would be equals, and we would make all decisions together. I like that. I am grown up and want to have my say."

"Anna," said Joses, "when have you ever not had your say—in anything? All your life, you've made it very clear what you think and what you want. My concern is that you would give Mother a hard time, and that's not going to happen! Mother is my concern, and I will watch carefully."

"Joses, you can watch me all you want. I'll be a good adult in this house, and I'll be a good wife and a good mother when the time comes. Just wait and see!"

"Okay. Just stating my opinion," replied Joses.

"Anyone else want to say something? Don't be afraid to say what's on your mind. We're all family and need to be open with each other," asked Timaeus.

The agreement was made, and plans were made to implement the changes. "I almost forgot something." Timaeus chuckled. "My father and mother kind of anticipated that you would all agree to this and have ordered supplies to be delivered to the pharmacy here in about two weeks. I hope that's okay."

The families were pleasantly surprised and assured him that it was just fine with them. "I'm sure the physician, and everyone else for that matter, will be very glad to have a pharmacy in town," said Simon.

***

Later that day Timaeus asked, "James and Lois, would you have time to talk with Anna and me?"

"Sure. The children are sleeping, so why don't we talk now?"

They walked outdoors a ways and sat under the oak tree. "I hope I'm not out of line here," began Timaeus. "But Anna and I have been discussing this and would like to run it by both of you. I'm a little embarrassed because I'm going to be talking about what I have seen of the two of you.

"I've seen that, financially, you help a lot of people. I assume that's because of who you are but also because you didn't need to pay for your home. Anna and I will be in the same position. It's our plan to build a small guesthouse for everyone who visits us, and that includes my family, Elizabeth and her family, Jesus, and anyone who needs a place to stay. Is that okay so far?"

"You're right about why we help others and I don't mind that you've said it. I also like it that you'll build a guesthouse on the family land. I think you have something more on your mind though, right?" asked James.

"Right. Anna's brothers and sister haven't had the advantage we've had and need to buy their homes. We'd like to find a way to help them. We haven't thought of a way yet but thought, if the four of us put our heads together, maybe we could find a way. What do you think? Are we out of line?" asked Timaeus.

"I've seen that some are having what seems to be limited finances. I think you're right. Right now, I can't think of how to do it. But Lois and I will do some praying, and we can talk again. Thank you, Timaeus. I'm sure the four of us can find a way to do this. Would you be available tomorrow when I get home from the Shop?" asked James.

"Yes. My parents want me to take a good look at the current pharmacy and tell them what I see. They don't want to have to do a lot of tearing down and building up. We'll see you at your house?" asked Timaeus.

"Sounds good. Come for dinner," said Lois.

"I'll come over in the afternoon and see what I can do to help you," said Anna.

***

Later that evening, after the others had left, Mary, Timaeus, and Anna took a glass of wine to the roof so they could further discuss the upcoming changes.

"Mary, may I ask you to start the conversation? Please tell us everything you're thinking—whether it's good or bad or scary or whatever," said Timaeus.

"It's a lot. And I've just heard of our living together, so I may feel or think things tonight that I won't feel or think tomorrow. I'll give it a shot though," began Mary.

"First, I will be glad to have others living here. There is a lot of work, what with daily chores and the animals, the garden, the sewing, and trying to prepare things for Japeth. So that's a very good thing. Next is the thing hardest for me to talk about."

"I know, Mother. It's about me and how I always want things my way, isn't it?" asked Anna.

"That's pretty harsh, but yes that is a great concern of mine. You've always been the youngest, and you've always had a very firm idea of what you want. So far, as your mother, I was able to help you see that there is another way that is more in keeping with the needs and wants of others. Now we would be equals, and I feel I would always need to be careful and alert about you and your mood changes. That could make life very hard for me and, in the long run, for all of us. Do you understand what I'm saying?" explained Mary.

"Wow, Mother! That's heavy! I just worry that you're going to boss me around. But from what you've just said, I need to really look at who I am. Timaeus, am I hard to get along with?" asked Anna.

"My girl, you are my delight! At times I need to stop and think and decide just how I want to say something to you to have you change your mind so that it appears to be your idea, but it has never been a difficult thing for me," Timaeus said, giving her shoulders a squeeze.

There was quiet for a time. After a bit, Anna spoke up. "I need more time for thinking. You're both right. I do want everything my way. But I'm thinking—things have all gone well, and if that's been different from my way, it sure worked out well. I don't know." She paused. "I feel that I really need to look at this, and I think I really want to look at this. I need to pray about it. Will you both pray with me?"

Anna prayed, "Father God, I feel that my eyes have been opened to something I've always done, and I really feel now that I want to change what I see as my selfish behavior. How do I do this? I know I can't do it. I think Timaeus and Mother will help me, but maybe it's time that I rely mostly on Your help. Father God, show me what to do and strengthen me to do it. Thank You for Your love and for the love of Timaeus and Mother. Amen."

A big three-way hug.

FORTY-NINE

28

James, Lois, Timaeus, and Anna met to discuss their concern. When they met over dinner the next day, everyone felt very comfortable. James started the conversation. "Lois and I prayed together, and then we each prayed on our own, and then today we prayed together again. We feel we may have an answer as to how to help the others so that they accept it. Have you two thought of anything?"

Timaeus answered, "Much like you, we also prayed together and then on our own and then again together today. We also feel we have an answer. James, please share your idea."

"We feel very strongly that Father God has given us an answer. When we agree on what we want to give them— whatever gift we decide—if they refuse it, we tell them that Father God told us to do it. And if they have a problem with that, they'll just have to discuss it with Him. We need to do His will!"

Anna squealed. "That's what we thought! We talked and talked about it like how would we feel? But it's the truth. Father God has laid it on our hearts, and that's what we are going to do!"

They all laughed. The rest of the meal was full of plan making. What kind of gift? The same gift for all? Money? Help fixing things? Replace worn out things?

A decision was made! Next Family Time, they would listen carefully and see if they could figure out what the others needed.

Anna said, "I know you would all like to tell me to be careful and not ask questions because that might give away our plans, and it might seem like we're interfering. I promise I'll be careful and just listen. After all, if we don't hear anything, we can all visit them and then decide."

"That's a great idea, Anna! Thank you for that suggestion. Let's make that a part of our plan," said James. "If we don't have suggestions for all of them, next week we'll find reasons to visit them at their homes! Thank you, Anna."

It didn't work out like that. When they met again, James said, "Lois and I have talked about this, and after trying to get a feeling for what each family would need, we feel that we're telling them what to do."

"We agree," said Timaeus. "We thought that, if we decide what they need, it sounds like we think we know more than they do. We don't want to do that."

"I wouldn't want anyone telling me what to do with any money, and I wouldn't want anyone to look at me and say, 'You need a new worktable, so here it is.' That's just not right. I know it's something I would have done a while ago, but that doesn't make it right," said Anna.

Timaeus gave her a hug.

"Do you have a suggestion?" asked James.

"We talked about it and feel we could give them enough to equal what the four of us have been given. Maybe figure the cost that our homes would have cost us and divide that by the four families and then give them that amount. That's just a suggestion. We're not set on it," said Timaeus.

James looked at Lois. She nodded. "That makes sense. Let's figure it out."

After a while, they came to an amount that sounded fair to the four of them.

"Now," said James. "When do we want to do this and how? Lois and I talked a little about it and thought maybe we should have everyone together when we do this."

"That seems like a good idea. That way, we have all of them together, and they all hear the same thing. I think there'll be less chance that they say no if they're all together."

Lois said, "I wonder if we should tell Mother Mary what we're doing, so she'll be ready. I think she would be with us on this."

"You're right, Lois. Timaeus and Anna, would you talk with Mother?" asked James.

"I won't talk though," said Anna. "I'm trying to do the right thing all the time. But if someone asks me something, I will say what I think!"

"Thank you, Anna. Thank you, James and Lois. We'll talk with her this week and do our best to get the entire family here Sabbath next. Or is that too early? I mean, will you have the money by then? Or should we wait a while?"

"Sabbath next will be perfect," said James. It was agreed.

Mary was delighted. "I am so proud of the four of you for thinking of this! I was just thinking that I need to go to Nain this week for supplies. If it would be okay with the two of you, Anna and I could ask Elizabeth and her family when we're there. Timaeus, I think you said you would be able to go with us, right?"

"Great idea. And yes, I am planning on going with you. I also need to look at some things I might want for the pharmacy."

They left early on Tuesday and reached Nain about the sixth hour—just in time for lunch. Elizabeth and the children were ecstatic! Combining the food Mary brought with what Elizabeth had already made was more than enough for all of them. Philip was able to join them for a few minutes.

Timaeus asked them if they could make it to the home this Sabbath. Philip and Elizabeth agreed but tried to tease and find out what was so special. There was no way they could get anyone to tell them.

On that Sabbath, after breakfast, Suzanna's sister and her close friend were asked to watch the children at the town square. Leah was told that, now that she was older, she should be the big helper and help keep the littlest children safe and help them if they cried.

After the children left and the smallest babies were put down for a nap, the family gathered on the roof. It was agreed that James would tell the family what they were doing and that Timaeus would back him up if needed. The two women, as Anna stated, would "only talk if asked a question. We need to do the right thing and let the men do most of the talking."

This was met with smiles.

"Family, Father God has laid something very heavy on our hearts—that's Timaeus's heart and Anna's heart and Lois's heart and mine. The four of us have been so blessed. We've been given our homes at no cost to us.

"I don't remember how it came up, but the four of us all had the same feeling at the same time. We all know that it is from our Father God. That is certain!

"We've talked about this a lot, and this is what we four feel is what Father God wants us to do. We've figured the amount our homes would have cost us and divided it by your four families. We are here today to present each of you four couples with this gift from Father God. Please, let us pray.

"Father God, You are our strength and our help. You guide us and You lead us to do Your will. We are so blessed that You have led us to do Your will today. Please continue to bless all of us and our children. Most importantly, stay with us Father God. We all need You so much. Thank You. Amen."

There was absolute silence. James passed a leather packet with money to each couple. Tears fell from everyone's eyes— especially Mary's.

After a few minutes, Simon said, "Pray with me please. Father God, how do I say Thank You? You know what this means to us. You always know, Father God. I don't know where to go from here. Help me. Help all of us to know and to love You more. Thank You, Father God, and please thank our families for us. Amen."

Hugs and tears and a lot of Thank-Yous were shared all around. Mary served everyone posca with fruit and cheese to celebrate.

Joses pulled James and Timaeus aside and told them, "I don't know how I feel about this. I understand what you were saying, but maybe it's my pride—I don't know. We can certainly use the money, but I don't know really why you're doing it."

James said, "Joses, you need to take this up with Father God. All we can tell you is that He laid it on our hearts to do this. We are only following His directions. Please try to understand. When Father God speaks, we obey."

Joses threw his arms around his two brothers and, with tears in his eyes, said, "Thank you! That's all I can say is thank you."

FIFTY

28

This week was the big week for planning the trip to Jerusalem! More than that, it was the time for Jesus to sort through his things and decide what he would need in Capernaum.

"Jesus, I've made this for you to take with you," said Mary.

"Thank you, Mother!" Jesus said as he picked her up and twirled her around.

"Jesus, I will certainly miss being picked up and twirled around by you! However, I will look forward to having you do that every time we see each other—even if that's in Jerusalem," said Mary laughing.

"Mother! This tunic is beautifully made. Thank you! What is this?"

"I wanted you to have something small that would remind you of home. I felt you would have a small table or a chair with a back on it, and this small sprang cloth would fit either one. I hope it's okay."

"What a great idea! It's a perfect size, and you're right, I should have either a table or a chair—I hope both—and it will fit either one. Thank you, Mother. You are the best mother any man has ever had. I am going to miss you more than anyone or anything else, but you've taught me so much that you'll be in my heart at all times. Thank you for being such a wonderful mother," Jesus said as he hugged her.

"Jesus, you are so very special. Thank you for being my son. Now! I have work to do, and you need to finish packing. Get going!" Mary turned to leave so Jesus wouldn't see the tears running down her cheeks.

Jesus was amazed that he really didn't need to take a lot of things with him. Mostly he wanted his Torah, the book of the Prophets, and his notes. His brothers had made two chests for him in which to pack his things. He would pack each in a separate sack to throw over the donkey as he traveled. It turned out that the two boxes were all he needed. "Thank you, Father God, for my parents and my brothers and of course my little sisters! Father God, You are so good to me. Continue to guide me please."

The families decided to take just four carts on the trip to Jerusalem, leaving most of the adults free to carry the small children. Leah was now six and decided that she should ride Jesus's donkey. James had let her ride a few times at home, so he agreed to let her try—but only if she let him walk alongside. She was ecstatic!

Almost the entire town was going to Jerusalem. Following Benjamin's example, private soldiers were hired to watch the town and to help take care of those who were left behind. As usual, those left behind were not able to travel—nor were they fully able to take care of themselves.

Miriam and her children and grandchildren stayed close to Mary and her families. That allowed Mary and Miriam to spend time together. Most of their conversations seemed to center around grandchildren. They were two grandmothers, enjoying life and enjoying each other.

The trip was uneventful—that is, until they reached Jerusalem the third hour of the Day of Preparation. After they set up their tents and unpacked, the men went to the temple to purchase the sacrificial lambs. They hoped to again be in the second group, and after the lambs were sacrificed, they would return to the tents in time for dinner to be prepared.

As they left the temple and were approaching their tents, they heard a man call, "Nazareth! Hey, Nazareth! Wait a minute!"

A man they didn't recognize was waving at them and running toward them. "Hi!" he called.

Jesus and his brothers stopped. They looked at each other, but no one seemed to know who this was—until suddenly, Simon took off running. He reached the man, and the two of them hugged and turned around and around, laughing and slapping each other's backs.

"Simon, I have found you! Oh, Father God is so good! I wasn't sure you'd recognize me. You've grown up to be a man."

Simon replied, "How could I possibly forget you? I've been praying for you! Come meet our families. Tell me how you are. You talk of Father God, so I assume you know Him now."

As they neared Simon's brothers, Simon said, "Do any of you recognize this man? He's one of the Greek men who Benjamin had watch the town years ago. I was so young."

They shook hands all around.

"I know you all need to be with your families to make preparations, but can we meet again this week? I told my family to plan nothing definite this trip, because if I found you, I wanted to spend time with you," said the Greek man.

"Of course!" said the brothers together.

They turned to look at each other and thought for a minute. "I think this is important," said Jesus. "Can our families all meet about the sixth hour tomorrow?"

It was decided that they would meet tomorrow about the sixth hour at a rocky place near where Mary and her families were settled. The Greek man hurried back to his family.

Simon shook his head. "He knows Father God! Thank you, Father God!" Simon was so excited that it seemed he floated on the way back to the tents. When he reached Suzanna, he pulled her to him in a big hug and said, "Remember me telling you about the Greek man I've been praying for?"

She nodded.

"Well, we just met him, and we're all going to meet him at the sixth hour tomorrow!"

Simon thought it would be hard to settle down for the ceremonial meal and the evening of the start of the festivals. The celebratory meal was so beautiful that he was caught up in its awesomeness.

That night at Family Time, Simon filled the family in on the story of the Greek man. The women reminded the men that the sixth hour was the time for a meal, so they would prepare a meal to be eaten with the other family. Of course, no one knew how many people were part of the Greek man's family, but that didn't seem to bother anyone.

After breakfast the next morning, the women talked and talked about everything and nothing as they prepared the meal. The men took a table for food and some beds to sit on, as the rocks would be uncomfortable. Philip had brought a large piece of tent material just in case it might be needed at some point. The men hung it across some tree limbs to provide more shade.

Mary and her families were just finishing setting up the food when the Greek man and his family arrived.

Simon ran to meet them and to help carry some of the things they were bringing. "Welcome!" he said. "Come meet my families! Forgive the noise. We're a noisy, loving family."

"Before I can introduce you, I need to know your name. You've always been the Greek man to me."

"My name is Yannis. It means 'God is gracious.' My mother didn't realize what she did when she gave me that name." The Greek man grinned.

Introductions were made all around. James chided, "Now we'll ask you to repeat everyone's name." At the look on Yannis's face, James said, "I'm just kidding! Sometimes I can't even remember all of our names."

Yannis introduced his wife and his five sons. "When I was in Nazareth, I left my wife and our then four sons because I needed the money. It was a pretty rough time for everyone back then. The food you gave us to eat on the way home—all four of us saved it to bring back to our families. My youngest son was born after my trip to Nazareth. His name," he said with a grin and a twinkle in his eyes, "is Simon!"

Simon and seven-year-old Simon shook hands. Simon smiled at the boy and ruffled his hair. "Are you a good boy?" he asked.

"Sometimes," admitted young Simon. Everyone grinned at that—honesty!

"Well, that's an honest answer. I hope the next time we meet that you can tell me that you are a good boy *most* of the time. Can we shake on it?"

The boy was hesitant, but he did shake Simon's hand. Simon clapped Yannis on the shoulder.

After eating, the young children—not Leah of course—were put down for a nap, and everyone relaxed, preparing to hear Yannis's story.

"Three of my friends and I heard about work in Nazareth taking care of the town and some of the townspeople who were unable to travel. We were desperate for money, so my wife and I agreed that I could be gone; we knew it would be two weeks or more.

"Things went well for us in Nazareth. A couple of the older people needed quite a bit of help, but it wasn't anything we couldn't handle. There was one woman who was so cranky— no matter what we did, it wasn't good enough for her. After about three days of this treatment, one of my friends told her that she was an old crab and that all the other people in town were nice. Why was she like this?

"She told him that she used to be very active in the town. She tried to greet everyone, bring meals if someone was sick, care for fussy small children, change dressings on open sores, and now she was just stuck in the corner of her room. She never saw anyone, and if that happened to him, he'd be cranky too. She said all she could do now was just sit in a chair all day, day after day. She asked him how he would be.

"My friends and I talked and decided that we should be able to help her—to bring out the person she used to be. We figured she needed to be around people more, but most of the remaining people were also housebound. Maybe we could find something for her to do, so she wouldn't be so bored.

"It took us a while, but we thought of something to try. First, we would take her, in her chair, outside the door where it was shady all day; we'd do the same with the other folks as they were able. We would go from person to person each day and share everyone's news. Then we would tell her what we knew about the other folks, what they were dealing with, and ask her if she had something we could tell the others. We asked, Would she like to do this every day? She huffed but said she'd try.

"It was a wonderful experience! Every morning after midmorning surveillance, we'd stop by her home take her outside, and she'd tell us what to tell the other shut-ins. In the afternoon, we would stop back, when it was time for her to go back inside, and tell her what the others were doing or thinking. Each time we went from person to person and told them what everyone was saying, their eyes would light up. Soon, we found ourselves in the middle of a messenger service. It seemed to raise everyone's spirits. Did anyone notice anything when you returned?" he asked.

Mary said, "We did. I believe I know who the woman was who was so cranky. Shortly after we returned, she told us what you'd done and that we needed to get the young girls to take messages to the others who were homebound. She even told us what time of day this should happen and how it should happen. It was a great idea. My friend Miriam is the one who organized the girls. We still do it!"

Yannis smiled and continued, "When all of you arrived back in Nazareth, you organized a town dinner in your town square, and you invited the four of us to attend. It was a great meal!

"I was seated at the table with Joseph and his family and really felt welcome. After we had eaten and were just sitting around talking, this very young man, Simon, looked at me and said, 'Do you know Father God?' I asked what His name was, and this kid tells me that the name is too holy and they can only say it in their hearts! I told him that I had many gods, and he asked me what happens if they disagree on something—like whether it should rain or not.

"I looked at Joseph, and he had a grin on his face and nodded at me, so I told Simon I didn't know—that we asked a god for what we wanted. If we got it, we were happy; if we didn't, it was like, oh well. Then this young kid tells me that Father God was the one true God and could do everything those gods said they could do and a lot more.

"I asked him how I could find out which of us was right, and he said, 'Just ask Father God.' I thought, *Just ask?* I asked Simon how his God would answer me. Would there be this booming voice? And this little kid tells me that I'll just know. I might be walking or working or something, and I would know.

"What a kid. But he didn't stop there. He asked if we could be friends, and I said sure. And this kid tells me we have a contract, and we need to shake hands on it like the men do. We did, and then I grabbed him in a great big hug!

"Now this young kid is this awesome young man. And if I may say so, I think he will soon be a father himself!" Yannis said with a grin.

Simon smiled and nodded.

"That's not the end of my story. When I returned home, things were harder than when I'd left. The money and the food I brought with me helped for several days, but I still could not find work. I became frustrated that I was not supporting my family in the way I should. One day, I told my wife I would go get wood instead of her going. I wanted to get away and do some thinking, so I walked quite far from home. As I was picking up wood, I began thinking about Nazareth and the young man who seemed to know so much.

"I dropped to my knees and I said, 'Father God, that young boy told me You are real. I need a real God. Please tell me if You are the only God. I have tried so hard to take care of my family, but as hard as I try, I can't find work. Father God, I need You to be the one true God. I need You. Please help me!' I then sat quietly. As I sat, I had this feeling of peace come over me. It stayed and stayed with me. I couldn't move. I couldn't open my eyes. I just stayed there feeling that I was completely safe. At that point, I knew that little Simon was right. At that moment, I knew that Father God was the one true God. And I knew I wanted to tell my family and everyone else I knew. I was so filled with joy and confidence.

"Did I have work waiting for me when I reached home? No. Did my family believe me? I think they wanted to, so I did kind of what Simon did. I told them that, as patriarch of this family, I wanted every one of them to, once a day for one week, ask Father God if He was real. I don't like saying, 'I'm the father, and you need to obey me.' But to me, this was far too important to leave any room for someone to not know Father God.

"We are now a family who loves and trusts our Father God. I am so blessed! We are so blessed!

"A few months later, a man came to the village and asked for me. He told me my uncle had died, and I was his only living relative. He left me a small house and quite a bit of land. He had been a leather maker, and his business would also be mine. We would need to move about five miles away. I hurriedly spoke with my wife, and we decided to accept and move.

"Two things about this—I didn't know I had an uncle. Also, when I was young, the training job I had as a young man was working in leather! Uncle had a man who had worked with him for many years. I asked him to stay and work with me. I also asked him to teach me. He agreed, and we have been working together now for more than six years.

"Thank you, Simon, for your challenge. Thank you for telling me about Father God. Oh, I should tell you that we now have a small group of people who get together every Sabbath, and we have an ancient rabbi who is guiding us. I need to stop talking and let all of you talk. But I can never say thank you enough for leading me and my family to Father God."

Simon stood up and clasped Yannis in a huge hug. Then he hugged Yannis's five sons. When he got to Yannis's wife, he waited a bit, but she shyly hugged him and whispered, "Thank you," in his ear.

A lot of grinning and then laughing were shared all around.

"Wait a minute! I almost forgot to tell all of you," Yannis said, beaming. "My two oldest sons are both bar mitzvahs, and the next two are studying and will be bar mitzvahs—one late next year and one in just a couple months!"

Later, Jesus found himself alone with the two "almost-bar-mitzvah" boys. He told them, "It's good to be a bar mitzvah. What kind of men will you be?"

The older one said, "I want to be an honest businessman. I'm thinking of doing masonry work. You know, a year ago, I had a whole bunch of questions about being a bar mitzvah. But as I'm getting closer, I feel more like I am being honored."

"You are being honored," said Jesus. "In my years of teaching, I have tried to impress on my boys the responsibilities. But more than that, I want them to know that, if they follow what they have learned and what they have promised, life will be a lot smoother for them. They will always have someone to talk with, even through the worst problems they face. It's probably one of the most important things we can learn. Life will not be perfect; that will be when we live with Father God. But putting Him in charge of our lives and letting Him work with us is very freeing. Do you understand what I'm saying?"

"I do. But nobody told me like that. It makes sense. I'll try to always remember. Thank you, Rabbi Jesus. Thank you for taking the time to talk to us."

"It is truly my pleasure. I want to always have time for everyone, especially youngsters." He turned to the younger boy. "What are you thinking, young man?"

"I think you are someone very important, and I don't know why. I know you are a rabbi but ... I don't know how to say it ... I feel you are more and that someday I'll look back at this time."

"I promise you that I too will always look back on our conversation today," replied Jesus. "If I can help you with something, you just have to tell me what it is."

The boy hesitated.

Jesus waited.

"Well, I don't know how Father God can do all He does. I mean people, animals, trees, grass, weather, everything. How does He have the time?" the younger boy asked.

"That is a very adult question. I think almost everyone asks that question. Let me see if I can give you an idea—just an idea. When you see a lamb or a goat, all they do all day is eat and sleep and run, and that keeps them very busy. They look at us and think, *How can they do all that?* That's a little of what it's like. What we do all day long is like what the sheep and the lambs do when we look at all that Father God does. He is so much more than we can even understand. That's where faith comes in. Faith is trusting that Father God knows what He's doing. Understand?"

"We are to what Father God does as the sheep are to what we do. That's pretty grown-up talk, but I'll remember it. I think I only understand a little right now, but I'm sure when I really think about it, it'll help me with my life. Thank you, Rabbi Jesus."

"Maybe this will help you a little bit more. A thousand of our years are like one day to Father God. Does that help?"

Yannis walked over to them. "Jesus, are these two talking your ears off?"

"No, Yannis. It has been my pleasure to speak with them. Children are so open and honest. They reawaken thoughts that I hadn't thought of in a long time." Jesus turned to the boys. "I pray we will see each other every time we all come to Jerusalem for celebrations. I look forward to hearing more as you both grow. Stay always with our Father God."

"We will!" the boys replied as they went with Yannis.

The younger one turned around and waved.

FIFTY-ONE

28

Monday morning about the second hour, two men came asking for Rabbi Jesus.

"I am he," replied Jesus. As he turned around, he recognized one of the men. "Zebedee! I'm glad to see you again!"

The two men clasped hands and hugged.

"How's the fishing business?"

"I'm glad you remember me. I was hoping for just this kind of surprise!" said Zebedee. "The fishing is great. Thank you for asking."

The younger man said, "I see you were right Zebedee. He did remember you." Turning to Jesus he said, "I am Rabbi Thaddeaus of Capernaum. Zebedee is an elder in our synagogue."

"I am so glad to meet you. I'm looking forward to spending some time with you—at your convenience of course," replied Jesus.

"We had hoped to meet with you earlier on our trip, but there was an emergency within our group, and we were needed there. Everything is fine now. I know this is last minute, but would you have time to meet with us now? And then come with us to meet our people and have lunch with us?" asked Rabbi Thaddeaus.

"That's fine. Zebedee, I see the family is trying not to interrupt us, but little Leah has broken free and is heading straight for you!"

Leah ran into Zebedee's arms and held on tight.

"Miss Leah," said Zebedee, "I am very glad to see you again. We men need to talk for just a couple of minutes. Could you be very quiet while I hold you and we talk?"

"Sure. I can be very quiet. When Benjamin is sleeping, Mother tells me to be the quietest person in the whole world," chattered Leah.

"That's a good girl. Now be very quiet for just a minute," Zebedee said. Turning to the men, he said, "Now where were we?"

While the men talked, Leah played with Zebedee's ears, beard, eyes, and hair. But, she did not talk!

Jesus said, "There is a quiet shady place where my family and I met friends yesterday. It's not far. Let's meet there. Do you have a minute to meet my family?"

"That place will be fine. Please tell your families that I would like to meet with them before we all leave for home," replied Thaddeaus.

"Rabbi Thaddeaus, would it be all right with you if I stayed here with the family while the two of you talk?" asked Zebedee.

"Of course. Thank you for coming with me today. We'll return here in just a little while," answered Thaddeaus.

The two rabbis walked over to the area where the family had met with Yannis and his family, found relatively flat rocks, and sat down to talk.

"This is a beautiful spot," said Thaddeaus.

He began, "Capernaum is a town a little larger than Nazareth. It lies on the northwestern shore of the Sea of Galilee. It's a beautiful place. Let me tell you a little about our people. A lot of our men are fishermen and are sometimes on the lake for more than a day at a time—sometimes several days. This leaves extra work for many of the women because they must act as both father and mother while the men are gone, and then they must become women only when the men are home. Most families have been here for generations, so for most of the families, this is not a hardship. I just wanted to tell you this as background.

"Our school is a bit larger than the one in Nazareth but not too much larger. We currently have twenty-seven boys under the age of becoming a bar mitzvah and another eighteen boys in the upper grades. We teach from the Torah and the Prophets. We are very fortunate to have another rabbi serving and teaching with us, so we are able to spend the time with each boy as he requires. There is an area outdoors where we encourage the boys to actively play a short time during the school day. We feel it's important to have them get exercise for their bodies, as well as for their minds.

"My father has served as the administrative rabbi for many years. He's been grooming me to take over for him. However, he died suddenly almost two months ago, and it is felt that, although I am twenty years old, I should have about two more years before assuming that position. I agree. That is why we sought someone to come in for about two years—until I can take over as administrator.

"We were concerned that, because it would only be about two years, we wouldn't be able to find someone who would take the position. Talking with the priests in Jerusalem, several of them mentioned that you would be the right person to take the position. When we heard that you had accepted, we were delighted!

"One of my concerns has been our interaction—yours and mine. I have been training with my father, and I must continue training so that I am able to take over. Yet I know that you are in charge of things, and I need to always be aware of that. And I accept that also. I've thought long and hard about that and I think I can do it—providing you're able to forgive me when I step out of bounds from time to time.

"I think that's what I wanted to say. I would appreciate it if you would tell me what you're thinking—the good and the bad. I think that will be the best way for us to work together."

Jesus smiled. "I was told that you are a very capable and knowledgeable young man, and you have certainly lived up to that. A little about me—I like to teach. When I teach, I look in the boys' eyes. I need to see that they understand. If they don't, I make a special effort to meet them someplace—maybe at the market—and try to say something that will help them understand, without them realizing what I'm doing. I love the Torah and the book of the Prophets. It fills me with love when I see the boys struggling with something, and then finally understanding.

"I'm assuming that I will be doing some teaching. Correct? It won't be all administration?" asked Jesus.

"We were hoping you'd say that. Yes, we would very much like to depend on you to teach. In fact, when I met with the other rabbi—Rabbi Sylvanus—we agreed that you may teach whatever grades you want to teach."

"Thank you! I love teaching every grade, but if I have to pick a favorite it would be the older boys—the ones preparing to become a bar mitzvah."

Thaddeaus grinned from ear to ear. "We were hoping you'd say that. Father taught that age and did such a wonderful job. However, I will need to learn your way. I never did work with father in the classroom. We were going to begin that part of my training when my father passed so I'll need to learn from you. Do you have other questions? Or should we greet your family and then move to have lunch with our rowdy bunch? Oh, a warning—fishermen don't always use the best language. Sometimes their expletives are a bit raw."

Jesus grinned. The two rabbis headed back to the families. Jesus gave a quick introduction to his family. He said, "Family this is Rabbi Thaddeaus. Rabbi, this is my mother, Mary, and these are my brothers and sisters and their families."

To the families, Jesus said, "We'll try to make time for all of us to get together with Rabbi Thaddeaus and his people in the next day or two, but for right now, I need to go with him. Mother, I will have lunch today with the Capernaum congregation so I'll see you later." Jesus kissed his mother on the cheek and waved to the families as he left with Thaddeaus.

Suddenly, there was a huge crash and a lot of screaming from a group to the south of them. Jesus and his brothers left what they were doing and began running toward the ruckus. Jesus called to Thaddeaus, "Come!"

As they reached the scene, they saw a cart that had apparently fallen from the top of the hill and landed on the group sitting there. Several people were hurt. Two older men were moving the cart away from the area.

Jesus and his brothers began examining the injured. Jesus was looking at a small girl who had simply been knocked down and had a few scratches. He looked in her eyes, smiled, and told her she was very brave and would be just fine.

James called, "Jesus! Come here!"

Jesus ran. "What is it?" he asked. There appeared to be blood around a man's head.

As Jesus examined him, James said, "He was directly under one of the wheels of the cart when it landed. He doesn't look good at all."

Jesus held the man's head, James rubbed the man's arm, and Jesus said, "Father God, please heal this man."

The man started to come around.

Jesus heard Joses call him. James told him to go. He'd stay with the man.

As Jesus reached Joses, he saw that a young man looked like he had several broken bones. He was not responding, but his arms and legs were lying at slightly strange angles. A man was standing with Joses, and he said, "Never mind this kid. He's nothin' but constant trouble for everyone. If it weren't for him, this wouldn't have happened."

Jesus smiled at the man and said, "I'm sorry about that. We need to heal his body right now. Then it will give you folks time to work on his soul. Understand?"

"When you put it like that, okay. But … ack," the man said and walked off.

Joses had already begun to try to straighten the young man's limbs. "Let's pray as we work. Father God, we've been told that this young man is a troubled soul. We ask that You heal him now and then send someone to help him to become the man You know he can be."

As they finished straightening the limbs, the young man stirred. He looked up at Jesus and Joses almost in terror and began to fight them off.

"Easy!" said Jesus. "You've been badly hurt, and we've asked Father God to heal you. You need to stay quiet for a while."

At that point, a woman ran over. "Now what have you done? Can you ever even pretend that you are a human being? Must you always be the cause of trouble?"

Jesus started to answer her, but Judas called him. He looked at Joses, and Joses nodded that he would stay and talk with the boy and his mother.

"What on earth?" said Jesus.

As he came up to Judas, he saw a disheveled elderly man rubbing his head and asking where his bed was, as he was tired. He was holding the hand of a boy about three. The boy had large red spots on his face and neck and arms.

Jesus and Judas smiled to each other. Judas took the man's hand and led him off to where most of the village seemed to be standing. A young girl met them and said, "Grandfather, where did you go? I couldn't find you!" To Judas, she said, "My grandfather is a little off in his head. He's a good man, and I take care of him. I went to see what happened, and then I couldn't find him or my brother. Have you seen my brother? He's kinda little."

"I have," said Judas. "Is there someone we can leave your grandfather with so I can take you to your brother?"

"No. It's just me," she replied.

"Then let's all go together."

Thaddeaus had gone over to where Jesus was, and the two were looking at the spots on the boy. As his sister came up to them, she said, "Did you have nuts again? Where did you get them?"

"Grandfather gave them to me," the boy said.

She turned to Jesus and Thaddeaus and said, "He always gets like this when he eats nuts. I hope when he's older he'll learn to say no." She looked more closely at her brother and said, "These are the most spots you've ever had!"

Jesus put his hand on her shoulder and told her, "Let's see what we can do about this. Will you help us?"

"I guess so. What do you want me to do?"

"You know Father God, don't you?"

"Yup! He can do anything, and He loves us and wants us to be good. That's why I try to take good care of Grandfather and Brother."

"That is very grown-up. Can you put your hand on Brother's hand and join us in praying for Brother?"

"Me? Really? I can help you big people pray?"

"It's extra special when children pray. Here, hold Brother's hand, and we'll put our hands on him too, and we'll pray.

"Father God, please heal this boy now and please remove this allergy from him. Father God, please strengthen this young girl. She is doing her best, and she trusts You. We know that is the best for her. Thank You."

Slowly the spots left, and the boy said, "Hey! I'm not itchin'! Hey," he said to Jesus and Thaddeaus, "thank you for prayin' for me."

His sister said, "Wow! He got well. I'll remember that next time he has the spots, and I'll pray that Father God takes them away."

Some of the villagers had been away from their camp and were now returning. After a lot of discussion, it turns out that what had happened was that the troubled boy had been goading three other boys into helping him get the cart to the top of the hill. When they reached the top, he ordered the boys to get in and ride it down. He got angry with the boys for refusing and kicked the front axle, and that sent him and the cart down the hill, landing on top of those sitting beneath.

The injured were all being attended to now, so Jesus, his brothers, and Thaddeaus returned to Jesus's family.

As they were walking, Thaddeus asked, "Rabbi Jesus, what just happened?"

"We heard the commotion, and we ran to help. You never know if you're needed or not, but we feel it's important to respond just in case. It's what we do," explained Jesus.

"I saw that, and I was amazed at what looked like the usual quick response by all of you. But what I'm asking is about the people all of you helped. How did you heal those people?"

"We didn't heal anyone. Father God does the healing. We've always done this. When someone needs help, we try to put our hands on him or her and ask Father God to heal them. You still look confused. Please, ask all the questions you want," said Jesus.

Thaddeaus turned to Jesus's brothers. "Can you help me understand?"

They looked confused as well. James said, "It's what we've always done. We just call to each other and run and pray. Father God is always near everyone."

"Can anyone do this? I mean—I don't know. I feel I've just seen something like a miracle—several miracles. I guess I need to think about this a while. Can we talk about this later?"

"Sure. Oh! Here comes Leah and the rest of the little ones right behind her. Prepare to scoop them up!"

As they returned to the families they could see that Zebedee was the center of attention. Rabbi Thaddeaus shook his head and said, "That is just like Zebedee. Children are drawn to him. Yet, see how he's playing with the children and still carrying on a conversation with the adults? How he does that I have no idea. Look! Now he's even chasing the children and still talking with the women. He is a wonder!"

The brothers would fill the families in on what had happened. Zebedee turned to Rabbi Thaddeaus and said, "Would you mind, Rabbi, if I stayed here a while with these friends? I promise to return by the evening meal."

"Of course. You all seem to be having a great time together."

Later as Jesus and Thaddeaus were walking to the Capernaum camp, Thaddeaus said, "Can we talk as we walk? I'd like to hear about each person who was healed. I would like you to tell me how each was healed. I really don't understand what I saw."

"Before we talk about them, let me ask a question of you. What did you do when you reached the sight of the accident?"

"Let's see. As I was running to the site, I asked Father God to take charge of the situation, whatever it might be, and to give help as needed. I prayed hard. When we got there, I saw a woman with a small baby, and the woman was hysterical. I went over to her, placed a hand on her shoulder, and asked if she and the baby were hurt. She said no, so I asked her to please stop crying because it was scaring her baby and that wasn't good for him. She looked at me and stopped crying, and she and the baby walked off. I don't think she was very happy with me."

Jesus smiled. "And then?"

"An older woman waved at me to come to her. She asked me to pick up a little one—maybe about a year old—and bring him to her. She couldn't walk, and the baby had crawled off. I did, and the baby was giggling and cooing, and that little guy tugged on my beard! The little rascal!

"The woman didn't look very comfortable, so I asked if she needed help. She said she sits on a cushion. But as she was trying to reach the baby, she wrinkled the cushion, and now it was knotted under her. I fixed it. She asked Father God to bless me.

"Next I found two sticks that looked like walking sticks, but I didn't see anyone around who might need them so I called out and asked if anyone needed help. A man had tripped and fallen down a small hill and landed under a fig tree, so he was hard to see. I took the sticks to him, and he told me that he was 'too old for this nonsense.' He said, 'I know I'm not supposed to rush, but I'm so nosey, I just had to hurry and see what happened. Well, I guess I didn't get to see, did I?' I helped him up, and he also asked Father God to bless me.

"I could see you and your brothers helping others, but there were others who I felt I could help. When I saw you go to the older man and the boy with spots, I felt I could come to where you were. I think that's all."

Jesus said, "Did you just listen to yourself? Think about it. You prayed hard on the way over there and Father God used you to help so many people. You were doing His work. You were doing His healing. Can you understand this? It's important that you do and that you recognize when Father God works through you. You too are a healer. All you need to do is pray constantly and then do what He directs you to do."

Thaddeaus stopped and turned to face Jesus and said, "The priests were right. You are the best teacher for me before I take over the administration of the school. I still have a lot to learn." Touching Jesus's shoulder, he said, "Father God, thank You for bringing us together."

FIFTY-TWO

28

The youngsters from the people of Capernaum ran to meet them. However as they approached the men, they looked toward the two rabbis and held back a little. *Just like kids all over*, thought Jesus. They did, however, accompany the men as they walked to join the others.

The entire group from Capernaum gathered around the two rabbis. Thaddeaus raised his hand to get their attention and said, "Everyone! Meet Rabbi Jesus. As you know, he will be with us for about two years. I was told that he was a good man. But let me tell you, I have already learned some amazing things from him. I promised him some lunch, so let's eat. And then you can all come and introduce yourselves—except you Peter. I know there is no way you'll wait, so come on over."

Jesus saw the man coming toward him. Peter was a solid man, a man of strength. "Hello, Rabbi. I am Peter, a fisherman of Capernaum, and I welcome you on behalf of all the good people and even the rascals of our town. Welcome." The man was a few years older than Jesus, but there was so much in his eyes. Jesus saw sadness, deep love, caring, and so much more.

Jesus reached his hand out and somehow knew he had just met not just a good man, but also a man who would be a good friend. The two looked into each other's eyes and seemed to know—this was meant to be.

What a wonderful group of people! They greeted Jesus as though he were an old friend. Jesus felt at home and comfortable among them. Things went very well. Lunch was delicious, children were noisy, and everyone laughed and talked. Sometimes it seemed like they all laughed and talked at the same time. *Just like home*, Jesus thought.

Jesus turned to Thaddeaus and said, "Is everyone here or are some doing something else? The reason I ask is because, as we were walking up to the group, I saw so many carts I thought the group would be maybe two or three times this size."

"That's Zebedee in action. He's a great man and a great asset to our synagogue. He thinks that no one should have to walk all the way from Capernaum to Jerusalem, so he ordered these carts about four years ago so we could all ride. They've cut our traveling time in half. We have so much to thank him for.

"Speaking of Zebedee, here come his two sons. I should warn you that they are a little tenacious! They love their Father God and feel that they're going to make sure that everyone else does. Sometimes, they're just plain overwhelming," Thaddeaus said as he was called away by one of his men.

As they approached, Jesus could see that, although they strongly resembled each other, there was quite an age gap. The older was probably about Jesus's age, but the younger was probably not yet a bar mitzvah?

The older one put out his hand and said, "Rabbi Jesus. I am James son of Zebedee, fisherman of Capernaum. This is my brother, John. He will be a bar mitzvah in about a year. You will be teaching him. Before you do, I would like to have a talk with you. We love Father God, and I need to know that you will be teaching him what is right not some ramblings."

"It's good to meet you, James, and you too, John." Turning to James, he said, "James, I don't think I have ever been introduced so wonderfully. I look forward to talking with you at the first minute possible. Perhaps the day after we arrive in Capernaum? Depending of course on your schedule."

"Fine. I'll check with Father and get back to you before we arrive home." He turned to John and said, "What would you like to say to the rabbi, John."

John looked Jesus right in the eyes. Jesus saw kindness. "Rabbi Jesus, I love Father God, and I've been studying hard. I would like you to talk with my brother, please. It is very important to me that I have the right schooling."

"Thank you. I promise you that you will have the right schooling. Tell me. What do you especially like studying in school?"

"The prophets! Father God worked with them and through them. It seems that each person He worked with, He worked with in a different way. They did His will. Can you imagine?! Doing the will of Father God? What must that be like? I don't think I can ever imagine it. But I feel that, if I just keep studying, I will someday be able to understand."

"You're a young man who is very wise beyond his years. It will be a blessing for me to have you in my class. I am honored to have met both of you."

Just then, Zebedee arrived. "I see you've met my two rascals, Jesus. Don't let them turn you away from the rest of our town. The rest of us have good manners," he said as he looked sternly at his sons.

"Hello again, Zebedee. I've enjoyed meeting them. To be truthful, I've never met anyone quite like either of them. I appreciate the honesty you have given them. In my mind, they're fine young men." Jesus watched as Zebedee and his sons tussled for a few seconds. *A strong family*, he thought.

"Rabbi Thaddeaus has been called to a rural area near our town for an emergency. I'm afraid he's left you in my care," Zebedee kidded. "Tomorrow we move out. I'll place your things in our cart. It's just the three of us, but the townspeople have decided that they want you to spend some time in each cart. That way, everyone can get to know you. I hope that's okay with you."

"That sounds like a good idea. I'll return to my family now and be here by sunup tomorrow." Jesus shook hands with Zebedee and his sons, waved to the rest of the group, and returned to spend the last night for a while with his family.

As he was walking, he thought about all that had happened since he'd met Rabbi Thaddeaus. Thaddeaus himself, Zebedee and his firm-speaking sons, Peter and his eyes of love and sadness, and the wonderful people of Capernaum who would be his family for the next two years.

"Father God, You have so blessed me. I can feel Your love and support through all of this. Thank You for guiding me here. I think about Mother and all our families and how I'm going to miss them. Take care of them for me. I know I'll see them at festival times here in Jerusalem, and that will be a blessing. So many people move and never see their families again. I thank You that I'll continue to see mine. Please bless my work and help me to show Your love. I love You, Father God. Amen."

Leah was the first to meet him as he neared the camp. "Uncle Jesus! We've been waiting for you. Grandma Mary said we can't eat until you get here, and I'm starved. I haven't had anything to eat since snacks this afternoon!"

Jesus held her hand, and as the younger children ran up, he tousled their hair and then picked up and carried the youngest two. As they reached the families, Jesus went to Mary and said, "Mother, you are my very favorite mother!" He put down the children and gave her a hug and a kiss on her cheek.

Leah said, "Grandmother Mary said we can eat when Jesus gets here. He's here, so can we eat? I'm hungry!"

James came up to her, bent down, and quietly said to her, "That wasn't very good manners. It would be best if you allowed the big people to make the decisions. Okay?"

"Okay, Father. I'm sorry. I'm just hungry."

"It's fine this time. This is just a time of learning for you. Remember how we've talked about your learning things as you grow up to be a big person?

"Yup! Now can we eat?"

After dinner, Jesus walked through the camp to visit with the people he'd known all his life. He wanted to talk with each one and to remember them as they were now. There were so many memories. He kept reminding himself that he would be seeing them again at festival days here in Jerusalem. Yet this felt like a time of growing apart for him. It felt like starting a whole new life.

Jesus joined his family as they were settling down for the evening.

Judas said, "This is going to be the last time we'll have Family Time with Jesus for a while, so how about if we make it special? I was thinking of making a fire, and we'll all just sit around it. We could bring out some of the children's beds—especially for the younger children—and we could just sing and then talk about whatever."

They soon had a blazing fire going, and James chuckled and said, "We can't see much of each other around the fire, as it's flaming like this. It's a good thing it'll burn down in a short time."

Jesus settled with his arm around Mary. He looked around at his brothers and sisters and their families and felt so at peace. *Thank you, Father God, for everything. I am so blessed,* he prayed silently.

It was quiet—as if everyone was content. Anna started weeping.

"Anna! What is the matter, sweetheart? Are you feeling all right?" asked Mary.

"It's just really happening. I don't know what, Mother. It's like my biggest brother won't be here, and it's like I never really paid much attention to him or to any of my big brothers because they seemed so old. But now I feel like I missed so much and that I was really so selfish all those years, and now there's nothing I can do about it," sobbed Anna.

"Anna," said Timaeus. "May I tell them? I know it's early, but I think it's time."

Anna nodded, crying into Timaeus's shoulder.

"I think this might be a little of what Anna is dealing with. We are with child. When we see you again, Jesus, we will have another child for you to hold."

Jesus walked over to his youngest sister, stood her up, and said, "You've been the very best annoying little sister in the world. I want you to know that all littlest sisters are like that. And like you, most of them grow out of it. I love you just the way you are, and I love you even better for the woman you are becoming. Carry that love with you wherever you go. Feel better?"

Anna nodded and held Jesus for a minute. The family now wanted to talk about the new baby who would come into the family. They shared another joyous, wonderful Family Time!

FIFTY-THREE

28

Jesus checked his boxes, slipped them into the sacks, and
tied them across the back of the donkey, before leaving the next
morning. It was going to be a sunny but cool morning with a
slight breeze. *It'll be a good day for traveling*, he thought. As he
walked, he did as he always did; he talked with Father God.
He talked about his family, his many friends and neighbors
in Nazareth, and what was coming up in this new part of his
life. "Father God, with You with me every step of the way, I'll
be able to do Your will. When I fail, please don't let anyone
else get hurt. Please help me to see what others need and help
them to find it. Especially help me as I teach these young men.
I thank You, Father God. I thank You for always being here for
me. Amen."

As he neared the people of Capernaum, young John walked
out to meet him. "Good morning, Rabbi Jesus." He held out his
hand, and Jesus shook hands with him. "Father said I should
greet you and bring you to breakfast with us this morning.
I would like to tell you that I think I will like having you as
my teacher. James and I talked for a while last night, and he
thought he was pretty sure too but wanted to talk to you some
more."

"Good morning to you also, John. Thank you for coming
to walk with me. I like that. I'm glad that you're accepting me.
That is probably the most important thing a teacher can hear.

You said breakfast. Can you tell me what we'll be eating? Or do I need to wait and see?" replied Jesus.

"I don't know if it's a secret or not, but my father is a very good cook—especially for a man."

"Good because I'm a very good eater—especially for a man. Oh! I smell something wonderful!" said Jesus.

As they reached the camp, Zebedee and James came toward them. "Perfect timing!" said Zebedee. "Breakfast is ready. I hope you're hungry. These two eat enough for a dozen men, so I figured I'd make that much for you too. See? Already I'm treating you like a son. I like you Rabbi Jesus," Zebedee said with a firm smack on Jesus's back.

Zebedee was right. James and John were healthy eaters. But he'd have to be honest; he also ate well. As they finished eating, James and John went to make a final check to see that everything was ready for the cart to pull out. Zebedee said that, while he cleaned up and finished putting things away, he'd like to fill Jesus in on what had been planned for him on this trip to Capernaum.

"The whole bunch of us got together and came up with a plan we hope will be okay with you. It will take us perhaps a little more than three days to arrive home. There are twelve carts in our group. We've agreed to keep to a certain lineup. So what that means is we'd like you to meet with our families one on one—two families in the mornings and two more in the afternoons.

"This is how we see it happening. We are the back cart. You will spend the nights and breakfasts with us here. Then you'll walk up to the next cart for perhaps two hours and then move on to the next cart. This second cart will serve lunch. After lunch, go to the next cart for about two hours and then move to the next cart. They will serve dinner. After dinner, we gather in groups and mostly talk—or joke or kid each other. It's usually a nice gathering. Then you'll come back here and spend the night with us. Questions?"

Jesus felt his eyes had never been opened so wide. The town had planned for him to spend time with each family individually, and he was amazed. "That's a wonderful plan! It'll give me a good chance to know everyone. When you can, please tell everyone that I am thankful."

"I will. I guess it's time to leave. So you're off to the next cart, and we'll see you back here for the night. By the way, you are welcome to come back here at any time. You just may need the rest!" joked Zebedee.

Jesus felt good. *What a wonderful way to meet everyone! I'll have one-on-one time with each family! Right from the beginning, I'll get to know them.* "Father God, I thank You. I know that this is Your plan. Thank You. Thank You for being You."

The first cart was filled with a family that reminded him of his family when he was young—a couple with five small children. The youngest child appeared to be weakly. Although he appeared to be about a year old, he just lay where he was laid. After talking with the family for a while, Jesus asked if he might talk with the children, as they were already gathered with the adults.

He spoke directly to the children, asking them to tell him anything they wanted to tell him. The older ones hesitated. But the third child, a little girl, said, "I want to sit in the front of the cart by Father and not sit in the back!"

"Really? Why is that?" asked Jesus.

"Because."

"I don't think 'because' is very helpful. Would you tell me more?"

"There is no more. I just want to do what I want to do."

"Do you think everyone should do what they want to do?" asked Jesus.

"Yes!"

"Well, what would happen if Mother didn't want to make dinner for you to eat or didn't want to make clothes for you to wear? Then what?"

She just looked at him.

She shrugged her shoulders, leaned on her father, and said, "She won't."

The older boys told Jesus that they were thinking things like, "I'm happy to be outside all the time," "I like being with my friends all day," and "I like eating at night with everyone and not going to school to sit all day."

When Jesus asked the littlest girl, about three, she said, "I like this cart and my new tunic."

Jesus smiled at Father and Mother as they chuckled. "Tell me about the little one," he said.

The father picked up the child and walked toward Jesus. He said, "No one seems to know what's wrong with him. He sleeps and eats but doesn't appear to be interested in anything else. Would you like to hold him?"

"That's one of my favorite things to do—hold children." Jesus held the little boy. Cradling him, Jesus looked at the baby with love. "I think he is just a little behind where most children are. Father God loves this little one and is strengthening him as we speak. This little one will be fine."

The father said, "Thank you Rabbi. We haven't found anyone who knew what was wrong. For some reason, I believe you're right." He took his small son and kissed his forehead as he lay him down again. "It's time for you to leave for the next cart, Rabbi Jesus. Thank you for stopping here. I look forward to worshiping with you."

They shook hands, and Jesus moved to the next cart.

After being in the next cart for a few minutes, Jesus prayed silently, "Father God, give me patience and wisdom, please!"

Two elderly sisters rode in this cart. The oldest appeared to be very sure of herself, very sure that she knew best, and very sure that what she thought was right was the only thing that was right. The younger sister was extremely timid.

"You see, Rabbi. It's just Sister and me in this cart," said the older sister. "That is the way we want it. You'll notice that our cart has the responsibility of carrying many of the supplies that may be needed. There was a special area built in back to hold important things. Some are foods, and some are parts for carts that may fail—things like that. You see, Sister and I are trusted with all of these items."

The rest of his visit went about the same way. When it came time for lunch, the older sister placed a small piece of bread and some water in front of him. "We don't believe in overeating. We eat and keep to our business," he was told.

Jesus prayed.

After lunch, Jesus moved to the next cart. As he walked, he said, "Thank You, Father God, for being with me during that experience. We'll have to work on that situation, I think."

The days moved quickly. He met so many people. The front cart was Peter's. Peter greeted him with a warm handclasp. "Come! Come! We've been waiting to have our time with you. This is my wonderful wife and my loving mother-in-law!"

"I am pleased to meet you. Thank you for having me as a visitor."

And so began a long and wonderful visit. The three of them had a lot of questions for Jesus: What was his family like? What did Jesus like to do? What was he good at? And many more questions.

After a while, they talked about themselves. It seems that, when Peter married, he and his wife planned on having at least a dozen children! However, that was not to be. She hadn't been able to carry some of the babies, and the three who had survived hadn't lived more than a few months. They now tried to unobtrusively help as many people as possible.

"We understand that we can't give people money or goods, but we have been given a way of seeing that something is going on. And as we run across folks, we try to gently bring the conversation to a place where we can maybe say something that will help them. We know they will never really see that we helped them, but we don't care. We want to help others to be all they can be, just as all parents do for their children," Peter said while lovingly looking at his wife.

Dinner was a feast.

That night, as Jesus was lying down, he thought back on the past three days. He thought of how much it seemed these people were much like people everywhere. Some reminded him of his people in Nazareth. "I'm going to like it here, aren't I, Father God?" He smiled as he fell asleep. It was their final night of traveling.

FIFTY-FOUR

28

At breakfast the next morning, James said, "We'd better tell you something about our town that maybe you didn't have in Nazareth. We have some Gentiles living near the town, and they are a bit of a problem. They come into our shops and act like they're doing us a favor. Other than that, they mostly ignore us. On the street, their kids jeer at us, and if we need to go to one of their shops, we feel like we're being watched every second."

"Why is that?" asked Jesus.

"They don't know Father God," stated John.

"James. John. Please give a fair answer. There's no purpose in giving only your side of the differences," stated Zebedee.

"Thank you, Father. You see, they worship many gods, and I have tried and tried to tell them that they're wrong. I tell them there is only one God, and He is the true God. Will they listen? No! They tell me to keep to myself, and then they walk away. Now the children see me coming, and they point at me and laugh. One day, I offered the children some dried figs if they would sit with me and listen to me. Those little urchins grabbed the figs and took off! I wanted to grab those kids and give them a good shake, but I remembered we need to show love, so I walked away."

Jesus asked, "Have any of them tried to tell you about their gods?"

"No! If they look like they're going to start, I just tell them I don't want to hear it, and I walk off," explained James.

"Do you understand what they might want to tell you? I mean do you really know their beliefs?" asked Jesus.

"I don't want to! Why would I want to know about that? I know the truth and that's what they need to hear!" stated James very emphatically.

"I see," said Jesus. He turned to Zebedee and said, "May I have another piece of that wonderful bread? It's about the best I've ever tasted." Jesus thought that it would be better to continue this conversation at another time—a time when Jesus knew James and the Gentiles a bit better.

The feeling among the entire Capernaum group was excitement! As they rode closer to home, there was really no way to keep the children inside the carts. About a mile before reaching home, the group stopped for lunch. Everyone ate together as a group. The time spent on the meal was short, and soon they were on their way again.

As they approached Capernaum, Jesus looked over his new, although temporary, home. He immediately saw the synagogue! It stood elevated near the lake. It was made of basalt rock, and it stood solid. The building was not beautiful in the usual way, but it showed strength and confidence—and safety. It was a building where you would seek comfort, hope, and friendship—a building meant to serve our Father God. "Father God, Thank You for bringing me here. Thank You for trusting me. I feel so full—full of Your love and full of hope. Thank You, Father God. Thank You!"

Zebedee leaned toward him and said, "What is your first impression of our little town?"

Jesus shook his head a little and said, "I don't know. I've only looked at the synagogue and it's—I don't have words. It's, it's like a synagogue should be—strong and welcoming. I have a good feeling about it."

Jesus looked over the town as they drew closer. As with most towns at the times of festivals, there weren't many people left in town. But that changed quickly. First the older children and then the younger children were allowed to run ahead to their own homes, many to see a grandparent. There was a lot of whooping and hollering. Home!

Zebedee said, "We'll drop you off at your quarters before we return home. See the small house to the right of the synagogue? There are separate quarters for three rabbis to stay and still have private space. Currently, there is just one other rabbi living there.

"The school is attached at the rear of the synagogue. There's a wide area behind the school that's a recreation area for the children and some of the men of the town. Right, Sons?" He laughed.

"A bunch of us guys meet there and work off some steam by playing games in competition with each other. It has to be fair. No cheating! We try to remember that we're Father God's people even in play," said John as he nudged his brother.

As they moved Jesus's boxes into the home, Zebedee told Jesus, "There is a woman who brings our rabbis their morning and evening meals. She will also do the heavy cleaning. You are asked to pick up after yourself and clean up after meals. She's a widow and lives close to the synagogue. She's been with us for several years now and is a really good cook.

"If you need anything, just tell her, and she'll see that you have it. Don't be afraid to ask. We want you to be comfortable and feel at home. Anything else we can do for you before we leave?" asked Zebedee.

"Father," said John, "may I stay and walk him through the synagogue and school? I've studied our history, so I can show him a lot."

"Great idea, John. Be home before dinner."

Zebedee and James left for home.

"Rabbi Jesus, I think the most interesting thing about the synagogue is that a Roman centurion built it for our Jewish congregation. We can't say who he is though. He says he doesn't want the attention. I see him in town once in a while," John began.

John did a great job of showing Jesus around the synagogue. They both laughed when Jesus got turned around and couldn't figure out how to return. John then took him to see the school area. Jesus nodded to himself. "I think things will be fine here. It looks like they have adequate space and supplies. *Thank You, Father God.*

After John left, Jesus unpacked and settled down to read his daily reading from the Torah—the book of the Law. There was a small rap on the door, and a woman called, "May I come in? I have your dinner."

Jesus went to the door and found a delightful woman standing there with a tray of bread and soup and fruit for him. "Come in!" he said as he opened the door. "Thank you! Could you come in and sit for a few minutes so we can get to know each other?"

"I'd like that rabbi. But you must eat your soup while it's hot. I'll just sit at the table with you. My name is Eunice. Tell me about yourself," she said.

They talked as old friends for a long while. She had been a widow for almost twelve years and had served the church for more than ten. Her children were all grown and had their own families. "They all live within about forty miles, so I see them a few times a year. I am so blessed!" she said.

Jesus insisted on walking her home. "It's past sundown, and I would feel much better if I saw you home directly. Will you always be coming at this time?"

"Usually I return home just before sundown. But tonight my neighbor was having a little trouble, so I went to help her for a minute. She's fine now, but we try to watch out for each other," explained Eunice.

He returned to his new home, finished his reading, and began rearranging a few things. The first thing he found a place for was the sprang, and it looked perfect on his small table. *I may want to put it on my chair from time to time,* he thought. As he looked for a place to put the picture of his mother he thought, *I'll see if I can find a piece of glass to cover it. That should keep it safe.*

The next day, he walked through the school area looking to see what materials were available for the students. Things looked good to him. He walked around what would be his administrative area. A bench large enough to seat three or four boys was against one wall. Behind his desk and chair were a good many shelves for his papers. He was surprised that three Torahs and three copies of the Prophets were on the shelves! *More than one person at a time will be able to look up references. That should be good for the boys,* he thought.

He placed his lesson materials where they would be within easy reach. As he was finishing, he heard someone calling him. "I'm in the school, James. Come on in. Welcome. I was just settling in."

"I see that. I hope things will work well for you," said James. He and John shook hands with Jesus.

Jesus motioned for them to sit on the bench. "John, before you leave today, perhaps you could show me where the various classes meet and maybe tell me a little of how the day is spent. All right?" Jesus asked.

"I'll do that, Rabbi Jesus," said John eagerly.

"Well now, men, could we start by you telling me your concerns?"

And there began a wonderful two hours discussing the Law and the Prophets and of moving around the school. The three parted with the beginning of a good friendship.

It seems I met James's requirements, Jesus thought.

***

Rabbi Thaddeaus returned midafternoon. "Rabbi Jesus, I'm glad you were able to get settled in. I knew Zebedee and his boys would take good care of you. Things worked out better for me than I had hoped.

"One of our local farmers began treating his family and neighbors very harshly, and when he threatened to kill someone, they called for me. He's a good man, and this was not like him at all. I talked with everyone concerned and then talked with him. He said he felt funny and wanted everyone to just leave him alone. When I questioned him, he admitted he had sores on his legs. I looked, and there were huge sores— covering almost all of his lower legs—all red and draining fluid. We tried to reach the physician, but he was in Cana. I had seen legs like this before and started the treatment I had seen then.

"Not only for him but for the safety of the family, I felt I should stay there for a few days until he came around. We all prayed—he, his family, his neighbors, and I. I showed him how to continue to treat the sores, and this morning, I noticed a good amount of healing. Right now, he's very embarrassed about the way he behaved. The neighbors come to visit him as they can—to show that they understand. Today, a couple of the neighbors even got him to chuckle about some of the things he had done.

"Father God is so incredible! We all prayed again as I left. I feel confident that everyone will be fine now. It's amazing what pain and illness can do to a person."

That evening, the Sabbath began. Rabbi Thaddeaus led the service. A good many of the townspeople who Jesus already knew were there. It felt good that he could greet them with a personal comment or a question.

Jesus met Rabbi Sylvanus before service that evening. Sylvanus had been staying with his parents as they recovered from a severe case of a flu-like illness. He was a short, almost round man with the merriest eyes Jesus had ever seen. Jesus smiled as he shook the man's hand. "It is nice to meet you Rabbi Sylvanus. I look forward to working with you. Are your parents well?"

Sylvanus seemed to giggle. "Yes. Thank you for asking. They've both lost a lot of weight, but they seem to be much better now. I've looked forward to meeting you for a while now. Welcome!" answered Sylvanus.

After the Sabbath service, Jesus asked the two rabbis if they could meet before and after school the first day of the week. "I'd like to start every school day with the three of us in prayer. After school tomorrow, I'd also like us to meet so you can update me on our curriculum. Would that be difficult?"

"Oh no, Rabbi. We've always met every day before school started," replied Sylvanus.

"Have a blessed Sabbath then, Rabbis. I think I'll spend tomorrow walking through the town and getting acclimated," Jesus said as he waved goodnight and walked to his new home. "Thank You, Father God. I am so blessed!"

Sabbath morning was beautiful—full sun and a slight breeze from the south across the water. Jesus finished his morning studies and prayers and began his walk around the town. "A beautiful day, Father God. Thank You!" he prayed as he walked.

The lake was just a short walk, so he walked there first. It looked like a good many people had had the same idea. *Maybe this is how they spend their Sabbaths,* he thought.

Peter and his wife saw Jesus and called to him. "Good Sabbath, Rabbi Jesus!" called Peter. "It's good to see you!"

"Good Sabbath, Peter and wife of Peter. This is a beautiful place to spend some time."

"It is. I think it must be one of the best spots our Father God ever created. It always seems different and yet the same every time we come here—the same by the shape of things and people walking or sitting, but different in that the sky and the water change. I've never had the same feeling twice while being here—and I'm here every day. It's like it's new every time," explained Peter.

Peter's wife said, "If he could, I think he would live here. He fishes here every day except Sabbath. Yet on Sabbath, this is where he wants to be." She shook her head and said, "I love this man!"

Peter put his arm around her shoulders and said, "You are my special blessing."

Peter's wife turned to Peter and said, "Peter, maybe it would be a good thing to tell Rabbi Jesus what we were just talking about."

Peter thought and said, "I agree. I think it would be better if you told him, rather than I do. You know, it's easier for a woman to talk of things like this. We men are always looking for quick fixes."

Peter's wife nodded. "Rabbi, we're concerned about the sisters. They seem to be getting further and further away from the rest of us, and the older sister seems to be getting so angry—so … tight."

"I did see that on our trip. Could you fill me in on what you've seen?"

"Both sisters were always active, helping in our synagogue and in our town. About the time the oldest one became of marriage age, their father was drowned in a sudden storm on the sea. Their mother just seemed to stop living, so the oldest girl took charge of the family. It didn't seem that she really wanted to—it was more like, 'I'll show everyone that I can take charge, and we won't need help.' She did keep things going for the three of them, but it appeared that she was very hard on both her mother and her sister. Their mother has since passed, and it seems like the younger sister has just withdrawn from life.

"Peter and I were just saying that we wish we could think of a way to bring the older sister back to the vibrant young woman she was and to bring back some life into the younger one. She seems to have just given up doing anything but what she's told."

Jesus thought for a minute. "I don't have an answer. I'm very glad you confided in me. I'll pray daily for Father God to help us with this. Will you also pray?"

"We have been, Rabbi. When we noticed on the trip that things were worse between them, we began praying then. We'll continue. Ah! Here come James and John. Good Sabbath!" Peter called to them.

"Good Sabbath!" they returned.

Peter explained, "We need to return home. We're having an early lunch with mother today, and then the three of us are going to visit a homebound friend. Good Sabbath, all!" Peter and his wife waved as they moved off.

John began, "Rabbi Jesus, most of the older guys like you aren't here today, but a few of us are going to be playing a game we call Loop. Would you like to join us?"

Jesus said, "I would very much like to do that."

As they were walking toward the synagogue, Jesus said, "I've never heard of the game of Loop, so you'll need to teach me as though I'm a very young boy."

John giggled and said, "That's funny! You're a grown man, but I'll do my best."

Jesus looked at James, and they both smiled.

Five other young men were also walking toward the synagogue. Jesus could see by the kidding and camaraderie that they were longtime friends and probably longtime playing buddies.

The men formed two teams. Each team had three balls— balls that were larger than Jesus had seen before. About maybe ten feet up on a sturdy pole, Jesus saw a round loop much like the bands that hold barrels together.

John said, "We just form two lines, and we compete against each other. One side tries to get more balls in the loop than the other." He went on to explain the intricacies of the game.

James added, "Just because you're new to the game does not mean that you're going to be allowed to let your team down. You need to catch on quickly!"

At the end, Jesus was exhausted. "Thank you all!" he said as they ended their three-game challenge. "That felt good. I hope you'll ask me to play again." He turned to John and said, "I didn't do too bad a job, did I? At least we won two of the games!"

"I don't think you had much to do with us winning though. But you were okay for a beginner," replied John.

"Thanks for the vote of confidence. Give me a while; I'll do my best to do my best. And that's a promise I make to you, John."

As the players returned to their usual Sabbath routines, Jesus decided to do some more walking around the town. He felt it would be a good idea to locate the various shops he might need. He met several of the people he had met on the trip home from Jerusalem.

When he returned to his new home, he thought, *I've not been here more than a couple of days and I'm beginning to feel comfortable. Thank You Father God.*

FIFTY-FIVE

28

The next morning, the three rabbis met in Jesus's area of the school. "Good morning, rabbis," he said. "Let's open with prayer. Father God, please let everything we say and do be to Your glory. Amen."

He turned to Thaddeaus. "Thaddeaus, thank you for giving me your father's work plans. I studied his notes, and feel I'll be able to step in. Thank you.

"I would like these meetings of ours to be open. I'm thinking that I'd like to start by going through all our lesson plans. The reason I'm thinking this is I want the three of us to be sure we are not teaching the same thing or check to see that we might be missing something altogether. When I make a suggestion like this, I am asking for honest feedback. Please don't hold back when I ask for your opinion."

Thaddeaus thought for a bit and then said, "About a year ago, Father said something like this, but we never followed through. I think we should review our lesson plans. However, I would also like to go through all of them. Maybe that could work?"

"I too," said Rabbi Sylvanus. "We should be able to find a way for all of us to look over things. I think it could really be a fun thing to do."

Jesus smiled. "Thank you both. Let's think. There has to be a way we can all work together on this." They talked for a while and came up with what they thought would be the perfect plan. It turned out it was.

The process took four meetings, but each of the rabbis felt he had learned something by going through this process, and each one made suggestions for changes. It took only two more meetings to work out the how and when the changes would be implemented. The boys themselves would probably never notice the changes, but the rabbis felt the process had given them a clearer picture of where they were and where they wanted to go.

Meanwhile, Jesus opened his first class in the Capernaum school. "Good morning, men. I've met some of you, and I look forward to getting to know all of you. I understand that you are all within two or so years of becoming a bar mitzvah. That is very exciting to me.

"Each day, I ask that one of you opens with prayer. I'll leave it up to you to decide who opens each day. I'll open today. Father God, please open our hearts and minds to know You and to do Your will. Thank You.

"The purpose of this class will be to make sure you understand who is Father God and how do we know. This will be a class of study and a class of asking questions and then together searching scripture to find the answers. Don't hold back. The questions you have are very likely the questions we all have or that we will have in the future. Let's begin."

Classes went well for all three rabbis. Rabbi Sylvanus taught nine boys ages six, seven, and eight, with the help of three boys from the post–bar mitzvah students. Rabbi Thaddeaus taught nine boys ages nine and ten, with the help of four older boys who took turns as helpers. Rabbi Jesus taught nine boys from eleven until they became a bar mitzvah at thirteen or so. He also taught with the help of four older boys. This seemed to work well for everyone. Sometimes one wondered who learned more—the students, the helpers, or the rabbis.

The weeks went by quickly. One afternoon, one of the students asked Jesus, "Rabbi Jesus? May I ask you something?"

"Of course."

"As you've told us, I've checked our Torah, and I can't find an answer. So I want to ask you. Many of our prophets, like Elijah and Joseph and Moses, were filled with Father God's Holy Spirit so they could do special things. The question I have is—how were they chosen? And then, why them? And once they had the Holy Spirit, did they have it for life or just for that one task?" he asked.

"In all my years of teaching, and that is a lot of years, I have never been asked those questions in exactly that way," said Jesus. "I want to tell you that I'm glad you first searched scripture. Let's think about this." He paused. "I think what we are going to do is have the entire class work on your questions.

"Let's work in three groups—the oldest three will form one group, the youngest three another group, and the three remaining will form the third group.

"There are only about twenty minutes left of school today, so we'll spend that time in our three groups to make sure we understand the questions. Then tonight each of you has a special assignment—you are to spend at least one hour on your own, thinking and studying these questions. This is pretty important. So our history test for tomorrow will be put off for a day."

The boys cheered!

"Tomorrow after opening prayer, we'll meet in our groups and talk about what we've been thinking. One thing to remember—no one has a bad idea. We will listen carefully to each other, and there will be no putting down or laughing at someone for what he says.

"Let's pray. Father God, we as a class are going to be discussing some important questions about Your Holy Spirit. We ask that You guide each one of us that we might come to know You better. Thank You, Father God. Amen."

The boys started talking immediately. Jesus prayed silently, *Father God these are difficult questions for the Pharisees and Sadducees. Please guide these young boys in their search. Please help me to say and do the things that will help guide them. Thank You.*

The next morning, Jesus greeted the boys. "Good morning, young men. I'm looking forward to watching you work on these questions and seeing what conclusions you reach. Will one of you please open with prayer?"

One of the youngest of the boys began, "Father God, this is an interesting subject for us. We have learned that You lead us where we need to go. Please help us to know what to say. Thank You, Father God. Amen."

The boys set up their three discussion areas. "I'm here if you have questions," said Jesus. "I will ask how you are doing in a about twenty or thirty minutes. You may begin now."

The discussions began slowly, but soon all the boys were actively involved. Jesus waited half an hour to ask how things were going.

They all answered at once. "Great!" "Good!"

"Let's begin with the younger group. How are you progressing?"

"We started out by each of us saying what we were thinking and, if we could, how we had come to think that way. We all had to say our thoughts—even if it was the same idea someone else already said. I guess what we did next is that we looked at what our prophets did when they were filled with God's Holy Spirit. We looked at Moses, Elijah, and King David."

"Good," said Jesus. "Can you tell us what you decided?

"They all did what our Father God wanted done. But they all made big mistakes! Like Moses taking credit for the water that ran from the rock and like King David when he took someone else's wife and had the man killed," he explained.

"And look at Moses's brother Aaron, who built that golden calf!" added another boy.

"What did that tell you?" asked Jesus.

"That's where we were when you stopped us," said the boys together.

"You did a good job. Now let's hear from the next group."

"We first talked about what each one was thinking and then we tried to figure out what the Holy Spirit does and how he does it," said one of the boys.

"Did you come up with an answer?" asked Jesus.

"Kind of. We know that the Holy Spirit directs men and strengthens them to do what Father God wants done. But we couldn't figure out how the men knew. We were just discussing it, and we thought that, somehow, the Holy Spirit made them just know—kind of like, he put the thoughts in their heads, and they did it."

"That is very good also. Thank you," said Jesus. "Now our last group."

"We pretty much started like the others—sharing what we were thinking. But then we looked at what kind of men the Holy Spirit used to do Father God's work. They were all just ordinary men. They weren't priests or Pharisees or Sadducees or even scribes—just men. But from what we know, they were all close to Father God, and they were prayerful, kind men. That's about where we were when you called us."

"I am proud of all of you. This is an important subject, and you have all done very well. I think that now that you've heard what the others have been thinking, it may give you other ideas to help all of you answer those questions we are exploring. The questions are:

1. How were the men who were guided by the Holy Spirit chosen?
2. Why were they the ones chosen?
3. And did they have Father God's Holy Spirit for life?

"Let's take an hour and see what we come up with. Begin now."

Jesus noticed in the middle group that two of the boys had a history of rarely getting along; at times they were almost hostile to each other. Today they were working well together, trying to work through these questions.

"Everyone finished? Let's all return to our usual seats and discuss our ideas. Would someone please start?"

"I will, but our group talked about it and decided that we want to make sure that our conclusions aren't the only ones, so we want to hear everything the others decided even if it was the same. Is that okay?" said one of the middle boys.

"What do you think, class?" asked Jesus.

As one, they all agreed.

The first boy then opened the discussion. It was a good discussion. They were all interested in hearing and asking questions of the other groups. Eventually it seemed they had reached their conclusions. They all agreed:

1. Some of these men were chosen because they lived near the problem that needed addressing.
2. These men already knew Father God and depended on Him.
3. And these men were filled with Father God's Holy Spirit for life.

"I was just thinking; there might be a fourth thing we've learned," said one of the older boys. "Some of these men did some pretty bad stuff, but Father God still used them to do His will. I think we should remember that, as humans, we will sin. But when we truly repent, Father God will forgive us and still love us and help us."

"You are right. Let's make that the fourth item we've learned from this study."

One of the older boys suggested:

4. We all do wrong, but if we repent, Father God forgives us and will continue to be with us.

One of the youngest said, "I hope someday Father God will fill everyone with His Holy Spirit. I know I'd like to do things for Him."

"Maybe someday He will," said Jesus. He turned back to the class and said, "You've come up with answers we can now all live with. There may be more and deeper answers to these questions. We don't know. We need to remember that there are things that we will never know for sure until we begin our eternal life and can then ask Father God."

"Rabbi Jesus, my first question to Father God is gonna be, "'Why did my sister have to die?' She was so little, and I loved her a lot, but she died. Mother had three more babies, but they were all boys. I still miss my sister, so that's what I'm going to ask Father God first thing when I see Him."

"I am very sorry about your little sister. I can tell you that she is happy now, she is well, and she is with Father God," said Jesus. He turned to the others. "You've all done a great job with these questions. I've been teaching since I was about ten or eleven years old, and I can tell you that this is one of the best class discussions I've heard. Thank you all! Let's go outside now and let off some steam. You may leave now—quietly! I'll be right behind you."

Following the boys outside, Jesus prayed, *Thank You, Father God, for leading these young men to better understand You. Father God they must know You and all that You are. Please continue to guide them and please continue to give them the courage to ask the hard questions and then to find the answers. Thank You for being our God! Amen.*

***

At the rabbis' morning meeting about a week later, Thaddeus said, "I want to tell you about something that happened in class yesterday. The boys were studying Exodus 28—God's command for what is proper to wear in the synagogue. When they finished verse 28, one of the younger boys asked, 'Was that the first time men wore pants?'

"I answered, 'I don't really know. It might be.'

"'Well, did men just wear tunics before that?' he insisted.

"'I don't know that for sure either,' I told him. 'But I don't think that it's very important, do you?'

"So then the first boy said, 'I just want to know why—if they didn't wear them before, why did they have to start wearing them in the new temple?'

"One of the older boys said, 'Because the marble floors were shiny, and Father God didn't want to see what would be reflected on the floor.'

"The boys roared! I just rolled my eyes and said, 'Let's get back to our studies. Continue reading chapter 29.'"

Chuckling, Rabbi Sylvanus said, "Boys will be boys, won't they!"

FIFTY-SIX

28

After a few weeks of getting to know the town, Jesus wanted to see the area where the two main north-south and east-west highways intersected. He had heard that these roads were important to the local economy. The north-south road led from Tyre to Egypt, while the east-west road led from Syria to the Mediterranean Sea. Huge caravans traveled almost continually through this intersection. There weren't many towns for quite some distance, so the caravans would supply themselves with dried meat and fruit; water; and, of course, dried fish. It was also the place where taxes were collected.

Jesus was amazed at the number of people, the animals, the hubbub, and the noise. As he walked around, he would stop to talk with people who appeared to be resting or waiting for something or someone.

One man looked utterly defeated. Jesus sat near him. "Good Sabbath!" said Jesus.

The man looked at him and then turned his head away. Jesus said, "If you don't mind, I'd like to sit here a bit to rest. We don't have to talk if you don't want to."

"Fine. Then sit and stop talking. I have enough problems without having to sit here and listen to yours," said the man.

Jesus nodded. They sat for a few minutes. The man said, "I can't believe that so much can go wrong all at the same time. It's just nuts!"

"I am a rabbi. Whatever you tell me goes no further. If you want to unleash, I will listen. You may be as angry as you wish to be," Jesus told him.

"Sure! You say that, but the language I would use would curl your ears," replied the man.

"I've heard worse. Sometimes it feels easier to talk if you use the words that make you feel better. Whatever is best for you."

"Okay! You asked for it! Here goes. My wife and I had two girls—little girls who had my heart. We lived in a small house I rented but was saving to buy. Well, she just takes the girls and up and leaves me! She takes my girls, my cart, and everything she could load up, and off they go with a seller of goods who lives in Egypt. Egypt! A —— traveling salesman! What kind of life will that be for my girls?!

"So I have —— nothin' left! So I hire on with a caravan to care for their stinkin' animals. I feed them, clean them; I even have to sleep with them. Do you know how —— much that stinks?

"Well, we get here—they're supposed to take me to Tyre— but we get to this —— place, and they tell me to get out. They say this is as far as I go, and they toss my sack out, and they —— leave! They didn't even —— pay me. So here I am—don't know anyone, don't have any money, and don't —— know how my girls are! I just give up! Everything's nothin'!"

Jesus nodded. "You're right. That is more than enough wrong. I'm sorry."

"Well, your being sorry isn't exactly going to help me, is it?" snapped the man.

They sat for a few minutes. Jesus was praying, *Father God help me reach out and help this man.*

The man turned to Jesus. "Well, got nothin' to say? You're a rabbi. Aren't you going to tell me all about God and tell me to pray, like all you rabbis do?"

"I've been praying," replied Jesus. "As of right now, I haven't anything to say."

"Well, that's a first! All you holy men go around saying everything will be perfect if you just pray. Well, let me —— tell you! I've been a praying man all my life. And what has it got me? Look where the —— it's gotten me. I have nothin'!"

Jesus waited. Jesus felt so bad for this man. *Father God,* he prayed, *Help this man. Help me understand.*

"Just leave me alone. You're no —— help. Go away!"

Jesus got up and walked away. He continued praying for the man. His heart felt so heavy. *Why, Father God? Why didn't I have the words to help him? I trust You. I trust that You're working to help him. I trust that You will help him. Thank You.*

As he walked around, he was hit from behind and almost landed on the ground. He turned to look and saw a young boy trying to stand up. He was breathing heavily and said, "Sorry! Please help me! Please! Keep him away!" He pointed to a man who was coming toward them.

Jesus put his hand across the shoulders of the young boy and asked the man, "What's going on?"

The man replied, "He's my son, and he's running from doing his chores. He does this regularly. You don't need to get involved. I'll get him home and deal with him."

The boy clung to Jesus. "He's not my father! He's trying to take me away! Don't let him! Please don't let him."

Jesus turned to the man. "It seems we have a disagreement here. Let's the three of us take a few minutes and talk about this."

"I see you're a rabbi, so I'm sure you want young boys to obey their parents. I'll take him home and deal with him. Come along, Son," said the man.

"No! No! Don't let him touch me! Please, Rabbi! He's not my father! My father died fishing, and I'm trying to help my mother and sisters! Please! Don't let him take me!"

Jesus said, "I see a soldier over there. Let's the three of us talk with him."

The man said, "I need to get home to chores. I'll get the boy later." And he started to walk away.

Jesus reached out and grabbed the man by the collar, twisted him around, and said, "You will come with me to the authorities. Now!" To the young boy he said, "Please come with me. I will help you."

The boy followed him.

The man struggled and struggled, but Jesus held him tightly until they reached the authorities. After questioning the man and the boy, the official said, "This man has been wanted for kidnapping children for years!" It turns out that this man would take strong-looking young boys and sell them on the slave market. None of the boys has ever been returned to his home.

When they were finished talking with the authorities, Jesus and the boy walked to the side of the road. "Tell me again what happened," Jesus said as he put an arm around the young man.

"Thank you, Rabbi! Thank you! I was so scared! Well, Mother does sewing and mending for some women, and I fetch water and goods for two families who can't leave their homes to shop. I went to get some water, and that man jumped out at me and tried to hold me. I ran away. I'm sorry I bumped you. Are you okay?"

"I'm fine. You are a very brave young man. May I walk home with you? I'm fairly new to the area, and I like to meet people. Would that be okay with you?"

They walked to the boy's home. It was a small house set among several other small houses in the town. "Mother!" called the boy, "I brought someone home with me."

A small woman met them at the door. "Welcome, Rabbi! Please come in."

It felt good inside. There wasn't a lot of furniture, but it looked homey. The woman's sewing was lying on a small table, and a chair sat near the window.

"I am Rabbi Jesus of the school at the synagogue," Jesus introduced himself. "I met this young man at the crossroads. He has quite a story to tell you."

The woman tousled the boy's hair and went to bring water for all of them. *A loving family,* thought Jesus.

The boy told his mother all that happened that day. His Mother grabbed the boy in a big hug. "Thomas! What would I do without you? You are my life!"

She turned to Jesus. "Will that man stay in jail or will they let him out again?"

Jesus assured her. "The authorities have been trying to find him for about three years. They assured me that he will probably never get out of jail. I think your son—and a lot of other young boys—will be safe now."

"Thank you, Rabbi. Can I do anything for you?" asked the woman.

"I don't think this young boy attends school. May I help with that?" asked Jesus.

"He's eight now, and I know he should be in school. But the people he helps need him mornings. We need the money, so he needs to stay home. He and my girls and I study from the Torah every day. He and I do a lot of discussing because we both have so many questions." She smiled. "We both learn."

"That's a very good plan. I'm assuming that you know Father God. May we pray?" asked Jesus.

"Rabbi! You are a man and a rabbi and you ask me if we may pray? I am honored. Yes! Please pray for us. My fervent prayer is that my son grows up to be a good and honest man."

"Father God, thank You for having me meet this wonderful family. Father God, Thomas belongs in school where he can learn of Your love. Help him, please. I ask You to please bless this family with Your love and Your peace. Thank You! Amen."

Jesus shook hands with Thomas and his Mother and turned to leave. "Good Sabbath!" he said. He turned to the boy and said, "I'll see you in school. Ask any of the boys to bring you to me when you arrive. I look forward to seeing you."

After classes two days later, there was a knock on Jesus's classroom door. Thinking it was one of the students returning, Jesus said, "Enter."

Rabbi Sylvanus walked in. "I have someone with me," he said as he turned, and Thomas entered the room.

Jesus rose from his desk and greeted them with handshakes. "I was wondering how soon I would see you! I'm so glad you're here. Are you starting your classes?"

"I am, Rabbi Jesus! I was in Rabbi Sylvanus's class today. He said he'd bring me to see you after school. I hope that's okay."

"That's fine." He turned to Rabbi Sylvanus. "How did the boy do?"

"He did very well. I talked with him after class. He's a little behind in some things, but he's ahead of us in others. I made a list of things he needs to work on, and he has assured me that he will catch up soon. I think he's going to be a fine student," said Rabbi Sylvanus.

Jesus turned to the boy. "I'm sure you will work hard, and I'm sure you'll catch up. How did you make arrangements with your people so that you could attend school?"

"I told them I would like to go to school and I still wanted to help them. It was easy! Both families worked with Mother and me, and we got it all worked out. I'm glad because I wanted to go to school. Mother's glad too."

Jesus told him, "Don't be afraid to go to Rabbi Sylvanus or one of the helpers for help. Don't try to catch up alone. Try your best and then ask for help. Do you think you can do that?"

"Won't people think I'm dumb if I ask for help?"

"Not if you've tried your best. That kind of asking for help is part of growing up," answered Jesus. "I'm very glad you're here and I'm very proud of the way you worked to make sure you could do your work for others and still attend school."

"Rabbi. I felt kind of like I was really light when I talked with my people. Mother says that what I felt was Father God helping me. I think she's right, don't you?"

"Absolutely! And He will help you every time you ask Him."

"Thank you, Rabbis. It's time for me to get home and get to my work and my studies. See you tomorrow," Thomas said to Rabbi Sylvanus.

***

It would soon be time to celebrate the Passover. At one of the morning meetings, the rabbis decided that the week before Passover, they would focus all studies on the eight days of Passover.

Rabbi Sylvanus said, "Every year when I explain about how we need to get rid of the leaven because the leaven permeates bread like sin permeates our lives, one of my young boys will always tell me, 'I'm not full of sin.' I love teaching this Passover story."

"I remember the first year one of my students asked me what would happen if they missed some leaven in the house. I hesitated a minute and said, 'What do you think would happen?'" replied Rabbi Thaddeaus. "I was happy when he thought for a minute and said, 'I guess that could mean that it was like if some of my sin stayed in my life. That wouldn't be good. I better help Mother clear the house.' I thought that was a good answer for kids of that age."

"It's such a Holy time," continued Rabbi Sylvanus. "It's the story of us as a people. Sometimes I'm overwhelmed by the thought of what our people went through. Yet, we forget it so often! I want to make sure the boys understand what this festival is all about. Oh, there I go—tears!"

Thaddeaus added, "I know what you mean. Year after year, we go through the rituals, but it's important that they understand why we have those rituals. I think it's a great idea that we all focus this week on Passover."

Sylvanus said, "Could we decide to stay here for Passover? I think we could make it something special right here. What do you think?"

They talked about the idea for a while and came up with what they thought might be a good plan. They would celebrate here at home; the Sabbath services from now until Passover would really concentrate on the meaning of the festival; and the Passover service would include a family acting out the meal while Rabbi Sylvanus explained each part of the meal.

They told everyone at the next Sabbath service and their overwhelming response was, "Yes!"

FIFTY-SEVEN

28

"Rabbi Thaddeaus," said Jesus as the two of them sat in his office, "I want to ask you a question." Thaddeaus nodded so Jesus continued. "Suppose you saw the sisters, each one alone, in a different part of the city. How would you approach them?"

"I'm not sure what you're asking," replied Thaddeaus.

"If you saw the elder sister walking alone, how would you approach her?" explained Jesus.

"I would nod and say something like, 'Good day.'"

"If you saw the younger sister walking alone, how would you approach her?" asked Jesus.

"I suppose I would smile and slow down to talk if she had the time. She is such a sweet person," replied Thaddeaus. "Why do you ask?"

"Let's look at the older sister. What is it about her that makes you want to avoid her?" asked Jesus.

"When I see her she is so—tight, I guess is the word I would use. She stands tall and erect and just focuses on what's straight in front of her," answered Thaddeaus.

"Are you ever like that?" asked Jesus.

"What do you mean? Like, tight?" asked Thaddeaus.

Jesus nodded.

"I never thought about it." He thought for a minute. "I guess I might be. I'm always trying to show everyone that I'm young, but I'm capable. I guess I do hold myself tight. My father wasn't like that. He—I don't know—he just seemed to love everyone, and they seemed to love him. I guess I just want to be seen as capable of filling his shoes."

"Do you think that's the message you're sending?" asked Jesus.

"I never thought about it. I'm so busy trying to show everyone I'm competent that I don't think about how I look to others. Now that you mention it, I guess I do appear tight." He paused for a moment. "I certainly don't want to appear like that, but I have no idea what to do to change that image. Where would I start?" asked Thaddeaus.

"May I make a suggestion. See how you're sitting? Straight up in the chair with your feet flat on the floor and your knees together? Relax! Sit back! Stretch out your legs! Maybe cross your ankles," suggested Jesus.

"Like this? Oh, that feels good! But I want people to see me not as a young rabbi but as a rabbi capable of leading the boys and of serving the synagogue," explained Thaddeaus, sitting up again.

"By being a friend, you'll show them. You are a very capable rabbi in every way. You do not need to prove it to anyone. I think it's hard for Father God to work with you if you're constantly focused on pretending—on trying to prove that you're good enough. Do you understand what I'm saying?" asked Jesus.

"I think so. What you're saying is that I am capable; now I need to be friendly. Is that about it?"

"I guess you could put it that way. But yes, you are capable. People do look to you, but ditch the uptight part. Remember your impression of meeting Older Sister. Be a friend. Smile a real smile. Look people in the eye. Relax!" offered Jesus.

"Thank you, Jesus. I'll try. You continue to amaze me! You know so much, and you have a kind and gentle way of teaching. I'd like to be more like you," said Thaddeaus.

"One more thing—don't try to be like anyone else. You are the person Father God needs you to be. Be you! That's the best," explained Jesus.

"You've given me a lot to think about. Mostly, I think you're right. Also, I feel very good about this conversation—like I've grown. Thank you," said Thaddeaus.

"You are most welcome. Now could we talk about the sisters? Peter and his wife have shared with me that Older Sister is getting more and more demanding. They feel it's hurting not only her but also her sister. I've been trying to think of a way to help them, but I've come up dry. Maybe if we put our heads together, we could find a way," explained Jesus.

"Of course, the first thing is that we pray. Maybe at our before-classes meetings every school day, the three of us could offer prayers," suggested Thaddeaus.

After more discussion, they were still unable to come up with any other suggestions. They decided that praying before classes each day was the way to handle this. In other words, they were leaving it completely in Father God's hands.

As usual, when Father God answered prayers, he really answered prayers. The three rabbis were just starting their meeting before classes a few days later when there was a knock at the school door. Thaddeaus went to see who was there and was amazed when he saw the younger sister and a man. He brought them to Jesus's office and Thaddeaus said, "Guess who's here! Come in! Come in," he told the couple.

"Sorry to bother the three of you, but we need your help," said the gentleman.

"Welcome! We're glad you came. Please be seated and take all the time you need. Just tell us why you're here," said Jesus.

The man turned to Sister and said, "I think you should tell them. It'll sound better if it comes from you."

Sister took a deep breath. "We met about two years ago when I tripped and fell and broke my water jar. Erastus saw me fall and came to my assistance. I was crying, but he was so kind. Over all this time, we've met as often as possible. Sister knows nothing of this. Now we want to marry, but we're not sure about Sister. Will she make a fuss? Will she try to split us? If she agrees to our marriage, will she try to take charge of our lives? Will she tell us what to do and how to do it?

"That's why we're here. Erastus is a farmer on the west side of town, and it would be hard for us to just move to a different location—one that was far away from Sister. But I don't want her meddling in my life any longer. I want the two of us to be a family. Can you help us?"

"Of course we can, and we will," said Jesus. "First let's all pray. Father God, we come before you today to ask You to help us solve a few problems for this couple. How can they start their lives together? And how do they work things out with Sister? We need Your wisdom, Father God. Please help this couple start this new part of their lives. Thank You for Your help. Amen."

"Rabbis, I forgot to tell you one thing. Erastus has two sons. Each one has his own family. Both are married, and soon one of them will be a parent again. I worry about Sister getting involved in their lives," said Sister.

"We understand," said Sylvanus. "First, I think you should go ahead and make plans to marry. The year of betrothal is not needed in your case, so make your plans remembering that. Then with all of us praying about Sister, Father God will take over, and everything will be just fine!"

Everyone smiled at that.

"From your mouth to Father God's ears!" said Thaddeaus. "It would be another one of His miracles if it works out that quickly. Let's assume that, with the five of us praying, we'll be able to understand what Father God's plan is. And we all know that following His will is really the best way to solve any problem."

Jesus said, "Why don't we plan on meeting one week from today and see what you have decided about your wedding, and let's talk about suggestions for making Sister a happier person. Okay?"

"I don't know if I can get away at this exact time," said Sister.

"Perhaps you could assert yourself. Perhaps you could try saying that you are going to be gone at this time. You do not need to say where you are going if you don't want to. Just say you will be away from home for a while. Could you do that?"

Sister took a deep breath and let it out slowly. "That's a little scary, but I need to do it. So, yes, if I need to, I will assert myself."

Erastus squeezed her shoulders.

As they were leaving, Sylvanus told them, "I have a very good feeling about this. I feel Father God's in your corner, and things will work out for everyone. So go with our blessings and stay close to Father God. Off you go!"

The next week, Erastus and Sister were waiting at the school when the rabbis arrived. "Good morning," said Sister. "We can't wait to talk with you!"

They went to Jesus' office and all sat down except Sister. "I am so excited! I'll try to tell you in the order things happened. I don't know what came over me, but just two days after we met, I told Sister 'no' when she told me to do something. She looked at me, and I said, 'I do enough around here. If you want that done, you'll have to do it yourself, or you'll have to wait until I feel like doing it.' You should have seen her!

"The next morning as I was cleaning up after breakfast—of course I had made the breakfast—I told her that, from now on, we were going to split the household chores. One week I would make meals, and she would clean up afterward. And the next week, she would make the meals, and I would clean up. I told her that there would be some times I would be going off by myself at a time that was convenient for me. But, I told her, I would still be doing my share of work, so we would continue to have our usual income. She just looked at me.

"Well, at noon that day, I made the meal and then went to my work, leaving the cleaning up to her. She did it! She cleaned up! Later that day, it was the usual time I went to town to pick up supplies, and that's when Erastus always tried to be there to meet me. So we met and I told him what was happening. I said that we should set a definite time to meet that would work for him and his farm schedule.

"We've met for two days now. I am so completely happy. Oh! Erastus and I have made plans for our wedding. We'd like to marry in three weeks just before Sabbath begins. We'd like all three of you to take part in the ceremony, if you would."

"Of course we will!" answered all three rabbis.

Sylvanus got up and hugged both Erastus and Sister. "Sister," he said, "could we please know your name so we don't have to call you Sister anymore?"

Sister giggled. "My name is Ruth. Mother named me after Ruth in the Bible because she wanted me to be kind. Sister's name is Naomi because Mother wanted her to be flexible and happy whatever her circumstances."

Erastus said, "We feel like we're getting to where we want to be, but I'm still a little leery of her sister's reaction and what she may try to do." He turned to Ruth and said, "I'm sorry to say that; I hope you don't mind that I spoke up."

"I'm glad you did." She turned to the rabbis. "I think I'm strong enough today to deal with day-to-day things, but how do I make sure she doesn't try to take over our lives? I don't want to cut her off completely—just make sure she minds her business and comes to see us when it is convenient for us. I want her to accept the boys and their families and not try to tell them what to do. Does that sound awful?"

"Not at all," said Jesus. "But I see you now as being able to handle her. Here's a suggestion. You can always tell the boys and their families—gently and with love—that your sister means well and they need to respect her. But they do not need to tell her things they're not comfortable sharing. And they do not need to make any changes that she suggests—unless they truly believe that they are changes that are good for all of them. Does that help you?"

Ruth turned to Erastus. "I think that sounds good. What do you think?"

"Ruth, I am so happy right now! You are so strong, and the rabbis are in our corner, and we're going to be a family! I feel Father God at work in all of this. I feel that, if we are diligent working *with* Sister, we'll all be happy," answered Erastus.

***

Because all three rabbis taught every day but the Sabbath and because, as Jesus said, "It is good to do good on the Sabbath, and this marriage is a very good thing," the wedding was held in the synagogue on the Sabbath. Afterward, everyone would go to Erastus's farm home for a dinner of celebration.

Erastus's sons and their families were all at the wedding. The oldest one told Ruth that, from now on, all the children would call her Grandmother. That made Ruth very happy; she shed a few tears.

Ruth asked Naomi if she would read the father's part during the ceremony. She was surprised to see tears in Naomi's eyes. "I would love to! Thank you!" And she gave Ruth a quick hug. Ruth said that her heart sang at that point.

Early the morning of the wedding, Naomi came to Ruth with a small package. "Sister, I want to know if you would like to have this today. Mother wore it on her wedding day. Maybe under your wedding tunic? Just to remind you of Mother. She can't be here, but maybe this could be a reminder. It's okay if you don't want to."

"Sister! This is a very fine and beautiful scarf. Thank you!" said Ruth as she hugged Naomi. "I would love to wear it. Would you help me decide where it would look best?" They tried several places and decided that she would wear it tied under the sprang, around her hair, and let the ends hang down her back. She felt so beautiful!

Was this a major change in Naomi? Yes! Was she now almost always nice? Yes! Did she stop her demanding ways? In a word, yes (for the most part, but this was new).

Was Naomi happy about these new circumstances? Yes. Did she respect Erastus and Ruth's privacy? Yes. Did she now reach out to help others? In a word, *yes!*

What happened to the small but steady business the sisters had been operating? It turned out that, with Ruth now on the other side of Capernaum, people there also wanted her to help them. Their business grew. Their newfound relationship grew. The sisters found they enjoyed being together. Naomi relearned how to laugh—at herself, as well as at circumstances. They both thanked Father God daily.

Erastus's son and his wife had a healthy baby boy. They asked Sylvanus if they might name the baby after him. Rabbi Sylvanus giggled. As the years went by, if you couldn't find the rabbi, you needed only to look for his namesake—you'd find them together.

One more beautiful outcome was that Naomi loved the little one as if he were her own grandchild. With the blessings of the baby's father and mother, Naomi became the maker of fine clothes for the child and eventually for all the children.

Erastus and Ruth quickly fell into work on the farm. The farm thrived. The animals thrived. And Ruth glowed. She was a wife and a grandmother!

Thank You, Father God, for Your miracles.

***

One morning as the rabbis were meeting, Jesus said, "I've noticed that we have several homebound elderly people in town. A few years ago, some visitors to Nazareth started a way of including the homebound in what's going on in town. It proved to be a wonderful idea and a great growing experience for everyone involved."

He then explained how the girls had been organized to bring the homebound elderly messages from one another and to keep them apprised of what was happening in town.

"If you think that this sounds like something that might be useful here, I'd like to perhaps implement it. What are your thoughts?"

Both rabbis agreed that it should be tried.

"I can think of three girls who could possibly do this. Maybe we should start with two lists—one of the homebound and one of the girls," said Thaddeaus. "Jesus, are you thinking that we would be in charge of organizing this in addition to what we're doing now?"

"I'm glad you asked. I think we have enough to do. I've noticed that the two of you do as I do. When you see someone needing additional attention, you stop and take the time to be with him or her. I don't think that should be stopped or even slowed down. Too many people need us. I was thinking of approaching Naomi. What do you think?"

They thought for a minute, and Thaddeaus said, "I think that's a good idea. Maybe we should talk to her first about this and then maybe talk with everyone after Sabbath services?"

"I think that sounds like a good idea. Jesus, you know how the plan works. So would you approach Naomi and explain it to the congregation?" asked Sylvanus.

"I can do that, but as I am soon starting perhaps my final year here, I was thinking that perhaps Thaddeaus could do the talking." Turning to Thaddeaus, Jesus said, "I can stand by if you want me to. But I think, if we talk about it some more, that you'll have no trouble explaining it. Does that sound okay to you?"

It was agreed.

After services, Thaddeaus approached Naomi and asked if he might stop in the next day and talk with her.

When they met, Naomi said, "I'm more than happy to do this! I can finally get back to helping others. Thank you for trusting me!"

Plans were made; homebound people were identified and girls chosen.

When Thaddeaus brought this to the congregation, they overwhelmingly felt that this was a great idea. It proved to be a success. As an aside, the girls learned a great deal about the history of the local families and about the history of the town. Everything went well, especially for the homebound; they once again became a part of the life in their city.

FIFTY-EIGHT

29

At the men's weekly Loop game, James and one of the other players got into a rather heated argument off to one side of the area.

"James, you're just a stuffed shirt! You have absolutely no idea what you're doing."

"I don't? I suppose you do?" asked James.

The rest of the players tried to change the subject and begin the games, but it seems that James and the man would not listen.

Jesus said, "Please tell us what the two of you are arguing about."

They both started talking at once, but at the look on the faces of the others, James told the man to go ahead and start.

"He is so rude! A Gentile man approached the two of us as we were walking here. He excused himself and asked if he could ask a question. Before he could ask, James began telling him that he was not worthy to be here in Capernaum and that he needed to first know our Father God. And then James walked up close to him and told him that Father God was watching him and that he and his family were going to burn in hell and he would be responsible.

"I tried to get between James and the man, and I tried to ask the man what I could do to help him. But James just kept going on and on."

James said, "They need to know Father God! If we don't take every opportunity to tell them about Him, how are they going to know? It's important! It's our duty to tell them!"

"I can see both sides of this argument," Jesus said. He turned to the rest of the players and asked, "What do you think? Should we discuss this here together? Or should it be done privately?"

The others sort of shuffled their feet and looked down. Finally one of the men said, "I'm embarrassed by this and would just like to get on with our games."

Another added, "But are they going to forget this? Or are they going to ruin the evening by being angry all night?"

Jesus turned to the two arguers. "What do the two of you want to do?"

The man said, "Someone needs to talk to this guy! He can't go on like this. It's not right, and it's rude. Jesus, you're our rabbi. Why don't you talk to him?"

"James?" Jesus asked.

James hesitated. "This really is not the time or place for this discussion. Maybe it would be good for you and me to talk about this, Jesus." He turned to the man. "Let's play the games. I promise I'll be nice tonight—that is, unless I need to make a point for my team," James said with a smile and a handshake.

After the next Sabbath services, Jesus approached James and asked, "How about if we go for a walk tomorrow and talk about the incident the other evening?"

James agreed.

The next morning, the two of them began walking. Jesus started the conversation, "James, tell me how you feel—how you react to seeing Gentiles."

"Jesus, our Father God is so awesome! I want everyone to know Him. These people are all going to hell! It's my job to tell them they're wrong and to tell them that what I know is right," began James.

"I understand. Could you take just a moment right now and pretend that you are one of the Gentiles and that you come up to you and talk the way you talk."

James was quiet for quite a while. After a while he said, "I need to continue to think about this. What I'm trying to visualize is if a Gentile walked up to me and acted as I do. I think this will take me a while. Do you want to continue walking while I think or should we split and meet later?"

"We're here at the crossroads, so I'm happy to just walk around and see the area. I was here only once before but didn't get to see very much."

"There's a bench over there that I think I'll just sit on and think. Why don't you come back in about an hour? I'll wait around here for you," decided James.

Jesus agreed and began walking around. He saw so many shops and so many services available. "I suppose all these things are needed for travelers before heading away from here. There really isn't much else for quite a distance."

He saw an area that he had never noticed in any other town. The sign read, "Taxes Collected Here." He walked over.

"Hello," Jesus said to the man sitting at a desk. "I'm not a traveler. I'm just staying in the area for a while, and I was wondering what this shop is."

"Welcome! My name is Matthew. I am a tax collector." They shook hands. "As our name says, we collect taxes here."

Jesus waited, not sure what to say or even why he'd stopped here.

"Tax collectors have a bad reputation. That's because most of them charge extra for the taxes and then take that extra money for themselves. That's probably what you've heard about us." As Jesus said nothing, Matthew continued. "I try hard not to do that. I try to make an honest assessment and charge a true amount. Still, I do make a nice living, and I do live in a very nice—although not elegant—home. Do you have questions for me?"

"I don't think so. I guess it's just that this is something I know nothing about. I was curious and just stopped in. Thank you for taking the time to explain things to me. I appreciate it," Jesus said as he shook the man's hand again and left the shop.

Jesus continued walking, occasionally greeting people. After a while, he returned to James. He sat near him and asked, "Are you okay? Would you like to walk or sit here? Or do you want to continue to be alone? Anything you need is all right with me."

James looked deeply at Jesus. "I've been wrong, haven't I? I love Father God so much, and I want everyone to know him. But when you suggested that I pretend that I'm the Gentile man and have me approach, I saw my way is not the right thing to do. If I approached me like that, it would just turn me off. I'd never listen to me. What I'm trying to figure out is what I should do. It really bothers me that they don't know Father God, but I'm going about it all wrong. I can't figure out what I should do. Maybe you know?"

"Let me ask you a question," said Jesus. "How did you feel when you pretended that you were approached by you?"

"I felt like a bat flew into my face! I just wanted to make me go away!" explained James.

"What does that tell you?"

"That's why they won't listen to me. They just want me to go away—kind of like I'm a threat to them," answered James.

"James, you are not a bad person. You love Father God and are trying to do His will. But now you've seen how others see you. Where do you go from here?" asked Jesus.

James thought for a minute. "I don't know, Jesus. I can talk to you. Is that because you're a rabbi?" He shook his head. "No, that's not it. Is it because I know you? Maybe that's it." He thought for a minute. "That's it, isn't it? I need to get to know them before they'll listen to what I have to say. How do I do that?"

"You're on the right track, James. As you think about this, I think you'll know what to do. Remember that, if you have questions, I'm here, and so is your father. He's a very wise man," said Jesus.

"He is. And you are. I can't think anymore. Let's walk. Oh, did I tell you? One of our servants died last night. He was in the fish house where we were cleaning and drying fish, and he just opened his eyes really wide and fell over backward. There was nothing we could do. Several of the other servants tried to help me take care of him, but he was gone. We took him to his family. As it was night, I was unsure what to do. But his family seemed to know. I felt a little helpless, but I told them I was sorry that he had died and asked if I could help. They said that, as a family, they would take care of him. I told them I'd pray for him and for them. I did. It was all I could do."

"You did well. Was he older?" asked Jesus.

"About Father's age I think. It was so sudden. He was working and just like that he died," explained James.

"Sometimes it happens that way. For him, it was probably a blessing; he didn't have a long time to suffer with some disease," said Jesus.

"You're right. I hadn't thought of that. Well, we're almost back at your place. Thank you, Jesus. I have a lot of thinking to do. I'm glad we had this time today. I feel like something's changing. I don't think I can explain it, but it's okay. Thank you!" said James.

"You're a good man, James. You may have once in a while done something the wrong way, but you did it for the right reason. Remember that. I'm sure I don't need to tell you to take this to Father God. I will as well. Good Sabbath, my friend."

"Thank you, my rabbi, my friend. I'll pray for you too," James said with a smile as he turned to walk home.

He began to talk to his Father God. "Please walk with me. I feel that today was a special gift from You. Help me as I learn. Thank You, Father God!"

James caught on rather quickly. The first thing he did was talk with his father and John, explaining the change he was making in his life. Both gladly offered their support.

The next day as they were hauling in their catch for the day, James took four of the largest fish to four of the family servants and directed them to families in town that he knew were having a difficult time.

That afternoon, he asked the servants to see if they could discreetly find out which of the Gentile families were having a rough time. Although they lived mainly outside of the town, the servants were able to identify seven families who were very poor and two others who were having a difficult time affording food to feed their families.

James purchased flour and oil to be given to these families. The next day when the day's catch was brought in, he added fresh and dried fish to the packages and instructed two of the servants to deliver the packages to the families. His instructions to the servants were, "Ask them to please accept these gifts. Only if they ask should you tell them it is from James the son of Zebedee, asking forgiveness for wrongs I have done to their people."

James joined the other servants in preparing the day's catch, working hard to take the place of the two servants he had sent to the Gentiles. This became a once-a-week service.

He didn't stop there. Daily, he made an effort to walk where Gentiles might be found shopping or needing services. He would smile and wave—making absolutely no effort to engage them in conversation. The first few days, he was avoided as much as possible. After that, some would nod in greeting. Before long, even the children stopped their harassment. James began to feel a bit better. He could see that it would take a while before the Gentiles would begin to trust him. *It's what I deserve*, he thought.

During the second week of these "travels," he heard a youngster screaming in terror. By the time he reached the child, other children were screaming. As he reached the area, he saw a young boy being chased by a goat with huge horns. James prayed and took off his robe as he ran. He threw his robe over the head of the goat, grabbed the child, rolled away, picked up the child, and ran behind a tree—the only thing in sight that might offer protection. He lifted the child to a branch and told him to climb and stay there until he told him to come down.

The goat had gotten the robe off his face and was looking around as if to say, *Who's next?* By now, several local adults had arrived, and between them they were able to capture the goat and calm the children. When it looked safe, James brought the child down. As soon as the boy touched the ground, he ran to his father.

James started to walk away. The man who appeared to be the father of the boy called to him. He turned to face the man.

"You saved my son. I want to thank you, but I don't want you to start yelling at me. I just want to say thank you," said the man.

"You are welcome," said James as he turned to walk toward the man. "Thank you for being so honest with me. I have changed. I no longer act like that. I found out it was not acceptable behavior. Please accept my apologies for every time I was out of line. From now on, I only want peace and possibly friendship. May we shake hands?"

The man looked at James for a minute and then accepted the handshake. The man said, "I am not sure where things go from here."

"That's okay. I know I was wrong, and I know it will take a lot of time before I prove myself. Thank you for speaking to me. Maybe we'll meet another day," James said as he waved and continued his walk.

Did that make James a friend to the Gentiles? In brief, not yet. However, the Gentiles began to smile or wave, and some even greeted him with, "Good day." He didn't push. He knew he had been wrong for a long time, and it would take a long time to make friends.

"I do want to make friends with the Gentiles don't I?" he asked himself.

"Yes!" he answered himself.

FIFTY-NINE

29

Preparations were being made for the trip to Jerusalem for the Festival of Booths. To say that Jesus was excited would be putting it mildly. He had not seen his mother for almost a year!

"Jesus, do you have a minute?" asked Thaddeaus as they were leaving school about a week before leaving.

"Sure," answered Jesus. "What's on your mind?"

"I'd like to talk about the trip to Jerusalem—just random thoughts. Naomi will be alone in a cart, and I don't think that's a good idea. And she's a woman, so we need to find a woman or a couple to ride with her.

"It's no surprise that Erastus and Ruth have asked Sylvanus to share their cart. I think that being close to baby Sylvanus is a great selling point for him.

"Peter and his wife have asked if you would share their cart. His mother-in-law will be staying with her sister, who is quite ill. That leaves me, but we have two other carts with only two or three persons, so I'll talk with them. What do you think?"

"I would love to ride with Peter and his wife. Are young Thomas and his mother and sisters going? They could probably use a driver. I wonder how it would work if we had Naomi ride with them?" suggested Jesus.

Sylvanus walked up at that moment. "Sorry I'm late, but one of my boys had what he thought was a problem. It's wonderful to see these young boys work toward their own solutions." He turned to Thaddeaus. "Have you told him yet?"

Thaddeaus smiled. "Not yet. I was stalling. I wanted you to be here. You were as big a part of this plan as I was."

Jesus looked from one to the other.

Sylvanus appeared to be almost giggly. "Jesus! There's a special surprise planned for you! You know that it doesn't take as long for all of us to ride to Jerusalem as it takes those from other towns to mostly walk. So we've decided that Peter and his wife and you will leave two days before the rest of us."

Jesus looked at him questioningly. "Go on," he said.

"You're going to Nazareth!" Sylvanus was almost bouncing. "Your family already knows you're coming. Some of your brothers said, 'Great! He can help with the packing!' They meant it in a good way though."

Jesus looked at the two of them. "Really? How will I ever be able to thank the two of you? This means a great deal to me!" he said as he clasped his arms around the shoulders of the rabbis. "Thank you! Thank you!"

"Jesus, the truth is that this was Peter and his wife's idea. They came to us. We wanted them here when we told you, but they wanted the three of us to talk together. They do so much for others, and they never want the credit. They're a wonderful couple. We are blessed to have them here."

"That Peter!" said Jesus, with tears beginning to form in his eyes. "He and his wife are like no one I've ever met." He closed his eyes and prayed, "Thank You, Father God!"

The next morning as James was taking his daily walk near Gentile territory, the father of the boy James had saved from the goat approached him and asked, "May I ask a question?"

"Of course," said James.

"I see that there's a lot of planning all over Capernaum. May I ask what all of you are preparing for?" he asked.

James explained in as few words as he could. "We have three festivals per year where our men are to travel to Jerusalem to worship our Father God. One is the Festival of Booths, but it's really our most important festival of the year. We must go. We decided a long time ago to take our families with us each year. It takes a lot of planning, but we feel it's worth it. That's what we're doing now—getting everything and everyone ready to go."

"Does everyone go?" the man asked.

James hesitated for a second. *Why is he asking these questions? Will our people who are left behind be safe?* As quickly as he thought these thoughts, he told himself, *Father God has arranged this. I will have faith.*

James answered, "Not everyone. Some are unable to travel because of age or physical conditions or because their babies are due now—things like that."

"James, you just stepped forward and trusted me. Thank you! You could have not trusted me and just walked away. You could have thought I would cause trouble and, for that reason, kept the information from me. I'm impressed, and I thank you.

"I would like to offer that my friends and I will stand available to help anyone in any way. If you would, please share with your people that, if they need help, they only need to talk with any one of us—to reach out. We will be ready to help in any way."

"Thank you! Yes I will tell everyone that you are ready to help with everything they might need. If it's all right with you, I'd like to give you a hug. But I'll settle for shaking hands. We need to be careful. We may become friends!" said James, grinning.

They shook hands and together reached out to the other one for a quick hug. Both men were amazed.

"Thank you," said James. "Again, I ask you to forgive me for all the times I wronged all of you."

"No more apologies needed, ever. I hope we can continue to work together," the man said.

"I hope so too. I'll work hard to do my part; I promise. I need to get back before the boats come in with the fish. I pray we'll see each other often. Thank you," said James. As he left, he turned back and waved. "Thank you, Father God. I feel so blessed right now. Protect all of us and all of our Gentile neighbors."

After Sabbath services, James asked the three rabbis if he could speak to them for a minute. He then told them about his meeting with the Gentile man and asked them what they thought.

There was a bit of silence. Jesus looked at Thaddeaus and nodded for Thaddeaus to begin talking.

"I think I like it—at least I feel comfortable about it." He thought for a minute and said, "Actually that could be a very good thing! They do business with our businesses, so they're known by many of us." He looked at Jesus and Sylvanus and said, "I think we should make it known to everyone. If it comes from the three of us, it'll be more easily accepted."

Sylvanus said, "Every time I've met one of the Gentiles, I've never felt threatened. I think this is good. Some of our people may really need help. Good job, James!"

As they spoke with people during this final week of preparations, most seemed to accept the possibility of help from the Gentiles. There were questions; there was uncertainty; there were some skeptics. It was interesting that those who were staying behind were the ones who seemed to like the idea the most. One elderly homebound woman said, "I'll feel protected even more now. Is that okay?" she asked.

***

Peter and his wife and Jesus made preparations to leave ahead of the others. "I will never be able to thank the two of you sufficiently for doing this. I don't have words to tell you what this means to me. Thank you!" said Jesus.

Using the cart, they were able to reach Nazareth before sundown. The trip was good. Both Peter and his wife loved to sing the psalms—as did Jesus. Jesus told them of the harmonizing he had learned at home, and they tried it. There ensued a lot of laughs and a lot of strange notes but a very enjoyable ride.

As they reached Nazareth, Jesus smiled as he saw his longtime friends all busy making travel plans. He waved and greeted each one he saw. As he reached home, Jesus called out, "Woman! Where are you?"

"Right here, my son!" answered Mary as she ran from the house.

Jesus picked her up and twirled her around.

"Oh, how I have missed that!" Mary said. "I have missed you a great deal, Son." She turned to his friends. "Welcome! Please come in."

"Mother, this is my friend Peter and his wonderful wife. They are the ones who've made it possible for me to come early and to stay for a daylong visit," Jesus said, introducing his friends.

Peter reached out his hand. "It is our pleasure. Jesus talks of you quite often. It's nice to finally meet you."

"Thank you." Mary turned to Jesus. "Timaeus and Anna should be back in a minute. Come in and make yourselves at home. I have posca and water. May I get some for you?"

As Mary was bringing the water, Timaeus and Anna arrived. Jesus greeted Anna with hugs, shook hands with Timaeus, slapped him on his shoulder, and introduced them to Peter and his wife. "Little sister, it looks like you're putting on weight! May I guess why?"

"Jesus, we are with child! You will be an uncle again," said Anna.

"Congratulations!" said Jesus to Timaeus as he shook his hand and again placed his hand on his shoulder. Turning to Anna, he said, "You're not too grown up now for a hug are you?"

Anna grabbed her big brother. "Oh, Jesus! My *old* brother!" she teased.

Mary said, "The entire family will be here tomorrow morning. I'm warning you, the kids are all growing and are very loud, especially when they're all together."

"We have dinner ready, so let's eat," said Timaeus.

After dinner, Timaeus showed Jesus and Peter the guesthouse he had built across the courtyard. Jesus was impressed. It wasn't very large, but it looked so comfortable!

The evening went well. Peter and his wife felt at home. Mary and Timaeus and Anna had made a few changes to the house and yard, but the changes they'd made seemed to make the home even more comfortable.

After a good night's sleep and a good breakfast, the men went to the roof while the women cleaned up and got ready for the arrival of the families.

Timaeus said, "Peter would you tell me about yourself? And would you tell me how our Jesus is behaving himself?"

Jesus rolled his eyes and shook his head.

Peter said, "First things first. Jesus has proven to be a great addition to our school and to our synagogue. The people love him, and the boys are pleased with his way of teaching them. So I would say that he has fit in well and is an asset to our town," he continued with a wink and a smile toward Jesus.

"I am a fisherman. My wife and I were not blessed with children, so we try to treat everyone as if they are our children. I've lived a good part of my life in Capernaum. I love Father God and try to always act as He would want me to act. I guess I'd have to say that I want everyone to like me. When I form a friendship, it's a friendship forever. It would take a lot for me to give up on someone. That's about it."

Timaeus smiled. "Thank you." Smiling again, he said, "I also want to thank you for making these arrangements for

Jesus to have time with all of us. We're all still packing for our trip to Jerusalem because we plan to leave at sunup tomorrow. When the families heard that you were coming, there was no way they were going to let these preparations get in the way of all of them spending today with Jesus."

Anna called, "The families are just down the road, so come on down!"

Jesus stood at the door, so he would be first to greet everyone. Joses and Claudia and James and Lois and their children were the first to arrive, as they lived closest to Mary. As each family neared, Jesus went to meet them. What a crowd!

There was a lot of commotion. The children had all grown at least two inches! Two of them Jesus had not seen, as they had been born this past year. Jesus was amazed at the changes in everyone. His brothers and sisters had matured. Little Leah was almost eight and seemed to feel that she was in charge, not only of her brother, but also of all the children.

Everyone was there! Everyone was talking—at the same time. Mary finally said, "Let's all go to the town square. The children will have a place to run around, and we'll be able to sit together and hear one another."

The women quickly packed up the lunch, and they all moved to the square.

Peter approached Jesus. "Years ago, my wife visited her uncle and aunt here and became quite close to some of the neighborhood children. Would you mind if we leave for a while? We'll probably only be gone a couple of hours."

"By all means," said Jesus. "Come back as soon as you want to. You're very welcome here! When you're here, you'll probably hear some tall tales of my life as a child. My brothers are known for their stories. Would you like one of the older boys to go with you? That way you won't get lost on the way!" Jesus teased.

"Thank you, but my wife has assured me that she remembers where to go, so we'll just take off for a while," answered Peter as he clasped Jesus's shoulder.

The families settled down at the square. Joses told the children his usual. "We adults want to talk for a long time. Behave yourselves. If you bother us, there will be additional chores and more studying to do. Understand?"

Of course they understood!

It was a time of bringing Jesus up to date on what had been going on in the family and the town. Joses recounted the gift of money from Timaeus and James and how that had changed their lives. "Our families are now able to reach out to others, and it feels so good to know that we are doing something to help those in need—to be able to act as Father God wants. We are so thankful!"

"Tell me about the Shop. What's new? Have you needed to hire help? If so, who did you hire? Joses, did you ever make those wheels? I want to hear everything!" said Jesus.

Joses replied, "The wheels are doing well. Japeth and his son take them on their trips. I've experimented with making them out of different woods. The different woods make some of them look nicer, but the best ones for racing are still the ones made of oak."

Simon added, "Japeth's eyesight is failing, but his son has matured, and the two of them make a wonderful team. So far, they've been able to sell everything that we men and our women have been able to make."

"One thing is a bit worrisome. We've had three families purchase land east of town who are people that we're kind of watching," said Judas. "So far, they're okay, but they're definitely different. They don't mingle, and they don't attend services. They are Jews but they seem to treat the rest of us as if we're beneath them. When they do mix with us, they treat us as though we're here to do their bidding. For instance, one day, they brought a broken table to the Shop. They just said,

'Have this ready before Sabbath on Friday.' No preliminary words—just an order."

James added, "It seems like they're creating an atmosphere of them versus us. We try to accept them, but they certainly are not friendly."

"They don't send their boys to our school. I think there are about five boys of school age. From what we can tell, it looks like they're teaching them themselves," said Simon. "Things might eventually be just fine, but right now, we feel that, as a town, we need to keep an eye on them."

"Let's talk about the good things that are happening," said Mary. "The girls and I have become almost as famous for our goods as the Shop has for all they create. We're working different colors into our work. We found that, if you wash them inside out and in salted water, they don't fade as quickly. So we've asked Japeth and his son to be sure to tell everyone to whom he sells things to wash them inside out and in salted water."

"New people are moving into town quite regularly," added James. "Their need for furniture, cooking and eating utensils, and storage boxes is keeping us more than busy. We've hired Abraham's younger son full-time and have two other young boys who come in about twice a week. So things at the Shop are going well."

Mary said, "There's been a little fuss about something we women have suggested. Some of us have noticed that repairs are needed in the synagogue. This time of year, the men do not have a lot of time to spare, so we've approached our husbands about a way we could be of help to them with the repairs. So far, they haven't gotten back to us with a yes or a no, but we keep hoping we can help."

"Things like what, Mother?" asked Jesus.

"We women can't actually do the repair work. But we've suggested that, when the men do the work, we women will bring water and meals to them so they don't need to stop work to go home to eat. We also talked about preparing food that can be eaten with hands so that, if the men don't want to take the time to sit down and eat, they can keep working. We understand that our men can't take a lot of time away from farming or from their businesses, so we're trying to do things that will help them make the best use of their time. We even suggested that they might do this during the two weeks the school is closed so that many of the boys would be able to help. Some repairs are really needed," Mary said.

Judas added, "The women are right. I'm hoping we can work it out. We still have a couple of men who oppose it just because it was suggested by the women. The thing is, the women talked with their husbands and it was the husbands who liked the idea and brought it forward. I guess we'll just have to let it work itself out. Personally, I think it's a great idea. Some of us have started a list of the repairs to make, and we feel it won't take more than three days, *if* we have enough men and *if* we gather the supplies ahead of time."

"I'm afraid that there will always be some who decide the value of a suggestion is based solely on who the suggestion comes from," said Jesus. "And it will always be a shame. It sounds like a great idea though. I hope you can work it out.

"By the way, how are Miriam and her families, Enoch's Mary, the school—everything?" added Jesus.

"Miriam is doing well. She had a lot of difficulty breathing and was really out of it about three months ago. She really scared me. I asked the boys to stop over there and pray for her, and the change was immediate! Father God is so good. I don't know what I'd do without her! Enoch's Mary is showing her age, I'm afraid. After her latest patient died, she also seemed to just fade. She still lives alone. But remember the girls we have who take messages between those who are homebound? Well, those girls also visit her. She really likes that and she seems to be doing relatively well," explained Mary.

Peter and his wife returned.

"Welcome! Did you find any of the people you knew?" Jesus asked Peter's wife.

"I knew my uncle and aunt had passed, but I wanted to look at the neighborhood and to see if I could find anyone I once knew. I did! One of the girls lives in that house now! She invited us in, and we had a nice chat. She has three boys who were in school, and her two daughters were taking messages from one homebound adult to the other, so we didn't get to meet her children. I told her that we were now doing that in Capernaum, and we talked about it for a bit. I'm afraid Peter was quite bored, but he survived. Didn't you, Peter?" she asked.

Peter just smiled and shook his head.

"That was wonderful!" said Jesus. "My families are filling me in on what's been going on this past year. Come sit with us." Jesus turned to Simon. "How are things at the school?"

"The school is doing well," said Simon. "We have three who will be bar mitzvahs during the next year; the youngest one is a questioner!" Simon smiled. "He wants to know why for everything. We rabbis have formed a solid front for him. He must prove that he has researched the answer to his questions before we take school time for discussion. It's been interesting because his questions are no longer simple. But we feel we're all growing, and we feel this is a good plan."

Judas said, "Remember the families who were coming through here—the ones who had their carts crash, and some of them were hurt?" asked James. "Well, the baby that was born that day is now a student at the school! His parents moved to a farm just outside of town that was once owned by the father's grandfather. The boy is almost eleven and is an okay student."

Simon added, "He's the only child his parents have, and they have pretty much coddled him. He feels he's a bit more important than the others, but we've been working on that. We've been stressing stories and pushing the idea that one person is not better than the other, but with different talents, and that we all need each other to get along in life. I think he'll come around."

"Philip and Elizabeth," asked Jesus, "I've not heard from you. What's going on in your lives?"

"Things are really going well for us," said Elizabeth. "The elderly woman near us died this past summer, and her husband isn't well. It's hard for him to walk. Jesus, you would be so proud of my little ones. Every morning our four- and six-year-old take the day's food to him. The couple has had a hard time the past few years, so I cautioned the children that they were not to take anything as a thank you. 'But, Mother! People always give people something! What should we do?' they asked me. I suggested they tell him they would like a hug. That's just what happened. So every morning they take the food and come back smiling, having had their hug."

"Your children are learning several lessons. You and Philip are doing well," said Jesus. "Philip, how is your father?"

Philip answered, "He's feeling well. I'll tell him you asked. Thank you. I should tell you that Elizabeth has become quite the homemaker and quite the cook. We had a town event where everyone—men, women, and children—were to bring items for others to taste. Elizabeth made a special dessert, and the town voted her dessert as the best of the town. She spoils me with her amazing food. I tell her I don't want to get fat!"

Jesus looked at Elizabeth and smiled. He turned to Timaeus, "Timaeus, how is the pharmacy doing?"

"It's also doing well. My parents and I made some changes to the interior of the building before we opened, and it seems those changes worked well. I keep busy. The physician suggested some things for me to carry that are not usually found in a pharmacy—things like vinegar and flax seeds. He was right. I'm happy, and so are my parents. So I guess I'd have to say it's a success.

"Oh! I almost forgot! My sister is betrothed. Her wedding will be in less than a year. I've met her future husband, and he seems to be okay—a little standoffish, but maybe that's because we just met. Anyway, that's my news!" added Timaeus.

Jesus loved this time with his families! He made sure that he took the time to speak one on one with each of the children. Leah asked him, "How is my friend Mister Zebedee?"

"He is doing well. He's looking forward to seeing you during the festival," answered Jesus.

It seemed that every time Jesus looked for Peter and his wife, they were deep in conversation with one or more families, laughing, talking, and listening. "They are awesome friends. Thank you Father God," Jesus prayed.

Too soon it was time for everyone to turn in for the night. It was well after sundown, and they would all be leaving early in the morning. The area was straightened up, and with a lot of hugs, the families left for their homes. Elizabeth and Philip and their children were staying with James, so Jesus stayed in the house, and Peter and his wife spent the night in the guesthouse

"Thank You, Father God, for this time together. We are all so very blessed! Thank You!" prayed Jesus as he finished his evening prayers.

SIXTY

29

Somehow, they were all on their way just as the sun came up.
Everyone was excited! The trip was uneventful except for the
usual—scrapes, bruises, broken cart wheels—and by the end of
three days, they were in the spot they loved to stay in for the
full days of the festivals.

While the women organized the campsite, the men went
to the synagogue to begin the process for this special Sabbath
meal.

On the way back to their families, Yannis found the men,
and after handshakes and hugs, Yannis asked them, "Do you
men know of a family from Nazareth about thirty or more years
ago who were terribly ill? As I understand it, many people were
ill, and some died. Most of this family died, but it's possible that
a girl of about fourteen survived.

The brothers stopped. "Why do you ask?" asked Joses.

"We met a member of that family, and she asked me to ask
those I knew from Nazareth. Does it sound familiar?"

This sounded a bit like the story their mother had told them
of her family. James said, "Our mother tells a similar story.
She has a younger sister who was taken to live with an uncle.
Maybe we should talk with this woman."

"If you have a few minutes, I can take you to her now. She
and her family are staying close to where we are," answered
Yannis.

The brothers looked at each other and nodded. James said, "I think this is important enough that we should take the time to look into this."

They went with Yannis to meet the woman. She was talking with friends, but as Yannis and the brothers approached, everyone turned toward them. The first thing Jesus and his brothers noticed was that two of the men looked a lot like Simon and James.

Yannis said, "Men, this is Rachel, the mother of these fine men. Miss Rachel, these are four brothers and two brothers-in-law from Nazareth. I told them your story and asked them if they would come to talk with you."

"Thank you, Yannis." She turned to the brothers and said, "I am honored that you would take the time to meet with me. Thank you."

James stepped forward. "I am James, son of Joseph of Nazareth, and these are my brothers, Judas, Joses, and Simon, and my sisters' husbands, Timaeus and Philip. May I ask if these are your sons?"

"They are," she said as she introduced the men. "I think I see a resemblance between my sons and two of you. Am I dreaming? Or do you see it also?"

James nodded. "I think we should all sit down and talk for a while. Right now, I'm trying not to be too excited! I have so many questions. I need to be certain before I mention this to Mother."

It was true! This family was Mary's younger sister and her family.

"It's close to time for us to prepare for the Sabbath meal, so we need to leave. How can we get together? We absolutely must get you and Mother together," said James.

It was decided that, at the fourth hour tomorrow, Yannis and his family would bring Rachel and her sons to the area where they had first met with Yannis.

As the brothers were returning to their families, they discussed the situation. Should they tell Mary? Should they try to have Jesus there? They would need to have a meal. After talking it over, they decided they would not tell Mary but let her think they were meeting with Yannis and his family—which they were. Joses would find Jesus and try to get him to come. The brothers would tell their wives what was really happening and ask them to take the lead on the meal.

Joses ran quickly to find Jesus who was with the folks from Capernaum. "Jesus, may I speak with you for a minute?" Joses asked after they had greeted each other with a hug and claps on the back.

They walked a little distance away. "Jesus, we've found Mother's sister Rachel. She's here with her family, and we're all going to meet tomorrow at the fourth hour. Can you try to come?"

"You've found Mother's sister? Are you sure?" asked Jesus.

"Positive!" answered Joses. "She has two sons, and they kind of look like Simon and James. We're sure. Can you get away?"

"I need to discuss this with the rabbis. Come visit with Zebedee, James, and John while I talk with the rabbis," said Jesus.

Thaddeaus and Sylvanus were happy for Jesus. It was agreed that he could of course go, and he could be free for the day.

When Joses returned, he said, "Mother, Jesus will be able to meet with Yannis and us tomorrow! I'm sure Yannis and his family will like that."

"I'm sure I will too. Thank you, Joses! It's almost time for the Sabbath meal. I am so hungry."

The next morning, plans were made much as they had been last time they had met Yannis and his family. Jesus tried to keep Mary busy with her back to the path that Yannis would take to reach them, but the children couldn't be held back and they saw Yannis.

Leah cried out, "There's Yannis and his family!" And off she and the older children ran.

Mary turned to greet Yannis and his family and then stopped. She looked at the woman with them. She ran and started to cry. "Rachel! I didn't know if you were still alive!" She crushed her sister in a hug.

The two women hugged and cried. Neither could talk for a bit. And then they both started talking at once as they walked back to the families.

"Oh, Rachel! How did Yannis find you?" began Mary. "Oh! First let's introduce our families. These must be your sons. I see a resemblance to mine."

Introductions were made down to the youngest child, and then the telling of the story began. Mary and Rachel sat side by side, holding hands.

Rachel began. "Our uncle and aunt sort of adopted me and took me to the city of Bethlehem and raised me as their own," she said. "They were kind people. Our aunt was a little overly fussy about almost everything—my clothes, my hair, my friends, the house, everything—but I knew she did it out of love. They both passed the year of my betrothal. That was hard. We delayed the wedding a few months, but then I was married, and I have these two wonderful sons! We still live on a rather large farm just outside of Bethlehem, where we raise sheep and goats. My eldest is betrothed and will marry in a few months."

"Bethlehem!" said Mary. "We lived in Bethlehem for almost two years! Jesus was born there. Why did we never see each other?"

"I rarely went into town. My friends and I usually met at one of our homes out in the country. Wouldn't it have been funny if we had seen each other and didn't know it? But we would have known each other, as it had only been two or three years. I want to believe that we'd have known each other anywhere we were," said Rachel.

It seems that Rachel had met Yannis's wife through mutual friends. During their talks Yannis's wife had mentioned that, while in Jerusalem, she had met a nice family from Nazareth. Rachel told her that she was from Nazareth a long time ago and that her parents and brother had died and she didn't know if her sister had survived. They talked for a while and then decided to get Yannis involved and have him talk to his friends when they went to Jerusalem. "And here we are!" said Rachel.

Jesus said, "I am the baby who was born in Bethlehem. That was a long time ago, wasn't it, Mother?" he teased as he squeezed her shoulder.

"Not so long, Jesus." She turned to Yannis. "Forgive me, Yannis! I've ignored you and your family. Please forgive me. How are you and your family?"

"There's nothing to forgive. This has been a very special time for us as well. To answer your question, we are doing well. Two more of my sons are now bar mitzvahs. I am so proud. I'm still working on and studying the Torah and the Prophets. It's hard, but I love it!

"Our young Simon has reminded us several times that he wanted to meet 'big Simon' and spend time with him. We assured him he would. I hope that's okay with you, Simon." As he looked for Simon, he saw that the two Simons were already together.

Young Simon was telling big Simon, "I'm not very old, and I have to start bar mitzvah schooling next year. It scares me."

"Can you tell me what scares you about becoming a bar mitzvah?" asked big Simon.

"I'm not grown up enough. My brothers are so grown up. I'm just little. How can I learn all the stuff they know?" asked young Simon.

"It sounds like you *are* growing up. You are asking a lot of questions. That's a good start to being a grown up. May I tell you a secret?" asked big Simon.

Young Simon shrugged his shoulders and said, "I guess."

"You have almost three years before you are a bar mitzvah. That's a long time to learn all you need to know. Now the secret—every boy feels that way three years before. Every boy! Including me!" explained big Simon.

"Really? Why didn't my brothers tell me?" asked young Simon.

"Did you ask them?" asked big Simon.

Young Simon looked down and said, "No. I didn't think about it."

"Young Simon, you are a wonderful young man. Your teachers will help you. And if you have questions, I'm sure your big brothers would help you. Your father is studying now. I'll bet he has a ton of questions, and I'll bet he'd be happy to help you. See? Already you know where to get answers! Don't worry, Simon. If you do the work assigned to you, you will have no trouble becoming a bar mitzvah. One more thing—you have enough things you are dealing with now. Don't worry about things you might worry about later. Do you understand?" asked big Simon.

Young Simon thought for a minute. "I think I understand. You mean that I have enough to learn now and that will get me ready to learn the bigger stuff later. So I shouldn't think about that stuff now, cuz I'll be ready when I get there. Is that right?" he asked.

Big Simon smiled at him. "Yes that is exactly what I mean. I want you to remember that. And I want you to remember something else—when you worry and when things are hard, talk with Father God. You can talk with Him all the time—not just during your usual prayers."

"I think my father told me that once, but I forgot. Thank you, big Simon. Thank you for not treating me like a little kid," said young Simon.

"You are welcome. You're a great young man. I'm glad I know you. Can we make a plan that we will do our best to meet whenever we can—especially when we're all in Jerusalem for festivals?" asked big Simon.

"Yes! Can we shake on it?" said young Simon, grinning.

Big Simon shook his hand and then picked him up and swung him around. "You are now officially my friend!" And they both laughed.

It was soon time to eat. Mary and Rachel couldn't get enough of each other. Rachel's boys fit right in with the family—just as though they had been cousins forever.

After dinner, Jesus looked for Yannis's third and fourth sons to follow up on their conversation of a year ago. He found them off by themselves. "Boys, you've grown quite a bit! Tell me, what's going on in your lives?"

The boys appeared shy.

Jesus tried again. "You are now bar mitzvahs, so that means you're adults. Has that changed anything in your lives?"

The boys smiled widely.

"I thought I'd have more time when I finished school, but I enrolled in more schooling, and I'm working now. When I can, I try to work with a kid who is having difficulty in one area of the Torah. It feels good when you've worked with someone and they catch on," said the older brother.

"I thought I'd feel different, but I really don't," said the younger brother. "I'm beginning to think that all your life long you're learning. I'm trying to see how I can grow with Father God and still be useful to all His people. I haven't found a way yet but I know I will one day. I've only been a bar mitzvah a couple of months, so I feel I have time to learn."

Jesus smiled. "You are awesome young men. Don't forget that. You're both thinkers, and you each have your own focus.

That's a good thing. You can always talk together and work things out. I'm proud of both of you, and so is Father God."

Leah came running up to them. "Uncle Jesus, could all of you please come back to the rest of us? Grandma Mary sent me to get you."

Jesus tussled her hair. "Of course, little Leah. Oops! I bet you don't want to be called little do you!"

"That's okay, Uncle Jesus. I don't get to see you very much, so you can call me whatever you want to.

"I love you, Uncle Jesus!" said Leah as she skipped beside him. The boys ran on ahead.

"Thank you, Leah. That means a lot to me. It makes me feel special. Know what? I love you tons!"

"How can you love me tons?"

"Think about it. A ton is very, very heavy. How much does love weigh?" asked Jesus.

Leah looked puzzled. "It doesn't weigh anything. Oh! So it takes a really, really lot of love to weigh a ton! Is that right?"

Jesus smiled. "That's right. That's how much I love you."

Leah took the hand of her Uncle Jesus.

Everybody was waiting for them. It was time for lunch.

After lunch, Mary turned to Jesus and said, "Remember when we used to all sing psalms in harmony?"

Jesus nodded.

"Well, we'd like to try it again. Are you ready?"

"Ah, Woman! I'm always ready to do whatever you ask of me." He looked at Joses and Claudia and said, "Let's do it."

After the first psalm, Rachel said, "How did you do that?"

Yannis's wife asked, "Can you show us how?"

Claudia and Joses and Jesus gave a quick explanation and then demonstrated how to do it. Even they created some weird sounds. "Just don't be afraid to try. You do not have to be perfect. Try it on this next psalm. Really. Try. We won't laugh at you."

Rachel and her sons caught on quickly. Yannis's wife was next. Eventually, they all tried singing in harmony. Some had much better results than others.

"You can always sing the melody," said Claudia. "If everyone sang harmony, I'm afraid it would sound a bit weird. Join us in a couple more psalms."

The younger children chimed in on the songs they knew. It was great time to remember—a time of love and a time of joy.

As with all things, it was time to return to their tents to prepare dinner. Mary and Rachel made plans to see each other often during these festival days. "Now that I've found you, I'm not going to let you get far away from me," said Mary.

Jesus needed to leave to be back by sundown. He took Mary aside and said, "Mother, all the things you and Father have taught me over the years have become a real part of me. Every day I find myself thinking, *This is something I learned from Mother*, or, *This is something Father taught me*. I want you to know how much you mean to me. Thank you, Mother!" And he hugged her. "I look forward to seeing you as soon as possible. Be well, Mother. I love you!"

***

Back with the people from Capernaum, Jesus ate dinner and then, as folks were gathering around a fire, he walked from group to group. One of the young girls asked him a very curious question. "What do your brothers and sisters look like?"

"I don't know how to answer that," said Jesus. "They look like my brothers and sisters I guess is all I can say. I don't think they look like me or like each other, and yet they do. Why do you ask?"

"Well, Father said I look like my brothers and sisters, but I don't think so. I've been looking at all the brothers and sisters in our group today, and I guess I can see a little bit that they maybe look alike. You weren't here today, so I was wondering about you."

"My, that was a lot of thinking! Not only that but you really did some checking up to see if what you thought was really true! I hope you're always like that. That's the best way to learn," answered Jesus.

That night as Jesus lay in bed, he prayed, "A wonderful day! Thank You, Father God. Thank you especially that Mother has found her sister Rachel."

The next morning, Jesus woke up feeling content. After breakfast, he met with Thaddeaus and Sylvanus to review the plans for the day. The people were all doing well, so they decided that, after their time in the temple, they would just be a part of their people—free to do as they wished.

During the week, the men of Capernaum and the men of Nazareth found themselves worshipping together at the temple and spending time together on the way back to their families. One day, Peter said, "Would it be a good idea to try to get all our families together? We men are getting to know each other and seem to get along fine. I think our families may get along as well."

"What a good idea!" said Judas. "Have you thought of any plans—like where and when we might get everyone together?"

The men stopped to talk about it. Peter said, "There's a rather large area just east of here. It's a little rough, but there are plenty of trees. Maybe we could meet at the fourth hour on the Sabbath day. What do you think?"

After discussion, it was decided to go with Peter's idea. Each family would talk with their townspeople tonight if possible, and then they'd talk again tomorrow after worship.

As expected, there were very few in either town who were not excited. It was agreed that the get-together was not mandatory, and people could certainly make up their own minds as to whether or not they would take part. Mostly, the people were excited!

Sabbath morning finally arrived. It seemed that no one could wait to start out for the day's adventure. Long before the fourth hour, almost everyone from both towns had gathered. Because the men already knew most of the other men, they were able to introduce everyone quite easily.

Matthew and Philip from the people of Nazareth and James and John from Capernaum took the boys for games shortly after the noon meal. The boys eagerly learned the games the boys from the other town had to teach them.

The older girls from both towns took the younger girls to a separate area, teaching each other to play the games each group was familiar with.

That left the adults to have a couple of hours to talk without interruption. But as with the children, the men went off by themselves, and the women stayed together.

Mary, Miriam, and Peter's wife got along as though they had known each other for years. Peter's wife told them of the changes Jesus had made in Capernaum. She told them about the man who kidnapped children, the girls and how they loved visiting the homebound, the changes in the sisters, and the change in Thaddeaus.

Thaddeaus approached Mary. "Mary mother of Jesus, may I speak to you for a minute?"

"Of course!" said Mary. "I was hoping you and I would have some time to talk."

Thaddeaus began. "I want you to know what a blessing Jesus has been to our town and especially to me. I have learned so much from him."

Mary smiled. "Thank you for telling me. I feel he's remarkable, but it's always nice to hear what he means to others."

"He seems to know what to say and when to say it. For instance, I was trying hard to show everyone that I was competent, not only to replace my father, but also to lead our congregation. Very gently, Jesus showed me what I was doing and how it looked to others and how that was not what I wanted. He helped me decide what I could do to make the changes I wanted to make. It's made a dramatic change in every part of my life. Yet when I look back on that conversation, I see that he made me feel that the changes I would make were my ideas. He's a remarkable man!" explained Thaddeaus.

"Thank you. He's always been that way. Ever since he was very small, he seemed to know what to say to make others feel comfortable. And from what I've seen, he's made them better people for it," said Mary.

"I'm looking forward to this next year. Jesus will be helping me learn to teach the boys during their final two or so years of preparation for their bar mitzvah. It's such an important time in the life of a young man. I've noticed that he's made the boys want to learn—not just to ask questions and get answers, but also to try to find the answer themselves. I love watching his interaction with others," Thaddeaus added.

Thaddeaus and Mary had been talking for a while longer, when suddenly there was a scream, followed by several screams and calls for help.

As was usual, Jesus, his brothers, and Thaddeaus ran to see what had happened. Peter, James, and John saw them run and ran after them.

As they reached the scene, Jesus took a quick look and said, "Take the girls!" And to others he said, "Get rocks!" He prayed, "Father God, please heal those little girls and keep these snakes away from the people, please!"

There were about eight or nine girls, ages probably about six to ten, all screaming and writhing in pain. Thaddeaus and the brothers began praying and trying to calm the girls. Peter, James, and John joined those looking for rocks and ran to take them to Jesus.

In the meantime, Jesus saw the snakes. It looked like a den had been disturbed. With no rocks nearby, Jesus began stomping on them just behind their heads.

As rocks were brought, Jesus and others began using them to kill the snakes. There were so many! Where had they come from? Finally, it looked like all the snakes were dead. Jesus went over to the girls.

"They've all been bitten. We've been praying and they're coming around," said Simon.

Jesus turned to the girl who appeared to be the oldest. "Please tell me what happened."

She was still crying, but she said, "We found a big stone, and we wanted to use it in a game we were playing. A bunch of us tried to lift it up, but a lot of snakes came out from under it."

One of the other girls said, "I wanted to play with them. They looked like the one by my grandfather's house. So I reached behind its head like he told me to, but it bit me. And then all the snakes started biting all of us, and we screamed, and then I got real dizzy and I hurt all over so bad."

By now, everyone had come to see what had happened. The parents gathered the girls in their arms.

Jesus said, "They'll all be okay. Right now, they need to rest—maybe until after dinner." He turned to the girls and said gently, "Did you learn anything?"

The smallest girl said, "I don't like snakes!"

Everyone smiled.

One of the older girls said, "I guess just because a snake looks like another snake, you can't be sure. So maybe we should leave all the snakes alone."

"I think we should not try to move rocks," said another.

Thaddeaus said, "Let's all pray. Father God, thank You for taking charge of these young girls and for healing them so quickly. Thank You for the new friends we've all made today. Thank You for the joy! Thank You for You!" He turned to everyone and said, "Now where were we? Let's get back to our getting acquainted."

Simon said, "I'll clean up here. Catch up to you in a bit."

"Thanks, Simon," said one of the men from Capernaum. "I'll help you. It'll get done faster and we can get back and settle that last game."

Jesus threw his arm around Thaddeaus's shoulders and said, "Great work!" He turned to Peter. "Peter, you looked like a veteran rock hunter today. Thank you."

Later, Matthew told Jesus, "Philip and I had just said to James and John how good it felt that there had been no big incidents this year. We were telling them about some of the other incidents from past years when we heard the girls screaming. I guess we definitely spoke too soon."

SIXTY-ONE

29

Back home. It was hard for Mary to leave Jesus, but she knew he was not hers alone. "Thank You, Father God, for giving me this extra time with Jesus. He's a good man, and I know I have You to thank for that. Thank You! Thank You also for bringing my Rachel back into my life! Please help us find a way to spend time together. I love You, Father God."

Back in Capernaum, Jesus, Thaddeaus, and Sylvanus were at their early morning meeting. After opening prayer, Jesus said, "We have a lot to talk about—our trip to Jerusalem and especially the changes we need to make to be sure everything is in place for me to leave in less than a year. Where would you like to start?"

Sylvanus said, "I am so excited about all that went on in these past few days! To me, the biggest thing was meeting your mother. What a woman! She is truly remarkable!"

"Thank you. She certainly is!" answered Jesus. "Thaddeaus, how or what are your thoughts and feelings? This will be a great year for you."

"I thought the festival went well. I was especially awed by the healing of the girls who were bitten by those snakes. Father God is so present for us.

"About these next few months, I feel excited—like I'm floating on a cloud! But then I realize how much I still need to learn, and that makes me know I need to keep focused," confessed Thaddeaus.

Jesus smiled.

Sylvanus clapped him on the back and said, "Aw, you'll do just fine. You're really your father's son, and everyone loves and respects you. Don't worry!"

"Let's make a list of things to do. We can start there and add and subtract as needed," suggested Jesus.

They worked until it was time for school to start. "I think we made a good start," said Thaddeaus. "I can't wait to begin teaching the bar mitzvah class. I can't wait until we meet to decide how we'll make these things happen."

Within four weeks, they had hired another rabbi, Rabbi Titus, who they hoped would stay with the synagogue and teach after Jesus left. As soon as Rabbi Titus was comfortable, possibly in about three weeks, Thaddeaus would begin teaching his bar mitzvah class.

Rabbi Titus worked out well and, from the beginning, joined the rabbis at their morning meetings. He was tall, looked and held himself like an athlete, laughed rather loudly, and was gentle but firm.

"Thaddeaus," asked Jesus one morning, "how do you want to work the transition from my teaching to your taking over?"

"I've been thinking about it, and I see two options. One, I watch you teach for a week or so, and then for a week or so you stand by while I teach. But that's really not what I'd feel comfortable with.

"As I see it another option would be for the two of us to meet in the evenings and go through the next day's classes, but I don't know if that would work either. What do you think?"

"Either is possible. Or we could be co-teachers for a while. We'd need to meet to set up how we'd implement it, but that way you'd be teaching right from the beginning. You would start out with a lesser share of the teaching but increase your responsibilities every few days—maybe each week depending on your comfort zone. Perhaps it would take three to four months—again, depending on your comfort level.

"We'll wait until you're completely comfortable teaching, and then I'll show you the duties in administration you haven't learned yet."

"I like that. Can you and I meet soon? I'd like to get started," answered Thaddeaus.

They did. After a few meetings, they felt they were ready, and they began. Thaddeaus said, "I feel like I'm starting something awesome!"

"You are," said Jesus. "This is your dream; it's what you were meant to be doing."

The co-teaching plan worked well. The boys accepted this new way of being taught, and each week Thaddeaus felt more comfortable and took on more of the teaching.

***

"Jesus, may we speak to you?" called Zebedee. He and John were approaching. It was a Sabbath afternoon, and there was, of course, no fishing.

Jesus smiled and said, "Of course! What can I do for you?"

John spoke up. "I would like to become a bar mitzvah. Father and I were talking about it, and we were wondering if we could hold the ceremony in two weeks? I will turn thirteen tomorrow, and I feel I am ready."

"I'll check with the other rabbis tomorrow at our meeting. I think it's a good time. You've done very well in class, and I know you'll be a great man in our town. I'll try to meet you at school tomorrow and let you know if the others have anything else scheduled," Jesus said, smiling as he put his hand on John's shoulder. "I'm proud of you John. If I had a son, I'd want him to be just like you!"

"Thank you. I'd like it if you and Rabbi Thaddeaus and Rabbi Sylvanus could all be a part of my ceremony. You were all my teachers, and you all mean a lot to me," said John.

"I'll check with them about that also. May Father God continue to bless you as you prepare for this part of your life," added Jesus.

The next morning, Jesus explained John's request to the rabbis. They agreed that two weeks before the start of the Sabbath service was a good time.

Jesus continued, "When I became a bar mitzvah, I had two parts in the service. I was wondering what all of you would think of John having the same parts. I was maftir and I chanted the haftorah."

"That is for special students," said Thaddeaus. "As I think about it, I agree. If we all agree, then John will be maftir and chant the haftorah. Thoughts?"

Sylvanus said, "He was the most earnest student I've ever taught in his early years. I remember that, one time, I had to assign him an hour of outdoor activity each day for one week just to get him to quit studying every moment. He's a good kid, and he'll make a great man. I agree. He deserves both of those parts."

Thaddeaus turned to Rabbi Titus. "Will you be feeling left out? I'm sure we can find a part for you that John would be very open to."

"This isn't about me; I won't feel left out. Perhaps I could stand at the door and greet our people as they enter," suggested Rabbi Titus.

"Great idea," said Thaddeaus. "Jesus, what do you think?"

"That is a good suggestion, Titus. I think that, every time we think of what might bother someone and strive to avert a possible problem, things will be better. Our synagogue and school are in very good hands with the three of you in charge. May I tell John after classes today? I told him I'd meet him then."

The three rabbis nodded their agreement.

"Of course. Thank you, Jesus. Let's pray and get to our classes." said Rabbi Sylvanus.

The ceremony went well. John had studied and practiced extra hard those last two weeks. At the end of the service, the synagogue at Capernaum had another remarkable man in its congregation.

Sixty-Two

29

One morning at the before-school meeting, Jesus mentioned to the rabbis that, while he was in Nazareth, the town was considering doing repairs on the synagogue. "I've never thought to look at this synagogue and school with eyes toward needed repairs. What do you think? A good idea?"

The four of them talked about it for a while and decided that this was something that should be done. Their first question was, should they take a first look or should they hire someone to do it? They decided to do both. After school, they would take a tour and make notes.

Their second question was who to ask to take a closer look. They decided to approach both Zebedee and Peter and see if either had the time or would want to be a part of this repair work.

That evening when Eunice brought dinner, Jesus asked her to sit a while and tell him how she was doing. She said she would stay only if he ate while they talked. It was like two old friends catching up on each other's lives. Jesus mentioned that the rabbis were looking into repairs that might be needed at the synagogue and school.

"Rabbi! That is such a good idea! May I say something?" asked Eunice.

"Of course."

"My neighbor and I were saying that it's difficult sometimes to stand so long for the Sabbath services. We thought that it would be nice to have benches for people to sit on—especially those who find it hard to stand that long. Is that something that could be discussed?" asked Eunice.

"Eunice, you are remarkable. What a good suggestion! I had never thought about it. We Rabbis stand, so I assumed no one would have a problem. But I see you're right. I promise that we'll discuss it. Thank you," said Jesus as he reached across the table and squeezed her hands. "Here. It's getting late. Let me walk you home. It may be better if you don't mention this to other folks until we've had a chance to check things out and then we'll tell everyone. Okay?"

"Of course. It's going to be a little hard because I'm so excited, but I can do it," promised Eunice.

The next morning, Jesus mentioned the benches to the rabbis. They liked the idea. It was decided to make this a part of the repair work at the synagogue and school. How would they pay for the needed repairs? They talked for a while and then decided that, when estimates for the repair work and the benches were in place, they would then update the congregation before one of the services and hold an open discussion.

At the daily meeting a few days later, Thaddeaus said, "I was able to meet with both Zebedee and Peter, and both are more than willing to work on the repairs. They also said they would set up their own schedules, get estimates, and bring us up to date. By the way, Peter's brother Andrew is back in town and is willing to help do any work needed."

That evening, while Jesus was studying, there was a knock on his door. He didn't recognize the man at the door but said, "Come in. You are most welcome. I am Rabbi Jesus of the synagogue."

The man entered and said, "I am Andrew, Peter's brother. Please forgive me for coming without being invited, but I've heard so much about you from so many people that I needed to come and see for myself. Am I forgiven?"

Jesus shook his hand with both of his. "You are forgiven, and you are most welcome. Here, sit a bit. Tell me about yourself."

"Okay, but I'd rather hear about you. I am Peter's brother. I am a fisherman by trade. For the past year or so, I've been in Cana to find new businesses for ours and possibly Zebedee's products. But after a few months—oh by the way, I was successful in reaching and contracting with several new businesses—so after a few months, I began to look into anything I could find that might have something to do with the fishing industry."

"Did you find anything?" asked Jesus.

"I did, but after a while, I began to see that almost anything could be applied to our fishing. Cement, leather, wooden items—all of them would make things easier either on shore or on the boat. But it was time for me to return home and put what I'd learned to good use. So I came home. Now, tell me about you."

Jesus filled him in on his family, his work as rabbi in Nazareth, and his work here.

"I think you left out a lot," said Andrew. "But maybe for tonight that's enough. Thank you for seeing me. I am really glad to have met you. I think we'll be seeing a lot more of each other. You intrigue me." They shook hands, and Andrew returned home.

Andrew's prediction was true. Within a week, the synagogue and school had been carefully gone over, and an extensive list of needed repairs was made. Andrew became a vital part of the work.

Peter, Andrew, and Zebedee reported to the rabbis during a morning meeting, "We've made two lists—one for repairs that really should be made as soon as we can start them and another list of the repairs that could be done later."

Andrew added, "We've also made a list of the probable costs of each repair. The total of all is overwhelming, but when we break it down to each repair, it's more manageable."

"Our family has agreed that we will cover the cost of labor, leaving the cost of materials yet to be covered," said Zebedee. "If it's all right with everyone, I'll use some of my servants. Most of them are very talented. What do you think?"

The rabbis looked at each other and nodded. Thaddeaus said, "That is truly amazing. Before service this Sabbath we'll talk with the people and get their input. Does it sound right that I open with the facts? And then maybe one of you can talk about the actual repairs?"

It was agreed that would be the plan.

After the others left, Jesus said to the rabbis, "I've been thinking. There are going to be a lot of things that come up during these repairs. The four of us can have all the questions about these repairs brought to us for decisions, or we could have one person responsible for everything day-to-day. I'm offering to be that person. As my responsibilities for the bar mitzvah classes are lessening, I'll have time. Any major decisions I would bring to the three of you. What are your thoughts?"

"I hadn't thought about it," said Sylvanus. "I certainly don't have time to spend working through these things on a daily basis. I don't know enough either."

Thaddeaus said, "With my new teaching responsibilities, I don't have the time either. I think it's a great idea. I say go for it,"

Rabbi Titus nodded.

They all agreed. Jesus would take the lead.

It was also decided that, before service this Sabbath, they would update the congregation. They did. As expected, there were questions, but everyone did agree that these repairs were needed and that each man would do all he could to help keep the costs down.

The work started the next Monday morning. It turned out that Zebedee's men were indeed very capable. Zebedee was able to set up a schedule that would keep his fishing business going as his workers worked on the repairs. The contacts Andrew had made in Cana proved helpful. The needed materials that couldn't be found locally were found in Cana.

Within four weeks, the list of the much-needed repairs was almost completed. On Sabbath morning, the rabbis, along with Zebedee, Peter, and Andrew, were looking over the repairs when two large carts pulled up. Jesus stood there for a moment. He couldn't believe his eyes! He ran and threw his arms around his brothers.

"What are you doing here and what's in these carts?" he asked.

Judas and Joses untied the covers and threw them off to show what was underneath—benches, a lot of benches! James said, "We were told you needed benches, a lot of benches, for the synagogue. So we made them and brought them here to see if they would meet with your approval."

The men gathered around, each one running his hands over the wood. "They are beautiful!" said Zebedee. "Amazing work! Thank you, men!"

Jesus looked at Zebedee. "You did this? You had my family make benches for our synagogue? You are an awesome friend, Zebedee! Thank you! Thank you! Let's get them inside and see how they look."

They looked great! Thaddeaus said, "Sabbath is almost a week away before the people would be able to see these. I don't know how I'm going to wait. Maybe we'll have to have a special meeting of some sort."

Peter said, "It doesn't look like we need a special meeting. Look." Several people had seen the carts roll in, and as they came to see what was happening, more joined them.

These men looked to Thaddeaus for an explanation. He waved at them and said, "Come on in! This is amazing!"

It was agreed; this was amazing.

Judas and Joses could only spend the night and then had to leave first thing the next morning. Jesus rode with his brothers for a mile or so outside the city.

"This was really a treat!" he said. "Thank you for the benches. They are wonderful! Thank you for visiting. Please give Mother a big hug and greet everyone for me." He hugged his brothers and waved goodbye.

"Another blessing from You, Father God. Keep them safe on their way home. Please continue to watch over all my families. Please continue to take charge of me. Thank You for all You do. Help me to know and do Your will. Amen."

Sixty-Three

29

Jesus's time in Capernaum was coming to an end. Rabbi Titus had fit in well. His students were learning, and any trouble that may have started to erupt—as a test of a new teacher of course—he handled readily. Thaddeaus was doing well, and his excitement seemed to be building as he taught the bar mitzvah preparation classes, while assuming more and more of the administrative work. The major repairs were completed on the synagogue, and several of the less urgent repairs were being worked on. The people were doing a great job of giving what they could.

"Father God, please lead me where You want me to go from here. Thank You for the blessings I have received while living and working here in Capernaum," became Jesus's daily prayer.

On Sabbath and some weekday afternoons, Jesus found himself walking along the roads at the crossroads and finding the many differences and the many similarities in people. He found so many people hungry for a purpose in their lives. He felt good when he found someone who just needed to talk, and he was there to listen. "Father God, is this where You're leading me? To reach out to people where they are? I'm willing to do Your work. Please let me know clearly Your will for me. I want to do Your will. Thank You, Father God."

One Sabbath, he returned home to pick up another robe, as it was cold and very windy and looked like it would rain. As he approached his home, he thought he saw his door close.

He walked carefully and opened the door slowly. His brother stood just inside the door.

"James! Welcome!" he said as he wrapped his arms around his brother. He stopped and said hesitantly, "Is everyone okay?"

"Everyone is fine! Let's see. Joses's son is a lot like Joses and was walking on a downed branch, fell off, and broke his arm. But he's fine now. Our Father God is amazing! I'm here with news. Timaeus's sister is being married in Cana in four weeks, and Timaeus was thinking that your time here may be ending and maybe you could join the family for the wedding. What do you think?"

"I think that would work out well. I'll need to talk with the rabbis, but as of now, it looks like perfect timing." The wind was really blowing, and now it was raining. Jesus said, "That wind is fierce. It seems to be coming almost directly from the south. That's unusual. I don't think you should plan on going back today."

"I talked with the brothers, and they agreed that I should stay a day or so and maybe meet some of the people you've been working with." James grinned.

Just then, there was a noise as if several rams' horns were being blown together. There was a knock at Jesus's door, and Sylvanus rushed in. "Jesus, that's the call for trouble on the sea. We must go. Now!"

James and Jesus joined Sylvanus and ran through the town, past the area of the fishing boats and shops, and into the area of the Gentiles. Many of the men of Capernaum were running in the same direction. The wind was fierce! As they rounded the north curve toward the east, they all slowed for just a second.

Apparently a huge wave had blown in from the sea and had risen more than a hundred feet above the water and been driven to shore. It had crumpled businesses along the shore and then hit several homes nearby. Gentile men, women, and children were all in need of help. The men of Capernaum ran toward them—not knowing what to do first but knowing they had to do something.

Zebedee spotted Jesus and called to him. As they ran forward, he said, "I have a warehouse a ways up the hill back there. We can move everyone up there. I've sent some of my men to make it as comfortable as possible, and the others are here with me. We'll do all we can."

By this time, they were in the center of the trouble. Jesus nodded to Zebedee and ran to a small girl whose head was at a strange angle. He said to the girl, "Hold very still! I need to look at your neck. No! No! Don't move! You don't need to be afraid of me. Look in my eyes. There. See? I'm going to make you feel better," he said as he prayed. "Father God, please heal this little girl. I know that none of these people know You but the ones I've met have been kind. Please, Father God, heal these people."

A woman approached. "She's my neighbor girl. Is she all right?" she asked.

"She needs to rest. She had quite an injury. Can you stay with her until we find her parents?" asked Jesus.

The woman looked at him sadly and nodded that she'd stay. She held the little girl's hand, and Jesus moved to the next person.

Two young boys had been sucked out to sea, lifted by the wave, and then thrown back to shore. One had hit his head and was not responding but was breathing. John was kneeling by him. The other appeared lifeless. Jesus turned the boy over, picked him up, held him over his arms, and gave him a few smacks on the back. The boy took a huge breath and began crying. When he saw Jesus, he began screaming. Jesus shook his head, put the boy down, and moved to the next person.

Zebedee, James, John, and their servants were taking people to the warehouse. After a while, Jesus and his brother James searched carefully for more people who might need help. No other injured were found. They joined the others at the warehouse.

Zebedee had sent two of his men to see if those remaining in Capernaum would be able to bring food or bedding or clothing—anything that might help. It seemed that all of the men from Capernaum were here to help. By the time Jesus and the others arrived at the warehouse, the servants were working hard to make the Gentiles as comfortable as the circumstances allowed.

Jesus saw James, the son of Zebedee, talking with one of the Gentile men. "Have we found everyone?" asked Jesus.

"Jesus, this man and I have become friends. He tells me that he's pretty sure that everyone is here. It appears there have been no deaths; we're all amazed at that. My father thinks the storm has eased and that by morning we can begin the cleanup," said James.

"Father God is so good! It is nice to meet you. Please let us know how we can help you put things back, help you repair things," said Jesus, shaking the man's hand. Turning to James, he said, "I'm going to walk around and look at everyone. I want to make sure that they're all well."

The children hid behind their parents—all but a little girl of about five. She walked up to Jesus and said, "Who are you? Are you going to hurt us?"

Jesus smiled and stooped down so he was eye to eye with her. "I am Jesus, son of Joseph of Nazareth. I would never hurt you, and that's a promise."

"My father says to stay away from all you Jews—that you're not worth our time. So I'd better go back."

"Before you leave, may I tell you something?"

She nodded.

"We Jews used to think the same thing of you. But as I can see, you are all very nice people. I think if we tried, we could maybe be friends. Is this your father?" Jesus asked as a man came up to them.

"I am her father. I want to thank you and your people for all you've done for us today. I'm surprised and very grateful. I don't know what to say except to say thank you."

Jesus reached out his hand in friendship. The man hesitated a few seconds and then took Jesus' hand. Some of those nearby murmured their amazement.

The little girl turned to her father and said, "I like him, Father. I'm glad you're going to be his friend."

The two men smiled at each other.

The Gentile's were now as comfortable as possible. The men of Capernaum were able to return to their homes.

"Our servants will stay here and bring them everything they need," said James. "Cook is already making a thick stew for later. We're having cook also make hot posca. I'm hoping it will help prevent any illnesses that might come from this."

Jesus said, "Thank you James. And be sure to thank Zebedee and John! The three of you are Father God's angels today. I think the rest of us will head back. Take care of yourself, my friend."

The storm had abated.

Thank You, Father God for helping these people. I'm unsure where this will lead, but I know You'll be in charge. Thank You! Jesus prayed.

As Jesus caught up to his brother and the rabbis, he heard his brother telling of other times Father God had been there when something drastic had happened. He thought, *Apparently Rabbi Titus was surprised at the healings.* Jesus smiled.

Brother James met with Jesus and the rabbis the next morning. Jesus told the rabbis, "My brother is here to tell me of a family wedding coming up in Cana in four weeks' time and is wondering if I might be able to attend. My time here is ending about that time, so I asked James to join us this morning, and perhaps we could discuss it."

The rabbis looked at one another and Thaddeaus said, "Jesus, I think that this is perfect timing. We don't like the thought of you leaving, but we realize that you have taught us so much and that you have shown us that we are now able to handle things here. If you're in agreement, let's say that you may end your time with us in time for you to travel to the wedding."

Sylvanus wiped his eyes and said, "I've never had a brother. And when I think of what a brother would be like, I always thought he would be just like you. I don't want you to go, but I know you need to get on with your life. I will miss you terribly, my brother!"

Rabbi Titus said, "My time knowing you has been very short compared to the others, but I have learned so much talking with you and just watching you and the way you handle people and situations. I also will miss you."

Jesus said, "Thank you all. I can tell you that I will miss each one of you. You have also taught me. You were left suddenly with a critical situation, but each of you pitched in and made it a smooth transition."

To James, he said, "I think we have our answer. Let's you and I leave these men to their discussions, and we'll walk a while before you leave." He turned to the rabbis, "Thank you. We'll make final plans later."

The brothers walked and talked easily until it was time for James to leave. Jesus walked with James about a mile out of town. "Please tell Mother that I love her and miss her. And tell the rest of the family I love them and I can hardly wait to see them!"

They hugged and parted with smiles.

SIXTY-FOUR

29

A few days later at the morning meeting, Thaddeaus said, "James came up to me after classes yesterday and said that one of the Gentile men wanted to know if someone could meet with a few of their men and explain who we are. Comments?"

There was quiet for a long time. Jesus waited, remembering that soon he would not be here for input and that this was the time to see how the rabbis handled a problem of this magnitude.

Rabbi Titus said, "I think Jesus should meet with them and answer their questions. I suggest this for two reasons. One, he has been the lead rabbi here for some time, and from what I have observed, he has a gentle way of explaining things. My second reason is—and I'm not proud of this—that he will be leaving soon, so if there are problems with either the Gentiles or with our people, it won't last long." He turned to Jesus. "I'm sorry to say that, but it's what I came up with."

"I take no offense," said Jesus.

Sylvanus said, "I don't know what to say. I think we should talk with them, but I don't want that responsibility."

"Jesus, I understand what the others have said. And if you would agree, I think you are the one to talk with them. What do you think?" said Thaddeaus.

"I think that is the perfect answer. One thing I want—no, I insist be understood—is that this is not part of a plan to try to convert them to Judaism. No one is to try to meet with them to convert them. If they have questions, those questions have to come from them. That has to be understood—clearly. After saying that, if some of them want to become one of us, let them take the lead. Just be there to answer questions and to help them as they request it. Don't deny them. Do you understand where I'm coming from?"

The rabbis nodded. "Should we tell our people?" asked Rabbi Titus.

Thaddeaus thought for a minute and said, "I think we should talk with Zebedee, his sons, and Peter and Andrew for sure. Probably either you, Jesus, or I should talk with them."

Jesus replied, "I'll do it. Why don't we just say that we'll leave this to me entirely? I will give all of you an update after the meeting with Zebedee and the others, and we can then talk about where to go from there. Okay?"

The three rabbis nodded.

While school was in session that morning, Jesus walked over to see if, by any chance, James was not fishing today and they could talk. He was working on shore.

"James, could you take a few minutes and talk with me?" asked Jesus.

James looked at the fish he was preparing and said, "Can you give me about fifteen minutes? Then you'll have my undivided attention."

Jesus nodded and walked along the shore. He spotted Peter and Andrew. "Hi!" he called. "I didn't expect to see you today! Are you feeling well?"

"We are. We fished late last night and decided to finish preparing the catch before going out. The wind is from the east today so the fishing won't be too good. What brings you here?" Peter asked.

Jesus asked if he could talk with them for a minute and then told them about the proposed meeting with the Gentile men and what the rabbis had decided.

Peter thought for a minute and then said, "I would never have thought this would happen. But I think that, as long as we don't try to make them one of us, it should be okay. In fact, now that I think about it, I think it's really awesome. And I think you're the one to do it.

"By the way, I can't tell you how much I'm going to miss you. I have asked Father God to be sure that you and I meet again."

Jesus held Peter and Andrew around their shoulders, looked them in the eyes, and said, "You are awesome friends. I am sure we will meet again. I want to thank you for your friendship. I don't know when, and I don't know where, but I have a good feeling that we will see each other again.

"I need to leave. I have a meeting with James. I'll see you again to make plans," Jesus said as he turned to leave.

James was waiting for him.

"I ran into Peter and Andrew and talked with them for a minute. I hope I didn't make you wait long. Thank you for seeing me."

"I'm assuming you want to talk about my being approached by the Gentile man to tell them what we're about. Right?" asked James.

Jesus nodded. "How do you feel about it?" he asked.

"At first I was hesitant, but after a while I thought that maybe it would be a good idea. I think we're more tolerant of people if we know more about them," said James.

"I think you're right. When I met with the other rabbis, we discussed this for a while and came to much the same conclusion. I'll be the one to talk with them, but I made it very clear that I would only do so if it was clear that this is not a plan to convert the Gentiles. This is just for clarity—to answer their questions," explained Jesus.

"What if they want to become one of us?" asked James.

"That would be wonderful; but it must come from them. We're in no way to push them. One thing we were a little cautious about is the reaction of our congregation. Will they accept this interaction? Will they be upset? Enough so that it could cause trouble? What kind of trouble?" Jesus grinned. "That's one reason we agreed to have me meet with them; I'll soon be gone!

"Also, I plan to tell the Gentiles that, if they have questions, they may ask any of the rabbis. I was hoping I could also mention you and Zebedee, as well as Peter and Andrew. What do you think?" continued Jesus.

James thought for a minute. "I'm trying to imagine what questions they might ask. Would I be able to answer? What if I say something wrong? I'd have to think about it, but I want you to know that I'm very excited that this is going to happen. I don't think you need to worry about it causing trouble with our people. I think that, when they understand the reason and our hoped for results, they'll realize that this is a good thing."

Jesus said, "You know that Father God has told us that He will give us the words if we trust in Him. If you can't answer a question, it's okay to tell them you need to do some research and get back to them. There's nothing wrong with that. It's better than trying to make up an answer. Do you understand what I'm saying?"

"I do. I guess I need to be reminded once in a while that Father God is there and will guide my words. Okay. You may tell the Gentiles that they may approach me and my father. I know he'll be more than willing. I was just thinking, if a youngster has questions, maybe John could answer them better than we could. What do you think?" asked James.

Jesus thought for a moment. "I think that might be a really good idea. Two things—I will need to run this by the rabbis, and we'll need to make sure that John knows he must not try to change anyone."

"I won't mention it to John until you let me know what the rabbis decide. Thank you, Jesus. As I said, I'm excited about this happening," said James.

At their morning meeting the next day, Jesus told the Rabbis, "I've spoken to Peter, Andrew, and James, and they've agreed that we should go ahead with the plan to answer the questions the Gentiles have. James says that, along with Peter, Andrew, and himself, Zebedee will be happy to be available if people want to ask questions."

Thaddeaus nodded. "I'm looking forward to this. Thank you for organizing this, Jesus. Really, I think this will benefit everyone."

"There is one other thing. James mentioned that, if some of the young people have questions, they may feel more comfortable talking with a younger person. He suggested that John could handle those questions. I told him I would need to run this past all of you. Personally, I think it's a great idea," said Jesus.

"I'm sure you'll talk with him ahead of time. He's a great young man. I also think he can handle this well," added Sylvanus.

"Thank you. I plan to meet with all of them and then set up a meeting with the Gentiles as soon as I can," replied Jesus.

That evening just before sundown, Jesus waited at the shore for the boats to return from the day's fishing. As he walked along the shore, he realized for the first time that the far ends of Peter and Zebedee's fishing areas were right next to each other. *No wonder they get along so well,* thought Jesus.

Peter and Andrew landed first. "Jesus! Good to see you so soon! Is everything all right?" asked Peter.

"I was hoping to get a chance to meet with the two of you and Zebedee and his sons later this evening about the meeting with the Gentiles," said Jesus.

Peter looked at Andrew and said, "Our catch wasn't all that great today, so we should be able to meet in about an hour. Will that work?"

Jesus smiled. "Perfectly," he said. "I'll wait and talk with Zebedee and then be back here in about an hour."

A few minutes later, Zebedee landed. "Jesus! What brings you here? Is everyone okay?"

Jesus explained why he was there, and Zebedee said he and James and John could also meet with him in about an hour. "Once we get things started, the servants can take over for a while."

Jesus walked home for dinner. He prayed for Father God's help and direction and then left to meet with the five fishermen.

"Thank you for meeting with me. I want to be sure we all understand what we're about to undertake. First, I spoke with the rabbis, and they agree that, if John wants to, he would be a great resource for the younger Gentiles."

They talked for a while, asked questions, and reviewed what Jesus would explain to the Gentiles. Then they tried to think of questions that might be asked.

Jesus turned to John. "John, we would like you to take on a special responsibility. We feel that many of the younger boys may feel more comfortable asking their questions of you. It's very important that you know for sure what you are saying. It's okay to tell them you don't know, but you'll ask and get the answer for them. You must be very careful that you do not try to tell them that they are wrong or tell them that they must be Jews. Do you understand what I'm saying?"

"Yes, Rabbi. What you're saying is to be honest about what I know and get the answers to the questions I don't know—not to guess. I'm not to tell them they must become Jews. Is that right?"

"Very good," said Jesus. "I'd like you to take the time to think about the questions the boys may ask you. Then think of your answers. When you have questions about the answers, ask me or any one of these men—whoever you wish to talk to. No one will feel left out or sad that you didn't talk with him." He turned to the others. "Right, men?"

They all nodded.

"James, the men contacted you. I'd like to meet with them soon. Would you tell me who I should contact to set up the meeting?" asked Jesus.

"Certainly. My friend is usually at our fish store about first hour every morning. He says he likes nicely prepared fresh fish. Then we talk for a minute. Perhaps you could be here one morning, and I could officially introduce you," said James.

"Tomorrow begins the Sabbath, and I want to meet with him when I have open time so I can meet with everyone on their schedules. I will be here the morning after Sabbath. Will that work for you as well?" asked Jesus.

It was agreed.

SIXTY-FIVE

29

Jesus was at the fish store early that morning, and James introduced Jesus and Damon. Damon said, "It's nice to meet you. I'm not sure what I should call you. I am called Damon."

Jesus shook his hand and said, "It's nice to meet you as well, Damon. You may call me Jesus. It's not necessary to use my title as rabbi." Jesus smiled. "I'm looking forward to meeting with you and your friends. Would it be okay if you and I talk for a while and let James get to his work?"

"Of course." Damon turned to James. "Thank you for introducing me. I like this man, so you can safely leave us alone." He grinned.

Jesus and Damon walked a short distance and sat in the shade of an oak tree. Jesus said, "Tell me how it came about that some of you are curious about who we are."

"This is a little uncomfortable. We've always thought that you people were a little weird," began Damon.

Jesus laughed. "Sometimes I think the same thing," he said.

Damon smiled. "All of you seem so orderly. You seem to be close to one another. You greet each other, and it appears that you're always there if someone needs help. Nobody I know does that. I'm having trouble defining it, but I can only say it's like you have a closeness—that you are totally self-sufficient. It's really not a bad thing, but it just makes us feel lesser somehow, so we want to say we're wonderful too."

"I never thought of it like that—that we might appear that way to others. We are a close group. We do respond immediately if someone is in trouble. Showing love to one another is very basic to our way of life. Tell me about you," Jesus said.

"I am a blacksmith by trade. My wife and I have four boys and one girl." Damon smiled. "Our girl is the youngest child and has the boys running all day long to do whatever she tells them to do.

"I have three brothers, but they live in the south near the Egyptian border. We were raised to be self-sufficient. We're told that you never know how long before someone is gone, and if you are depending on someone for something, when that person is gone, you're in trouble. So each one of us must be able to do as much as possible.

"As a people, we try to help those needing help, but we give of our excess. That means that we will help when our work is done, and we give what we have that's above what we need. We need to be sure that we take care of our families first. Does that help you understand?"

"It does," said Jesus. "Thank you for telling me. Can you tell me how it came about that you want to know more about us?"

"I'll be honest with you. James and a few others were always trying to yell at us. We got to the point where we started avoiding you folks. The children would overhear us talking, and they began to be openly rude. Then James started walking in what we call our area. He'd smile and wave.

"I'll never forget the day an angry goat was chasing the children. My son was that boy. James saw it happening, took off his robe and threw it over the goat, and then hid the boy in a tree until some men ran up and tackled the goat. It was to us men that he apologized for his previous behavior and quietly walked away. We men talked and decided we'd wait and see what would happen. I see him now almost daily, and now we feel easy talking with each other.

"Some of us men were talking, and we wondered about the change in James. We began to talk about all you people. We know nothing about you, so we thought that maybe we could ask James if it were possible to have someone nice and patient talk with us about who you are. So here we are," said Damon.

Jesus nodded. "Thank you. You're right about James—he has changed. Do you know when your men would like to meet with me?"

"We don't know what your schedule is, so we talked about three dates." He mentioned the dates. They talked for a minute and decided to meet at sundown a week from today in a fairly large nearby building owned by one of the Gentiles.

Jesus said, "Are any of your young men curious? Would they like to meet with us?"

Damon said, "Three of our young men, ages about thirteen and fifteen, have asked to be a part of the group if you're open to that."

"I am. Children have a special place in my heart. We have a young man who we have asked to be available to answer questions that might come from your young men. We felt it's sometimes easier for youth to speak to someone their own age. I'd like to have him come to the meeting, if that's fine with you."

Damon nodded. "I think we'd all like that. So it's agreed. We'll meet here at sundown next week. We'll allow our young men to attend, and you'll bring your young man. Thank you, Jesus. We all look forward to this meeting."

They shook hands. "As do I. I'll be here. Oh, the young man's name is John. He and I will be here. Thank you."

***

Jesus was excited about the prospect of the meeting with the Gentiles. "Father God, I need Your help. I have no idea what this meeting will lead to, but when You are in charge of things, there are always positive results. Please fill my head and heart with Your wisdom that I say and do only the things You want me to say and do. Thank You, Father God," Jesus prayed.

Next Sabbath after the noon meal, he met with Peter, Andrew, Zebedee, James, and John to talk about this upcoming meeting. Jesus gave them an overview of what he planned to say, after which they talked about the questions that might be asked and the answers they would likely give. John was cautioned that, although he would be attending the meeting, he was not to speak unless Jesus gave him a nod. He would be in attendance to learn and to perhaps meet some of the younger men. He readily agreed.

***

Just before sundown, Jesus met John, and they walked to the building where the meeting would be held. They were amazed by the number of men in attendance—seventeen men and five young men!

Introductions were made, and Jesus was asked to begin. He said, "We are of the Jewish faith. We believe in one God, and we call him Father God." He gave them a quick overview of their history, from Abraham through the flight from Egypt to the current day.

"I'd like to tell you about life as a Jew by telling you my story."

Jesus talked for more than half an hour, but the Gentiles seemed to be very interested. "I'm sure you have questions. Please ask them. I'll do my best to answer them."

One of the men spoke up. "I was in Egypt for a few years, and they have all kinds of gods. You have only one. Why is that? Isn't there a lot to do for only one God?"

"That's a very good question. We know that others have other gods. In our minds, these gods are made of wood or metal or stone. They are not able to move, so we don't see how they can help people," replied Jesus.

"How do you know that your God does things?" asked another.

"We feel Him. We see the miracles He works in our daily lives and the miracles he works in the troubles that we have. Feeling His love and seeing His works are how we know," explained Jesus.

"You told us about how you grew up. But how does your faith in your Father God work daily. I mean, what does He have you do every day?"

"A fair question. I am a rabbi—that is, I'm a teacher. My daily routine is a little different from the members of our synagogue. Our people begin each day with a reading from the Torah and then eat breakfast and go to work or tend the animals or the crops on their farms—depending upon what they do for a living. There are times during the day when we take just a few minutes to ask Father God to strengthen us.

"We are usually home for dinner at sundown and then have a bit of free time to spend with family and friends. Most of our people have what our family calls Family Time, where the problems or joys of the day are reviewed and where questions are asked."

"What kind of education do you have?"

So continued the evening and the questions. When the last question was asked and answered, Damon asked Jesus and John if they would spend a few minutes shaking hands or just having conversations with some of the men.

The young men walked bravely over to John. "What do you do?" they asked.

Jesus nodded at him.

"I have finished the schooling that I must take, and I have become a man in our faith. I am responsible for everything I say and do. I attend an advanced class now; several are offered. They help us learn more and more about our faith. I also work with my father, who is a fisherman," answered John.

The young men talked amicably—mostly about fishing—until Jesus said it was time to leave.

Jesus turned to the men, "We welcome all of your questions. None of them is a dumb question. Besides John and me, we have others you may freely ask your questions. I believe you know Peter, Andrew, Zebedee, and James—all fishermen. Please do not hesitate to ask me or any of them any question you may have. Thank you for meeting with John and me here tonight. Please remember, don't be afraid to ask your questions of any of us."

Jesus walked John home.

"What are you thinking, John?" asked Jesus.

"I feel kind of like I just made a big jump in learning. I'm glad the men didn't ask any questions of me. I know I can talk with the young men, but I'd be a little hesitant to answer questions from the men," answered John.

"You're a wise young man. I can give you a little hint," said Jesus.

"What's that?" asked John.

"At any time all you need to do is quietly in your mind say, *Father God, help me.* Do you think you can do that?" asked Jesus.

John smiled. "Yes, I can. Thank you, Rabbi Jesus."

They shook hands as they parted for the night.

"I'll see you soon," said Jesus as he gave John a quick hug.

Next Friday after services, John approached Jesus and asked if he had a moment to talk.

"Right now is a good time for me. You seem pretty excited. I'm all ears," said Jesus.

"The last two evenings, some of the Gentile boys have come to me with questions. I wanted to tell you what they're asking. I'm kind of surprised," began John. "The questions they're asking me are, 'Can you play?' 'Do you have to pray all day?' 'Can you go out with girls or do your parents pick a wife for you?' 'Can you eat regular food or are there a lot of foods you can't eat?' And then they ask things like, 'How do you know your God is listening to you? Does He talk to you? What does His voice sound like?' 'What do you do in your synagogue?' 'What do you learn in school?'" said John.

"You've been able to answer all of their questions, haven't you?" Jesus said with a smile. He was pleased with John.

"I have. I remembered what you said about asking Father God to help me, and I do that every time I talk with them. They seem really nice. Is that okay to say?" asked John.

Jesus nodded. "Yes it's okay. Father God created everything, even the people and animals and plants that don't know Him. I do need to caution you about something though."

"What's that?" asked John.

"Many things other people do may seem a lot of fun and may seem like something you want to try. You must talk with Father God. The first thing you do could lead to things you don't want to do. But because you've done other things without a problem, you'll think it's probably okay.

"Let me give you an example. They show you a new trick. It's fun, and you'll be able to show others how to do it. That's okay. Next, they show you something they've made, maybe a whistle or some toy and give you one. That's okay. Over the weeks, you share things with them, and you receive little gifts or some knowledge much like you'd do with our boys.

"But one day they offer to share their lunch with you. Do you know if it contains pork? Or the blood of an animal? Will you be strong enough to say no to the boys you've become friends with? Standing here now, it might seem like a clear-cut answer. But when you're there, it's not easy. These are now friends. You've shared a lot with them. You need to be alert to this. It could be harmful to you and to your relationship with Father God. You need to be strong enough to say no and stand by it."

"So I shouldn't be friends with them?" asked John.

"It's not that easy. Yes you can be friends with them. I don't know of anyone who has been their friend, except maybe

James. Mostly we're businesses that they have learned to trust. You are now at a crossroads—sharing who we are without proselytizing. Does this make any sense to you?" asked Jesus.

"It's confusing. I'll do some thinking about what you've said, and I'll talk with Father God. Thank you for taking time for me. I appreciate it," answered John.

"You are welcome. Remember you are a man in our congregation. You may come to me any time you want. What you are dealing with is new. I want you to keep me apprised of everything that happens. Okay?" said Jesus.

"Thank you for telling me that. I feel better. I need to get home. I still have some studying to do. Good night," said John.

"Good night, my friend," said Jesus. "You are quite a man!"

Jesus spoke to the rabbis about what he and John had talked about, and it was agreed to let things work themselves out for now but to watch the situation closely.

The questions from the Gentile men and the boys dwindled quickly. It soon became a wave and a hi when they saw each other. Apparently, their questions—their curiosity—had been answered. Whew!

SIXTY-SIX

30

One week remained until Jesus would be leaving Capernaum. "Father God, only with You by my side will I be able to do this. Where You are leading me is so different from what I've experienced. Please take complete charge of all I do and say. May I only do and say what You want me to do. Thank You for Your amazing help," became Jesus' continual prayer.

Before services that Friday, the congregation arrived at the synagogue early. Thaddeaus asked Jesus to come up to him. He turned to Jesus and said, "Please stand right here."

Sylvanus, Titus, Zebedee, James, John, Peter, and Andrew joined them.

"What's going on?" asked Jesus.

Sylvanus said, "It's a going away celebration! We've all been working together to get something that will let you know in just a little way how much we love you and how much you have taught all of us."

To his amazement, the congregation applauded.

Zebedee said, "You are going to be so missed, but we want you to remember us forever! This is a small gift from us, and this gift is from the congregation."

Jesus opened the packages. The one from the rabbis held two changes of clothing! The package from the congregation held three new pair of sandals! The entire congregation exploded. There were many calls of, "Thank you, Jesus." Jesus was overwhelmed.

"This will last me for years. Thank you!" he hugged everyone he could reach. "You are very special friends. I will never forget any of you! How could I? You are all such wonderful people! I promise I'll do my best to return and see all of you again."

After the service and after the congregation had left for home, the rabbis and Jesus's close friends stayed for a moment to say their final goodbyes. Sylvanus was not the only person with tears in his eyes.

"I hope I see all of you again before I leave. Thank you, my friends! In these almost two years, I've come to think of all of you as my brothers. Father God is so good! I will carry each of you in my heart wherever I go. Thank you!"

Hugs were shared all around.

Jesus spent his final two evenings in Capernaum visiting those he fondly thought of as his fishing brothers. Zebedee and his sons presented a strong young donkey to Jesus. He'll make your travels a lot easier," said James.

"Thank you so very much! You and your sons have done so much for me these two years. Thank you, my friends."

The four of them laughed, reminisced, and then joined the other men for their regular weekly game.

John said, "Rabbi Jesus, just because you're leaving us doesn't mean anyone's going to let you win tonight! You'll have to work really hard!"

The game was tied going for the final point—the one that would break the tie. Andrew said, "Jesus, this point is yours. We win or lose as you play!"

There was the usual hot sweaty play, and just as Jesus reached to make that final play, Andrew ran in and made the point. Everyone stopped. They all looked at Andrew with disbelief.

Andrew explained, "If he didn't make it, I didn't want him to leave with that memory. I didn't want that to be his last memory of Capernaum. Besides, I made sure I spoke loudly enough that the other team would hear me, so I figured their attention would be on Jesus, and I could go in easily!"

They all laughed.

Both teams went up to Jesus to say their goodbyes. James said, "I have an idea. Why don't we all sign the ball and give it to Jesus? Every time he sees that dirty old scruffy ball, he'll remember all of us!"

John ran to the school and brought back pen and ink. What a fun way to say goodbye.

Sixty-seven

30

Jesus left Capernaum about the third hour. He'd packed his items the night before, eaten a wonderful breakfast, straightened his rooms, loaded his donkey, and begun walking. He walked around town, wanting to make sure he remembered everything. "I'll be back. I promise," he said to the town as he walked.

It was time to start on his way to meet his families in Cana; it was time to begin his new life. "Father God, thank You for You. Thank You for my time in Capernaum and the people I have met here. Thank You for my wonderful family! Father God, please take my entire future in Your hands. Help me to go where You want me to go and help me to do all that You want me to do. I want to do Your will. Thank You!"

As he reached the crossroads, he saw Matthew standing just outside his office. "Good morning, Matthew. A fine day, isn't it?" Jesus called.

Matthew waved and walked toward Jesus.

"How are things going for you?" Jesus asked.

He stopped for a minute to just talk. He told Matthew of his leaving Capernaum and the wedding he would be attending in Cana.

Matthew said, "You're a good man, Jesus. I've enjoyed the short time we've had together. Thank you! Enjoy your family. Capernaum will miss you."

They shook hands and Jesus continued his walk to Cana.

His pack was heavy, so he was thankful for the donkey. The days were hot but tolerable. The two nights spent in inns were barely tolerable. *Why can't inns be friendlier? Oh well, I'll see my family soon,* he thought.

The next afternoon, about the eighth hour, he could see that he was close to Cana. He was elated. *Almost there!* he thought.

He noticed two little girls and three small boys running toward him. As they neared, he saw that it was Leah in the lead! He ran to her, scooped her up in his arms, and spun her around. When he put her down, he bent down and gathered the rest of the children to him.

Lots of "Uncle Jesus! Uncle Jesus!" greeted his ears. And they all began talking at once.

"Thank you for coming to meet me!" he said. "Let's go see all the others."

Little Bartholomew, now almost six, said, "I can help carry your stuff. I'm bigger now."

"You are bigger now, but everything I have is in these two bags. And I need to let the donkey carry them. Would that be okay? I'll tell you a secret: there's nothing in there that's very interesting."

Jesus picked up the two youngest and started toward town. Almost at the city gates, he saw his mother coming toward him. He set down the children and told them to run with him and he ran to his mother.

"Woman!" he called. "Mother, I have missed you!" He picked her up and spun her around as he always did. They both laughed. "Mother, are you well?"

"I am, my son. I am so glad to see you. Come, the others are waiting. I told them they could not meet you before I did," said Mary as the children gathered around and they all walked to meet the family.

And there they were—every one of them. So many hugs! So many kisses! So much commotion! He was home.

"Okay!" Jesus said. "Tell me who all these children are."

Everyone laughed, and each of the men introduced their children.

"Let's see. James you have three, Judas two, Elizabeth four, Joses three, Simon two, and Anna twins. Did I get that right?"

They agreed that he was right.

Jesus turned to Mary and said, "Woman, you have a very large family!" And they all laughed.

It took the rest of the day both before and after the evening meal to catch up with each family. Of course during each telling of a story, there were many "additions" from the other families. All in all, it was a fun family get-together.

SIXTY-EIGHT

30

The wedding would be the next day—the beginning of a week of celebration. Timaeus's sister was a beautiful bride, the wedding was beautiful, and the feast afterward was absolutely wonderful. Foods had been brought in from as far away as Syria and Egypt.

During the days, Mary and her daughters and daughters-in-law helped with preparations for each evening's celebration. Jesus and his brothers found businesses in town doing work that interested them and spent the days with those men at their work.

Timaeus's mother had hired three of the town's young women to care for all of Mary's grandchildren, leaving the adults fairly free. It was a time of new meetings and of fun and relaxation for everyone involved in the wedding festivities.

The fourth evening, Mary asked Jesus, "Could you and I have some time alone tomorrow? There's something I want to talk with you about."

"Of course, Mother. You don't ever need a reason to talk with me. How about right after breakfast?"

"Thank you, Jesus."

Late that afternoon, the brothers found themselves alone.

Simon asked, "Jesus, where do you plan on going from here?"

Jesus replied, "Our cousin John is staying near the Jordan River just south of the Sea of Galilee. I understand he knows

Father God and is doing a lot of teaching there. I thought I'd go to see him and hear his ministry."

Joses said, "Our cousin John? I hope you find him. I wonder what his ministry is about."

Jesus smiled. "I hope to find out. From what I've heard of him, he intrigues me."

"What have you heard?" asked Simon.

"Not a lot. Apparently he's a little unusual in his dress and in his eating. I've heard that he eats mainly locusts and honey and wears a short leather cloak. And he lives in the country and baptizes people for Father God by immersing them in the Jordan River. I don't know anything else, and I can't explain why he does those things. So I'll go and see," answered Jesus.

James said, "Jesus, we'd like to bring you up to date on what's going on back home. Remember that we told you about the people who moved into Nazareth who say they are Jews but are not friendly and will not mix with us."

Judas added, "There are a few more who've moved in near town. They are really difficult to deal with. It's as if they think we are beneath them. They're demanding and will not talk to any of us."

Joses said, "It's getting so bad that we're thinking about possibly moving the Shop to another town."

"What have you tried?" asked Jesus.

"At the Shop, we pray daily. We pray for understanding, and we pray that they and we can learn to live together," said James.

"When they come into the Shop, we are pleasant. We welcome them, and one of us walks toward them to let them know we have time to work with them. As angry as they make us feel, we treat them with respect. It's not always easy," said Joses.

"They seem to like our work, but they are still so rude— almost nasty. We just try to ignore it. We know we have each other, and that support is a great strength to us," said Judas.

"I'm finding the same thing at the pharmacy. When these new people are near, you can just feel the tension in the air," added Timaeus.

"What do you think is going to happen?" asked Jesus.

"We don't know. There may still be something we can do. Or maybe something will happen and that will change things. We haven't given up yet, but we really don't have much hope that anything will happen soon," James admitted.

"I'm sorry. Nazareth was such a loving community. Keep me apprised of things, will you?" asked Jesus.

Judas said, "That reminds me. What are your plans after you visit with John? Are you coming home?"

"I don't think so—at least not at this time. I've been praying a lot about where I go from here, and I believe Father God is having me go from town to town to talk with people. I've found that most people really want to talk about something. It's almost like there is a big hole or a big hurt in an awful lot of people. I'm going to walk around and see if that's where Father God wants me," Jesus explained.

Mary had approached without Jesus seeing her. Coming up to Jesus, she said, "I'll have to pray for you even harder. That's certainly a different kind of life. Somehow, I think it suits you." She turned to the others. "We were wondering if you would like to join us before we go to the celebration. The children would like to do some singing."

She turned to Jesus. "Claudia has written songs for the children based on the psalms and has Leah singing the harmony. It's really quite beautiful. We adults join in on many of the songs. Come!"

SIXTY-NINE

30

It was a beautiful morning. There were just a few scudding clouds with a light breeze. Mary and Jesus walked off to a spot near where sheep were grazing.

"Jesus, I know that you're thirty years old, but I want to tell you the story of your birth. Joseph and I had decided we would tell you when you were on your own. So this seems like the prefect time. I'm just sorry Joseph isn't here. He loved you so much," Mary began.

"I know he did. Our family is so blessed to have had the parents we've had. I've seen how hard other families have had it."

"Thank you, Jesus. Let me start at the beginning. Joseph and I fell in love when I was barely fifteen and became betrothed a few months later. I was so happy! My parents had passed shortly before, and I was living with my uncles.

"One day after I had finished my chores and it wasn't quite time to start dinner, I was just sitting under a tree in the yard. An angel from Father God came to me and told me I would be with child, and the child I would have would be the promised Messiah."

"Mother!" said Jesus.

"Please let me finish. I told Joseph. I could tell he was upset. He told me that he didn't know what he should do, as he knew that he could not possibly be the child's father. But we agreed that we would both pray and ask Father God to guide us. This was pretty heavy stuff! The promised Messiah!

"The next day when we met, he told me that the previous night after prayers, an angel came to him and told him not to worry but to go ahead with our marriage and create a family. We cried together. We laughed together. And we prayed together. We decided that we would be married after our betrothal as planned.

"I lived with my uncles, but I wanted to talk with a woman, so I went to visit my cousin Elizabeth until it was closer to my wedding. Elizabeth was really quite old, but she was also with child! Her child would be just a few months older than you. We talked and laughed and made baby cloths for swaddling our babies. She had a lot of friends, and they were forever telling us about the pain of childbirth and how we should raise our children. Elizabeth said to pay no attention to them—that if things were as bad as they said, Father God would not allow it. And, most importantly, no woman would have more than one child! When I returned home, Joseph and I were married.

"About that time, Caesar decided that everyone needed to be registered in their hometown, which meant we needed to go to Bethlehem because Joseph is a descendent of King David. This was about the time you were to be born, but we had to go. So Joseph bought a donkey for me to ride on, and he placed extra bedding on the donkey's back so I would be more comfortable. I would walk a ways, and then I'd ride. It wasn't easy, but Joseph did his best to make it easy and even fun for me.

"As expected, you wanted to be born, and we just barely made it to Bethlehem. It seems a bit funny now, but no matter where we looked, we couldn't find a place to stay. Finally, we found an innkeeper who could see the condition I was in and told us the only room he had was in his barn. Joseph looked at me so sadly. I said that would be fine, and we settled in his barn.

"There were no midwives available, so Joseph helped me. Being a first-time mother myself, I didn't know much. But we prayed and prayed, and you were born. And you were perfect, and you were beautiful! Joseph and I held you and laughed and cried. We did remember to thank Father God. Looking back on that day, it was really quite beautiful.

"The very next day, we had visitors! Some shepherds came to the inn, and the innkeeper directed them to the barn. It seems that an angel, surrounded by what they said was a legion of angels, had come to them in the night and told them the Messiah had been born. They decided to come and see you for themselves. They were so nice. One of the sheep came up to the manger we had laid you in and tried to smell you.

"I picked you up and held you so that all the sheep could smell your feet. It was amazing. You didn't mind at all. The shepherds only stayed a couple of hours. They had so many questions about who we were and why we were there. And then they told us about themselves. It seems they were two young brothers and their grandfather. They explained that their grandfather did not like living with his daughter and would much rather live outdoors with the boys. It was an amazing visit.

"After registering your birth, we found a small house in Bethlehem and settled in. You were circumcised at eight days, and thirty-three days later, we took you to the temple in Jerusalem to be dedicated to Father God. While we were in the temple, we met some extraordinary people. An older man named Simeon was there. Father God had told him that he would live to see the promised Messiah, and he waited every day in the temple. When he saw you, he took you right out of my arms. And with tears in his eyes, he thanked Father God for showing him the Messiah. He then blessed Joseph and me and told us you would be responsible for tumult for many people and told me that I would also feel a deep hurt.

"As we were leaving, an older woman named Anna approached. She was a widow who lived in the temple. When she saw you, she thanked Father God for allowing her to see the promised Messiah. Later, we heard that she would tell everyone she met that she had seen the Messiah.

"We loved Bethlehem. Our little home was so comfortable. Joseph was known as a carpenter and began to work in the local shop. We were making friends and felt very comfortable living there and worshiping in the synagogue.

"You were in your second year when we had the most unexpected visitors. Joseph was just about to leave for work when we heard a commotion outside. When we looked, several townspeople were laughing and talking around some men on camels. It turned out that they were wise men from towns way to the east of town. They stopped at our house and asked to see our baby. Joseph held you. The men dismounted and bowed down on their knees in front of you! They said they had heard of the birth of the Messiah and had come to see him. Joseph and I looked at each other. One of the men told us not to worry; they were here only for the honor of meeting the boy and to give him gifts that they had brought with them.

"We accepted the gifts on your behalf. We asked the men to come inside to sit awhile and have something to eat and drink, but they said they needed to be on their way. The journey had taken longer than expected, and they were needed at home. After they left, Joseph needed to go to work and said we'd talk about things that evening.

"After dinner and after you were in bed, Joseph and I talked and talked about the visitors. We talked about all that had happened to us and to you since the angel first visited each of us. We had agreed when we first knew you were coming that we would raise you and all our children in the most loving way we could, especially staying close to Father God. We also decided that we would keep the gifts and would give them to you when you went off on your own. I brought them with me, and I'll give them to you before you leave.

"Shortly after the men left, King Herod ordered the killing of all the children two years of age and younger. An angel appeared to Joseph and told him to take us and go quickly to Egypt and stay there until Herod died. That night, we took everything we owned, loaded our donkey, and left for Egypt. While on the journey, I discovered we were going to have another child, who would then be born in Egypt.

"We settled in Egypt. Many Jews had already migrated to Egypt, so we had no problem adjusting to life there—except for the sand that got into everything! James was born there.

"When we heard that Herod had died, we went back home to Bethlehem. Before we reached Bethlehem, we heard that Herod's son Archelaus was now king. We were as afraid of him as we had been of Herod, so we continued to our hometown of Nazareth.

"I'm sure you have a lot of questions. I'll do my best to answer them. As I said before, I wish Joseph could have been here for this. He loved you so much, and he was very proud of the man you've become. Do you have questions, Son?"

Jesus reached over and held his mother. With tears in his eyes, he said, "Mother, thank you—not just for telling me all of this but also for being such an awesome mother and Joseph for being the world's best father.

"This answers so many questions for me. When I was quite young, I told Father that I felt I was different. He listened to me and then explained that I was a special person and should stay close to Father God. I've never forgotten that. Torah and the book of the Prophets were always so easy for me to understand. My brothers and I seemed to be able to pray for people who were ill or hurt, and they would recover—things like that. I felt blessed that we could do these things as a family—that we could help so many people—but I took it as just a normal part of our lives. I often wondered why others didn't pray and heal one another. I see more clearly now.

"Mother, this is pretty—I don't know—scary? Astounding? Heavy? I've taught the coming of the promised Messiah for so many years. And now … I question, yet somehow I know this is true. Elizabeth and Anna—my sisters' names. That's so nice.

"I need to talk with Father God for a while, Mother. Would it be okay if I went off by myself, just for a short time? Right now, I feel that I am so full of love that I am going to explode. Thank you, Mother. Thank you for all you are; I love you so much!" Jesus held his mother for a moment, kissed her cheek, and then went off to think and pray. He found a huge rock near a large tree and sat to let everything soak in.

When he returned, the entire family was wondering what was going on. He pulled his mother aside and asked her, "Should we tell the family now? I feel that we should tell them, but I think the words should come from you. Would you be okay with telling them today?"

"That would be perfect. How about if we tell them now while the youngest children are still down for their naps and the others are at the square with the sitters? I think I'll tell them much like I told you. Does that seem right?"

"Thank you, Mother. Oh! Please make sure they don't treat me any differently. I couldn't stand it if they didn't tease me and treat me as they always have!"

Mary smiled. "Yes, Jesus. I'll tell them in no uncertain terms!"

Jesus returned to his family and said, "Could I have everyone's attention, please? Thank you. Mother has something she wants to tell all of us today. It's going to take several minutes, and you'll all have questions afterward. So while the babies are all down, let's listen to Mother! Okay?"

Mary told the story much as she had told Jesus—ending with the admonition that she would not tolerate them being any different to Jesus. "He's still our Jesus, and he's still the same. Don't forget that! I mean it!"

James said, "You're still my big brother, and although I'm shocked, this doesn't surprise me in the least. It's like you were born a rabbi. So, big brother," he said affectionately, wrapping Jesus in a big hug.

"You've always kind of known everything—not that you've acted like it, but somehow you've always known things. I still love you!" Joses said as he punched Jesus in the upper arm.

Anna said, "I don't know what to do. You're just my brother, but the Messiah? How can I touch the Messiah? How can I tease the Messiah? Shouldn't I be afraid of the Messiah? Jesus, please hold me," she said.

Jesus held her. "This is news to me as well. But to me the news feels right. Little Anna, I am still your brother. Father God put us all together. We need to trust Him and do His will. Please know that I love you."

He turned to the others. "I don't know what I feel, let alone what all of you feel. We need to let Father God direct us. Just know that you are the best family any man has ever had. We have all been blessed."

Simon said, "Let's pray. Father God, we are all startled by the news that our Jesus is Your promised Messiah. We need You to take each and every one of us in Your arms and show us how to deal with this news. We trust You, Father God! Hold us and show us Your way. Amen."

"Thank you, Simon." Jesus turned to everyone. "Please don't tell others of this. Let's let Father God determine when this should become known. Okay?"

They all agreed. James said, "I think that we've always been coming to this point in our lives. When I look back at certain things, I feel this has all been a part of Father God's plan. Jesus, I love you as my brother, and I don't think it will be difficult to think of or love you as the promised Messiah. As I look back, I can see it clearly. I'd like to say thank you for being my brother." James held Jesus. He had tears in his eyes.

Jesus turned to Elizabeth. "What do you think, my sister?" He noticed she was crying.

"Oh, Jesus!" she said. "Father God does so much for me. I've loved Him so long. I've loved the stories of the promised Messiah, but now I know that He is here and that He is my own brother. All I can do is breathe. I feel so full! Could you hold me, please?"

Jesus held her and told her he loved her.

The rest of the family added their love and their feelings. The family spent a long time talking with each other and sharing what this could mean not only for them but also for all of Israel—for the entire Jewish community.

***

There was just this evening and one more for the week of celebration.

Mary and her family were seated at a table just finishing their meal when a servant approached Timaeus. "Sir, may I speak to you in private?"

"You may speak freely here," replied Timaeus.

"We are almost out of wine. What would you have me do?" asked the servant.

Mary overheard and said to Jesus, "They are almost out of wine."

"Woman." Jesus leaned toward her, smiled, and said, "What is it you want me to do?"

Mary turned to the servant and said, "Do as he tells you."

***

Continued in the New Testament of the Holy Bible.

ACKNOWLEDGMENTS

I only have the words *thank You* **to our One God, our Father** God, our Lord Jesus, and God's Holy Spirit, who has been with me every moment. Thank You!

Thank you to my daughter, Patricia Jo Wandersee, for being my first editor. Your backing and your suggestions were a great help.

Thank you to my son Paul Dunlop for being my very patient photographer.